Journey to the Black City

Keith R. Mueller

WALDORF PUBLISHING

Published by Waldorf Publishing
2140 Hall Johnson Road
#102-345
Grapevine, Texas 76051
www.WaldorfPublishing.com

Journey to the Black City
Book One: After: The New Earth

ISBN: 978-1-943847-58-7
Library of Congress Control Number: 2015957014

Dedication

I would like to dedicate this book to those fighting to stop human trafficking and child prostitution, and to those who come after; those who work to lead the abused back into the Light.

Table of Contents

Preface

On an Earth very like our own, the shining civilizations of ancient man have been crushed; the glaciers keep moving ever south, grinding the cities of men beneath them. Neither science nor magic has been able to stop them. In long years past, warfare and a virulent influenza killed most of the human population.

Now, almost two thousand years later, humans have again gathered together in a few vast city-states. In the wild lands between the cities, the free tribes roam in the company of saber-tooth cats, mammoths, and dire wolves. But there is only a tentative peace; though the zeppelin raids for slaves are long since over, there are those in the Black City of the West for whom only one thing matters. That thing is power; the power to dominate and subjugate; the power to kidnap and enslave children and women into a sexual bondage purporting to save their souls, but in reality to supply wealth to a priesthood whose hearts are as black as the zeppelins they fly.

Into this world of steam-powered war machines and crystal ships, two young people must journey. It will be a journey from innocence and light that will carry them from their tribe into the black heart of the basalt city, and then into Green Hell, the vast, jungle-covered, virtually unknown land far to the south. On this journey they will discover the power of love and the power of hate, the power of magic and the power of science. It will be a journey that will change them forever, and bring them closer together than they'd thought possible.

Chapter 1

It was almost dark by the time Kel had climbed to the top of the path through the mountains. He stood atop the ridge and gazed down into the valley below him. It was hard to see in the deepening twilight and even harder to understand what it was he was looking at. To Kel it seemed that the plain below him was covered with black rocks, but the rocks seemed impossibly large and they were arranged in more or less straight lines with what seemed to be pathways between them. At the nexus of this orderly tangle of rocks, they soared into the sky.

Even at this distance, he could tell that the tallest of the standing stones were over a hundred feet tall and that there were many of them. He looked to the north and he saw the ice wall. Though it was some distance away, Kel knew it was coming. The great glacier that had been grinding the world of men for over a thousand years was still slowly moving south.

He looked back at the dark plain, and as the wonder of what he was looking at gradually subsided, he saw a light in the midst of the blackness. This light was pure white, not a reflection of the ice lights that flickered in red, green, and purple curtains to the north. It was small—like the smallest pinprick of light in an otherwise empty sky. To Kel it seemed as if a star had come to Earth and was dwelling in the terrifying blackness below him. He suddenly knew that his destiny lay amid these sinister black stones. And he finally realized what he was seeing. It was the Black City of the West—the nation city that was named Los Angeles...

~

Kel awoke suddenly. He lay still in his small tent absorbing the content of his dream. More than others, he realized the importance of dreams of this kind and he knew that he must memorize it immediately—dreams and visions fade quickly in the physical world.

Though he was only a shaman-in-training under the guidance of his grandfather, he knew that the city in the dream was real—and the white light was symbolic, though of what he couldn't say. He hated it when something like this happened to him. Here he was, being trained as a shaman and he has a dream he can't figure out. He sighed. It was very frustrating. He lay a moment longer, feeling sorry for himself, listening to the world outside his tent. He heard the sounds of very early morning—the distant calls of birds and the muffled sound of footsteps outside the tent.

Kel rose reluctantly, knowing that it would be chilly this morning. He saw the north side of his tent depressing and relaxing rhythmically as

1

though the leather hide still lived after the animal was long dead. With the wind from the north he knew the air would be cool outside. He pushed back his sleeping furs and crawled out of the small shelter into the dawn.

Geog and Mart were already tending a small fire, preparing to make breakfast. Geog looked over at Kel and snickered. "Seers spend too much time dreaming and not enough time cooking."

Kel laughed. "We all do what we do best…and nobody makes a breakfast like you, Geog. You will make someone a fine wife one day."

Now it was Mart's turn to snicker, though he made no reply.

The three of them had been friends since childhood, so they were natural companions for hunting expeditions. They'd captured their share of prey this trip, both with the spear and the snare, and bags of wild herbs and berries sat full on the ground.

Today they'd begin the trek back to their tribal town. They all knew the people were depending on them and the other hunting expeditions to supply them with enough food for the coming winter. Small game this year had been a bit scarcer than the year before and Kel's tribe was too small to mount expeditions to the north to hunt the really large prey animals—what the northern tribes called mammoths.

Kel imagined the huge animals of which he'd only seen pictures and read descriptions in the books in his father's small library. He was now grateful that his father had insisted that he learn to read and write. While neither skill actually involved magic, there was still a vague sense of power in the words and images he'd seen in those books over the years. Imagine a shaggy beast, taller than three men, with giant curving ivory tusks, auburn to black hair hanging down its sides to shield it from the cold, and feet so large—just being near one would be a terror.

It was said that in ages long past, men herded these animals as men now did sheep in the more stable communities farther to the south. This was back even before the ocean war between the mighty tribes of this land mass and that of the lands across the eastern seas. Kel was no stranger to magic and tried to imagine the great powers and knowledge of those long-gone city men. He could not.

He made the silent prayer of thanks to the Gods and his ancestors for allowing them to capture the food necessary for their people to survive. Then he said another silent prayer of thanks to the spirits of the animals that lost their lives so that his tribe would live. Respect for all life was the most important thing shamans were taught, something they passed on to the rest of the members of the tribe as well. Take no more than you need, be grateful, and give thanks. The three of them ate the venison and roots that Geog had cooked in silence. The trek back to the tribal town would be long, probably four days with the load they were bearing. The meat was salted and packed into the small wagon; all that remained to be done was harness the two horses to the rig and be off.

As the sun rose over the horizon, they all instinctively looked to the north. It was something people did without thinking. Kel imagined that the people of the Black City looked toward the ice wall as well. The glacier was still there, of course, no matter how much one wished it to be otherwise.

Now with the sun still low in the sky, the distant ice face—almost a mile tall—reflected the light into the land, illuminating the ground that would have been in twilight shadows if the ice hadn't been there. In places where the ice was thinner, flashes of startling greens and blues could be seen. *It was quite beautiful in its own way*, Kel thought, *like the ice tiger, deadly but beautiful*. He suddenly thought of Lyria and smiled. The ice tiger was her spirit animal. He missed her.

He felt a renewed energy as he thought of Lyria and said, "Well, let us be off…the tribe awaits us."

To this Mart replied, "Don't you mean Lyria awaits you?"

Before Kel could reply, Geog laughed and said, "Now I know what you were dreaming about this morning. I heard you moan in your tent."

Both Geog and Mart guffawed as Kel reddened and kicked a clod of dirt in their direction. Then he shivered. That star he saw in the Black City…could that have been Lyria? He shook off the thought and helped his friends hook the horses to the cart.

As they progressed south and west along the rocky trail, they were silent for a time.

"Do you think the ice will reach us here, Kel?" Geog asked.

Kel had no answer, but he spoke the truth when he said, "If it does, it won't be in our lifetimes. Maybe the Gods will see fit to finally stop this."

"The Gods didn't stop it for the great city men those ages past," Mart replied.

Kel looked at his friend in mock disgust, "You must have slept through your schooling, Mart! The Gods brought the ice because of those men. It is said that in this world there is but one evil and that is greed. Everything else we call evil grows from that greed. When someone steals

3

or murders or rapes or desires conquest, they are taking something that is not theirs to take. It matters not in which God's name they pillage—they know only one word and that word is 'mine.' The truly frightening thing about this dark force is that it is passive. It does not seek out men and corrupt them as some of the religions of the city-states teach. It simply is. Sadly, men seek it eagerly and when they finally find it they are consumed by it."

Geog spoke after considering what Kel had said. "So what you are saying is that the glacier is like that greed made solid. It is a display of how greed works in the world, consuming and destroying all before it, like a man who is not hungry though he continues to eat."

Kel looked at his friend in surprise and said, "You are a great hunter, but I never realized you had the potential to be a teacher as well. I think that when you finally settle down you will make a fine father with strong, well taught, and well fed children!"

Geog laughed, "If I ever get the chance. It seems the young women of our tribe and the others surrounding us only have eyes for Mart."

Mart grinned, "It isn't my fault that I was born beautiful."

He shook his long mane of blonde hair and struck a pose with one hand on his hip. At that, they all roared with laughter as they worked their way down the pathway toward home.

The rest of the day, as well as the next, passed uneventfully, as the three young men had hoped it would. Boredom is, well…boring. Still, when one is finished with his task, a boring trip back home can be a welcome thing. It's far better than the excitement of having a snake frighten the horses like the last time they went afield. Mart laughed at the memory, though at the time he had some choice words for the horses that included no laughter.

"What's so funny, Mart?" Geog asked.

Mart told him what he had been thinking about, and Geog said, "Well, if it is so funny, the next time it happens we will let you follow the horses, picking up bags of berries and herbs as you go!"

Kel laughed. "I do not know about that. Knowing Mart, he might pick up the horse droppings by mistake."

Mart responded in a hurt voice, "Hey, I might not be as good a cook as Geog, but I know a real pie from a horse pie."

They all laughed again as the wagon rolled and the sun rose in the sky and then began to set.

When they stopped that evening to eat supper and camp for the night, they were in high spirits. By the evening after next, at the latest, they'd be home. Geog freed the horses from their harnesses and tied them to a long line so they could graze freely but not wander too far.

Kel made dinner for the three and as they ate, Mart commented, "Yep...the person who should make the food is definitely Geog!"

The others laughed and Kel's reply was simply, "Told you so!"

After eating, Geog and Mart went out into the wilderness to set some snares, hoping to add to their food cache for the winter. When they returned, Geog asked Kel to tell them more stories he'd heard from his grandfather and read in the wondrous books his father owned.

"Tell us about the ancient city people whose greed brought the ice into the world."

"You've heard the story about how the Gods made the stars and all of this." He gestured with his hands to the world around him. "You also remember the story of the great Divine dragons whose magic fires made the stars and the Earth, and how the story said that the dragons danced to the music of the Divine and as they spun, they spewed out great fires that made the spirals of stars?"

The two nodded in agreement, eager for more as Kel continued, "It is said that the city men made windows of curved glass, some with silvered backs like the hand mirrors the ladies seem to like so much...I wonder if Mart has one of those?"

Geog and Kel laughed heartily at this, but Mart didn't seem to see any humor at all.

"With these giant mirrors and bent glass they could look deeply into the heavens. But they were greedy men and even with everything they knew, they claimed knowledge they did not really possess. They claimed that they had acquired the knowledge of how the stars were made and that the dragons were mere myth, bedtime stories for children. They tried to replace one religion with another, one of their own creation. Religions come and go; that is a fact. So, the creation of one religion to replace another seems the way of men and should not have made that much difference in the world."

"But the dragons really existed, didn't they?" Geog asked with a worried look on his face and Kel laughed.

"Who knows for certain? That is one of the ways of religion—the use of story to make a point. Whether the story is true is not important, what is important is the point the story makes. It is like giving medicine within food to a child. The medicine is what is important. The food just carried it to where it will do some good!"

They both laughed with Kel.

"So if religions replacing one another is the way of things, what happened?" Geog asked.

Kel looked at him and answered, "This is one of the big problems with religions. It is the same problem that plagues men in all of their enterprises. Because religions are the inventions of men, greed comes into the picture."

Geog interrupted Kel. "You are saying religion is made by men and not the Gods—this sounds like blasphemy to me."

Kel laughed. "Calm down, Geog. You'll break something."

Geog smiled worriedly and Kel went on.

"Think of it this way. Let's say that two men of differing religions look at a mountain. One says that the mountain is a God named 'Rock,' while the other insists that is not so and the mountain is a God named 'Stone.' So the followers of each faith make war upon each other. Now be the mountain for a moment. Do you care what these men say about you? Do any of their comments diminish you in any way? Of course not! The Gods simply are, like the mountain. Men tell stories about Them to try to understand Them, but in the end They still are who and what They are, and the stories are just that…stories."

The others nodded in understanding.

"This is what happened. The men of the ancient cities beheld the heavens…and wanted them. It did not matter to them how far away the stars or how empty the blackness between them. They wanted them, and in their greed they made mighty machines that could leave the Earth and fly toward the stars. They attempted to claim the heavens as their personal tribal territories. Then the ice came and the great cities used their magic to try to stop it. They used their sky windows to attempt to melt the ice by reflecting the sun onto the face of the glacier. They also set up great steam engines near the face of the ice to make heat, hoping to melt the ice that way. But nothing worked and the ice, a symbol of the greed of men, ate the great cities and their magic, and said, 'Mine!'"

Mart whoofed out a breath of air saying, "Well, nothing like a cheerful story to send us all off to bed…makes me wonder if you should wed Lyria and have children after all. Poor little kids probably wouldn't want to poke their heads out from under their blankets."

The small fire reflected the mirth in their faces as they laughed in unison. They decided to sleep under the wagon instead of setting their tents so they could make a quicker departure in the morning.

Chapter 2

...It was almost dark by the time Kel had climbed to the top of the path through the mountains. He stood atop the ridge and gazed down into the valley below him. It was hard to see in the deepening twilight and even harder to understand what it was he was looking at. To Kel it seemed that the plain below him was covered with black rocks, but the rocks seemed impossibly large and they were arranged in more or less straight lines with pathways between them. At the nexus of this orderly tangle of rocks, the stones soared into the sky. Even at this distance, he could tell that the tallest of the standing stones were over a hundred feet tall and that there were many of them! And he realized finally what he was seeing. It was the Black City of the West—the nation city that was named Los Angeles. Kel noticed a tiny spark of white light down in all that blackness, but he'd seen that before. Something else was calling to him.

Kel then looked to the south and he beheld a great forest extending as far as the eye could see. The great trees stood taller than most buildings and they were so densely packed it was impossible to see between them. Occasionally he could see the flutter of birds at the top of the canopy, but that was the only movement visible. The green was dark and solid, seemingly impenetrable. He couldn't believe his eyes—there surely could be no such place as vast and green as this! Then he looked at the edge of the mighty forest, hoping to see at least the trunks of a few of the trees. There he beheld a small city being built on the very edge of the forest several miles from an incredibly wide river. Again, he was shocked by the enormity of scale. The river was far wider than any he'd ever seen or could have imagined. The far bank faded into the mist that hung over the slowly moving black waters.

Kel looked at the small city and saw that it was a walled city of black stone. He saw that slaves were building the city. He was shocked by the distant sound of whips and the cries of the tormented people lifting one stone atop another, using great wooden poles and ropes. Two large black shapes hung over the city—they were gigantic cylinders vaguely pointed at each end. Under them was some kind of compartment that extended half the length of the objects. Kel realized with a shock that they were zeppelins. And in the farthest distance, he heard a noise the like of which he'd never before heard. Barely audible at this great distance, it was an animal noise—shockingly ancient, utterly alien and terrifying.

~

8

Kel awoke with a start. It was barely dawn. He was sweating even though the air was cool. He shivered. Last night he'd been sure his destiny lay in the Black City. Now he was no longer so sure. Imagine! Two black cities! He tried to return to sleep, but he found himself wide-awake staring at the bottom of the wagon. After he'd counted the knots in the wooden planks three times in the early morning twilight, he quietly arose and prodded the embers of the fire and added some dry grass. He looked up into the predawn sky, watching as a group of giant fireflies drifted over their camp. He watched them with curiosity—they were traveling in a straight line, he noticed. He counted twenty in all, and all heading in a southerly direction. How strange it was, for he knew the ways of fireflies—and they didn't fly in a straight line. Soon they were gone from sight, distance and the coming dawn blotting them from his vision.

When the flames of the fire returned, he put some wood into the blaze and began to prepare their breakfast. He smiled as he thought about Mart. He'd be pleased that his turn at making breakfast had been usurped. In the distance, he heard the howl of a Dire Wolf. He added a few more sticks to the fire and shivered, as the howl of the wolf seemed to change into that strange animal cry he'd heard in his sleep.

While breakfast was cooking, he walked over to the wagon and kicked the sole of Mart's boot.

"Get up, Mart! This is your day to cook."

Mart mumbled something about where Kel could put the sticks to build the fire, and then arose. He was surprised to find breakfast waiting for him. Geog awoke by himself. It seemed he was always hungry and could smell food while asleep.

They ate faster than they normally did, as each man was eager to get on the road and get home all the quicker. After breakfast, Kel told Mart to clean the plates and put out the fire. He could, after all, do some of his cooking chores this morning. As Mart cleaned up, Kel and Geog went to get the horses. They seemed a bit nervous this morning, though neither man could detect any reason why they should be skittish.

"Even the horses are anxious to be on the way home!" Geog said.

Kel, not so calm after his dream, glanced around nervously but saw nothing.

He thought about the wolf, but it had been at least a league away from where they'd camped. They struggled for a little while to get the horses in harness, but finally the job was done. The fire was cold and Mart packed the breakfast gear into the wagon— everything else was already packed. Tomorrow they'd eat with their families in their tribal town. Kel whispered to the horses and they calmed a bit. Though the horse wasn't his spirit animal, he had the ability to talk to them. He took the lead and they headed off away from the rising sun, toward home.

The small horses were stout and built for this kind of travel, so Kel and his companions made good time. After the first hour of travel, the horses again became skittish. Kel turned the lead line over to Geog and took his spear from the wagon. With the long iron head pointed toward the sky, Kel used the spear as a walking staff as he walked cautiously ahead of the horses, scanning the surrounding brush and rocks for anything that might pose a threat.

"Watch for snakes," Mart said.

That brought a chuckle from both of the other men, but Kel still stopped and listened intently. All he heard was the clopping of the horses' hooves, the creak of the wagon, and the subdued conversation of Geog and Mart. Kel himself was starting to feel a bit nervous—he felt as though he was not seeing something that he should be seeing, something that was right in front of his eyes. He sniffed the air, trying for a scent. There was nothing. As the wagon came up behind him, Geog halted the horses. One horse neighed and the other jerked in his harness.

Kel looked up from their path and for an instant he thought the air shimmered in front of his eyes. He blinked and then he did see something. Standing directly in their path was a huge ice tiger. He was shocked. This was too far south for the large predators to roam. The land didn't hold enough game for these large animals. The sun glinted off the big cat's giant incisors hanging like daggers from its jaws. The cat's tawny, slightly striped flanks rose and fell with its breathing. Kel instinctively lowered his heavy spear, firmly planting the iron-shod butt into the soft earth. If the cat jumped, it would impale itself.

Strangely, the horses began moving forward toward the large animal. Kel glanced at the horses as Geog jerked at the lead, turning one of the horse's heads so they'd both stop again. Why weren't the horses afraid of the tiger he wondered? He turned back quickly and the tiger was gone. All at once the truth came to him. The tiger was a 'sent thought,' a warning or message of some kind from Lyria.

"Did you see that?" Kel shouted.

Geog and Mart stared blankly at each other and then at Kel. It was clear that neither had seen the apparition Kel and the horses had seen. He now understood why the horses were not afraid—they'd instinctively recognized Lyria before he had. Kel was mortified; it seemed that a horse was a better shaman than he was!

As the day progressed, they discussed the vision and what it might mean. Kel had never had this happen before, though all three had heard stories. "I have always heard that something like this happens in time of extreme stress or danger..." Geog said nervously, but he cut himself off after seeing the rebuke in Mart's expression.

He turned to Kel self-consciously and murmured, "Uh...I'm sorry, Kel. You know I don't know anything about magic or the ways of a shaman."

Kel looked at him seriously. "What you say is true, there is no denying it. Something important has happened back home."

Mart suggested that to speed things along, they not stop for a midday meal. The others agreed with him and so they ate cold meat and the last of the bread that they'd brought with them on this expedition. Through midday and into the afternoon they moved on, not stopping or resting. Their pace wasn't especially fast and the horses had the endurance to go long distances at the speed at which they were traveling.

Mart finally spoke for the first time in over an hour, "Too bad we don't have one of those steam engines to take us back home like the cities have. We could be there in two hours."

"It would do no good unless you also had the iron ribbons that they roll on. If you build them, I will see what I can do about getting us a steam engine." Geog retorted.

Kel laughed at the thought of the three of them in the front of one of the long steam-snakes. He'd seen one such engine when he was a child of no more than six summers, but he remembered it vividly. Mostly he remembered the noise it made and the billowing black smoke that poured out of the top of it. He remembered being frightened, and being consoled by his grandfather and father as they explained to him how the snake could only follow the iron ribbons and that they were as safe as if they had been at home. Though the ribbons still lay to the north of their tribal town, there hadn't been a steam-snake pass in many years. It would seem that whatever lay to the east of them was no longer of interest to the men of the Black City.

They camped under the stars their last night, not wanting to take the time to pull the tents down in the morning. After rising, they found themselves again on the path home, riding at a steady pace. They were all eager to be home—and fearful of what the mysterious vision might mean. As they topped a low rise, they saw a faint wisp of smoke near the horizon. Finally! Home!

Geog looked at Mart and grinned, "Almost there, I can taste dinner already!"

Mart looked at Kel and said with a smirk, "If Geog has a spirit animal, I wonder what it might be? What kind of animal is hungry all the time?"

"I do not know of any animal that is hungry all the time except Geog. Perhaps he is his own spirit animal."

Geog made a threatening gesture with his hand and growled.

"Apparently it also has indigestion," Kel said, chuckling. And they all laughed at that.

The terrain was mildly downhill now and they set a brisk pace, each man keeping to his own thoughts. Once again the horses were calm as they trekked along patiently behind Kel and Mart. Here the vegetation was mainly low scrub. There was a lot of sage and calf-high grass. As they moved along, Kel cut some of the sage branches they passed. The small, dull green leaves made fine incense when dried and ground into a powder. He knew his grandfather would be proud of him for thinking of this. Kel smiled, rather pleased with himself.

By late afternoon they could see the small village ahead. Nothing looked better than home after several days away. Even the horses seemed eager to be home and they began moving a little quicker without Geog giving them any encouragement. As they advanced, Kel saw someone on horseback approaching from the village. He shielded his eyes with his hand as he tried to see who it might be. The sun, coming down in the west directly in front of him, allowed him to see only an indistinct black silhouette in the blazing glare.

Hunters and rider met about a thousand yards from the tribal town. The young woman on horseback leaped nimbly to the ground, her hair flaring in a dark cloud around her head as she dismounted. She approached at a run. Kel started forward as well. He'd recognized Lyria even before her arrival and he was both worried and glad at the same time—worried about the spirit animal he had seen and glad that Lyria was safe.

Lyria was dressed in the simple garb of the flatland tribes. She wore an unbleached linen top with long sleeves that could be detached at the shoulders and trousers with leggings that could be detached just above the knees by simply unhooking the small bone rods from the sewn loops through which they passed. In this manner the people of the flatlands could adapt their clothing to the temperature and the season. Around her neck she wore a simple necklace of tiny shells the inland tribes favored as decoration and for which they traded with others at the annual summer festival. At her waist she wore a leather belt trimmed in fur. On each side of her belt a long, curved dagger was sheathed.

Lyria looked at the three hunters. Kel saw both anger and, strangely, fear in her blue eyes. Lyria's breathing was fast from her run, but she was in excellent condition and prided herself on her physical stamina. "Kel, the day after you left on the hunt we were attacked."

Geog snarled, asking, "Bandits like three years ago?"

Lyria shook her head emphatically and said, "They stole from us, yes, but those who attacked us came from the air, not the land."

"How can this be?" Kel asked. "There has not been an airship raid in many years. I thought the Black City was done with us. They no longer even run their steam-snakes through our territory."

"It was an airship nevertheless. They came at night when the sky was filled with clouds and very dark. They carried no lights and we hardly heard them as they approached us from upwind. They must have circled around a distance away so they could come at us from the northeast."

She paused, looking into Kel's eyes, and then said, "The men of the airship brought a cloud with them. They dropped it on our town and the cloud put us all to sleep. Most people dropped right where they were—a few like Garn, your grandfather, managed to take a few steps before they fell."

She looked at him with sorrow in her eyes and she glanced quickly at the others.

"We did not awaken until the evening of the next day. By then the airship was far away. We did not understand what had happened and everyone felt as though they had been up a long day and had gotten no sleep rather than a full day of it."

"Kel," she spoke flatly now, "when the first of us awoke we began helping the others, it was then that we noticed that Garn was gone."

A tear slid silently down her cheek as she moved closer to Kel and hugged him. "Nothing else was taken from us. This was no slave raid such as the Black City used to do, nothing gone but your grandfather. Kel, why would they take just an old man and no one else? Poor Pela has been beside herself with worry."

Kel thought about his grandmother. It wasn't proper for someone of her age to endure something like this. The Gods took everyone eventually—that was natural and right. But this...this was unforgivable.

Lyria was not yet finished. She whispered, "Kel? Some of the tribe never awoke. Three babes and two of the old men, Ado and Vars were dead. Pela said it was the cloud, that it must have a more dangerous effect on the very young and the very old."

Now she was crying as he held her against him.

"This will not stand," Kel hissed between clenched teeth, "I will not allow it."

He held Lyria at arm's length and looked into her eyes.

"Let us be off to town so that we may plan what we must do."

Geog and Mart started the horses forward as Lyria mounted her golden mare. She rode beside Kel as they rode toward the town.

Chapter 3

At the outskirts, a small crowd of worried people met them. With Garn taken, the job of tribal shaman fell to Kel—a job he was as yet unprepared to take. The village seemed quite normal—there was no damage, nothing burned, nothing pillaged. It looked as though the zeppelin raid had been imagined. The people who'd met the group at the edge of town followed behind them silently. Kel knew he couldn't let the people see how unready he felt. What they needed now was a sure hand, and the confidence that things would be made right again. He decided he'd give it his best effort.

Pela met Kel and his little group in the central area of the village, which was clear of structures and used for town meetings and ceremonies. She was dressed much like Lyria, though she wore no jewelry of any kind. Kel knew what this meant. She was mourning as though she already considered her husband of fifty-five years to be dead. Lyria also made this observation and she looked at him with sadness in her eyes.

Kel hugged his grandmother and kissed her brow. She led them to the benches that bordered the open area and she sat heavily. For a short time, nobody spoke.

Then Pela sighed, "Why would they take my Garn, Kel?"

The plaintive note in her voice broke Lyria's heart and she quickly brushed away the tears. There would be time enough for tears later.

Kel hugged his grandmother again and said, "I do not know...I have never heard of this before. It would almost seem as though they came looking for him, but how is that possible? The men of the city do not pay attention to the ways of the tribes. At least they haven't up to now."

"It was a stealthy raid," Pela said. "They came in silent and dark, and the cloud they dropped upon us was like nothing I have ever heard of. In the past, the raids by the Black City have been in daylight with much sound and fury. They rely on fear and their superior weapons to subdue the tribes so they may take whomever they wish with little fighting. Still, the slave raids stopped years ago." Her voice trailed off in uncertainty.

Kel shook his head and said, "We need more information so we may form some plan of action. Tonight I will journey with Hawk to the west to see what I can see. Maybe there will be some clue as to what is going on."

He struck his fist against his thigh and Lyria gently covered it with her hand. "We will get the ceremonial materials ready for you," Lyria whispered. "Tonight I am confident we will learn something important."

Kel wished he were that sure. Once he and his friends were fed, they each headed home. Kel went to his family home and walked inside. He hadn't lived there for six years. When he was picked at eleven to serve as his grandfather's apprentice, he'd moved in with Garn and Pela.

Now, standing in the cool interior of his parent's home, he relaxed a little. He knew his part in the ceremonies well, having participated many times with Garn and then later on his own. Spirit travel tonight would be easy, although interpreting what he saw might require a bit more work. He sighed and lay down on the bed in his old room.

He smiled at the thought that his parents hadn't moved his bed out and used the room for something else. In a moment, he was asleep and slept dreamlessly until his father came into the house to wake him for the ceremony.

Kel walked across the clearing to Garn's house and entered. He was alone. He knew Pela wouldn't be there. She'd been the wife of the shaman for a very long time and she knew he needed solitude to begin his work. He removed his shirt and washed himself with the water in the tray that had been left for him. He dried himself with a linen towel and put on his ceremonial shirt. This shirt was made of finely tanned deer hide and was decorated with hawk feathers along both sleeves. When he was ready, he took a deep breath and went outside to do what should have been his grandfather's job.

The sun was just below the horizon and the sky was darkening quickly. The fire pit at the center of the open area was filled with wood and was now burning brightly. White smoke writhed toward the heavens—his spirit and that of his guide would travel that path very shortly.

Near the fire, the drum was set up. Upon the tightly stretched hide that made the head of the drum were painted the symbols of the spirit animals of the tribe. Those who wished to do so were assisted in a journey to find their spirit animal. Some chose not to and that was fine. It was a personal choice that bore no stigma if one chose not to test that path.

Kel searched the drumhead and saw the hawk symbol that belonged to him. He looked at the central symbol as well—the outline of the mastodon, their tribal totem. He walked slowly around the fire, feeling the heat.

Lyria moved up and sat at the drum. This was the first time she'd done so for a village ceremony. Lyria had come as a 'gift' of sorts from another tribe. She'd been having visions as a young girl and the shaman of her village hadn't been able to help her. This sometimes happened and when it does, the person goes to another tribe to have a different shaman work with him or her.

Sometimes a fresh look showed a path that hadn't been visible at the beginning. In Lyria's case, her path was discovered and she found that she'd been journeying without the drum—something very rare indeed. As Garn and Pela nurtured her skills, she and Kel developed a childhood liking for each other that evolved into more than friendship as they entered their teen years. By then they were inseparable, so they were betrothed to be wedded after Kel had done his shadow walk and had truly become a man of knowledge. Lyria knew that both the shadow walk and their marriage would probably be postponed indefinitely now that Garn was gone.

As Kel walked around the fire, Lyria began to strike the drum with the large leather-padded drumstick. The drum's voice boomed out at a steady pace. From her training she knew what was necessary—a steady beat that wasn't fast or slow. It was the heartbeat of the Earth—it was the heartbeat of the Mother. As he moved he began to take on the movements of a bird. He stalked around the fire jerking his head one direction, then the other. He lifted his arms and the hawk feathers hanging from them made his arms look almost like wings. Lyria watched his face, looking for the fixed, distant look that signaled the beginning of the trance.

The drum boomed…

Kel slowed his pace. He moved, stopped, and then moved again as though he had forgotten that he was walking. He stumbled a bit and came to a halt, staring into the fire, seemingly confused. Pela, who had returned to assist in the ceremony, threw some sage into the fire and the smell of the incense filled the air.

The drum boomed…

Pela went to Kel and helped him gently to the ground. He looked in her direction but he didn't see her—he was beginning to be somewhere else. Once he was lying safely on the ground, Pela gently laid his hands across his chest. She tapped his forehead with a hawk feather once, twice, three times. Kel inhaled deeply and relaxed. His breathing became shallow and regular as he became one with the Earth. His eyes glazed and then closed. Now it was time to see.

The drum boomed...

...Kel was walking along a forest pathway. He was following a very small stream that meandered between the trees. He could hear the soft murmur of the water as it played over small rocks and fallen twigs. He looked up and saw the sunlight filtering through the trees bathing everything in a gentle green light. He saw bright butterflies flitting between the glowing branches and when they moved into the sunlight they lit up as though they were made of gold. He returned his attention to the small stream. He'd been this way many times and he knew that if he followed the water, he'd find the clearing.

He moved around a large boulder set in the forest floor, stepping into the quietly flowing water. He passed the stone and a short distance farther he stepped over a fallen tree that lay across the water. He was almost there now. In the distance, barely audible, the drum boomed. He walked through a low hedge and was in the clearing. Now he could begin the real work...

The drum boomed...

...Kel walked once around the standing stone in the center of the clearing. He touched it. He'd found this place one day during a journey. Up until that time, he'd always entered a tunnel or cave to reach the Otherworld. Each time he'd only had limited success. Then Garn had told him to look for his own way. That was when he'd found the forest and the stone. He walked slowly back to where he'd come into the clearing, sitting in the grass. A light breeze moved the grass around him and he felt it caress his face like the gentle touch of the Divine.

A quick movement attracted Kel's attention. He looked at the top of the standing stone; a hawk stood there looking at him with black eyes. They stared into each other's eyes for a moment and then he spoke to the hawk.

"Great Hawk, master of all hawks, please hear me. My family has been struck, my nest raided. I need your clear seeing and your high flying to help me set things right again."

Kel stared into the hawk's eyes and the hawk stared into his, and then the bird nodded and...

The drum boomed…

…now he was moving very fast. He felt disoriented and confused. Why were the trees tipping like that? Why was the ground moving from side to side? He looked left and saw the great brown wing of Hawk. Sudden awareness struck him—the trees weren't tipping, he was. He was negotiating the trees at a fantastic rate of speed. Suddenly he burst through the green canopy and he was in free air. He soared into the incredible blueness of the sky. With a few flaps of his great wings he was above the clouds swimming through an ocean of clear air. The drum was gone. The forest clearing was gone. All that was left was the ecstasy of flight. Kel soared into the sun.

Suddenly his path changed. He was descending but he wanted to continue upward. He banked hard to the left and turned. He looked down and, with the acute vision of Hawk, saw a village very like his own. He dropped quickly, circling as he went. He passed low over the central clearing. There were a number of people standing there and they looked worried. He recognized Jos, the tribal leader of the village north of his own. Jos was speaking to several men and women.

Kel landed lightly on a rooftop. A small child gazed up at him and smiled. He knew this child could see him in spirit. This boy would be a shaman one day.

He then returned his attention to Jos. What he heard disturbed him greatly. "Why would the airship come like this, poison our children, and take our spiritual leader? What does the Black City want with our shaman? It just doesn't make any sense…"

Kel heard others speaking, but he'd heard enough—it was time to return home. He opened his mighty wings and soared into the air. He made one very low pass over the head of the smiling child, much to the child's delight, and then he soared off to the south. This information, whatever it may mean, was important. The Black City was kidnapping men of knowledge and magic…

…As Kel circled over the forest and began his descent back to the standing stone, he again could hear the drum in the distance. It was Lyria calling him home. He circled once more and dropped at lightning speed into the clearing. The Earth eagerly reached up for him, but he felt no fear. It was simply the Mother welcoming him back into Her arms…

The drum boomed...

...Kel was suddenly sitting on the ground again, staring up at the hawk. The hawk's black eyes found his. The great bird seemed to nod and then without further fanfare it took wing, soaring over the trees, and was gone. Kel wandered back along the path he'd taken into the forest. Over the fallen tree, going around the rock, he again stepped into the water of the small stream. The birds were singing and he smiled in spite of what he now knew. Spirit was a truly magnificent thing.

The drum boomed...

Chapter 4

Kel was once more lying on the ground. The drum boomed one final time and he opened his eyes. He was back in his world again, a world of weight, an earthbound world. He sat up suddenly and his head swam. He didn't care. He'd learned something important: The men of the Black City were stealing magic. There could be no other explanation.

Lyria and Pela came to him and helped him up. Lyria lifted a cup to his lips and he allowed the clear, cool water to flow down his throat. It always surprised him what thirsty work flying was. He looked around and the world came into focus more clearly. Lyria and Pela helped him to his feet. Ler, his father, was suddenly at his side adding his strength to assist him to the benches where the people of his tribe eagerly awaited his information. What he had to tell them would frighten them as it had frightened him.

Though he was exhausted, Kel couldn't sit down. His agitation of spirit made him pace back and forth in front of the people of his village. He gathered his thoughts and, with the fire silhouetting him, he looked into the eyes of everyone present. To the people, Kel seemed to glow. The firelight passing through the hawk feathers on his arms backlit them and the brown and white striped patterns shifted, blended, merged, and separated once again.

"I saw in a vision what is happening. I went up to Jos's village, and the people there had also been visited by the airship." He paused to let that information sink in before he continued. "Galv was taken in the night, just as was Garn."

The people looked at one another, though none dared speak their thoughts.

"Some of their babes also died in the attack from the sleeping cloud. What happened to us happened to Jos's tribe one night after our village was attacked."

Again Kel paused, and then continued, "This is going to happen again. The men of the Black City are stealing magic. They are taking the source of magic from the tribes. Why, I do not know. They have never been interested in our beliefs before this."

Adria, a young woman slightly older than Lyria, asked, "How? How do they know which of us are people of spirit and which are not?"

She looked at Kel, and her eyes spoke for her—she didn't believe him. Kel knew this would be a problem for some of the tribal members—

especially for Adria. People grew accustomed to their lives, even the dangers that might be present. What some feared more than danger was change and uncertainty. Now several others were beginning to look at Kel skeptically. He realized that if he couldn't move them, his journey had been for nothing and whatever the Black City was doing would go unchallenged.

"If they wanted magic, why did they not take Pela as well...or Lyria for that matter?"

Adria was jealous of Lyria and her position with the tribe, particularly with Garn and Kel. This was especially true since the bandit raid a few years earlier when Lyria discovered her spirit animal and had visited blood and death upon the bandits. That night she'd killed five men with her own hands using their own weapons.

"Surely if they wanted just magical power they would have taken them as well."

Kel was shocked. He felt the tone of Adria's voice—she half wished they'd taken Lyria. He didn't know how to reply to her, so Lyria filled the void in the conversation.

She rose and walked over to stand next to Kel. She was almost as tall as he and she knew they made a formidable pair—and she knew that Adria knew it as well. She looked steadily into Adria's eyes for a moment. The other woman dropped her gaze. Lyria was satisfied—she knew she'd won.

Finally Lyria spoke, her voice strong as she gazed at the entire gathering. "Think for a minute about the life of the people in the City of the West. Their beliefs are not ours. Their religion is not ours. In their belief, women are merely the property of men. They are bonded to their husbands in a kind of slavery, like a work horse and its master."

She looked around at the gathering. The firelight reflected in their eyes and Lyria couldn't tell if she was reaching them. Nevertheless, she continued.

"When people of the Black City wed, do you know how they refer to the couple about to be married? No? Here the man and woman are simply 'the betrothed,' they are equal—each one bringing something of worth to the relationship. When we wed it is a bonding of the God and Goddess, earth and sky, sun and moon. We are equal partners in the dance of life."

She paused, looking around her. "In the Black City a couple that is to be married are called a 'bride' and 'groom.' Think about this! Remember the horse I mentioned before? Is not a horse controlled with a bridle? Is not the master of the horse called the groom?"

Lyria noticed with some satisfaction that she still had their attention.

"The women of the Black City are treated like pack animals. They are nothing but mares whose purpose is to give birth to more men who will be taught to continue the tradition of superiority of men over women."

She stopped for a breath, as this was a topic near and dear to her.

Kel then spoke, taking what Lyria had said and adding to it. "The people of the Black City do not know that women can have power or work the magic between the worlds. Women are simply for pleasure, labor, and giving boy babies."

He glanced around quickly, adding, "They probably looked right past both Lyria and Pela never realizing what they were not seeing. Not seeing is the way of the religion of the Black City."

Lyria noticed with some satisfaction that Adria suddenly had nothing to say.

Llo, the elderly village blacksmith, asked, "Why are the airships stealing men of magic from the tribes? Are they trying to weaken us with the intent of raiding us for slaves again? They didn't do this before when they were taking men and women into the city. Why now?"

Kel shook his head and then he remembered the dreams that had disturbed him while on the hunting expedition with Mart and Geog. He remembered the walled city being built on the edge of an impossible forest. He spoke haltingly as he couldn't be sure.

"I think…I think the men of the Black City have found something. I think they have found something their religion can't explain and with which their science cannot deal."

He looked around at his people.

"There is a place far to the south. It is a land of forests as far as the eye can see. Even if you could walk through it, and I am by no means sure that you could, it would take many months to reach the other side. It might even take years."

The gathered people looked at one another in disbelief. They knew of forests, of course, but nothing similar to what Kel was describing.

Again, it was Adria who spoke in a challenging way, "There is no such place! It surely sounds like a dream."

"Yes, Adria it was a dream, but it was not an ordinary dream. This I know." Kel stared steadily at the young woman. She dared not directly contradict the young man who was now the tribe's shaman.

It was Llo who spoke next. He walked over to where Kel and Lyria stood. He cleared his throat and said, "There is indeed such a place as Kel describes."

He paused, looking around defiantly—as though looking for a challenge. His eyes paused momentarily on Adria and she lowered her gaze a second time that night.

"Far to the south this forest lies. I have heard tell of it from traders from whom I have bought iron."

He cleared his throat again, and then chuckled, "The fire of the forge is not good for one's throat!"

The group laughed and some of the tension was lifted from the gathering. Kel admired Llo's way with people—if only he had that kind of skill. Llo not only forged iron, he forged words. "Very far south of here the land tapers and narrows into a sort of funnel. At the narrow end, a great land spreads out in all directions. This land is nothing but forest, just as Kel described."

He looked around at the people whom he considered his family. "Even in the days of the old cities, before the ice crushed them, even as the war between the great tribes of the black cross and white star raged along the eastern coast, this land was unknown and unknowable. Strange diseases and even stranger creatures, both very small and very large would kill, maim, and eat the men of the cities. This area they called 'Green Hell' and they came to fear and avoid it…and what dwells within it."

When Llo quit speaking, no one else picked up the conversation. Everyone was struck dumb by the story they'd just heard. Kel heard again in his mind that strange, alien animal noise he'd heard in his dream *…and what dwells within it…* He shivered.

Again, Llo spoke. "All this is fine, but what are we to do about it? Garn is probably in the Black City by now."

"Then we must go to the Black City and bring him back," Kel said grimly.

Llo stared at him in disbelief and asked, "You will go into that place looking for him?"

"I will." Kel nodded.

Lyria added, "And I shall go with him to keep him safe and out of trouble."

There was some laughter.

Llo turned to her. "This is not a safe journey, and it is even less safe for a woman. Remember, bandits don't just steal money."

Lyria gave him a sarcastic snort; "I am as good with a blade as any man alive." A brief smile crossed her face, as she added, "And better than some who are not."

Llo could not argue against this and remained silent, remembering that night three years ago when the bandits attacked the village.

Chapter 5

That night came back to Kel vividly. It had been the time of the evening meal. Everyone was completely unprepared for an attack. Why should it have been otherwise? They hadn't experienced a bandit raid in twelve years and that had consisted of three men entering a storage building and making off with some salted venison. This last time though…

Kel remembered the confusion and the shouting. Twelve wild men descended upon the village, weapons ready. It didn't take them long to round up the unarmed villagers. Many of the men were gone on hunting expeditions at the time. He'd been fourteen summers and Lyria had been thirteen. As seven of the men went through the homes, five remained guarding the villagers with spears lowered. One of them noticed Lyria and a savage grin spread across his face. "While they are taking your food, I will take this pretty young thing."

He grabbed Lyria by the arm, pulling her roughly out of the circle. She jerked her arm free of his grasp, spitting into his face. Rage filled him then and he swung his fist into Lyria's stomach. She whimpered in pain, sank to the ground, semi-conscious. Kel moved forward, but a spear point pressed against his throat stopped him. The men all began laughing and taunting the man who'd taken Lyria from the circle to rape her right there in front of the villagers.

He grinned and said, "I will show you all what you have been missing."

His men cheered. He managed to move one step closer when the ice tiger took Lyria.

Suddenly she was up. She crouched before the man, with the soles of her feet and the palms of her hands flat on the ground. Her gaze swept past Kel and he shivered. Her eyes were suddenly an uncanny green. She growled low in her throat and hissed. Then she was on the man. Leaping straight into his face, she grabbed the shaft of his short spear, shoving the point under his chin. Then she settled on him and her weight drove him to his knees. The point of his spear burst through the top of his skull in a crimson fountain. Lyria leaped off of the man, bringing his spear with her. One of the other men turned toward her and she delivered a savage blow with the iron butt of the spear into his groin. He grunted but he never really had time to feel the pain. Lyria leaped straight up into the air with a scream no human throat could utter. She lifted the spear in both hands high above her head and, using her weight she drove the spear all the way

26

through his body and into the earth behind him. He was dead but still standing—held vertical by the spear.

She whirled to face the remaining three men. Quick as lightning she snatched the impaled bandit's long knife from its sheath, leaping again. She flew through the air toward the two bandits who stood side by side. She snarled, sweeping one man's spear out of her way with disdain as the heavy dagger in her hand met the man's throat, virtually decapitating him.

Before he had time to fall, Lyria's dagger caught the man next to her on his right shoulder. The curved blade was pointing down, the dagger sunk deeply into the man's shoulder, severing his brachial artery. He turned pale as his blood pressure dropped and he was unconscious before he hit the ground. It took him two minutes more to die as his blood pulsed out of his body into the dirt of the village meeting ground.

The fifth man turned to run, but it was too late. The ice tiger took him from behind, the long heavy dagger cutting through his spine. He dropped heavily to his knees. He was completely paralyzed. Lyria moved sinuously around him, holding one hand on his shoulder until she was kneeling directly in front of him. She leaned in close to his face, tipping her head in a quizzical manner, and then slashed once more with the dagger and the man was dead.

Five armed men slain with their own weapons in mere seconds. The villagers picked up the weapons of the fallen bandits and when the other seven came out of the houses to see what the noise was all about, they dropped their booty and fled into the night that had brought them. Lyria uttered a savage animal cry of triumph and victory, and then she collapsed. Kel was stunned. He'd never known that a spirit animal could just…take you.

Pela and some of the other women picked Lyria up and carried her into Garn and Pela's home. They laid her on a bed and tried to revive her. When they couldn't accomplish that, they removed her clothing and bathed her. They were astounded that none of the blood on her was hers. She'd moved through the battle unscathed, physically anyway. The next day she regained a sort of semi-consciousness that allowed the women to give her water and broth. Garn worked in his way to help her return completely to the physical world. He was in awe; he'd never seen anyone suddenly possessed by his or her totem like that. This girl was special that was for sure!

During those three days when Lyria lay between the worlds, Llo worked feverishly in his forge. He worked alone, stopping only to eat the meals his wife left on a table outside his forge. Three days later he left the forge with a linen bag in his hand. He told no one what was inside. On the fourth day, Lyria left the house for the first time. She was weak, but otherwise fine. As she sat in the sunlight, Llo approached her, handing her the linen bag.

He only said, "You will need this."

She looked up at him and smiled. Then she turned her attention to the gift he'd brought. She gasped in surprise when she drew out the leather and fur belt with two daggers mounted thereupon. She reverently removed one of the knives from the sheath, looking at the blade. It was fourteen inches long, curved, and the inside edge was razor sharp. She noticed that the point was thicker than the rest of the blade and she had no doubt these daggers could easily pierce the soft iron armor most tribal warriors wore, if indeed they had any armor at all.

She jumped up, strapping the daggers to her waist—then withdrawing them in a smooth, quick motion. She smiled at Llo and said, "No gift of any kind could be better than this."

Impulsively she hugged the old man, kissing his forehead. Llo blushed and mumbled something about being glad to have done it for her. She was admiring the blades when Kel walked up. She handed him one of the daggers and he examined it carefully. In spite of its length and weight, it was very well balanced and seemed light in the hand. Llo explained that the metal was all one piece, blade, guard, and pommel, and very strong. He told her how he'd shaped the blade using an ice tiger's tooth as his model. He presented her with the tooth as well. Though the steel blade had the same curvature and a bit more length than the giant cat's incisor, it was of course much thinner.

"The grip plates look like ivory, Llo. Is that correct?" Kel asked.

Llo beamed saying, "I used the ivory of an actual mammoth—the mammoth is a natural prey animal of the ice tigers."

Both Lyria and Kel were overwhelmed. Lyria thanked Llo again telling him the daggers would be called 'Teeth of the Ice Tiger.'" Much to Llo's pleasure, she began wearing the daggers every day.

Kel's distant thoughts of that long ago day were interrupted by Geog. "Well, if you two are going, I am going also. Somebody has to do the cooking." He grinned, and Lyria and Kel laughed.

Then Lyria, dreamily, said, "No Geog...this journey is not for you, it is ours alone." Her eyes were glazed, fixed into a stare that saw none of the physical world. Then it passed.

"I agree with Lyria," Kel said. "We will have to move fast and invisibly. The more feet on the trail, the more a track is left."

Geog looked disappointed.

"Look, Geog, someone has to spread the word to the other tribes. Everyone who has not yet been visited by the Black City must prepare for that eventuality. Your job must be to organize this task. It is vital. Whatever they are doing, we must prevent them from getting their hands on other shamans."

Geog nodded his agreement. He knew that Kel and Lyria were right. Now all that remained to be done was to devise a plan whereby Kel and Lyria could enter the city and do what needed to be done...and then get out again.

Chapter 6

The next morning Kel arose late. His journey and the aftermath tired him greatly after everything that had happened. He lay in bed a moment longer; then realized he was in his father's house, not Garn's where he normally slept. The events of the previous day came crashing in on him again. He felt as though he would burn the Black City to the ground if he could. As he started getting dressed, he heard an argument outside. He smiled, hearing Geog's voice.

"We need to figure out what they will need to pass through the great mountains. We already know what they will need for the westward trip to the mountains!"

Mart disagreed, "We need to plan for the whole trip, not just for the mountains."

"There are hundreds of miles to traverse and we cannot assume there will be much food in the mountains, so we must plan for that part of the trip first!" Geog said.

"If they don't make it to the mountains, it will not matter if they have provisions for that part of the trip," Mart retorted.

Kel opened the door, stepping into the early morning sunlight. Squinting as his eyes became accustomed to the light, he walked over to his friends, putting a hand on each one's shoulder. He smiled at each in turn and said, "Geog, I want you to plan the provisions for the mountainous part of the journey, and Mart you figure out the flatlands between here and there. Then both of you can try to discern what we should have for the other side of the great mountains."

Geog looked at Mart and said, "You know, he's got something there."

Mart agreed, "Yes, he does."

They both hurried off to take care of their business.

Kel smiled, shaking his head.

"Those two..." he mumbled.

Kel walked across the clearing, past the now smoldering fire pit, to Garn and Pela's home. He refused to call it simply Pela's home. He was certain he'd find Garn. Pela met him at the doorway with a smile.

"Come in, come in," she coaxed, "I have breakfast ready for you."

Kel entered his grandparents' home. There was cooked meat and eggs on a polished wooden dish along with fresh homemade bread. Kel's mouth watered. He hadn't realized how hungry he was.

He smiled at Pela. "This looks really good! Thank you."

He pulled out his chair and sat down.

"Well, eat then! We have more," Pela said and smiled at him.

She seemed to be in better spirits than yesterday. Kel supposed having him back was a welcome distraction. He knew she also held a secret hope that Kel might find and bring Garn home. After giving thanks to the Gods, his ancestors, and the spirit of the animal slain to supply the meat, he dug in. He was ravenous!

After he'd eaten, Pela asked, "With the books you have read in your father's house, have you learned anything about the civilizations to the west of us? Have you learned anything about the Black City?"

She was concerned that once Kel and Lyria got to the city, they might have trouble getting around without raising suspicion.

Kel thought about this a moment, and then said, "I have read a little of the city in the west. I know something of their religion and their style of dress. I think clothing will be the most difficult thing for us; they do not dress as we do."

Pela went over to a chest by the wall. She took out a bag that was tied at the top with a leather thong, opened it, and poured the contents onto the table—a profusion of copper and silver, along with a few gold coins, spilled over the tabletop.

"Take this money with you. With it you can buy what you may need in clothing as you draw near to the city."

Kel looked at the coins, and then looked up at Pela. "Where on Earth did you come by all of this money?"

"Garn and I have lived long and have seen much. Before you were born, Garn did his shadow walk with a tribe on the other side of the great mountain range." She pointed to the west.

"He never told me where he did his shadow walk," Kel said. "This comes as a complete surprise."

Pela laughed, "Life is full of surprises, young one."

"But this does not explain the coins."

"Of course it does!"

Pela looked sideways at Kel, and then said, "Can't you figure this out?"

Kel thought, and then ventured, "The other side of the great mountains is close to the Black City. I'll wager they trade some with Los Angeles if they are that close."

Pela smiled at him. "See? That wasn't so hard, was it?"

31

Kel laughed and nodded, "Not when you think about it, I guess."

"If you are to one day be a man of knowledge, you need to be able to think. Take the money; it has no value here and may have great value to you on your way."

When Kel opened the door and walked out into the morning air, he listened to see if Geog and Mart were arguing again. He heard nothing and smiled to himself, figuring they must be at opposite ends of the village. As he crossed the open area in the village's center, he saw Lyria talking with several of the women. He changed direction and walked toward them. Adria was with the group, and Kel was concerned that she might be making trouble for Lyria.

Quite to the contrary, Adria was in an animated conversation with Lyria. They were discussing what clothing Lyria should take for the long journey that lay before her. He noticed that Lyria was allowing Adria to lead the conversation. *Smart woman,* he thought, *why have an enemy if an ally can be had instead?* He passed them, making his greetings to all the women, and specifically to Lyria and Adria. He listened to the conversation as he continued on his way.

"Well, I think you should take enough extra undergarments. In the mountains there may be no streams in which you can wash your clothing," Adria said.

Lyria laughed, "That is sound advice! After all, women have a problem every so often that men do not."

The women in the group laughed, glancing coyly at Kel, who was looking over his shoulder at Lyria, and he reddened. He turned his head quickly back in the direction he was walking. Maybe he shouldn't listen quite so closely to the talk of women!

Later in the morning, Geog hurried toward Kel and said, "I have seen to it that four messengers have been sent to warn the other tribes in the area. I expect they will complete the task within six days and will need another four to return."

"That is all we can do," Kel responded.

"I wish we could travel faster." Geog sounded frustrated.

"We do what we can, Geog. Nobody can ask more of us."

"Hopefully we will not be too late."

Geog shook his head in anger and said, "Your trip to the Black City will take a long time as well. I have never known anyone who has traveled that far to the west."

Kel nodded, "Garn has, but his advice is beyond us now. I expect it will take fifteen to twenty days just to get there, depending on the conditions in the mountains. We can only trust our instincts and hope we make no mistakes."

"Oh, I think Lyria will keep you on course," Geog chortled.

"No doubt," Kel said with a smile.

Geog went off to make sure Mart wasn't wasting his time on foolishness, so Kel wandered back home to look in his father's books. He was seeking maps that might show a pathway through the great snowcapped peaks he knew awaited him just over the horizon. All he found were general maps showing a great area of land. While they were interesting, they gave him no real information on the lay of the land, where low passes might be and what travel conditions might be like in that part of the world.

He began to realize how little he really knew of the world outside the small area he called home. He wasn't fit for this task, he felt. But it fell to him nevertheless and he would do his best or die trying—he owed that much to his Grandfather and his tribe. He shut the book of maps, returned it to the shelf, and then sat in a chair for a time to reflect.

A sudden thought brought him to his feet. Of course! Why hadn't he thought of this right away? He remembered the old blacksmith's words about trading with men from the far south. Surely if he dealt with such widely traveled individuals, he must have heard something of the way west. Kel mentally patted himself on the back and headed out the door. He'd go see Llo immediately.

When he arrived at Llo's forge on the fringe of the village, he could hear Llo and his sons working. The ring of the heavy hammer on the anvil reverberated through the walls of the forge. He heard the rhythmic breathing of the great leather bellows Llo used to raise the temperature of the flame in the forge, which allowed him to work the iron. Kel walked up to the door and knocked. He knocked again, and Llo's wife, Danni, opened the door. She smiled at Kel.

"Well...so you are going on a journey soon?"

Kel laughed, "If I can figure out where I am going and how I will get there."

"Ahh..."

"Would it be possible for me to have a word with Llo?"

She stepped away from the door and motioned for Kel to come inside. He walked into their home. Sunlight streamed in through the large window at the front of the house.

"Please, sit down," Danni said. "I will go to the forge and ask if he can get away."

Kel nodded, smiled, and sat in a comfortable chair with carved wooden arms and a padded leather seat. He settled back. This was a very nice chair. He looked around as he always did whenever he came to visit Llo and his wife. The objects hanging from the walls in Llo's home had fascinated him from the time he was very young. The display always seemed to change, and it was always interesting.

Mechanical traps hung next to long and very sharp spearheads. Daggers of different lengths and shapes hung next to objects made of copper, silver, and iron that served no purpose other than decoration. Finely sculpted dragonheads of several sizes hung beside very realistic iron trees. Copper and occasionally silver-forged likenesses of animal footprints hung next to birds forged and welded with such skill and artistry they looked as though they would take flight at any moment. Llo was a true master at his art. When the summer gathering happened in a couple of months, he would take most of these objects, using them as trade for more iron, copper, and perhaps some of the exotic fabrics that came from the Far East or the southern regions where men spoke with different words. Both Kel and Llo knew the universal language of art and barter could bridge any language barrier between groups of people. Kel's happiness faded slightly when he realized that for the first time in his life he would miss the summer gathering of the tribes.

Chapter 7

His thoughts were interrupted when Llo walked in and went to the large copper basin to wash his face and hands. He dried his hands on a linen towel, glancing at Kel as he did. He walked over and sat in a chair facing the younger man.

"So…Danni says you would like to talk with me."

"Yes. I seek advice."

Llo smiled. "You are wondering about what lies ahead of you, are you not?"

Kel looked at Llo seriously. "I have no knowledge of what lies to the west. I thought you might be able to give me some information."

"That I can, young Kel. In years past I have traveled even beyond the western mountains…with your grandfather."

Kel started with surprise.

"You traveled with my grandfather? I just recently found out from Pela that he had traveled that far."

"People get involved in what they are doing in the present and forget that those around them have not experienced what they have."

"I can see that," Kel replied with a smile.

Llo chuckled and began his story.

"West of us all the way to the mountains, the land is pretty much as you see it here. There is sage, scrub, some trees, and grasses; the climate is pleasant most of the year, as it is here. Before the ice, this area was a desert and living was hard then, or so I have been told. Closer to the mountains you will begin to see more trees. They will be smaller at first, but as you go up, the trees get bigger and taller. It seems they like the cold air more than we do."

Kel laughed and asked, "How many days do we travel before the land changes?"

"Oh…let me see…it has been a while since I have taken that journey." Llo paused and Kel waited patiently. "It will take you at least six days riding to get to the low hills that lead into the mountains."

He looked hard at Kel and said, "If you push the horses more than six or seven hours a day, you will lose them. It will take much longer to reach the Black City if you are on foot."

He paused for effect, and then added, "Impatience is a path you must not travel, Kel."

Kel nodded, "The horses will need time to sleep and feed, just as we will. I understand what you say."

"Make sure you heed this advice. It could mean your life if you do not—and the life of your Ice Tiger."

Llo rose, walked to a corner of the room, and picked up a heavy wooden box. He brought it back and set it on the floor between them. He looked at the young man, and then opened the box. Kel saw a variety of wrapped objects. Llo took one out of the box, and unwrapped the cloth that padded and hid what was within.

In his hand Llo held a magnificently forged and carved darkened copper and silver eagle. The russet brown patina on the copper was very like the dark brown of an eagle and the silver in the design represented the white feathers of the great bird. Though the sculpture was small, the detail was exquisite. He looked up and said, "These items you will take with you to use in trade for what you might need as you travel."

"Llo, I cannot take these items…are they not what you have made for the summer gathering?"

"Yes, but I have more. Look around you, boy, we have many items to trade."

Kel slowly nodded, overwhelmed by the enormity of the gift. "I will trade wisely, that I promise you."

"I believe you will, especially with Lyria watching."

They both laughed. It seemed everyone in the village thought Kel needed Lyria's guidance for everything he had to accomplish.

Llo went on with his description of what he and Lyria might encounter on their way to the Black City. He warned of the huge, tawny mountain cats that might catch one unaware from rocks overhead. He told him of the mountain snakes that carried poison in their jaws similar to the rattling snakes he was familiar with around his village.

Then he told him about the great village on the other side of the mountains. Kel was astounded when he heard what Llo was telling him. He listened intently, knowing his fate and perhaps the fate of his entire village depended on him.

"The village is huge," Llo began. "Imagine this village increased by about twenty times."

"Is it a village or a city?" Kel asked in wonder.

Llo laughed, "It is a village just like ours, but over the years many of the smaller tribes have banded together and consolidated their living arrangement."

Kel thought about it, and then said, "They would have many hunters they could field at one time and there would still be warriors left in the village to protect it from bandits."

Llo nodded knowingly, "This they have learned from trading with the Black City."

"They have dealings with…them?" Kel's voice was scornful.

"When you walk out into the wide world, your opinion of things must widen as well. Not everything black is evil, and not everything white is good."

Kel nodded. He could see Llo's point—he just didn't want to believe it. It was simpler to think of Los Angeles as an evil entity, a monolithic unit of darkness.

While the men were silently thinking about what had been said, Danni approached with honey cakes and hot tea. They thanked her and tasted the cakes. Kel always had a liking for Danni's honey cakes.

"These are very good, Danni," he said. "Each time I taste one, it is better than the time before, impossible as that might be."

She smiled at Kel. "Thank you, sweet thing. Maybe you simply recognize the honey within yourself."

Kel blushed and Llo guffawed. After they'd eaten a cake or two and sampled the tea, they set their dishes aside and Llo continued his explanation of what he might encounter on his journey.

When they finished their conversation, Llo handed Kel a rolled up piece of tanned sheepskin. When he unrolled it, he found a detailed map of a way through the great mountains. Landmarks were clearly indicated and distances roughly annotated. "Well," Llo said with a sly smile, "You didn't think Garn and I traveled blindly did you?"

Kel laughed, "No, but I had no idea he or you might have a map."

"This map is old," Llo warned. "Some of it might no longer be true. But the major landmarks and the location of the tribe we talked about should still hold after all this time."

Kel thanked Llo, rolled the precious map, and put it in the box with the trade items he had been given. They finished their cake and tea, Kel said his goodbyes to Llo and Danni, and then he was back outside walking slowly toward his grandparents' house. He was deep in thought.

He walked in and put the box Llo had given him on the floor. He then went back outside to find Geog and Mart. He could hear them arguing and moved toward the sound of their voices. He found his friends behind the building used to store the food supply for winter. They were loading a small, two-wheeled wagon.

"The heavy things should go to the front so they will help balance the cart."

"No," Mart retorted, "the heavy things should go near the back so they can be more easily loaded and unloaded."

"How about putting the heavy items in the center over the axle—that is where the greatest support will be."

Kel smiled when his two friends looked up at him.

"That is not a bad idea."

"Actually, it isn't," agreed Mart.

Kel watched them for a moment as they first put some very soft tanned hides to the front of the cart along with rolls of tribal woven linen. As they were tying this to the front of the cart, his curiosity finally got the better of him.

"Um, why are you loading the cart with pelts, hides, and linen rolls?"

"Oh, that is not all we're going to load on," said Geog, very sure of himself, "but don't worry, we will leave ample room for food."

"We have it all planned," Mart added, "and we did leave room for the food."

Kel was mildly exasperated; neither man had answered the question he'd asked.

"But why are you loading the cart?"

"Oh…we thought that would be obvious."

"Yes! Plain as the sun in the sky," Geog agreed.

"Well…assume the day is cloudy and the sun is not at all plain."

Geog and Mart looked at each other in surprise.

"When you and Lyria leave, you will be riding horses. You will take a third horse with the goods in this cart to use as trade items."

Geog looked at Kel sympathetically, as though he thought Kel would find this complex idea to be confusing.

"That way when you get to other tribes or even the Black City, you will look like a simple trader and, in fact, you will have something to trade," Mart said, looking at Kel seriously.

"And you can take tents and enough food for both of you and even some grain for the horses should grass be in short supply," said Geog, finishing Mart's thought.

Kel looked at his friends in surprise. They'd figured this out in spite of themselves. He was actually proud of them.

"You know," he said, clapping both men on the shoulders, "that is a brilliant idea."

"We thought so, too. We can be brilliant if we put our minds to it." Geog finished.

"I have one other box you can fit in. Llo gave me some iron and soft metal work he had prepared for the summer gathering. He suggested the same thing."

Mart and Geog looked at each other.

"Now don't go thinking you are all THAT brilliant," Kel said with a laugh.

His two friends laughed as well and then went back to loading the cart. Feeling ignored again, Kel went off to find Lyria. She was always good with horses and he wanted her opinion of which horses they might take.

"We need sturdy horses, rather than really fast ones," Lyria stated.

"I agree," said Kel. "We should also get a stronger one to pull the cart. It might get a bit heavy if Geog and Mart have anything to say about it."

Lyria rolled her eyes, "Are those two going to do that?"

"They are doing it right now."

"Well, that may be for the best, it will keep them occupied for a while."

"That it will," Kel said knowingly. "That it will."

They looked over the horses and Lyria made her selections. She chose three young ones, Fog, Mist, and Morning, and was certain the tribe would agree. Everyone wanted them to bring Garn back. Llo, whose job it was to make and fit the horseshoes, said he would re-shoe the three selected horses. It could mean the difference between crossing the mountains with three healthy horses, or the possibility of one or more throwing a shoe and turning up lame.

Mart and Geog rolled the little cart into a storage shed for the night. Clouds were building and it looked like it might rain. Everything was ready. If it didn't storm tomorrow, Kel and Lyria would set out on the first leg of their long journey.

Chapter 8

That evening, the tribe gathered beside the fire pit. They had a small fire this time, with everyone sitting around, talking as though everything were normal. Their fears were held back this night. It was a time for last camaraderie with soon to be parted friends.

"Well, everything is in readiness," Lyria said.

The firelight cast an orange glow over her face. Her dark hair enhanced the effect. To Kel she seemed to be almost ethereal.

"We will do what we are setting out to do," Kel said with certainty in his voice. "They will never suspect that we might follow them and attempt a rescue."

"We packed two bows and about forty arrows," Geog stated.

"And plenty of food—and tinder for cooking fires," Mart added. "I wish we were going with you."

"Me, too," Geog stated matter-of-factly.

Kel smiled at his friends. "I know you do, but someone has to be here when the riders you sent out come back. Until we hear their news, we don't have any idea what you may need to do next."

"You are right," Geog agreed. "But that doesn't make the wishing any less."

The three of them laughed in the glow of the fire. They'd be friends for life, and hopefully their lives would all be long ones.

Lyria glanced up into the sky, but then her head remained tilted up. Her gaze captured Kel's attention. He looked up and asked, "What is it you are looking at?"

"Are those fireflies?"

Kel strained his eyes. "They might be," he said, finally catching sight of the pinpoints of light, "but they look very high."

"They are all flying to the south. Did you notice?"

"Yes, but fireflies don't usually fly together like that. Still, I have seen such a thing when we were preparing to return from our hunting expedition."

They continued to watch silently with the others as the lights moved slowly south. It was strange—they were more or less following a straight line south. Why were they moving like that? They watched as several groups of ten to a dozen lazily drifted over their village. The lights disappeared south of the village. Kel shook his head; there were mysteries enough on the Earth right now for them to worry about.

Finally, it was time for everyone to sleep. Kel looked to the north. It was too dark to see the clouds, but he did see an occasional flicker of lightning. Tomorrow would bring what it would bring. Kel rose from his seat and started toward Garn and Pela's home. He'd sleep there tonight, in the house he'd lived in since his training began. Maybe he would dream.

Lyria got up and walked with him.

They briefly touched hands but there was nothing to add to what had already been said, except, "I love you, Lyria. Please take care. Promise me you won't go rushing into battle on the spur of the moment."

"I love you too, Kel," she said, smiling at him in the darkness, "and I will be careful and cautious throughout our travels."

They parted company. Kel went into Garn's home. He was tired. He lay on his bed, looking at the ceiling of his second home. He sighed and drifted off to sleep. Two houses away, Lyria was also descending into a deep slumber. She was tired and tomorrow would be the first very long day of many yet to come.

~

... It was almost dark by the time Kel had climbed to the top of the path through the mountains. He stood atop the ridge, gazing down into the valley below him. It was hard to see in the deepening twilight and even harder to understand what it was he was looking at. Then he suddenly realized what he was seeing. It was the Black City of the West—the nation city that was named Los Angeles.

Kel turned, looking to the south; he saw an endless vista of trees. The dark green canopy was impenetrable. Below him, he saw a small city standing on the edge of The Green. That city, like its northern counterpart, was also made largely of black stone. The city was very far away. To the east of the city flowed a river of impossible size, whose farther shore was obscured by mist and humidity. Kel thought it odd that he could see so well, even though it was long after nightfall.

Suddenly, the great black river was close, so close he could see a ship on it. He soared in the night sky on silent wings watching what the men on the ship were doing. What were they doing? He didn't understand what he was looking at. The ship sailed quietly down the river, into the widening mouth. As the great river flowed into the ocean, the craft made a turn, following the coast toward the city. Kel looked over in the direction of the city. It was night. Everyone was asleep. No eyes would see this silent ship as it passed them.

He recognized it as a crystal ship by the array of huge quartz crystals over the stern of the vessel. He'd read how the crystals would focus the sunlight, heating the water, which made the steam to run the large craft. The top of the ship seemed strange, even though he'd never before actually seen a crystal ship. He was distracted a moment later by something that was happening on the deck.

Kel saw vast canvas tarpaulins stretched tightly over some huge object. Whatever it was, it tapered to both ends and was massive in the center. What the tarpaulins hid, he could not guess. The strange thing that originally attracted his attention was the smoke. It seemed that roughly every ten minutes or thereabouts, slight puffs of white smoke would drift out from under the concealing cover. What could that mean? Was something afire on the ship?

The ship slid placidly past the sleeping city to dock at a second wharf on the shore. This wharf belonged to the great church that the priests built before work had begun on the city. Kel saw men throwing lines to other men on the dock. They were securing the ship prior to unloading it. But what was the cargo? He strained his eyes to see...

~

The first birds of dawn were singing cheerfully when Kel awoke. He thought briefly of his odd dream, going through it mentally before he opened his eyes. This was another of those enigmatic dreams he felt must be remembered, though why that was the case, he didn't know.

Now he could smell food cooking in the main room. He smiled, opening his eyes, his dream temporarily forgotten—Pela was making him breakfast. He rose, put on his trousers and shirt, washed his face and hands in the copper basin in his room, and then opened the door. Lyria stood by the cooking fire, smiling at him. It was Lyria who had made his breakfast. He saw Pela standing nearby, smiling broadly. Kel smiled at the two of them.

Lyria smiled brightly, her blue eyes sparkling. "I thought since we would be traveling together, I should get some practice making the kinds of food you like."

Pela asked jokingly, "Are you awake yet, Kel?"

Kel yawned. "Awake enough to notice Lyria's hair," he said with interest. "I rather like that look."

Lyria smiled, "In the tribe I came from originally, the women would put up their hair like this when battle loomed."

43

"Are we going into battle?" Kel, asked.

"Hopefully not," she answered, "but with my hair like this, it will not get in my way should we need to fight."

"Well, I find your…battle braids to be very attractive."

Lyria shook her head, grinning.

"I like it this way as well," she said, "maybe I will keep it this way from now on."

She'd braided her dark hair into many narrow, tight braids that hung in rows on both sides of her face. The braiding shortened her hair, keeping it close to her head, even when she shook it.

Kel became serious, saying, "I have had yet another strange dream of the city in the south."

"Tell us," Lyria said, now very serious as well.

They sat at the table, and as they ate breakfast, he told the two women about the dream he'd awakened from.

"Something important was aboard that ship," Lyria mused.

"If it was burning, why were the men so calm?" Pela asked.

Kel answered, "I do not think that the smoke I saw was a fire."

"The sleeping cloud," Pela suddenly suggested, adding, "it came down on us like white smoke."

"She's right," Lyria, added, "could they have been making prisoners sleep under the covering? Perhaps the shape you saw was some kind of cell for prisoners."

"Does the Cathedral of the Black City take prisoners? I have never heard of such things. Surely the zeppelin raids we have suffered could only have come from a large, powerful place like Los Angeles."

"You are probably right," Pela agreed.

"We will find out soon enough, once we get to the Black City of the West," Lyria said, shuddering.

They ate the rest of their meal in silence, each lost in their own thoughts.

After breakfast, Kel and Lyria walked out into a gloomy morning. The sky was grey and overcast, but the possibility of rain seemed remote. It would seem the fury of the storm had been spent farther to the north. They both looked up at the sky. A cool wind was blowing in from the west. It would actually be a pleasant day to begin their long journey. The breeze from the west promised clearer skies later in the day; the clouds that had come in from the north would probably be swept away by noon.

"I expect we might as well say our goodbyes and be on our way," Lyria said.

"I suppose so…the way will not be any shorter this afternoon."

Kel went back to his father's home. Ler greeted his son warmly, and said, "Kel, I have something I want you to take with you."

"What is that, father?"

Ler handed his son two of the precious books from his library. One was a history of the nation cities. It told how they came to be in the days after the ice crushed the unity of the land. The second was of the religion of the west. Kel thought both books would come in handy, supplying valuable information they might need when they reached Los Angeles.

"You are going into a snake pit, Kel."

"I am afraid you may be right about that."

"Read. Learn. If you can make yourself look like a snake and act like a snake you will pass unnoticed by the real snakes."

Kel smiled. "That is very sound advice, father."

They embraced and Ler patted Kel on the shoulder.

"Take care of her, Kel. She is a rare kind of woman."

Kel nodded in agreement, "I have no argument with that."

"Find your grandfather. Take your shadow walk, whatever that may be, and live to wed your Ice Tiger."

When Kel pulled back, he saw his father's eyes bright with tears almost shed.

"I wish your mother had lived to see what a fine young man her son has become."

Kel smiled at his father and stepped out of the house into the open air.

Geog and Mart approached, leading the strong workhorse that was harnessed to the small two-wheeled cart. "Your food and fire-making equipment are at the very back so they will be easy to get to."

"And your tents are right behind them," Mart finished the sentence Geog had begun.

Kel smiled at them and embraced each of them warmly.

"Take care of the tribe, my friends, the people need you."

Mart smiled, "You'll be back before too much can happen to us here."

"See that you are right about that," Kel replied.

Lyria came riding up to the three men. The women of the tribe followed in a line behind her. She rode a light grey stallion that pulled at the reins. The horse was as ready to go as she was. Lyria handed another

45

set of reins to Kel. His horse was almost the same light grey color as the one she rode. Both had subtle mottling of darker gray irregular patterns—the reason for their names—Fog and Mist. Being brother and sister, they were good companions for each other and for the humans who'd be riding them. On the left side of Kel's saddle a scabbard was attached in which a light spear was set, tip down. It was in a convenient location should it be needed quickly. There was another on Lyria's saddle as well, and she wore her two beloved daggers, the Teeth of the Ice Tiger.

Now there was nothing left to do but the one thing they wanted least to do. They were ready to leave. Kel mounted Mist, pulling her reins to turn his spirited animal to face into the wind coming from the west. He took the reins of the workhorse, Morning, from Mart. The horse took two steps forward. She'd been well trained and would follow them even if Kel dropped the reins. Faithful Morning was named so because as a very young filly, she'd always been up early, always eager to be around people. With a flick of the reins, they took the first steps of a very long journey. Neither envisioned how long it would actually be.

They rode out of the village side by side. As they passed the last building, they both looked back. They missed the village already. They turned again, heading slowly out into the scrub brush, heading ever west.

The people of the village followed at first—sixty adults and twelve children of varying age. Only a dozen stayed in their homes, too old or sick to take the walk. The people of the village strung out behind Kel and Lyria, chatting among themselves, laughing at quips some of them made. The children were laughing and running about. Today was just another day of adventure to them.

As distance from the village grew, the crowd thinned. A mile from the village, only a dozen or so still trailed behind the two people who were the hope of the tribe. Then, after another mile, they shouted final goodbyes, waving at the departing couple.

Kel and Lyria turned in their saddles, waving back at them. They turned back to the front and sadness descended upon them—mixed with the sadness was the excitement of the journey and the knowledge of its importance to the tribe.

Chapter 9

The last of the villagers began walking back home slowly. Now there was no laughing or banter. The immensity of what was transpiring set in. They walked quietly back to the village and their homes. Only one person lingered. She walked slower than the others and soon they'd left her behind. She didn't mind. It seemed she was always being left behind.

Adria kicked at a rock she felt was in her way and it skittered out into the brush. Of all the people of the village, she thought, she was probably the only one who was happy that that woman was gone. She kicked at another stone and missed. She stopped, went back and kicked it a good one, sending it sailing away. She smiled grimly. Now that Lyria was gone, perhaps she could come into her own. No, that wasn't right. Now that Lyria was gone she WOULD finally come into her own. Her mind raced. She thought back to those bitter years, back to when she was a child. She snorted in disgust, remembering all of it...

She remembered how her father and mother told her they thought she had the talent to be a shaman. She was too young then to fully realize what that meant, but she knew it was important. She wanted to be important. She had dreams back then, dreams that might be foretelling dreams, and her father told her he was going to take her to Garn, the shaman of the tribe to see what he thought. She remembered how excited she was.

Garn listened patiently to her father, and then he had asked her to tell him her dreams. She told what she could remember and Garn asked her what she thought they might mean. She wasn't so sure about that, but Garn didn't seem concerned. Interpretation of dreams was frequently guesswork at the best of times. Who could say what the Gods were trying to communicate with the special dreams they sent from time to time? Only after much practice could the most talented shamans become really good at that kind of interpretation.

Garn accepted her on a preliminary basis and her instruction began. She could tell, even back then, that she would be great. But the feeling was not to last very long. Garn set the time for a drumming ritual. He wanted to see how she would do in a journey beyond the physical. He wanted her to seek her totem. He instructed her carefully how to visualize a cavern in the Earth as she listened to the rhythm of the drum. She'd travel through the tunnel, and come out into the bright sunlight. She'd seek the animal that would be her spirit guide. She smiled a bitter smile remembering how she felt that day.

The drumming ritual had worked. Adria had indeed left her body behind and found the other world—and she found insects. She found centipedes and scorpions. She became frightened, jumping out of the journey without following the drum back as she'd been told to do.

Garn then suggested that she receive more training before they try again. She thought he was being unfair, but she agreed to go along with him. She studied with Garn, and then with Kel for a year. She liked Kel because he was easygoing. He didn't judge her the way her parents had, and now the way Garn seemed to be judging her all the time.

That was about the time SHE came.

It wasn't fair. Her father was tribe born and so were both of his parents. Shouldn't the student of the shaman be a person from the tribe? She thought so. But then that incompetent, so-called 'shaman' from the northernmost tribe of their trading circle had come with the girl. They traveled all the way from the face of the ice in the north to talk to Garn. An outsider—two outsiders—had usurped her position. If the northern shaman had been competent, he could have solved Lyria's problem himself, but no! He couldn't deal with the girl, so she was 'gifted' to Adria's tribe for assistance.

Adria kicked at another stone and it too went flying off, making a satisfying clatter as it struck some larger rocks. Everything had been going so well up to that point. Adria was about thirteen at the time, Kel was twelve, and that girl had been eleven. Things deteriorated quickly after that. Garn discovered that Lyria could journey without the use of the drum. It seemed that was a rare talent that needed attention and guidance. It was true that Garn kept Adria in training at the time as well. She'd been progressing some, but the next time she journeyed, she'd again seen insects—stinging insects. Very large scorpions and centipedes this time, four or five times their normal size in the world. She knew Garn was becoming concerned; she vowed to herself to try harder.

The three of them continued training together for a while longer. Adria remembered how she'd fallen in love with Kel. Garn said he would be a good shaman, and with Adria by his side, who knew what they might accomplish. Then something went wrong. Kel suddenly discovered Lyria in 'that' way. She knew he was falling in love with her, and she was furious.

Then there was the night of the bandit raid. While Kel tried bravely to defend Lyria, she'd turned into something ferocious, saving the entire tribe as well as her virtue. She, on the other hand, had stood by and done nothing but shiver in fear, afraid that one of the men would see her and take her, too. She'd been glad, actually, when that bandit said he was going to rape Lyria. That would've taught her a lesson in humility.

She'd decided she needed to do something big, something big that would recapture Kel's attention—and Garn's. She decided she would do a journey on her own. If Lyria could do it, why couldn't she? She asked a friend to help since she still needed the drum, or something like it to reach the other reality. She fumed—how was it that THAT woman didn't need a drum? In the end there was nothing she could do except steal one of Garn's rattles. She'd had enough training to know that a rattle would work for journeying almost as well as a drum. The two of them went a short distance into the scrub. She didn't want anyone to hear the rattle.

Adria laid the blanket on the sand just out of the firelight from the village. Adria had been afraid to use someone older for fear she'd tattle, so she chose a friend who was a giggling young girl of eight. As Adria laid out the blanket, she instructed the young girl on how to use the rattle—how to be rhythmic.

"You have to keep up the steady pace until I wake up again, do you understand?"

"Yes," the girl answered, her voice soft with fear.

She was actually doing what they'd planned.

"Good. Then let us begin. I'm just as good as that tiger girl," Adria said spitefully, "even better!"

She lay down on the blanket, shifting around until she was reasonably comfortable. A cool breeze blew through the air—it was a pleasant evening for this. She smiled. Now she would show them!

She glanced at the young girl and nodded her head. The other girl began shaking the rattle. She was very steady with the rhythm. Adria relaxed, took a deep breath, held it a moment, and then let it out. She did this two, and then three times, as her body lost all the tension she'd held inside. She was beginning to see.

There was the tunnel! It was working. She would show them all! She walked through the tunnel and when she came out the other side, it was night. Shouldn't it be bright daylight? She could hardly see, but she could hear quite well. She heard the dry slithering and clicking of hard little claws on stones. The whisper of many small feet in the sand...

She heard a distant sound, like the wailing shriek of a very young child. She felt as though her skin was tingling. Something very sharp poked her in the arm. Another sharp stab in the leg...

And suddenly Garn was there. Adria opened her eyes, once again coming out of the journey world directly into the physical world. Several people were holding torches aloft to supply light. Garn was slapping her. Why was Garn slapping her? She was a good girl. She was a powerful girl. Again she felt a sharp poke on her arm.

Now totally in the waking world, she looked down at herself and began screaming in horror. Centipedes and scorpions swarmed over her body. Garn was not striking her; he was striking the insects that crawled over her body—over her face and her legs and under her clothing.

Garn stood her up and then he was undressing her, right in front of everyone. Kel was there. Garn ripped off her shirt, slapping the insects from her neck and her naked breasts. Then her pants were gone and Garn was slapping the things from her lower body—from everywhere.

Finally it was done. Pela came forward, covering her with a blanket. Never in her life had she been more humiliated. That old man and Kel had seen her naked and screaming in fear. Now they'd never think of her as strong. Now they'd never let her finish her training. Crying, she turned and ran into the village.

Over the next few days, she allowed Pela to treat the insect stings. Fortunately there had only been four or five. She was lucky and she knew it. It could have been much worse. *It was*, she thought, *almost like the scorpions and centipedes were worshipping me.* She knew the stings were probably accidental, caused by Garn's meddling. She'd have to think about this a while.

When she was completely healed, she left her parent's house with her head held high. If some of the others looked at her with scorn—that was their problem. Then there were the ones who looked at her with just a little bit of fear—now they were the interesting ones.

Garn's rattle had been broken. During the tumult someone stepped on it. Hmph! That wasn't her fault. The old man probably stepped on it himself just so he could blame her—not to her face, of course—he didn't work that way. So the rattle had been passed down from his grandfather— so what. It was just a gourd with some dried beans inside and attached to a stick. She couldn't understand why he cared so much. He'd told her it wasn't the rattle, but the fact she'd stolen it that concerned him. Well, anyone could see that she hadn't stolen it. She was going to put it back when she was finished with it. Oh well…

But now the old man was gone. That woman was gone and Kel was gone. She'd thought she loved him but now she knew that he was just as insincere as Garn and the rest of them. She didn't need him either. She could play that game of insincerity too.

She was the last to return to the village that morning. As she passed through the common ground, she smiled at folks and expressed her deepest, most sincere concern for the travelers. She expressed only the very best wishes for the two of them on their journey. She smiled at Pela, telling her she was convinced Lyria and Kel would bring her husband home—as if they could. She opened the door to her home, walked in, and closed the door behind her. This was going to be her time.

Chapter 10

Lyria and Kel rode in silence for another mile. To the far west the sky was blue. Kel looked up. Though the sky was still overcast, he could now see bright spots in the clouds where the sun was trying to come through. He sighed.

"Things will work out," Lyria said calmly.

"I know. I just hope I will be up to the tasks that lie ahead."

"You know what I think? I think the very fact that you can doubt yourself a little shows me that you are thinking rather than just going blindly into this. That is reassuring, Kel."

"My doubt reassures you?" Kel asked skeptically.

Lyria laughed and answered, "Sort of."

Kel laughed. "If you must know, I am rather sure of my doubts."

That set them both off in gales of laughter.

"Still…we have been on our way for almost an hour now and nothing bad has happened," said Lyria. "I believe we are going to be all right."

Four hours later they stopped for their midday meal. Kel tied the horses on long leads so they could forage in the brush but not wander too far. He wanted them to graze long enough each day to maintain their strength, remembering what Llo said about not pushing too hard. Near the trees was a small pool of water. It must have rained here last night. The horses drank the water and when they were done, the pool was dry.

When he returned to the cart, Lyria had unwrapped some of the food that Mart and Geog had packed for them. She handed him a sandwich of homemade bread, butter, and rabbit meat. He looked at the packages his two friends had put in the cart.

"Just how much food did Geog and Mart pack for us," he wondered aloud.

"There is a surprising amount. Your friends don't do things halfway, do they?"

"Nothing they do…even arguing…is ever done halfway!"

He took a big bite of the sandwich. It was good!

"It looks like they got half the village to make food for us," Lyria commented.

"I can see that!"

"We have honey cakes for dessert."

Kel, surprised, exclaimed, "Really? I bet they were made by Danni."

Lyria showed him the wrapping around the honey cakes. On the top of the linen was the mark of the long-horned bison, Llo's totem.

Kel smiled, thinking of the old blacksmith and his wife. "That was very nice of her to do this."

"She's a thoughtful person. We are lucky to know her and Llo."

"That we are," agreed Kel.

They finished their meal and ate some of the honey cakes with great delight. This wasn't turning out to be such a bad adventure…yet.

The next four hours they traveled both in silence and in conversation. They discussed where they would live when they were finally married and whether they should have five children or only three. They discussed the possible meaning of the mysterious 'shadow walk' that would be required of Kel before he could be a shaman. Sometimes they were serious and sometimes they laughed and jested as they traveled.

Time passed more swiftly than they'd imagined it would. In the next hour they'd have to find someplace to camp for the night. Ahead was a rise, and Kel suggested that when they crested the rise, they might see a place to camp.

They chose the base of the largest tree in the area. Heavy branches hung overhead, shielding them somewhat from the wind and maybe a bit from rain, should some come in the night. Kel tied the horses' lead ropes to the next tree.

Kel built a small fire while Lyria worked to get some food together for their supper. While the food was cooking, he and Lyria put up the two small tents they'd brought. They were both very tired. After they'd eaten, he banked the fire. They crawled into their tents and were asleep almost immediately.

It was dawn when they awoke.

As Lyria made breakfast, Kel packed the tents and put them in the wagon. He hitched Morning between the shafts of the cart and saddled both of their horses. By the time Kel finished with the horses, breakfast was cooked. They ate the eggs, pork, and toasted bread in silence. Both were anxious to be on their way.

"As long as the ground is level, I am going to try to read while we ride."

"Don't fall off," Lyria snickered.

"I never fall off," Kel retorted. "I just dismount very quickly."

They both laughed. He tied Morning's lead to his saddle horn and they were off on the second day of their long journey.

Once they were steadily on their way, he pulled one of the books his father had given him out of his saddlebag. He opened it, and began to read. After an hour of silence, curiosity got the better of Lyria.

"So what are you reading about?"

"This is an old book. It is a copy made a hundred years ago of an original that was written over five hundred years ago!"

"What is it called?"

"It is called *The Way Things Were*. It's a history of the World before the ice came."

"So have you learned anything from it yet?"

"Some. I have been reading here and there through the book."

"Well?" Lyria said impatiently, "Tell me, so I know too."

He began describing the world before the ice came, as told in the book.

"In the years before the ice moved, the Earth had been populated by large united tribes. Those civilizations built great cities that thrived in temperate regions of the Earth. It was so all around the world. In the vast, cold regions of the northern reaches, individual small tribes existed in the company of the great animals of these regions.

"Among them were the wooly mammoths and rhinoceros as well as giant cave bears and large bison. It was far too cold that close to the great ice pack and the animals far too dangerous to think about building cities, so the far north was left to its own devices and its own tribal rule.

"Far to the south the lands were all wild and densely forested in a most inhospitable way. Men from the cities went into Green Hell, but they didn't come back. It was surmised that hostile tribes, animals, or diseases that civilized medicines could not cure had killed them all. So they stayed away.

"In the central temperate zone, however, great cities grew into the skies. Not cities like Los Angeles—those were cities of stone, metal, and glass. There were libraries where books such as the one he now held could be read and studied. There were schools where people studied for years to learn medicine and science. It was so across both great seas as well. The city tribes thrived and they united together.

"Across the eastern sea, the united tribes there chose as their symbol a black cross that represented the four elements under the control of God.

The religion of the black cross tribes was that of the Liberated God. According to their belief, when their God and Goddess made the dragons that formed the Universe and everything in it, God was displeased. The Goddess had added the concepts of beauty and love to creation. All of that frivolous and unnecessary thought would take the minds of His creation— men—away from a constant devotion to Him. In anger he tricked the Goddess with a magical drink putting Her in a deep sleep. When She awakened, She found Herself bound, and God, who was now Her master, planted one foot upon Her and declared himself liberated from the wiles, deceptiveness, and lies of His feminine half. This was why the religion called their deity the Liberated God."

"That is awful," Lyria said in shock. "How could anyone follow a faith as unbalanced as that?"

"It says here that many didn't. Many fled across the sea to this land to escape the horrors of the land of the black cross. It says in here that thousands fled the domination of the Cathedral across the sea and the priests who ruled there."

"Tell me more."

"This next part is a bit more pleasant," Kel said with a chuckle.

"In this land, the people were free to follow what faith they chose. Most followed the old religious ways of the God and Goddess in harmony. In fact, the symbol chosen to represent the united tribes of this region was a banner dedicated mostly in honor of the Goddess, for it is She who brings people together as a family.

"Their banner bore three colors, red and white stripes alternating— thirteen stripes in all for the thirteen full moons of the year. In one corner, on a field of dark blue, were several five-pointed stars; pentagrams representing the four elements ruled by Spirit to protect each tribal region. Of course you know the significance for these colors…"

"Certainly! They are the colors of the Goddess in Her three faces: Maiden, Mother, and Crone," Lyria responded, smiling at Kel. "I know something of our tribe's religious beliefs."

"I know you do!"

Kel continued with his description of that ancient time as told in the book.

"This was a time of great magic, it seems. The magicians of this land discovered how to take air apart."

"What?"

Kel laughed as he said, "I can only repeat what is in the book!"

"Using magic, they were able to take out of the air the 'gas,' it is called, that makes the air float above the ground. This 'gas' they called 'hydrogen.' This is what makes the zeppelins float in the air. They also discovered that this hydrogen would burn quickly and was very destructive if it ignited. They discovered how to make large steam machines that would hold the steam and then release it suddenly. With this device, apparently, they were able to launch large arrows they called 'rockets' up into the sky. Inside these rockets they had hydrogen that would light once the rocket was safely away from the Earth, and when it burned, the fire and force all came out the back end so the rocket would travel very quickly. The book said they got some of these hydrogen rockets beyond the air of Earth, and that they stayed up there and never came back. The men of that time wanted to try to claim the stars as tribal territories, but they never had the chance. It was about then that the ice began to move.

"Now here is where it gets interesting. When the ice began to crush the civilizations of the world, the black cross tribes said it was the fault of the unified tribes on this side of the great sea because we didn't make people follow the teaching of their Liberated God. They sent fleets of crystal ships across the sea with zeppelins attached to them. The ships would land soldiers—all warriors used ballistic weapons at that time, and the airships would drop what they called 'bombs.' Apparently they were metal objects that used the magic of the ballistic weapons to make great detonations on the land. They could knock down whole buildings with these bombs. Eventually, neither side could continue the war due to some kind of lung illness that swept the lands, killing soldiers, wives, husbands and children by the score.

"The black cross army retreated back across the sea. Within a hundred years, most of their lands were under the ice. Many fled here to escape. They brought their religion with them. It was never widely accepted in the free lands but when the ice destroyed the unity of the tribes and each began to go their own way again, this religion took hold in several places. The land by the western sea was one of them. The Cathedral of the Black City is of that religion."

"That is a lot to think about," Lyria said in wonder, "I will need several days to make sense of it all!"

"I am thinking that many of the deeds of men do not make sense."

"I think that people decide what to do without thinking what the results will be. Or maybe they don't care," Lyria responded. "Maybe they only do these kinds of things because they can and it makes them feel powerful."

"Those are words of wisdom, Lyria!"

When the sun reached its zenith, they stopped for their midday meal.

Lyria looked into one of the food packages and found eggs. She delightedly said, "We have boiled eggs." Each had been wrapped individually so the shells would not crack prematurely.

Kel found the loaf of bread they had started in the morning and separated two pieces for each of them. They spread some butter on the bread and then ate.

"The butter will be good for only a couple days, so we should eat it soon."

"That's a good point!" Kel replied, and spread more of it on his bread.

"Are you sure your totem is not the hog," Lyria asked with a grin.

"I am certain," he replied. "Besides, who ever heard of a butter hog?"

"I was quite certain I was looking at one just then…I must have been mistaken."

"I suspect you were," Kel retorted with a snicker.

He held out the ceramic pot that contained the butter. "Would you like some more?"

"I would at that," Lyria laughed. "I guess you are not a butter hog after all."

Kel made a snorting sound—Lyria laughed and playfully shoved him.

After they ate, they waited a bit so the horses could graze for a while longer. The day was sunny and only mildly warm. The heat of summer was still a few months away. This was a good time of the year for traveling.

Kel began reading again. He shook his head in wonder and looked up at Lyria.

"In days past, the people of the cities were able to talk to each other over very long distances by using something they called a 'telephone.' Somehow, by connecting boxes all over the city with very thin pieces of copper, they opened gateways for talking. Imagine being able to talk to someone all the way on the other side of the village."

"By all the Gods and Goddesses," Lyria exclaimed, "that would be a disaster!"

"Why would you say that?"

"Can't you just see it? Mart and Geog arguing with each other into the night on little boxes?"

"Hmm," Kel said thoughtfully, "I had not thought of that possibility!"

"They would never get any sleep and they would be grumpy all the time."

"You are right, Lyria. We are better off without talking boxes."

"I think so too."

They both laughed as they hooked Morning to the cart, mounted up, and began heading westward again. It was the second day of the trip and everything was going well. Kel thought to himself that this was not so bad after all. They came to the top of a rise, and looking down, they saw a dry streambed. They'd have to cross it if they were to continue. Kel stood in his stirrups, looking in both directions, hoping to find an easy path. He could see none.

They moved down the western side of the rise, slowly approaching the streambed. At the bank, they stopped to survey the situation.

"Can we take the cart across?" Lyria was worried.

"Not here, that is for certain, it is far too steep."

"Which way do you suggest?"

Kel looked left and right. Both seemed just as promising—or just as unpromising, depending on how he thought about it.

"Let us go south for a while and see what we can see."

They turned south and began following the stream. About a mile later they found a spot where the bank had collapsed into the stream, making a shallow embankment. Kel was sure he could get their cart down into the streambed; all that remained was getting it out the other side.

"This won't do," Lyria said, "we won't be able to get up again on the other side."

Reluctantly, they continued heading to the south. Two miles farther, they found what they were looking for. The stream forked—neither of the two smaller streams was nearly as deep as the main one. Kel smiled—he knew they could cross.

Lyria crossed first, leading Mist. Kel followed, holding Morning's lead line as she pulled the cart. They traveled cautiously through the first stream. Once across, Kel breathed a sigh of relief. The second small tributary was even shallower than the first; crossing it was easy. He remounted his horse and they were again on their way. Kel looked at the sky and the position of the sun. They'd lost almost two hours of travel time. He sighed. He supposed this was to be expected.

By the time they'd stopped for the night, they'd encountered no other serious obstacles in their journey. They built a small fire and, as the evening before, they tied the horses to a tree and set their tents.

They ate in silence; both of them were exhausted from the additional work at the streambed. Kel hoped they'd not have a problem like that again. Still, as problems go, that one had been solved relatively painlessly. He banked the fire and they crawled into their tents and were soon asleep—and so passed the second day of their journey west.

Chapter 11

Four days after Kel and Lyria left their village, the first rider sent to contact the other villages returned. Pars rode into the village early in the morning, reining in at the corral. He tied his horse to the fence just as Geog was passing. He was clearly tired from the long ride and as he shook the dust from his long, braided hair, Geog ran over to assist him.

"I will see to your horse," Geog said. "Go into the village and gather everyone together that we may hear what you have to say."

"Thank you. It has been a long ride, though not as long as I had thought it would be."

"Not as long as I thought it would be either," Geog responded as he untied the reins from the fence. He led the horse into their large community barn where he put the tired animal into a stall with freshly cut grass. He took a few more minutes to wipe down the horse—any news could wait long enough for the horse to be made comfortable. When he was finished, he gave the horse a pat on his side and stroked his forehead. The horse neighed, shaking his head. He figured the horse wanted to be left in peace to eat; he knew that was how he'd feel, so he closed the stall and headed into the village to hear what Pars had to report.

When he arrived, he found Mart and about twenty people already gathered around Pars waiting impatiently for the rest of the village to arrive. While they waited, some tried to coax Pars into revealing at least some of his story. He just shook his head, saying he'd tell it once everyone was present. Mart was surprised that Pars had returned so quickly. He'd not expected any of the riders to return for at least two more days. Finally most of the villagers were gathered and Pela, speaking for the village, asked Pars to tell his story.

"I am back early because I encountered riders from the village to the north of us coming this way; they were on their way here with news of the abduction of Galv. I told to them about Kel's journey and what he had seen in a vision. We talked for a short time and I returned here with their news. They continued east to seek the villages in that direction. The riders were three in number—they were in armor and carrying weapons."

Pars stopped to take a drink of water from a cup Pela offered to him.

"We already know their shaman Galv was taken by the black airship. What further news did they bring?" Mart eagerly asked.

Pars finished drinking, wiped his lips on the back of his hand, and continued his story. "They told me of yet another shaman who had been taken! That is three so far of which we have heard tell."

"This is news, indeed," said Pela in a worried voice.

"We must wait for the rest of our riders. But we cannot expect their news will be any better. The warriors I met told me that the tribe to the far north where Lyria was born has not yet been raided. Galv was taken captive when traders from that northern village were visiting—that is how they found out about the attacks."

Pars paused for a breath and another drink of water.

"The tribal villages are planning a gathering. They told me at least three tribes were going to meet. Now, after hearing my news, they said they would all come here. They all revere Garn and would make this the center of decision. We must assume more will be coming and even though they will bring food and shelter, we must nevertheless prepare for their arrival."

Pars looked at Geog, Mart, and Pela. He knew there would be many things to do and just days in which to do them.

Toward the rear of the gathering, Adria stood with her four most trusted friends. None of the three girls, or the boy for that matter, was more than ten summers of age. She instinctively knew that younger children were more easily led, and perhaps misled. She smiled to herself, not misled exactly—used for the greater good—*her* good. This was going to be her time. That horrible woman was gone and now no one would stand in her way. Well, almost no one. She moved away from the gathering and her friends followed.

"It is no wonder that the northern village was not raided," she scoffed. "They are seeking shamans who are not weak bunglers."

Two of the young girls snickered. Adria smiled to herself. It was nice to have friends. It was nice to have followers. "The village is making plans for the gathering and so must we." She looked at each in turn, "We must make certain that no one finds out what we are going to do, so we will help the village as much as they ask, and meet in secret at night." She then looked at the young boy who looked at her quizzically. "It is much more fun when it is secret," she confided in a whisper. Her companions nodded solemnly in agreement. Then each went back to their families to help the village prepare for the coming tribal gathering.

~

61

Far overhead a zeppelin drifted in the bright sky. There was a storm coming from the north, but it still seemed a day away, which might possibly give them enough time to complete their mission. This zeppelin was different from the others, as it was painted a very light gray so that in the bright skies of day it would be invisible. Only four of its engines were running and they were operating at half speed. Nobody on the ground would hear or see it. Though their movement through the air was slow, they were at such a high altitude they could see great distances thanks to the brass telescopes mounted fore and aft in the gondola.

"There's been an unusual amount of traveling by horsemen these last few days," said the priest. "I'm suspicious of this."

"If the half-humans are planning anything, we'll see it from up here," the commander of the airship said confidently.

Father Woods, who was in charge of this surveillance operation, liked a confident crew. They were superior in every way to the half-humans running around on horses on the ground. Why should they not be confident?

The airship continued east. In two days they'd have their mission completed and then they could head back to the Cathedral and Los Angeles. The commander looked to the north again. He saw lightning flickering in the dark clouds in that direction. The ice was invisible now due to the dense cloud formations. This wasn't a good sign—the cloudbanks were very low and heavily laden with rain. He knew that the airship would probably have to turn back this evening; zeppelins didn't fare well in high winds or storms.

"Ensign Johns," the commander said, "keep an eye on those clouds as well as the half-humans. We don't want to have that storm sneak up on us."

"Aye, sir." This was the Ensign's first long distance cruise and he was eager to do everything right. This was a good assignment, long distance flying with almost nothing to do but spy on the half-humans on the Earth below and watch the clouds above. He turned his telescope toward the north, studying the cloud formations. The storm would reach them in twenty-four hours if it continued at the present rate. He checked the large brass-cased wind-speed gauges that told him both their airspeed and the relative speed of the wind striking the port side of the zeppelin. He did the calculations, quickly determining the approximate speed of the oncoming storm. He took his pocket watch from his uniform blouse and opened it.

The watch, mounted in silver, was a gift from his parents when he'd graduated from the aviation academy. He was as proud of the watch as his parents were proud of him. It was ten in the morning. He looked again at the oncoming storm.

By late that afternoon they changed the airship's course and were now flying south and west. All engines were operating at cruising speed and they were at maximum altitude. The commander doubted anyone on the ground would hear them as they passed; the wind was picking up and it would be making noises in the vegetation on the ground, masking any faint engine noises that might make it all the way down there.

They could outrun the storm, but they'd have to abandon the mission at this point if they were to return safely to the city with the intelligence they had to report. The priest was worried; they'd seen five groups of horsemen traveling rapidly between the villages, and the men were not traveling alone. They went in groups of two and three. None were traders—there was not a wagon or cart to be seen. Using the large telescope in the aft of the gondola, the priest saw the spears, shields, and iron and leather armor the male riders were wearing. They were warriors. Could it be the tribes were preparing for war? If so, against whom would they campaign? He knew there could only be one answer. The villages had stopped fighting each other in favor of trading almost two hundred years ago.

"We need to return to the Cathedral with all available speed!"

The commander looked at the priest, and then turned to the engine master. "You heard him. We travel at emergency speed as long as the engines will hold, and then drop to cruising speed again. We need to get back as quickly as possible." He looked at the priest out of the corner of his eye. He was jeopardizing the safety of the crew and the ship. If the engines overheated, they could catch fire—and with all that hydrogen above them it didn't take much imagination to guess what would happen to the men in the gondola, even if they somehow survived the six thousand foot fall to earth.

"Keep a steady eye on the heat readings," he said to the engine master. "If you see any dangerous spikes in temperature, lower the speed immediately." He looked steadily at the priest expecting a challenge. There was none.

"You know best how to run this ship. It's vital we get back as soon as possible, but we do need to get there in one piece!" Father Woods smiled, flashing very white teeth, adding, "I defer to your judgment on how we can best accomplish that."

The engine master opened the main throttle controlling all eight engines. It would be twelve hours before they were back at the Cathedral if they could hold their present speed.

~

By evening, work was well underway as the village began to prepare space for the influx of visitors they were expecting the following week. This would be the greatest gathering of the tribes in a hundred years, if the rumor was to be believed. The villagers were excited but tired, so it was decided that they'd turn in early this evening and start again at dawn. Tomorrow the construction of new corrals would begin. The incoming folk would have large tents with them to use as temporary homes, but their horses would also need accommodations.

Chapter 12

Adria listened intently to her parent's snoring. She hated living at home and had been planning to move out on her own when this news came. Once again, the issue of shamans who apparently couldn't even protect themselves had effectively foiled her plans. It was ridiculous. Now that her parents were sleeping, she rose quietly and slunk out into the night. The sky had gradually clouded as the afternoon wore on and now none of the twinkling sky lights, not even the moon, illuminated the ground where she walked. The central fire in the common area was burning low after the final meeting of the day. Its ruddy light was enough to guide Adria to the corrals and the barn where the horses were kept.

Her four friends met her behind the barn. She knew they'd have to find a new meeting place tomorrow. Work was to begin on extending the corrals, so the earth would be turned and softened due to the work being done. The footprints of children who walked there at night might be seen and Adria would take no chances of being discovered. Not now.

Glorr was the first to arrive. He was ten, the oldest of the four. He came sneaking up through the shadows like a young panther—being secret *was* exciting. Adria greeted him quietly and he nodded in response. They had to wait only a short time before Palom, her sister Lorra, and Abi arrived. Palom was nine summers. Her sister and Abi were both eight, though Abi constantly insisted she was almost nine. Once they were gathered together, Adria led them a short distance away, behind a hedge of sage the tribe tended and nurtured.

"Did anyone have trouble getting away?" Adria frowned at her companions. As leader, she needed to maintain control.

"I thought my parents would NEVER go to bed tonight," Glorr complained.

"Our parents were in bed early," said Palom.

Lorra laughed, "They were put in charge of organizing the food warehouse, moving everything so they could take an accurate tally of what we have in ready food—and that's hard work. They started today, so they were really tired tonight. We didn't have any problem getting out."

"My grandparents are old and they always go to bed early," Abi said giggling.

"Good," Adria exclaimed, "now, here is what I am planning."

An owl hooted in one of the nearby trees and all of the conspirators flinched. Amid giggles and playful swats, they finally got down to business.

"Remember my telling you about that man I have been studying with during the summer gathering?"

The others nodded in silence.

She had told them about the mysterious man she'd met two years previously at the summer gathering. He never told her his real name, saying it was both for his protection and hers. She delighted in the secrecy. She couldn't even remember exactly how she'd found him—or had he found her? Well, it didn't matter, did it? He was telling her things she'd always wanted to know. Things she'd always suspected of herself. Great power was available to great people, if the proper price was paid. If the rest of a person's tribe refused to see their greatness or deliberately tried to stifle it, as Garn surely had in her case, it didn't matter. The wind was turning now in her favor, wasn't it?

The man always sat in the shadows on the nights when they'd talked. She wondered why she couldn't recall his face, though. They'd originally met on a very bright and sunny day; surely she should remember. It was funny, but not all that important in the scheme of things. She just shrugged it off.

At a summer gathering, getting away alone was easy; there were hundreds of people and many dozens of camps. Wandering off was simple, and nobody really paid much attention to a person who seemed to want to be left alone since so many were eager for companionship. The man told her that there were ways of finding power much more quickly than the ways taught by the shaman or healer.

There were other powers beyond the Light. Powers beyond the animal spirits and guides that might be summoned by magic if one has properly prepared oneself. That summer, the man had hinted at many things, making suggestions. But he'd told her only one really useful bit of knowledge: power had a cost. If one was willing to pay the price, power and respect could be taken by force. Adria knew she was ready.

Then last summer the man told her what she needed to do for the initial ritual of power. At first she'd been shocked, but as the man discussed the issue with her, she began to see the logic in what he said. Actually, she was amazed she hadn't figured this out for herself long ago. It was so simple, really—elegant, in fact. Once, she'd taken Garn's rattle and it had been destroyed, but something actually happened, hadn't it? She had actually traveled between the worlds, but now she realized that the problem she'd had then was one of control, and of preparing for the magic with an appropriate ritual beforehand.

He'd explained the ritual to her in detail and shown her certain things she would need, but it took her until now to realize that this was her time. If Kel and that woman or Garn returned, it would be all over. If she waited until the tribes were gathered, the same would surely be true. Shamans would again be present in her life to block her rise to power. What needed to be done had to be done now. She resolved that it would happen before the sun rose the day after tomorrow.

"Tonight we take an oath," Adria stated.

She looked levelly at each of the children. "This is very serious," she cautioned.

Adria withdrew a small knife from her belt.

"Glorr, would you build us a small fire?"

She smiled. Her dreams were finally becoming reality.

Glorr quickly gathered thin twigs and sticks, putting them in a small pile. He looked at Adria inquisitively. She nodded, adding bits of dry grass she'd cut with her knife while the boy laid the fire. She struck a spark and the flame caught the first time; that had to be a good sign.

"Now we take a blood oath. Each of us has to cut ourselves on our hand or fingers."

Lorra pulled back a bit, a look of fear on her face.

"Don't be stupid, Lorra. We each cut ourselves. We need only enough blood to put a drop or two into the fire—that is all. You will hardly feel it."

Adria went first. "With this, my blood, I swear my life to secrecy." She stabbed the small knife into her thumb, letting the blood drip into the fire. "Violation of this secrecy brings death. This I cannot escape, whatever power I may grasp." One, two, three—the drops sizzled in the flame and the smoke that rose from the fire seemed almost to have a shape. She felt lightheaded though the blood she lost was very minimal. Each of the children did the same, repeating the words Adria had learned last summer. Each in turn seemed to sway; and then it was done.

She looked at each of the children in turn. "By this oath, you have sworn anything we discuss here and from now on will not be told to anyone for any reason," she said sternly.

She glared at the children. "If you tell what we do or say, the bloodsmoke will come to you and it will kill you!"

Giggling nervously, Glorr asked, "Really?"

Adria turned on him like a wild beast. The firelight and maybe something more—she wouldn't have liked the word mania—flashed in her eyes, flaring around her head as it lit her blonde hair.

"Test it," she said. "Test it." She gave him a predatory smile. He shivered, nodding his understanding.

"When you looked into the flame as your blood fell, did you see anything?"

Abi and Lorra had seen nothing other than white smoke curling up, but they were young so Adria would forgive them their lack of vision.

"I did see something," Glorr replied tentatively. "I'm not sure what it was exactly, but through the smoke I could see something—something alive with a long tail."

"I saw it too," Palom whispered. "It was a scorpion!"

Adria began laughing and the children shrank from her in fear. That was good! Fear was good, especially when it gave power. As the children backed away from her, she dismissed them with a curt turn of her head. She'd seen a scorpion too, and on other occasions as well, she remembered. Scorpions sting people in their beds when they sleep. She knew then how she would accomplish the ritual. She laughed again—it was all so simple. Quietly she extinguished the fire, carefully spread out the blackened sticks and twigs, stamping them into the ground, making them invisible. She returned to her parents' house.

~

Fourteen hours after aborting their mission, the gray zeppelin was descending toward the vast airfield just beyond the Cathedral. Six other ships, all black, were moored there as well. A storm was approaching Los Angeles so all the zeppelins were grounded. The huge barns were already open and men, looking like ants from the height of the descending airship, were slowly moving the giant crafts into their berths to wait out the storm.

They'd gotten back in time, but not by much. After the initial run at top speed, a port engine overheated spectacularly, spewing jets of flame from a ruptured gas line. The valve had been closed just in time, shutting down the flow of hydrogen before the flames could blow back and burn through the gasbag of the zeppelin. Though it couldn't be seen from inside the airship, the commander was certain there'd be scorch marks along the gray flanks of the ship. The remaining engines were reduced to cruising speed and its rudder trimmed sufficiently to compensate for the ship running with only three engines on the port side.

As the airship approached the ground, windows of the gondola were opened. Heavy guide ropes were tossed down to the ground crew who attached them to hand-cranked winches, which brought the ship the rest of the way to earth. It was moored to a large wheeled wagon that would be used to tow it to its berth in the zeppelin barn. A wheeled ladder was quickly brought to the open door of the gondola for everyone to disembark.

Ensign Johns was surprised at how glad he felt when his feet touched solid ground; he'd been close to dying, he'd been sure. The engine master said everything was fine, but Ensign Johns was not completely convinced. With the storm coming, the ship would be grounded for at least a day— maybe two, since the faulty engine would need to be repaired. That'd be enough time to regain lost confidence. The commander glanced at the side of the gasbag and was mildly surprised to see no black stain from the fire. Obviously the Redeemed God was on their side.

As the crew climbed into a steam-powered truck, a Cathedral automobile was waiting for the priest. He had to tell the Bishop what he'd seen. Both vehicles moved away from the giant airship. The truck headed toward the crew's quarters while the black automobile turned toward the Cathedral and the zeppelin began its slow trip to the barn.

The automobile came to a halt by the side door in the huge stone structure. The driver quickly stepped out from behind the wheel, scurried to the passenger's side, and opened the door for the priest. He lowered his head as the priest stepped out.

"I hope you had a safe trip, Your Grace."

"Thank you. We did have a nice, uneventful flight, except for when one of the engines almost exploded!" He laughed.

"I'm certain the Redeemed God was with you," the driver said in shock.

"He was. May He be with you also."

The priest briefly put his hand on his driver's shoulder; then he turned, walking quickly to the bronze door. He opened it and went inside.

As it happened, the Bishop was just getting ready to eat supper so he invited the priest to dine with him. The man accepted—it was quite a privilege. They dined at a long table, much too large for two. The room was softly lit by gaslight and large candelabras stationed at intervals along the table. The waiters came and went, bringing several courses of beef, vegetables, and breads. Afterward, wine was served. Once the first glass was poured, the Bishop dismissed his servants—finally he and the priest were alone.

"So, tell me of your journey."

"Your Eminence, I've important information. First though, I want to say your idea of painting the zeppelin gray was brilliant. It was obvious that no one on the ground either heard or saw us. It makes spying on the tribes, at least from a distance, very easy."

"I'm glad you approve. Now, what of your message and your mission?"

"Your Eminence, the tribes appear to be gathering. Over the last several days we observed a number of small groups heading from one village or another, heading in all directions. It was like a relay race, if you will."

"Do you think they're planning a tribal gathering?"

"I believe that's certain."

"Perhaps they're preparing for their summer 'thing.' They seem to hold such events in high regard."

"Your Eminence, it's months too early, all of the travelers we witnessed were in groups of only two or three. There were no carts, wagons, or any indication of trade goods—and all the men were armed."

The Bishop yawned, "The half-humans are always armed."

"Not like this."

Father Woods paused for effect. "They were heavily armed with bows and arrows, multiple spears, and slings. I personally saw a ballistic weapon slung to the back of one warrior. They were also in armor—or most of them were."

"This is indeed somewhat disturbing news," the Bishop said, stroking his jaw in thought. "Ballistic weapons are forbidden to the half-humans. We must find out if they have more, and how they acquired them. That, above all, could be the most dangerous thing you're reporting. We'll have to find some way to visit this meeting, wherever it's to be held."

"Well, that may be easier said than done, Your Eminence," the priest retorted.

"We shall see…we shall see," the Bishop responded.

The Bishop dismissed Father Woods but told him to remain on Cathedral grounds in case he needed him further in the next day or two. The priest nodded his understanding and left the dining room where the Bishop sat, deep in thought.

Chapter 13

Adria managed to sneak back into her parents' house without being noticed. She smiled. It was her house, actually. As she undressed and climbed back into bed, she continued making plans, but quickly dropped into the peaceful sleep reserved only for the righteous.

Early in the morning, her parents, Ama and Torr, woke her. They wanted her to help in the gardens—cutting out some weeds or something. She arose with a smile and dressed quickly. Her family ate breakfast together; afterwards, her parents walked to the village common ground, leaving Adria to work in their garden. In back of most homes were small gardens. Each family grew one crop. Some grew corn, others, tomatoes or lettuce. Some grew grapes for the wine they made. Many seeds were gotten in trade, and the climate seemed to be very good for most plants. The problem concerning the village was that the freshly planted gardens would produce nothing in the way of food before the anticipated meeting of the tribes. The crops had just been sown and summer was still a couple of months ahead. Even so, weeding had to be done—so Adria put herself into it. She didn't mind this work, actually. It gave her time to think, and the food they were growing would benefit her along with the others. As long as she got something out of it, just about any endeavor was worthy.

Approximately two hours later, Glorr wandered over to see if he could help. He looked worried. He squatted down next to her and began picking at weeds sprouting from the turned earth of the garden. He glanced at Adria a couple times and finally she couldn't take the suspense any longer.

"What's wrong, Glorr?"

"Last night I had bad dreams," he confided. "I dreamed I was standing in front of a tribal council. I was being accused of something, but I could not tell what. I was very scared and confused."

"Silly! Everyone has scary dreams sometimes. You are not backing out of your oath, are you?"

Glorr paled, "No! No! I would never do that! The dream just scared me is all."

"If we let scary dreams be our guides in the world, nothing great would ever get done."

"I guess you're right, Adria. And, I would NEVER back out on our oath! I don't want to die."

"As long as you keep our secrets, nothing bad will happen to you."

Glorr nodded in silence and that is how they worked the rest of the morning—in silence. Adria gave him a couple of surreptitious glances, but he seemed to be fine now. He better be.

After the midday meal, Adria and Glorr wandered away, looking for the three girls. Palom was the only one they found who'd been able to sneak away from the workers to whom she'd been assigned. Adria was not worried that this would be a problem, as kids snuck away from work from time to time. People expected it to some degree and this was important. She had to find a certain plant, and could only think of one place it would be. They made their way gradually toward Pela's house. What Adria needed was probably hanging behind the house, and old Pela would never notice if a few were to disappear.

"You go and look through the window," Adria said to Palom. "See if she's in there."

"Why me?" Palom was obviously frightened.

"This is part of the secret. If you don't do it, something bad might happen to you—or maybe to your parents."

Palom shivered, nodded, and reluctantly walked around the side of the house. Adria and Glorr moved quietly to the rear; here there was only one window, and Adria could see a drape covering it. She waited nevertheless.

"There's nobody home." Palom whispered, out of breath from running and from excitement. "What do we do now?"

"You two watch on either side and tell me if anyone is coming."

The two children dutifully took up their posts as Adria quickly scanned the drying herbs and seeds that hung from trellises and lay in various pots and baskets. It didn't take her long to find the poppy seeds. She knew what to look for; the man at their summer gathering had shown her examples. She took a small handful, dropping them into a leather pouch she'd tied at her waist.

When she was done, she quietly called the two children back to her. "Remember, you tell anybody what we did and you will die. Or maybe someone in your family will die. I don't know. Just know this: The bloodsmoke will find someone if you betray our secret pact."

Adria turned and walked back toward the center of the village, leaving her friends to wander back home on their own.

One reason the village was built where it was, was the stream. It wasn't a big stream as such things go, but it supplied their village with the water they needed. It was said that the water came from near the ice in the north, and that if the glacier came much closer, their water supply would dry up. But that was a problem for those living in years to come.

Right now there was plenty. Adria lowered an earthenware jug into the stream to let it fill halfway to the top. Then she put in the poppy seeds. She knew her parents would be dutifully helping the village, so she'd have the house to herself. Once home, she set the jug on an iron platter and placed it in the hearth over the fire. The water needed to be hot to leech out the lethal magic from the seeds.

Soon the water was boiling. She watched it carefully, not getting so close that she might accidentally breathe any vapors. Thirty minutes later, using a heavy well-worn leather glove, she lifted the jug from the fire and carried it outside. She set it in the dirt behind her house to cool. Her house. Yes—that had a nice sound to it.

She found the smaller ceramic jar her father had given as a gift a couple years ago. Into this she carefully poured the sludge from the jug, and when no more would come out, she carefully carried the ceramic jar into her house, hiding it in her room. She pulled the iron platter out of the hearth; no reason to let anyone know she'd been cooking. She snickered, knowing how clever she was. She went back outside to find that a butterfly had landed on the jug and tasted its contents. It lay on the ground curled up, never to fly again. She was pleased—it was the proof she hadn't even realized she was looking for. It actually worked.

Now all that remained was to dispose of the jug. She carried it a short distance to where the village buried their refuse. Here she smashed the jug and carefully buried it. Now nobody would be able to tell what she'd done, or know she was to blame.

She headed back into the village and found her parents near the horse barn. They were digging holes for new posts that would support the enlarged corral. She helped with the digging, smiling a lot while she worked and jesting with her parents and the others working there, but her thoughts were elsewhere.

~

The Bishop called his servant Harold into his rooms. "Send for Father Woods, please. I have need of his presence."

"Yes, Your Eminence," Harold answered, hurrying to carry out the Bishop's order.

While he waited, the Bishop glanced at the papers he was holding. It had taken him all night to figure everything out. It was his plan, with many scrawls and scratched out sections. He'd formulated this idea just the night before and he was pleased with it, but he wanted to know what Father Woods might think. He was a valuable asset to the Cathedral; he had brains and charisma. The Bishop could think of no other word to describe what he saw in the young priest—a flashing smile, well-groomed hair, and a way with words—and with the minds of people. If anyone could pull this mission off, Father Woods would be the one.

Close to thirty minutes later there was a knock on the Bishop's door.

"Come in, Father Woods."

The door opened and the young priest entered the room, bowed, and then knelt. He waited silently, patiently.

"Rise," the Bishop said in a kindly voice, "I've something here I want your opinion on."

He handed two sheets of paper to the priest; a rewriting of the scrawling that had been their predecessor. He waited with his hands folded on the desk before him.

The priest looked up with a smile on his face. He handed the papers back to the Bishop. He allowed himself to relax back into his chair; after all, it was now obvious he wouldn't have such luxury for very much longer.

"I think this is an excellent idea," the priest said enthusiastically.

"I thought you might. Do you feel you can bring this off?"

"Me?" The priest looked at the Bishop in mock horror; then laughed, "If not me, then who?"

They both laughed, and the Bishop knew he was on the right path. It would be a dangerous path, but if they managed this, it would go a long way in helping their cause—and protecting themselves.

"Now none of what I've written there is set in stone, Father Woods. Any suggestions or changes will be welcome, though we need to have this thoroughly worked out before you leave."

"That'll not be a problem, Your Eminence. I've checked with the ground crew on our zeppelin, and they tell me it'll take at least three days to replace the engine and properly test it."

"That's fine, the half-humans will take at least two weeks to gather together properly."

"There is one snag, Your Eminence, we don't yet know where this gathering will take place."

"I think we'll have that figured out as well."

"Can you tell me how?"

"Of course, my boy, of course. We'll be sending another zeppelin up tomorrow; it's already been painted gray for the mission."

"So, another spy ship?"

"Exactly! In four days, we should be able to detect the movement of a large number of half-humans from a fair distance away. They make a lot of dust when they travel, don't they?" He gave the priest a superior smile.

"That they do, Your Eminence. But if we have two gray ships, why bother waiting for the one being repaired?"

"That can be answered simply. The second craft is still a warship and bears all of its weaponry. An envoy of peace wouldn't come in a warship."

Father Woods nodded. That was a canny observation.

The priest left the Bishop, returning to his own quarters. He needed to put some of his own touches to the Bishop's plan. It was a good plan, but it needed to be humanized. Also, he needed time to think about what questions the half-humans might ask him, so he'd have completely spontaneous answers. He entered his room and closed the door. He glanced up at the image of the Redeemed God on the wall above his bed. God stood triumphant, one foot resting on the subdued and bound Feminine. It was a comforting image.

He walked to his desk and sat. The gaslight jutting from the wall over his desk was ablaze, and in the relatively bright light, he read again the Bishop's proposal. He shuffled the two sheets for a moment, set them down, and then took a blank paper and began to write. He worked for several hours, finally deciding to take a break. Deception was dangerous and tricky work; it had to be planned carefully.

He left his room, going down the stone steps to the dining hall. Most of the priests were gathered here for the midday meal. He ate in silence, listening to the conversations around him. It seemed he was always spying. He smiled, was that not his mission? His attention was attracted by the talk of two priests across the table from him. As he ate, he listened in.

"I hear the Bishop has some mysterious plans for the south."

"You hear many things," the second priest said with a smirk. "Tell me this one."

"Well," the man leaned toward his companion in a conspiratorial manner, "I hear stories of a new city being built, and it's IN Green Hell!"

"That's nonsense," the second priest said, "nobody can live in that."

"Well I heard that there's something important there that the Bishop's looking for."

"Pfff…f," the second priest scoffed. "There's The Green, bugs, and man-eating animals; that's all there is waiting for us in that stinking morass."

"Well, I'm only repeating what I've heard."

"Where have you heard this?" Father Woods asked quietly.

The two priests looked suspiciously at Father Woods. He smiled, flashing his very sincere eyes and his very white teeth. Rumors usually didn't make people suspicious; they were just stories, after all. Everyone heard rumors—and spread them. The suspicion led him to believe the perpetrator of this rumor must be someone of influence.

"Well…the truth of a rumor depends greatly on its origin, does it not?" He smiled again, innocently.

The two glanced at each other quickly as the second man shrugged.

Again, the first priest leaned toward Father Woods and loudly whispered, "I heard it from Father Caven, and you know how close he is to the Bishop. If what he says isn't true, then what might be?"

"Very well thought out, Father Green," Woods said with a disarming smile. "I'll tell you what, I know Father Caven very well. Let me talk to him and I'll let you know what the real story is. In the meantime, it might not be a good idea to spread this rumor—you know how people fear that part of the world."

"That's a good thought. Mum's the word!"

Father Woods smiled again at the two priests, and rose and walked out of the dining hall.

The Bishop heard a knock on his door. He sighed. Would he never get some time to just read and enjoy himself? "Come in."

He was surprised to see Father Woods kneeling in front of him.

"Rise, please, and tell me your business."

Father Woods stood, telling the Bishop what he'd heard in the dining hall. The Bishop frowned. He stood, paced the length of the room twice with his hands clasped behind his back, walked back to his chair, and sat down again.

"I'll tell you that the rumor is true. For now, I'll not divulge any details."

Father Woods nodded solemnly; he understood security.

"Hearing that this leak has come from Father Caven is disturbing. I'll take care of this personally. You may go back to formulating your presentation for the half-humans. That's your task right now. After I take care of a few things, I'll send for you again."

Father Woods nodded.

"Send in my servant when you leave, would you?"

"Certainly, Your Eminence!"

Father Woods left the Bishop, informed his servant of the Bishop's request, and then left the apartments.

Chapter 14

In the evening, Adria returned home with her parents. They ate dinner together, happy with the day's work. When they'd finished, she asked to be excused so she could go talk to her friends. Her parents told her it was fine with them, so she left the house. It was getting dark now; this was the right time to find the second ingredient she'd need for the ritual. She hurried around the side of her house, past the garden, and walked a short distance into more wild regions surrounding the village. Soon she was near the stream, so she began hunting in earnest. It took her a long time to find a scorpion. She trapped it in a jar she'd brought for this purpose. Then she looked for another, and yet another.

Scorpions weren't all that common in areas where men built fires and placed magic rituals to block their entry. It took Adria over an hour and a half to find three of the small arthropods. She returned home and placed the jar on the sill of her open window. Then she went in the front door, a big smile on her face.

"I hope I didn't miss our evening tea," she said. "I thought perhaps I should make it today, since both of you worked so hard and I was off with my friends for a while."

"That would be very nice, dear," her mother said.

Adria went into her room, quickly returning with the small ceramic jar containing the concentrated sleeping drug hidden in the pocket of her tribal trousers. She brewed the tea carefully. While she was alone by the fire, she removed the ceramic jar from her pocket and using a small smooth stick, she smeared a bit of the sticky paste into two of the cups. There. That should be enough. The third cup she left untouched. With the ceramic jar again safely hidden from view, she walked into the living area with the tea and the cups on a tray. She poured the tea, handing cups to each of her parents. They smiled at her, proud of how well behaved she was. *One day soon, she should have a husband,* her mother thought. Then Adria poured her own cup of tea. She watched her parents over the top of the cup as she sipped.

Her mother took a sip, stopped, and then looked at the cup. Adria's heart skipped a beat. But then the woman drank the rest of the tea without comment. When they'd finished, she took the tray back to the kitchen area, washing the cups and quickly putting them away. She was listening to the conversation coming from the living area.

"Torr? I am very tired this evening."

"I am too," Adria's father responded. "Digging holes is harder work than I remember."

"We are not as young as we once were, either!"

"Don't remind me! We have more holes to dig in the morning."

They both yawned as Adria came back into the living area.

"We are going to bed, dear," her mother said with a smile. "I just can't believe how tired I have become."

Both of them yawned again.

"Well, have pleasant dreams!" Adria said, smiling at them.

Now Adria was once again alone in her room. The final part of the ritual was about to begin. She suddenly felt fear; not fear regarding what she was planning, but fear that she might not actually be strong enough to do this. Doubting herself had never before occurred to her. She shook her head with stubborn resolve. She'd come this far, she would complete the ritual and then SHE would be the woman of power. She walked softly across the living area, listening carefully at the entrance to her parents' bedroom. Snoring. She stifled a snicker. The poppies worked better than she'd hoped.

"Mother?" she called tentatively, "Father?"

There was no response at all from her sleeping parents. She quietly went back to her room, picking up the jar of scorpions. She returned to her parent's bedroom, silently entering.

The first to go was her mother. It was easier than she thought it would be. She simply held the jar against her mother's neck and shook it. The scorpions stung. She pulled back the blanket, putting the jar on her mother's stomach, then on her right breast.

"There, that should be enough," she whispered.

Then it was her father's turn. When she was finished, she dumped the scorpions on their bed. She quickly scooped two of them back into the jar and drew up the blanket. She knew that thing would stay in the warm darkness until it could be discovered the next morning.

She returned to her room and excitedly began reciting the ritual words she'd learned the summer before. "With this blood sacrifice, I pass the line between childhood and power. What has been done cannot be undone—a life taken cannot be given back. What power I now wield is mine and mine alone. Come into me now. Fill me with that power that I may stand in glory and have all who see me tremble."

Suddenly the power was in her...and then she screamed, and screamed....

~

"Father Caven, welcome!"

The Bishop smiled. The priest bowed, and then knelt. The Bishop gently touched his shoulder.

"Arise, my friend."

Father Caven and the Bishop ate a leisurely dinner in the Bishop's rooms. Afterward, over some wine, the Bishop told Father Caven why he'd been summoned.

"I have need of some information, my friend, and since it deals with a rather sensitive subject, I felt you'd be the best one to help me."

"Certainly," Father Caven answered, he was eager to help his friend.

"I need you to do two things for me. When the first is accomplished, I'll tell you the second."

Father Caven nodded.

"This is very secret—that's why I'm only entrusting you with this information."

Again the priest nodded.

"We've a traitor in our midst. There's a priest by the name of Green; do you know him?"

"Vaguely," Father Caven answered.

The look of suspicion in his eyes was all the proof the Bishop needed that here indeed was the source of the information leak.

"Somehow he's learned of our plans for the south. He's spreading rumors."

Father Caven, seeming to be genuinely surprised, "About that?"

"Yes." The Bishop smiled inwardly. If one was going to talk of secret things that should be kept in silence, telling them to rumor spreaders was very poor judgment indeed.

"I want you to personally execute this traitor to our cause and to our God. He's a blasphemer and an unbeliever. He's supplying information, no doubt to the underground dissidents in the City. He needs to be gone. Tonight. Do you think you can handle that? Once he's taken care of, our little problem is solved."

"Yes, Your Eminence!"

There'd been a look of relief on the priest's face. Good. That meant he'd do what was asked of him and do it efficiently. He suggested the two

81

of them should go into the city tonight to relax a bit. He gave Father Caven a dagger of half-human craftsmanship. When the good father was found, there'd be a tribal dagger in his back. He smiled and waited for Father Caven's return.

It didn't take long. Father Caven wanted to prove his loyalty and hide his involvement in this fiasco. The knock came on the door two hours later. It was only about nine in the evening; plenty of time for the second half of the operation.

"It's been done. I cut his throat and then left the dagger in his back. It'll look like a cowardly attack by one of the half-humans."

"Excellent!" The Bishop beamed. This problem was practically solving itself. "Did anyone see you with Father Green?"

"Won't matter, I wore a dark cloak of the kind the tribes fancy when they're in the city. If anyone saw me, they would've taken me for one of the half-humans."

The Bishop smiled, shaking his head. Such talent, wasted on a rumor. Stealthily, Father Woods came out of a side room. He was behind Caven, who never saw the heavy iron rod descending. The rod hit him hard on the back of his neck and he slumped forward onto the table. A second blow broke the vertebrae and the traitorous creature was dead—and it was a virtually bloodless operation as well. Father Woods looked up at the Bishop.

"Take him out the side door and get rid of him where he'll never be found."

"Yes, Your Eminence."

The Bishop nodded, satisfied. Father Woods knew where to take the body.

"I'll say he was sent on a special mission to the north and—well, things happen. People disappear."

The Bishop looked up into Father Woods' eyes. Was that a threat, he wondered?

He carried the body out the side entrance where an automobile waited for him. This one had no driver; this was totally his job. The body was wrapped in a heavy tarpaulin and he shoved it into the back of his automobile. He started the small hydrogen engine and waited for a moment for the steam pressure to build. He then moved away from the Cathedral along cobblestone streets into the heart of the city.

The tall building looked like many others that lined the streets here in the downtown area. Gaslights illuminated the streets so driving was actually easier in the city than on the road between it and the Cathedral. As the vehicle came to a stop in front of the iron gate, chains immediately started rattling and soon the gate was rising. Once he was inside, the gate was again lowered.

Two men met Father Woods in the open courtyard where he'd come to a stop. Without comment they opened the vehicle's doors allowing the priest to exit and his cargo to be unloaded.

The first man asked, "The usual way?"

The priest nodded, "Just another dead vagabond to be cleaned up."

"How come a priest is bringing us this fertilizer?"

"The poor man died on the steps of the Cathedral. It was the least we could do."

The second man gave the priest a skeptical look, but nevertheless took his end of the heavy bundle, loading it onto a cart. The priest nodded to them, got back in his vehicle and turned for the exit, which was already being raised.

The men took the cart to a large basin. One opened the tarp—that shouldn't go in, after all. The body, as requested, was naked. As they slid the body closer to the side of the cauldron-like iron basin, one of the workers pointed to the man's neck.

"This one was killed!"

"Not any of our business, now is it?"

"No, but look here."

Both men strained to see in the dim light. Around the neck of the corpse, only partly hidden by the massive bruising from the blows the man had received, the men saw the faintest of lines. The corpse's face was well tanned; but the whiteness of his body extended very far up his neck.

"This one looks like he was a priest!"

"Still none of our business," the second man said nervously.

"Have they begun killing each other?"

"Who knows? Who cares?"

The first man nodded. He made a mental note of the event, however. He knew some people who might be very interested in this kind of information. Then the body slid into the basin to be processed with the rest of its contents to make the fertile solutions used in the great food growing tanks on each of the sixty levels above them. To feed a large city, you had to have efficient food production and processing.

Chapter 15

Her neighbors heard Adria's screams. It was still not very late and not everyone had retired for the evening. Mart was the first to arrive with his father. They lived right next door. Mart pounded on the doorframe.

"Adria! What is wrong?"

She came to the door and then suddenly was very calm. She held it open and Mart entered. His father waited outside to talk to the others who were arriving.

"I...I went into their room to ask them something and I couldn't raise them." Adria was now sobbing. Pretty convincingly, too, she thought.

"I lit the lamp and I found them like that." She pointed to the bedroom and whimpered.

Mart walked in cautiously, approaching the bed. He saw two people there, but he had a hard time identifying them. Their faces were swollen and blackened. Mart gasped. Both were obviously dead. The stink of death-released bowels filled the room. Mart stepped outside for a moment.

That was when Pela arrived.

Pela went into the house with confidence. She was a healer, and if it was beyond her healing, it fell to her to take care of the dead. She approached the bed, looking at the two still corpses.

"This is not natural."

She looked closer at the blackened, swollen skin and then removed the blanket. She pulled her hand back quickly and the scorpion that was about to sting her fell to the floor where she quickly killed it.

"A scorpion."

She looked at Adria. The young woman recognized the suspicion and responded with tears.

Pela examined the sting wounds on the bodies.

"You saw no other insects?"

"No," Adria said tearfully, "I didn't even see that one until you killed it."

Pela pulled back the blankets completely. The reek of death intensified, but she examined both bodies carefully, counting the stinger wounds.

"They like to sleep with their window open; they do it all the time," Adria sobbed. "The bug must have come in that way."

"Yes," Pela said, looking at Adria with an even stare, "that surely is what must have happened."

As Adria continued to cry in her room, Pela organized some help from the people gathered outside. They quickly removed the bodies from the house. Then they removed the bed; it would be burned later. For now, the corpses must be prepared for burial. That aspect of the Goddess who escorts the dead to the Otherworld must be called upon; this would be Pela's work. Preparing the bodies fell to the women of the tribe. It was going to be a very long night.

Pela glanced once at the house where the deaths had happened. The girl was not even going to participate in the death ceremony—that told her all she needed to know.

The women of the village took the bodies behind Pela's house, cleaning them carefully. She again counted the sting marks, too many for one scorpion. After cleaning, the bodies were wrapped tightly in new linen along with sage and other herbs; then the heavy cloth was sewn shut. The bodies were put inside a small building near the horse barn where they'd wait until morning for the burial ceremony.

A couple of the village women offered to stay the night with Adria, but she refused them saying she'd feel better alone this night. She'd been sobbing again when she talked with the women. She knew she'd have to attend the funeral services in the morning, regardless of how she felt. She had to maintain the secret; she had to retain the power.

She watched furtively from her window as the two women walked away. She wanted to be alone, though in reality she was not. She smiled when the scorpion crawled out from under her hair and rested on her shoulder—seeming to look out the window with her.

She put the scorpion back in the jar, promising it that in the morning she'd release it and its companion. She apologized for the death of their third companion, but sometimes sacrifices had to be made—not by her of course, always by others. The scorpions seemed to understand. She quietly got undressed and slept soundly until the birds of dawn awakened her.

Adria arose and quickly dressed. She wanted to make a good appearance in front of the village during the funeral rites for her parents. She put on her best clothing; then she put on her mother's jewelry. Why not? It was hers now. She paused and thought better of it. *Wait a few days*, she thought to herself, *this has to be believable*. That pest Pela is already suspicious. Something might eventually have to be done about that, too. She ate a quick breakfast, and then left the house. She passed Pela in the meeting area near her house. Was that sneaky old woman spying on her? She sobbed as she passed the old woman.

Out beyond the fields to the north, she saw black smoke rising. Her parents' bed was burning. Good. She didn't think any of the poppy tea could have leaked out onto the bed; still, one of them could have vomited at the very end. Well, that little piece of evidence was gone now, as would her parents' bodies be very soon. Despite what Pela may think, she'd gotten away with it.

Pela led the funeral ceremony. Normally it would've been Garn's task, but with the shaman gone, the task fell to her. She didn't mind; she'd liked Adria's parents very much. As the circle was being drawn around the bodies raised on a pyre of wood and grass, Pela saw Adria approaching. She was surprised—she'd not expected the girl to come. But now wasn't the time for questions about the girl. Her parents needed to be cared for first.

Pela raised her arms toward the rising sun. A drum was beating slowly from some hidden location. Incense burned in a small iron cauldron on its tripod stand. It was placed near the bodies inside the circle that had been drawn around them. And then Pela spoke.

> "Shining Lord of the brilliant sky,
> You time our lives as the seasons fly.
> The spark. The flame. The cooling ember
> That flares again in deep December.
> Horned one; Lord of the Earth untamed,
> I have seen Your antlers O thousand named.
> Take these souls in Your wild fire;
> Bring them home from this funeral pyre."

Geog and Mart had volunteered to be fire bearers for this ceremony. Pela smiled at them; sometimes they actually could work together. They moved forward solemnly, thrusting their torches into the base of the pyre. As they lived their lives with the Divine, so would they return to the Divine—together.

Adria was sobbing loudly now. Some of the other women were crying as well, but somehow her display seemed forced. Pela shook her head. She had to finish this before she thought of anything more; she owed it to

Adria's parents to see them into their afterlife. As flames roared up to consume the bodies of Adria's parents, Pela spoke again.

> "Bless them, Mother, each your child.
> Bless them, Splendid Lady, young and wild.
> On this day let them be born anew.
> Starting fresh with the dawn and dew.
> Bless them Mother, with wings to fly.
> Bless them, Splendid Lady, the battle's nigh.
> The flaming sword in Your name they hold,
> They stood their ground for love, not gold.
> Bless them Mother, take them back this night.
> Bathe them in Your Otherworld Light.
> The field is quiet, their battle done.
> Hold them 'til their lives are again begun."

The fires roared, quickly consuming the bodies of the departed. As the pyre collapsed into a smoldering ruin, Geog and Mart remained. They'd lit the fire and would stay to clean up the ashes and bury them. Pela would tend to the grave ritual before the bodies were covered. Adria offered to help.

There were small, specialized, shovel-like tools dedicated to this purpose, and the ashes were quickly and reverently scooped up. Within the hour, most of the ashes had been cleaned up and placed on a large linen tarpaulin. This was securely rolled up and carried to the burial plot two hundred yards from the cremation site.

The burial site was old and sacred. Geog and Mart walked slowly toward the giant boulder standing by itself on the flat earth. They could feel the air change somehow as they approached the stone. Both of them knew that here was a gateway to the Otherworld—a gateway that should be approached with reverence. The rock stood ten feet above the ground, looking as if the Gods Themselves had dropped it there. Their tribe had buried their dead on this site for hundreds of years. Nobody knew for sure how long ago the first grave had been dug—some said more than a thousand years ago. The great stone was also a landmark that could be seen from several miles away. Standing there alone on the plain, it guided traders and travelers alike to a welcoming meal and a welcoming roof.

A shallow grave had already been dug and the ashes of Adria's parents were put into the ground; most of the ashes, that is. Mart and Geog had been too busy to notice Adria as she had surreptitiously put a small amount of the white ash from the bodies into a small leather bag. She started to smile, thinking of the power and prestige she'd have when she showed this trophy to the nameless man when they met again at the coming gathering; but then she remembered this was a solemn occasion, so she started crying again.

Pela went forward to the grave and then, to Adria's dismay, she began putting a few of her parent's things into the grave. Gifts for the dead were always given, she knew, but by the family. Pela had no right to sneak into the house, HER house to steal her things. She watched carefully as Pela reverently placed some of Ama's... no, Adria's gold jewelry atop the linen wrap. Pela whispered more words as she laid Torr's spear and long-bladed dagger next to the jewelry.

She stood, and Geog and Mart proceeded to shovel the excavated dirt back into the grave from where it had been taken. When they were done, a small mound was the only marking spot for two lives well spent and prematurely ended. They turned away sadly, returning to the village.

Considering the slight mound, Adria was sure she'd be able to return in a couple nights to quietly dig up her jewelry and secret it in her house. She sobbed loudly as Pela turned to look at her.

~

After their work shift, the two men who'd helped Father Woods stopped at a nearby tavern for a quick drink before heading home. The place was dark, even with the gaslights ringing the room. It was dark outside at this hour as well and in concession to the darkness, extra oil lanterns were placed on the tables. They supplied only a little more light. The two men sat down at a table near the door.

"So, George, have you been thinking any more about that body?"

George answered with a shake of his head, "Nope. Like you said, it's none of our business."

"So, what're you drinking tonight, gentlemen?"

The waitress smiled down at them. She was about twenty summers old and very fit. Her clothing made that very apparent.

George looked quickly over his shoulder, and then he turned back, smiling. "Oh, were you talking to us?"

"Well, I don't see anyone else at your table."

"Oh, well," George said, as though he was confused, "I thought I heard you say 'gentlemen' and I just figured someone else must be standing behind us."

She smiled. Harry thought she was pretty.

"Okay, assholes, what do you want? Does that sound more like you?"

George and Harry roared with laughter and ordered two whiskeys. The drinks arrived quickly and as they drank, they talked of the trade, and of the rumors spreading at work, and if their waitress would be available after hours.

An older man, a magician, was just packing up his paraphernalia from a show he'd just performed. He looked over the crowd and his eyes fixed momentarily on George.

George took a sip of his whiskey, saying, "I'm going to the bathroom; must be getting old—this is happening much too often."

Harry laughed, "Maybe you shouldn't drink so much!"

"I haven't…yet, but the night's still young!"

Harry was laughing as George made his way toward the bathrooms at the rear of the tavern near the stage.

He glanced back at the table when he reached the bathrooms, noticing that Harry was again engaged in conversation with their waitress. Instead of going through the bathroom door, he bypassed it, stepping quickly behind the heavy curtain that shielded the back stage area from tavern patrons. There he found the magician waiting for him. He glanced around; nobody was within earshot.

"A priest was killed tonight," he said, looking around again. "I think he was killed by the Cathedral. He was beaten to death and brought to us for processing by another priest. Something is going on."

The magician looked thoughtfully at George. "How do you know he was a priest?""I could see the mark of his high collar. Nobody but a priest would wear something that uncomfortable."

The magician laughed, nodding. George was a keen observer.

"Thank you for this information, it may somehow attach to the rumors we've been hearing regarding the Cathedral adventuring into the far south."

"Why would anyone want to go there? The Green holds only death for our kind."

"Well, the rumors have been persistent, and the crystal ships have been sailing regularly from port, with soldiers, engineers, and construction people aboard."

"They could be going anywhere," George said disgustedly.

"But the rumors aren't about anywhere, are they?"

"No," George agreed, "they seem to be consistently about the south."

"One thing you may not have heard," the old stage magician said, glancing around furtively, "One rumor says that this particular rumor came directly from the Cathedral, from a priest."

"And now a priest has been slain," said George thoughtfully.

"It may not be the strongest verification, but it's still suggestive, is it not?"

"I agree, but I don't know what it means."

"Neither do we. Yet."

George saw one of the stagehands coming toward them. He grabbed the magician's hand and began pumping it furiously, slurring his words as he spoke.

"That waazsh a fine show you juss' put on for us, yesh it was…"

The stagehand walked over and said, "Sir, you are not allowed backstage."

George turned toward him, grabbing his hand, shaking it as well.

"Well, I'll go back out front then…wahdt ye say yer name were?"

"I didn't," the stagehand said stiffly, "you better go now."

"Oh, okay," George, said jovially. He turned, walking back past the edge of the curtain; almost stumbling over his own feet as he made the turn to go back into the tavern.

"I'm sorry about that," the stagehand apologized, "I'll try to keep a quicker eye out back here for drunks."

"It's fine," the magician reassured him, "at least he liked the show!"

Both men laughed, then the stagehand went back into the shadows to prepare for the next show; the magician went to his dressing room. This was his last show for the evening, but he was not yet done working this night.

George walked back to his table, sitting down with Harry. They each had two more drinks while Harry tried again to pick up their waitress, but she was having none of it.

"Looks like I'm not the only one getting old." George chuckled.

Harry laughed, "I'm not old. I just look that way from having to work with you all the time."

They laughed jovially.

"Besides Harry, what would your wife say if you came home with that waitress?"

It was obvious from the look on Harry's face that he hadn't considered that part of the problem.

Chapter 16

It was evening of the sixth day since Lyria and Kel began their journey west; they reined in their horses by a wide stream. Kel dismounted, carefully approaching the water's edge. He stepped out into the current.

"I can still see sand and rocks on the bottom," he shouted to Lyria, "I do not think the water here is more than two feet at its deepest."

"At least we won't have to look for a place to cross in the morning."

Kel laughed and pointed to the west. "Oh no…crossing will be easy!"

Lyria looked at the line of mountains looming quite close now. She could tell they'd be in the low hills below the mountains by the coming evening. She considered the mountains for a moment. "Walking across the mountains is just like walking here on the flat."

Kel looked at her with a quizzical expression, his head tilted to one side—it made Lyria's heart warm. What a delightful, smart, and funny man he was; and soon, hopefully, they would be wed.

"The walking is the same—it will just be vertical instead of horizontal," he said jokingly. "Let's see if you retain this jovial mood once we are a day or two into that vertical walk."

She laughed as she loosened her saddle, sliding it from Fog's back to the ground. The animal seemed happy to be rid of that burden for a while. Kel waded back to shore and removed Mist's saddle as well. Both horses wandered down to the stream, lowered their heads, and began drinking; they hadn't come upon any water for two days and the horses were thirsty. Kel released Morning from the cart. She too went to the water to slake her thirst. He then walked down and tied their leads to a tree by the gently sloping bank. Here there was grass and water for the horses, and grass for Kel and Lyria to sleep on as well—they had become tired of rocky ground.

Lyria prepared the fire while Kel walked down to the stream to fill their water skins. It was likely they'd find water in the mountains, but there was no point in taking chances. Both of them were worried about what lay ahead.

That evening they ate a little salted pork with bread—what remained of the butter had spoiled several days ago—amid a few more oinks, snorts, and playful shoving. After eating, they sat together holding hands, watching the moon rise.

"When we get to the mountains tomorrow evening, I will journey and see what I can see."

"That would not be a bad idea. I am sure Hawk will be able to see ahead and above very well." replied Lyria.

"The map Llo has given us has led us well, so far," Kel confirmed.

He pulled the map out of the leather bag at his side. He unfolded it, placing it on his lap. Lyria moved closer and leaned against him so she could see as well.

"If we continue as we did today, due west, we should find a very large boulder that is much bigger than the burial rock of our tribe."

Kel pointed out the rock on their map. Lyria pointed to the landmark as well.

"That should not be hard to find. If the drawing is correct, the rock will look something like a dog's head."

Kel nodded silently. He was very aware of Lyria's warmth as she leaned against him. How he wished right now that they were married. He sighed and Lyria smiled and moved a short distance away from him.

"I am in agreement with your thoughts," she said and giggled.

Kel thought she sounded as she had when she was eleven.

"So, you can read minds?"

She laughed, "Not minds, but the language of your body."

He put his arm around her and drew her close, hugging her.

"I really love you, Lyria. Once my Shadow Walk is done and we are wed, then you can read all of my bodily language you can stand."

She snuggled against him, looked up coyly, and whispered, "Is that a promise?"

"If ever there was one."

In the morning they again set out just after dawn. Some of the excitement of the journey had worn off, and after six days of walking steadily west, they were bored.

"Look there," Lyria said, shielding her eyes with her right hand, pointing with her left. "Buzzards, several of them. I would say we will see what they are feasting upon in a couple of hours."

"That will give us a diversion from what we have been doing for six days!"

Lyria laughed at that, nodding in agreement.

As they plodded on, Kel read more of *The Way Things Were*, occasionally reciting something out loud he found to be of special interest.

"It says here that long before the ice came, the first outlanders arrived on the eastern shores of our lands from cold regions to the north of the area that would become the unified tribes of the Black Cross."

"They didn't follow that horrible religion, did they?"

"No, this was well before the Redeemed God became redeemed."Kel continued, "When these explorers arrived from across the eastern sea they came in boats with monsters on the bows and they made war on the original peoples who lived here."

"They brought monsters with them?" Lyria asked.

"I don't think they were real monsters; it sounds like they were carved onto the ships to make them appear fierce before their enemies."

"That sounds interesting. I wonder what they really looked like?"

"The book does not say. Anyway, it says the original peoples were nomadic and small in numbers and very soon they were overwhelmed all along the eastern part of the land. They were conquered, it says here, 'by magic swords of great power forged in the lands across the sea.' The new men also brought sicknesses that killed many of the original people—especially the young. The original people were pushed back and back until they were either all killed or brought into the tribes coming from across the water. A thousand years before the ice moved, they were all gone, though it says their blood is mingled with ours, as many of the invaders took them for brides and bore children with them."

"So they really do live on then," Lyria said, "in us."

"I suppose that is true," Kel answered thoughtfully.

When the sun was nearly at the top of the sky, they came upon the buzzards at their feast. Kel saw them first for he was riding a little ahead, making sure they were still on the right trail. Lyria came up over the low rise leading their cart and looked down on the scene. There was a four-wheel wagon tipped on one side. She saw from her elevated position that the wagon had been pulled by two horses, but the carcass of only one could be seen, its bones showing whitely through rends in its hide. She rode down to sit next to Kel.

The buzzards weren't happy with their visitors, taking quickly to the air. Their ten-foot wingspan cast flitting shadows over the scene below them. Two ravens, however, were not intimidated by the presence of the recent intruders. They stood their ground on the rim of the upper front wheel of the wagon, croaking their defiance.

Kel tied their horses to the back wheel of the overturned wagon and walked over to examine the carcass of the horse. He stooped and picked up a broken arrow. The feathers and maybe a foot of the shaft were all that remained. Though the horse had been dead for many days, he could still see the wounds in its neck and flanks; wounds made with arrows that had been removed.

"This is the work of bandits," he said with surety. "The horse was slain with arrows."

"And so too were the people who traveled with them."

Kel walked around the wagon and there he saw the bodies of three individuals. Though the sun and time had desiccated them, and buzzards had ravaged them, the wounds on their bodies were clearly visible. The three bodies lay on their backs, stripped of their clothing. A number of arrow wounds could be seen on each body. Each victim's throat had also been slit. A man, woman, and boy child of about eight summers lay dead before them, their blood long dried and brown against the soil and grass.

"The wagon is empty, Kel."

"I am not surprised at that."

"The lower back wheel is broken," Kel commented.

"I saw. It must have broken as they fled, tipping their wagon and leaving them at the mercy of those bandits."

"Precious little mercy," Kel spat.

"We can't just leave them like this."

"No, we can't. I will get the shovel and we will bury them. We do not have time for a proper cremation and there is no sacred site for the ashes to rest, but perhaps the Gods will allow this to be a sacred site for these unfortunate people."

Kel turned, walking back to their cart. Before he picked up the shovel, he fastened a quiver of arrows to his waist, bringing the other to Lyria. She strapped it on wordlessly, taking the bow he offered. He walked back one more time to their cart to get the shovel.

An hour later, the grave was dug and the three bodies were laid side-by-side, hands folded peacefully across their chests. In the grave, they left a small amount of food as an offering.

It was then Kel thought of something. "Wait here. I will only be a minute."

He ran back to their cart, climbing into the back, moving a few things to expose the wooden trunk that Llo had given him to take for trading. He opened it and looked through the various bundles until he found the one he was looking for. He hurried back to the gravesite. He looked at Lyria and opened the wrapping.

"When I was his age, this would surely have delighted me."

In his hand was a bronze, copper, and silver eagle with a wingspan of perhaps a foot. He looked at Lyria and moved the tail of the eagle. Cleverly hinged and articulated, the wings flapped up and down. Lyria's eyes opened wide in delight and surprise.

"Oh, Kel," Lyria said, tears forming in her eyes when she realized what Kel was planning, "what a lovely, thoughtful thing you are doing."

He laid the toy eagle gently on the young boy's breast.

"May your spirit soar with the eagle in the Light of the Otherworld, young one."

He readjusted the bodies. The woman was in the center, so Kel moved her hands to her sides. Then he moved the left hand of the boy and the right hand of the man, so they now lay holding hands; a family forever.

He began shoveling the dirt and rocks back into the grave. When the grave was closed, they examined the wagon one more time to see if perhaps the bandits had inadvertently left something useful, but it had been thoroughly searched and stripped. The wagon would surely have been taken as well if it hadn't broken a wheel when it tipped. Clearly the second horse that had been pulling the wagon was now with the bandits. They could be close by, or perhaps in the mountains ahead of them. Kel scanned the surrounding territory but saw nothing threatening. However, with the hills and rocks of the region, he couldn't see very far at all. They decided to carry the bows and arrows on their persons from now on.

As they rode off, Lyria was still drying tears on the cuff of her shirt.

They rode on in silence for some distance—the sight of the murders cast a pall over their travels. Still, they both knew that in life, the future was uncertain at best and the end was always near. Now they rode side by side, each scanning the terrain for any sign of movement that might indicate the presence of a raiding band.

The journey became uneventful again. Lyria maintained a special alertness; she knew that complacency would bring disaster. By the time the sun was heading toward the mountains in front of them, they'd reached the foothills of the mighty mountain range. Kel could feel the extra exertion Mist was putting into walking as the grade increased. Their days would cover fewer miles until they crossed the mountains, descending on the other side where the Black City crouched waiting for them.

Lyria was the first to spot it. She pointed eagerly. "Look, the dog-head stone!"

Kel looked where she was pointing, "Amazing! It really does look like a dog's head, does it not?

"Yes it does," Lyria responded excitedly.

"We should be able to reach it before nightfall."

"This is seven days on the path, and I think we are making good time."

"We are, or we were. Now we begin your 'vertical' walking and the horses will need more rest."

"We can walk some of the distance leading the horses," Lyria suggested.

"I imagine we will have to."

They camped by the landmark so clearly marked on Llo's old map. The dog-shaped rock was huge; it stood thirty feet tall, to the tips of its pointed ears. There was a small stream running clear and cool directly past the large boulder. Fog, Mist, and Morning were tethered with long lines to a sturdy tree. Kel looked up at the rock and wondered if it had been an actual dog at one time.

"Do you suppose the whole body of the dog is under the ground?"

Lyria, looking at him in amazement, said, "I really doubt that."

"I was just wondering," he mused, "if it had been alive at some time and turned to stone by magic."

"If that were true, it would have made an excellent guard for the village."

Kel laughed again at the image of the giant dog sitting outside his home.

"I, for one, would hate to have to feed it. I don't think we have enough meat in the entire village for that."

"Maybe," said Lyria, "it is a good thing it is just a stone."

"Maybe?"

Kel looked at her out of the corner of his eye.

"Definitely!"

"It is a good thing we settled that before we eat."

"Are you hungry again?"

"Not again," Kel responded. "Still!"

They laughed as they prepared their evening meal; the somber mood of earlier in the day was finally cast off.

After eating, they drank from the stream and refilled their water skins.

They packed everything they wouldn't need this night back into the wagon so they could make a quicker start in the morning; they still had a long way to go. Then Kel removed from the wagon a rattle he'd made several years ago under Garn's guidance. He'd decided to use the rattle since it wouldn't make as much noise as his drum and they didn't know who might be close by. He handed the rattle to Lyria. She took it without comment, settling herself comfortably on her blanket. He then reclined on his blanket just outside his tent, closing his eyes. One breath, then another, and the tensions of the day faded rapidly; he heard the soft sound of the rattle as Lyria shook it.

Chapter 17

Kel entered the dense woods, following the stream further into the forest. The sun was filtering through the trees, casting a wondrous green light over all he saw. Birds twittered in the trees. He noticed with some surprise that he was wearing a sword; he'd never been armed in a journey before. He passed the boulder, again getting his foot wet in the shallow stream. He found the fallen tree and negotiated that obstacle, and then he was in the clearing, looking at the stone in the center. He sat down in his usual spot and could just barely hear the rattle Lyria was shaking. He looked at the stone for a moment, expecting to see Hawk, but his totem was nowhere to be found.

He was suddenly aware of a presence to his left. He looked in that direction. Monsters! There were monsters coming! He scrambled to his feet, his hand instinctively going to the hilt of his sword. Strange creatures were floating in the air, coming toward him. Their faces were neither animal nor man, but they were unspeakably hideous, with twisted features that seemed to change as they moved. It almost seemed that, under their flesh, yet other unseen creatures were moving. He'd just begun to draw the sword, and he stopped.

Nothing ever threatened him on a journey and suddenly his fear was gone. He let the sword drop back all the way into the scabbard and stood, hands at his side as the creatures approached him. Suddenly they were gone! They vanished, and to his astonishment, there was Hawk, less than a foot in front of him, staring directly into his eyes. There was something…some message…but he couldn't quite get it. Hawk turned, flying to the standing stone in the middle of the clearing. He looked once more at Kel, nodded in his peculiar way and was gone, through the trees, leaving Kel to figure out the mystery for himself. He heard the frequency of the rattle change; he knew it was time to return to the physical world once again. He retraced his steps through the forest, finally opening his eyes…

Lyria, sitting cross-legged on her blanket, stopped shaking the rattle. She looked at him quizzically. He sat up, then rose and stretched. When he felt like he was fully back, he turned to her and told her of his vision.

"I can't imagine what that might mean," she said. "But then, you are the shaman!"

She smirked at that and Kel laughed.

"I suddenly felt that, despite their ugliness, the monsters were not a threat."

"And, if you had drawn and wielded your sword," Lyria said. "You would have cut Hawk!"

"That is what it looked like, though I doubt anything could harm Hawk."

"So what or who are the monsters and why should you not be afraid of them?"

He thought for a moment and then it came to him! Of course! Why had he not seen it immediately?

"Before we left on this journey, Llo told me something. He said that when one goes out into the wide world, one's impressions of things must widen too."

"That makes sense," Lyria said, "but what does that have to do with monsters?"

"He also told me something else. He said not everything that is black is evil and not everything that is white is good."

Lyria silently looked at him.

He continued his thought, "The monsters are something—or someone—we will see as dangerous, only it will turn out not to be so. I don't see any other explanation. Hawk was reminding me of what Llo said, but in his own way!"

"So somewhere along our path we will find friendly monsters?"

Kel laughed, "Something like that."

By this time the sky was dark. There was cloud cover hiding the stars and the moon. It would be a dark night. They sat together for a few minutes, enjoying the closeness; then they retired to their tents for the night. The fire was burning low and it was banked properly so it wouldn't spread before it went out. They both knew the next day would be a long and hard one. The climb was coming.

~

The Bishop paced back and forth across the length of his office, deep in thought. In mid-stride he suddenly stopped, turned, and walked quickly to the telephone mounted on the wall beside his desk. As the polished brass cradle on the right side of the oak box lifted with the handset, somewhere in the Cathedral there was a click as the line was opened.

"May I help you, Your Eminence?"

"Connect me with the head of the repair division in the zeppelin barns."

"Yes, Your Eminence."

The line went dead for a moment; then another voice spoke.

"This is Franklin, Your Eminence, what can I do for you?"

"How long will it be before the engine on my gray zeppelin is repaired?""Another two days, Your Eminence," Franklin said apologetically. "We have to mount it and thoroughly test it; though upon your order, the other gray ship was dispatched yesterday."

"That's fine. There's one more thing I'd like you to do for me."

"What's that, Your Eminence?"

"I want the zeppelin repainted."

There was a slight pause, then, "What color this time?"

Franklin sounded a bit…miffed.

The Bishop smiled. He'd gotten it painted gray only a few weeks earlier.

"I want you to paint it white."

"White? Yes, Your Eminence. We can do that in the morning so it'll be dry by the time the engine is ready to install tomorrow afternoon."

"Excellent! Thank you. I know how hard you and your men work to keep me happy!"

"It's for the glory of the Redeemed God," Franklin said without hesitation.

"Yes it is," the Bishop responded.

He hung up the phone, thought a moment, and picked it up again. Once the connection was open he told the operator to connect him with Father Woods.

There was a knock on his door about a half hour later. The Bishop glanced at the large clock on the wall; Father Woods had made good time, considering he was all the way over in the zeppelin barn when he'd been summoned.

"Come in."

The Bishop's servant opened the door, saying, "Father Woods to see you, Your Eminence."

"Thank you, Harold, send him in."

A moment later, Father Woods was kneeling before the Bishop.

"Rise, Father Woods."

The priest stood. "You asked for me, Your Eminence?"

"Yes, I did. I want you to do something. I want you to go to our tailor's shop in the city and have him make you two new robes."

"New robes?"

Father Woods was so surprised he forgot to address the Bishop properly.

Good, thought the Bishop, *maybe it'll surprise others as well.*

"Yes, Father. I want you to have two white robes made to fit you, and make sure the collar's left open. I don't want these robes to have the priest's collar."

"Yes, Your Eminence," Father Woods responded, sounding confused.

The Bishop was pacing again. He ended back at his desk where he picked up several papers, turned, and offered them to Father Woods.

"These are some ideas I've had regarding your upcoming mission. I want you to read through them and let me know what you think."

Father Woods accepted the papers and turned to go.

"Actually, would you mind sitting here to read them? I'm very anxious to hear your opinion."

"Certainly, Your Eminence."

Father Woods sat in a padded chair near one wall and began reading the papers. It didn't take long. He was smiling. The Bishop liked to see that.

"This is a very good idea!"

Clearly from his expression, Father Woods was impressed.

"Now you may go for your evening meal. Over the next few days, I want you to re-read this; see if there are any alterations or suggestions you can think of."

"I shall, Your Eminence."

"Excellent! Remember, we'll have only one opportunity to do this…and it'll be your life and that of your crew on the line! This has to be done perfectly."

"With the guidance of the Redeemed God, it shall be!" Father Woods answered enthusiastically.

~

Kel and Lyria began early the next morning. While Kel saddled Fog and Mist, Lyria restarted the fire to cook breakfast. Today they'd have eggs! Lyria found some quail eggs earlier and had brought them back to the camp. After Kel said the appropriate prayer, Lyria began preparing them. They still had some cheese left, so this went into the mix along with cut up salted pork. She made two quail egg omelets, which pleased Kel greatly.

"These are really good," Kel said with a smile.

"I'm glad you like them. Not a bad change, is it?"

"Not bad at all," Kel responded with his mouth filled to capacity.

"Oink! Snort!" Lyria whispered.

Kel laughed and some egg yolk ran down his chin.

"I am never going to live down the butter hog, am I?"

When they were finished eating, he took their bowls to the stream to wash them while Lyria made sure the fire was extinguished. He returned, packed their eating utensils and bowls in the basket and put it back in the cart. He removed the map again and briefly sat down to study it. Lyria came over to sit with him in the grass.

"It looks like we go south for a while; then the trail should be more obvious as the ground gets rockier."

"It almost looks like the trail is an old stream bed," Lyria suggested.

"I believe you are right! That makes things much easier."

"Why would that be?"

"Well, if we imagine we are flowing water, we can judge where the hill would take us, and that will be the trail."

"What if there is a waterfall?" Lyria smiled slightly.

"Then we can practice your vertical walking."

They both laughed as he put the map away and they mounted up for the day's journey.

As they began their ascent into the mountains, they kept a sharp eye on the terrain, looking for a telltale smudge of darkness against the sky that would indicate a campfire. Once, very near the trail, they found an old campsite. By the condition and scent of the ashes they determined that it was at least a few weeks old. It could just as easily have been the last campfire of the bandits' victims, assuming they'd come across the mountains, or that of the bandits themselves. They moved on.

At midday they stopped, resting by a calm pool of very deep water. The horses needed to feed, and water wouldn't hurt them either. Kel again filled their water skins though they'd not drunk very much since he'd filled them last. The three horses calmly grazed by the pool's edge while Lyria prepared a quick meal that wouldn't require a fire. They didn't want to take the time to build a fire, and they didn't want to give away their position.

As they ate, Kel looked again at the map. From now on, the path should be easy to follow. It looked as though it had been merely a game trail at one time, but now it was a horse trail as well. From what they'd seen so far, though, it wasn't a trail often used by humans.

"I am glad we brought only a small two-wheeled cart," he said to Lyria. "It looks like some areas ahead will be narrow and have tight turns."

"It seems that the path is very plain since we have begun to climb."

"And it should stay that way until we are well over the top and headed down the other side."

"I can't wait to see this huge village we are headed toward."

Kel smiled. He was eager to see it as well.

"Imagine, a village with over a thousand inhabitants. Actually, it is rather hard to imagine."

"I am anxious to see it as well. Llo is not one to exaggerate, but this is something one must see to believe."

Lyria laughed, "That is my feeling as well. It must seem like a summer gathering every day."

"Hopefully we can get information regarding the Black City from the people."

"If they trade with the City, they will know more than we do now."

Kel nodded, popping the last bit of bread into his mouth.

"You will notice, Lyria, that my final bite was actually quite small and not piggish at all."

"Yes, I saw, but you could have chewed it a bit longer."

He bumped her shoulder with his and she laughed.

Kel saddled the horses while Lyria shook out and folded their blankets before putting them in the cart. They rode for about two hours then dismounted to lead Fog and Mist by their reins. They'd decided to walk an hour for every two or three hours they rode. The pace was slower now than it had been in the flatlands they'd left behind them. Just as Llo had said, trees were becoming more prevalent. They weren't yet walking in a forest, but if they climbed much higher, they soon would be.

Kel pointed up the slope to the horizon. "The trail moves off to the south a little bit; that is good."

"I can see the top is not as high in that direction," Lyria said. "I was beginning to fear we might have to go all the way up into the high mountains to find a way through."

"Llo mentioned that crossing would be hard, but not as hard as it would look from the start."

"I am glad he traveled this way before."

"I know! A person could wander around up here in the mountains for days before finding a way through without a map such as this one."

Somewhere overhead a hawk cried out. They both looked up, straining their eyes against the bright blue. Finally Kel pointed toward a dark spot in the heavens. The hawk was traveling parallel to their direction. It called out one more time; then disappeared far above the trees.

"Well," Lyria stated with finality, "that surely is a good omen."

"I agree; I was rather surprised that up to this point we had not seen a hawk."

"Well, we have seen one now—and he was going the same way as we are."

"Then everything should be fine."

They rounded a bend in the trail where it ran between rather steep embankments, and then came to a halt—the path ahead of them was blocked by a fallen tree.

Kel groaned. This was going to take even more of their time. He sighed and dismounted.

"I will have to pull the tree out of the way."

"It looks too big for us to move," Lyria said.

"I will use my rope and try to let Mist pull it to one side."

"I think that might work. And if not, we have two other horses that can pull as well."

Faithful Morning gave what sounded like a sarcastic snort and Kel laughed. He walked over to the horse and patted her on the forehead.

"Never fear, Morning, you are pulling enough for all of us on this journey."

Morning flicked her tail from side to side and seemed to have nothing more to say about the matter.

"Well, it's not going to move itself, I suppose."

Kel removed his rope from Mist's saddle, looping it around one end of the fallen tree. The other end he wrapped around the saddle horn and clucked at the horse. Mist moved forward and slowly the tree began sliding. Only one end needed to be moved; the path would be wide enough for them to pass if the tree was merely moved to the side. Mist pulled again; the tree turned, then it was sliding freely. As soon as it was parallel with the trail, he removed the rope, rolled it, and hooked it back on the saddle.

"Well, that could have been worse."

"Yes it could have. We do not have the hawk's ability to soar over obstacles with ease."

Kel took Morning's lead rope, slowly guiding the wagon around the tree. That would be the most difficult part of the operation. Lyria dismounted to watch where the right wheel passed the tree. It would be a disaster if they broke a spoke in the wheel because of a fallen tree. Finally the cart was around the obstacle. Lyria led Fog and Mist around the tree; then they remounted and once again began moving uphill. They'd be close to the top of this ridge by nightfall. Kel was hoping to cross it this day.

"The top of this ridge is near," Lyria stated, giving speech to Kel's thought.

"It is. I am hoping we can cross it before we make camp."

"That would be wonderful!"

"Once we reach the other side, everything will be new. Even when we look back where we have been, we will no longer be able to see any of the flatlands we have crossed to get here."

Lyria looked back the way they'd come. From their present position, she could see no more than a hundred feet or so behind them; trees and rocks prevented seeing any farther.

"I understand what you are saying."

Lyria also felt that it would be nice to put the destroyed wagon and its slain occupants on the other side of the mountain. He smiled at her. It was almost as though she could read his mind.

Chapter 18

The next morning Father Woods arose early. He said his morning invocations to the Redeemed God; then ate a quick breakfast in the dining hall. He descended the steps to the ground floor of the Cathedral. He used the telephone by the side door to call for an automobile. He opened the heavy bronze door, walking outside to wait for the chauffeured machine to arrive. He thought about the Bishop's plan. It was risky, but under the circumstances it was clearly the best option available to them.

With all that was happening far to the south, they didn't need some kind of tribal uprising. He imagined thousands of half-humans crossing the mountains and storming the Cathedral. They wouldn't succeed, of course, but still, many of their soldiers were away and couldn't be summoned back from the south very quickly. No, it would be up to him. He smiled. He knew he could pull this off.

After about twenty minutes, the steam-auto drove up and stopped. The driver quickly stepped out, running around the vehicle to open the door for the priest. He held it with his face lowered as Father Woods climbed into the back seat. He shut the door and was quickly behind the wheel once again.

"Where would you like to go, Your Grace?"

Father Woods didn't recognize his chauffeur; it seemed to him the servant staff was constantly changing. He'd heard that some of them had gone south to try their fortunes in a new world.

"I'd like to go into the city. Take me to the tailor's shop run by Thomas Kantner."

"I know the place, Your Grace. It's called Thomas Tailors."

"Not very imaginative, but I guess it gets all the important information across."

The driver laughed, "It certainly does, Your Grace."

The vehicle pulled away from the Cathedral. Father Woods sat back into the leather seat. The auto was comfortable, at least. As they entered Los Angeles proper, they had to slow down. Traffic in this part of the city was heavy; horses, carts, large wagons, steam-autos, and delivery trucks moved this way and that, sometimes seemingly at random. They drove down Sun Boulevard past shops and taverns and tall hydroponic buildings that grew most of the food the city consumed. They continued on their way, passing mounted half-human traders dressed in fur with iron plate and boiled leather armor, and society women walking their exotic animals on leashes as they shopped for the very latest in irrelevant styles. Overhead to the north, the aurora flashed and flickered, a steady reminder of the cold death moving toward them.

When they arrived at Glacier Street, the driver pulled to the curb and put the boiler fire on a low setting to keep the engine hot and the steam pressure up but without using excess water or hydrogen. Again the driver quickly exited the vehicle, running around to open the door for the priest.

"Would you like me to come with you, Your Grace?"

"That will not be necessary. You wait with the automobile; I'll be only a short time."

"As you wish, Your Grace," the driver said, bowing his head.

As the priest walked toward the entrance of the tailor's shop, the driver got back into the auto. He settled back into his seat. Official autos were very nice inside, and comfortable. He couldn't imagine why anyone would want to ride horses.

Father Woods opened the glass and wood frame door. A bell attached at the top jangled its notice to those inside that a customer had arrived. As the priest walked to the counter, a short, squat older man came bustling out of the back room and nodded to him. His hair was a bit long on the sides and rather nonexistent on the top of his head. He wore a long sleeved shirt, vest, and slacks. Father Woods noticed the cloth tape measure dangling from his pocket, and the gold chain draped across his chest attached to a pocket watch.

"How can I be of service, Your Grace?"

The man was properly subservient, Father Woods noticed with satisfaction.

"I'd like you to measure me for some new clothing."

"Yes, Your Grace," Thomas Kantner said, "but we have a number of priest garments already made up that we could alter to fit you."

"That will not do."

The tailor bowed, answering, "I'll do what you ask, Your Grace."

"Thank you. I need two robes made in a heavy white material."

The tailor looked up in surprise and said, "White, Your Grace?"

"That's correct. The whitest you have."

"Fine. Fine."

The tailor opened a door to the back room slightly—shouting to his assistant to come to the front.

The second man was younger than the tailor and Father Woods noticed he was certainly no relative of Thomas Kantner. *Must not be a family business*, he thought.

"Lars, I want you to measure Father…" he looked enquiringly at the priest.

The priest flashed his very brightest smile, answering, "I'm Father Caven!"

"Very well, Father Caven," the tailor's assistant said, "if you will just stand over here, I can take your measurements."

The priest obliged, and in a short period of time they had the work finished. Father Woods made sure they understood how the collar was to be fashioned, even making a drawing for them to use as a model. The tailor showed the priest several kinds of fabric, but not being knowledgeable on the subject, the priest simply told them to use their judgment. The only stipulation, he added, was that he wanted them completed in three days. He handed both the tailor and his assistant a silver coin to speed things up. They smiled, saying the robes would be ready in just two days. The priest smiled back at them and walked out. The bell on the door jangled yet again.

When the chauffeur saw the door of the shop opening, he quickly got out of the car and went around to open the passenger door for the priest. After the priest was settled into his seat, the driver returned to his position in the cab and increased the fire level. Steam pressure quickly built and they were once again moving down the street.

"Where would you like to go now, Your Grace?"

"Take me just around the corner to the right, pull in, and wait for me."

"Yes, Your Grace."

The driver knew where the priest wanted to go; he'd taken priests there numerous times. He turned the corner, pulling to the curb outside a tall apartment building. He knew some apartments in this building were kept for the priests. This was where women were brought for the priests, some willing, some not. He smiled as he picked up his book. Apparently priests liked to dominate the feminine, just as did the Redeemed God— just as he himself did on occasion.

~

Once the priest left the tailor's shop, Lars came to his employer.

"I've checked in the rear storage room and we've no white thread with which to make these robes."

The older man thought for a moment, responding, "Very well. Run over to the wholesale supplier around the corner and get what you think we'll need to finish the job."

"Yes, sir," Lars responded with a smile.

He hurried out and around the corner. Half a block ahead of him he recognized the priest's steam-car at the curb. He stopped, looked both ways, and crossed to the other side of the street. He continued on his way up a block before returning to the other side of the street again.

He reached into his pocket and pulled out the two rolls of white thread he'd removed from the storage room at the tailor's shop. He deposited them in a street corner trash receptacle and made his way another half block to the wholesaler who supplied most of the tailor shops in this part of Los Angeles. He pushed open the door, walking inside. He quickly found what he was looking for, two rolls of white thread identical to the ones he'd thrown away. The proprietor knew him and let him take the thread, adding the cost to the bill Thomas Kantner paid monthly. He dropped the thread in his pocket with the receipt and left the shop again.

Lars started back the way he'd come, but before passing the priest's steam-car still parked in front of the apartment building, he turned into a rather disreputable tavern nearby. Hurrying inside, he brushed off the approach of several prostitutes who came slinking out of the narrow walkway between the tavern and the building next to it. He sat down at a table just inside the front door, letting his eyes become accustomed to the dimness of the interior.

Day and night the gaslights burned in this place as it had no windows, but it still seemed dark inside. This early in the morning there were few patrons. The waitresses were sweeping the floor and sprinkling sawdust over the freshly swept areas to absorb the remains of the frequently spilled drinks as well as the occasionally spilled blood. One of the tavern's entertainers, a magician and storyteller, saw him and walked over. He sat down just as a waitress walked up.

"What can I get for you fellows?"

"Nothing for me," said the tailor's assistant smiling, "I'm still working; just stopped in to say hi to a friend."

"What about you, oh wise and wonderful worker of magic?" She said, grinning at the magician.

"I'll have an ale, if you don't mind, Abby."

"If you don't mind, I don't mind," she replied with a snort.

Then she turned to Lars saying, "He actually knows what the ale in this place tastes like, and he still drinks it."

The three of them laughed, and the waitress left to get the drink. The men were alone once again.

The tailor looked swiftly in both directions to make sure nobody was within earshot. Leaning across the table he spoke in a low voice to the magician.

"A priest came in the shop today, said his name was Caven."

"Strange," the magician said, "the word from the Cathedral is that Father Caven left yesterday on an important mission to the north of here. He was supposed to be gone a fair amount of time too."

"I don't know about that," Lars said. "But I distinctly heard the name."

"Very well. Thank you for coming to me this quickly."

"Any idea why a priest assuming the name of another priest would want a white robe?"

"I haven't the slightest idea," responded the magician. "You better get back to work now before your boss decides you're slacking off!"

Lars laughed, rose, and walked out of the tavern. This time he walked right past the Cathedral steam-car. He was, after all, on a mission for the Bishop—wasn't he?

~

It was almost dusk by the time Kel and Lyria crossed the ridge. They paused briefly at the brink, looking down into a shallow valley. The terrain rose again on the other side, but the top of that ridge was lower than the one they were standing on. It would seem they'd made it over the mountains.

"Well," Lyria said in a happy voice, "We did it! It looks like we're finally over the top and it was not nearly as bad as I had imagined."

"It does at that," Kel answered, and pointing said, "I think we should descend to that rock outcropping there to make our camp. I can see trees and grass; there must be water there as well."

"I can see it, too."

They rode down the trail about one hundred yards to the outcropping. There they made camp between two large boulders; it would help shield them from wind if it came up that night. It would also somewhat shield their position should someone else come down the trail; in the dark they'd be virtually invisible.

They unsaddled their horses and led them to the water. A narrow stream meandered between the rocks then disappeared into the trees to their right. There was plenty of fresh green grass for the horses to eat as well and they wasted no time in getting started.

"Mart and Geog sure worried a lot about nothing," Kel said with a laugh.

"They had our best interests at heart."

"Yes, they did. They argue about everything, but for them arguing seems to be what thinking would be to us."

"That is an interesting way to look at it!"

They both laughed, and then as Kel set up the tents, Lyria prepared a cold dinner. No fire tonight, either.

The next morning they started out once more. Now they were actually walking downhill, at least for the time being. Soon they were in the little valley and by midday they'd made it to the rising ground on the far side. Here they rested once again, eating their noon meal. After this, they moved steadily downhill once more.

"Llo's map shows this giant village to be more or less on this trail," Kel stated.

"If it is the size he says, we should be able to see it easily enough."

"I imagine even the smoke trails from cook fires and the like will be visible from a long distance."

"We will never find out sitting here on our horses discussing it."

"You are right," chuckled Kel, as he heeled his horse into motion.

Lyria quickly followed, leading faithful Morning and her cart.

Chapter 19

They traveled another two days uneventfully, traveling steadily downhill. The mountains were now behind them as they followed the trail through pine and aspen trees that, while not dense enough to actually be considered a forest, still obstructed their view over a distance and occasionally obstructed the passage of the cart. Another fallen tree had to be moved off the trail the third day of travel this side of the mountain.

On the morning of the tenth day since they'd left their village, they found themselves moving into a shallow, winding canyon. The rocky outcrops forming the barriers on both sides of the trail stood no more than forty feet tall. With the meandering path of the old streambed they were following, they couldn't see very far in front of them.

Their first notice of trouble came from Fog. He'd suddenly stopped in his tracks and snorted. He seemed nervous, reluctant to move ahead.

"Something is wrong," Lyria, said to Kel. "This is not how he usually acts."

Kel was dismounting, taking his bow with him. Once on his feet, he removed the spear from its scabbard as well.

"I will scout ahead," he said.

"Not without me you won't." Lyria whispered as she dismounted.

Slowly they led their horses around the next turn. Kel was ready with his spear and Lyria had an arrow nocked to her bowstring. She held Fog's reins loosely, ready to let them fall at an instant's notice. They came around the bend to find they were in a slightly wider area. In the eons that it had flowed, the stream had eroded away a large area of land, making a tight turn in this spot. They slowly made their way into the widening canyon. Just as their cart came out of the narrower region behind them, there was movement on the rocks above them.

Kel and Lyria looked up. There were five men standing in the rocks and they were all armed. They looked down on the travelers silently for a moment. Silhouetted against the brilliant cerulean of the sky, they were hardly more than shadows.

Kel stood, spear in hand ready; Lyria had drawn her bow fully, ready to release her bolt of death. He heard her snarl and glanced over. Her eyes flickered to his and he shivered. Her eyes were no longer blue; they'd become green. The tiger was coming.

"Hold!"

The shout came from somewhere above them.

"Lower your weapons. These are not the bandits we seek."

The men in the rocks relaxed their bowstrings and lowered their spears. Kel and Lyria did the same. Then another man appeared in the rocks; he was much closer to them, having hidden behind a boulder a short distance ahead.

"Forgive us, travelers," the stranger said. "We are seeking bandits who ambushed some of our village a couple weeks ago."

The man walked closer. He was staring at Lyria. When he saw she'd noticed, he shifted his gaze quickly to Kel and bowed; it was an odd gesture rarely seen in the tribes.

"My name is Dan," he said smiling, "I hope you will forgive us."

Dan walked to Kel, holding out his hand. Kel stared at the offered hand in confusion. Dan laughed.

"I am sorry," he said, "old habits die hard."

He bowed again and began introducing the members of his group. Where do you come from?" Kel asked.

Dan looked quickly again at Lyria, taking a half-step back.

"We come from Mountain Village; it is only a day's walk ahead of you," Dan offered.

"We found a wagon with its occupants slaughtered on the other side of the mountains," Lyria said. "Were those some of your people?"

The man dropped his head.

"I believe that to be the truth," Dan said. "We had two wagons of trade goods headed east. We'd hoped to open trading routes with the eastern tribes. We found one wagon, stripped of its cargo and the men slaughtered."

"This wagon of which we speak carried three—a man, a woman, and a young boy of about eight summers," Lyria said.

"That is the Pan family. They were the lead traders in our village and had taken their family with them. Tell me. What of the girl?"

"We found only three bodies," Lyria said. "If there was another, they took her with them."

"They will take her into the city and trade her," Dan said with certainty. "Her name is Noria and she is nine summers of age. She has the most startling hair; it is beyond blonde—almost white in color."

The other men were gathered a short distance away, talking. It was decided that they should spend no more time here and should return to their village. Dan agreed.

"Well," Dan said to Kel and Lyria, "we have gone from weapon pointing to becoming bodyguards."

The other men laughed as they formed up on both sides of Kel and Lyria. Dan took Morning's reins, leading the wagon at the rear of the group. They made their way a short distance through the river-cut canyon; then they were in more open, rolling hills. Ahead they could see many columns of smoke.

Lyria asked in awe, "Can there be that many cook fires?"

Dan answered from behind them.

"Oh those are just the ones that burn wood. We also have some homes that run on gas."

"Gas?" Kel asked in surprise.

"Natural gas. Though they all still have wood-burning stoves as well. Sometimes the gas runs out before we can bring more from the city."

Kel turned in his saddle and looked at Dan in surprise.

"Trading with the Black City has gotten to that level?"

"Of course, it can make life easier."

Kel turned back to the front and they rode on for a time in silence. He and Lyria both had a lot to think about.

Crossing over the top of a hill, they came upon an overturned wagon.

"This is where the bandits ambushed our traders," Dan said. "While they were picking over this wagon, the other must have escaped, at least for a little while."

They stared silently at the wagon as they passed. Kel noticed an arrow protruding from the rear wheel. He looked at it closely; then reined up and stopped. He reached into his saddlebag, removing the broken arrow he'd picked up at the massacre on the other side of the mountains. He dismounted and walked to the wagon. The fletching on both arrows was identical—red-dyed eagle feathers. He turned and looked at Dan, then the others.

"These were the same who killed the people we found. This arrow is identical."

"So now the suspicion is fact. And little Noria is in the grasp of the Black City."

"How can you be so sure of that?" Lyria seemed skeptical.

"That is how it is done. Girls, young women, maidens…they are all valuable property to some in the city. They are sold to men who refer to themselves as pimps. They then…rent their captives' bodies to whoever will pay the going price."

"That is terrible," Lyria said in shock.

"Come," one of the men said.

Kel remounted his horse and resumed his position beside Lyria.

"We can do no good here. We should return to the village so Noria's relatives can be told the sad news."

They rode on in silence, the men in the group spread out into the countryside. They carried their spears upright with the butts in a small cup suspended from a leather strap on the right side of their saddles. The tips were left bare and ready for instantaneous use. Lyria watched the way they spread out. If a large obstruction such as a low hill was ahead, two of them would ride out and reconnoiter the back side of the hill before the main body of travelers approached it. Lyria noticed that Dan stayed close to them as he led Morning and the cart. They continued on this way until they were finally on top of a low rise looking down onto Mountain Village. Kel and Lyria stared in disbelief.

It was almost a small city. There was a main street that was wide and paved with small stones. On both sides of the main street were shops and open-air vendor areas. In the center of the main road there was a large circular open space with raised benches around the perimeter. The benches went up five levels. Obviously this was for town meetings and festivals, a place where many could gather. Extending out from this main thoroughfare, other smaller streets meandered through large areas of wood and straw-mud homes. Neither Kel nor Lyria had ever seen anything like it.

"This…this is…amazing," Lyria gasped, her voice reflecting her awe. "It is much more than a tribal gathering. I have never seen so many finely made homes in one area before."

"Where do you get your water?" Kel asked.

"There's a stream from the high mountains that runs underground. In this area it comes near the surface."

"Near? How do you get to it if it is underground?" Kel asked in confusion.

"We dig what are called 'wells.' They are holes in the ground that go into the water."

"With buckets we can bring up as much as we need," one of the other men offered. "It would seem this area is a huge lake, but under the land.

There are many wells both large and small through the village and they all bring up fresh water."

"As you can see," Dan said, "over there to our left are large community farms. We grow everything we need year round."

"The Gods have blessed you surely," Lyria said.

"The Gods and hard work," the first man said with a smile. "But then, the Gods have always favored those who are willing to work for what they want."

They began their descent into the village and soon they were riding on the cobblestone main road. Nobody gave them much of a look; Kel figured that with so many people, a couple of strangers would hardly be noticed. They reached the central open circle after about a half hour. Here the men stopped. They dismounted, as did Kel and Lyria. On one side of the area, there were long wooden troughs. Several horses were tied there already and the men led all the horses over so that they could drink.

"We will care for your horses while they are here, if you like." Dan smiled at them.

Several young boys were approaching from one of the large barns along the street past the open area. They took the horses, leading them away.

"What of our wagon?" Kel sounded concerned and Lyria looked worried as well.

Dan laughed and said, "Here we have a sacred bond. There is no theft in this village, none. Your wagon will be untouched once it is unhitched. It will be stored in the barn with your horses, out of the elements."

Dan thought for a moment and said, "If my memory serves me, two bandits rode through and stole from one of the merchants."

One of the other men said, "They did not get very far. Because we are such a large community, we can dispatch large numbers of armed men within minutes of their being called."

"An emergency call, using that bell," Dan pointed to the top of a double story building to their right, "will bring no less than one hundred armed men to this location in two minutes. Those bandits didn't stand a chance and the merchant got his things back as well."

"Come, we can finish our talk inside."

Chapter 20

The building they entered was built like a dining hall; it was a large open room with many trestle tables and chairs. Dan led them to a smaller table near the corner. They all sat and, amazingly, a man came up and asked them what they'd like to eat. He told them what was available today and stood patiently while they thought. After everyone ordered their food, the man hustled off to prepare the meals.

"Do they make everyone's meals?" Lyria asked.

"Only those who come in. Most people prepare their own food at home. This roadhouse is mainly for travelers."

"After we have eaten, there are smaller rooms in the back where we can talk privately," Dan said. "We have some things to discuss."

Kel and Lyria looked at each other, but before they could speak, the food arrived and then it was time for eating and drinking—not talking.

After they'd eaten, the other men left by the front door leaving Dan and his two companions by themselves. Dan rose and motioned for Kel and Lyria to follow. He opened a wooden door and motioned for the other two to enter. They complied and Dan closed the door behind them. They took seats in chairs they moved to the center of the room so they could talk face to face as was the tribal style.

"I will begin by telling you something of myself."

He looked at Kel, then Lyria, though for a shorter span. Then he sighed and looked back into Lyria's eyes saying, "There is one thing I would like you to do for me first."

"What is that?" Lyria asked suspiciously.

"Part of what I am going to tell you will make you angry. I would like a promise on the Goddess and God that you will not kill me until I have finished my story."

Lyria looked at the man in disbelief.

"This I do swear on all the names of the Goddess and God," she said sincerely.

Dan sighed, apparently relieved, and began his story.

"I was once known as Dan Hendricks. I was born and raised in Los Angeles. My mother was a society woman, and her husband would not have liked knowing that she had a lover. When she became aware that she was with child, she hid the fact as long as possible and then went on a vacation to visit relatives. She had the baby—me—without my father knowing, and for five summers my mother's sister raised me as her child.

119

"When she died, I was put into an orphanage—that is a building for housing unwanted children who have no family. I suppose they did the best they could, but there is little money spent for these things in the city and so, when I became a little older I began roaming the streets. I did this until I was twelve summers—and then I ran away from the orphanage entirely. After that, I was on my own.

"Early on, I discovered two things about myself. One is that I am a coward. When my friends were threatened on the street, I was somehow never there; I would have suddenly wandered off or had just gone into a shop nearby. I have come to accept this in my personality. The other thing I found out about myself is that I am an exceptional thief. I could get a woman's purse or a man's wallet from his pocket without getting caught, almost never getting caught—people are very careless when they are out in public. I suddenly had money to spend and I knew I could always get more. True to my coward's nature, I never robbed anyone who appeared to be armed. This way, when I was discovered, as was the case every once in a while, the most they could do was to try to beat me—but being a coward, I am a very fast runner.

"When I left the orphanage for good, I eventually found other men and women like myself who fed off of what those around us had too much of. We never robbed poor people on the street and we never broke into their houses. The more affluent homes on the hills just to the south of the city proper, however, were fair game. We made so much money...stealing and selling to merchants, that pretty soon we were very well dressed. We had pocket watches and vests and button-up shoes. We were kings then—believe me.

"It got to where we were able to rob some of the museums; those are large storage areas where old and valuable things are displayed for people to come in and see and perhaps learn from. This we did only on occasion as the museums were well guarded and I wasn't keen on facing any armed men.

"We hung about in taverns in the more...disreputable parts of town and there made friends, connections, and met merchants willing to buy items that technically belonged to someone else. Among these friends and connections we discovered a secret group within the city who were fighting against the Cathedral, which is located just outside the city. The priests of the Cathedral want Los Angeles under their dominion. They say they want to 'convert' people to save them, but largely they are after property and the domination of women."

Lyria said, "So far you have told me nothing that would make me want to kill you."

"Let's see if you feel like that when I am done with my story."

"We have read of the Black Cross church across the eastern sea and what they believed in. This religion is still in effect in the City, is it not?"

"Only partly," Dan said. "Let me finish my story; it is soon told."

"This secret organization had a number of interesting members. Some listened, some looked, some thought. Because of my talents, they wanted me to go into the Cathedral and see if I could ferret out any plans they might have for taking over the city. They managed to forge papers that made me...ME...a priest! Imagine! Anyway, I dressed as a priest and with my papers, I was allowed inside. What I saw in there amazed even me. There are basements in that building under basements. They have entire libraries of ancient books, many from before the ice came."

Kel interrupted, asking, "Is it possible to see this library? That must be a real treasure."

"That it is, but nobody but the priests can see it. They're afraid of what the books have to say."

"If they are afraid of them, why do they not burn them?" Lyria asked.

Dan turned to Lyria and said, "The same old reason—power and greed. Though they hate and despise and fear what the books have to say, they keep them because they can, because they are theirs and no one else's.

"Now let me finish my story and then you can kill me if you wish. But let me finish quickly because a coward does not often offer to die. I found some papers the organization wanted and a few books, too. I could go into the libraries and storage rooms because I was a research priest from a church far to the east in a city called 'Atlanta.' It was far enough away they could not check easily, even with their damned black airships."

Again Kel interrupted and asked, "The black ships come from the Cathedral? I thought they came from the city."

"They do not come from the city. The black ones leave and return to the Cathedral and the barns that store the zeppelins are on their grounds."

"There have been kidnappings recently from some of the tribes," Kel said. "The victims were taken in black airships."

"Then it is the priests who have them."

"They took my grandfather. He is our village shaman and my teacher. We journey to the Black City to find him."

"Then you'll have to look to the priests," Dan said. "The city has a few zeppelins but they are painted various colors; never black, and they never cross the mountains."

"Now," Dan said, "back to my story."

Kel and Lyria again sat back to listen.

"I stole the books and papers and I stole something else. I brought it with me here and if I do not die this evening, it is yours," he said, looking directly at Lyria.

"I gave the papers and books to the man I was supposed to deliver them to and several days later I was told priests were asking after me. The men of this conspiracy offered to hide me, but being a coward I chose to run.

"I left the city and traveled east until I ended up here, and here I stayed for a time. I had never been somewhere where people actually cared about each other, a place where everyone was fed and everyone worked at what they could do. I was welcomed for the first time in my life. By then I was all of nineteen summers, but I felt as though I had come home. Then, some years later, I made a mistake. I was in the village roadhouse when some men came in. They looked like a rough bunch, but I was used to that from when I lived in the city. There were ten in the group; later I met two more who had stayed with the horses. They said they were traders and they were looking for a guide across the mountains. There was no reason for me not to believe them. They offered to pay me to guide them and I agreed. We crossed the mountains and once on the other side, they continued east. I could not seem to get them to pay me, so I just rode along. I was afraid to confront them about our bargain.

"One night we came upon a village. They left me holding the horses and told me they were going to sneak into some of the storage rooms to steal food. We had not eaten in several days, so I did not disagree; besides, I had not yet been paid. From my vantage point I could see part of the village. I noticed the men were surrounding the place and I became fearful they were not going to just steal a little food. I moved a bit closer, and then they attacked. I had not expected this; you must believe me. To this point, I did not know they were bandits. They rounded up the villagers, and as some were robbing the homes, one man pulled a young woman from the hedgerow of spears. That was when she attacked."

He got no further before Lyria had him by the throat, snarling, "You were part of the raid on my village!"

"Yes, and no," Dan stammered desperately. "Like I said, I didn't know this was what they were planning; I didn't know they were bandits. I was an outsider, remember? And you promised not to kill me until I finished my story."

Lyria shoved him roughly back into his chair.

"Speak then," she spat.

"I saw how you began killing the bandits I'd been traveling with. By then I knew I would not be paid, so I ran. I took three of the bandits' best horses with me. I knew they would not need them. I rode fast and I rode scared. Mostly I was frightened that you would somehow find out I was there and come after me. Something magical happened that night, didn't it? The way you killed those men so quickly? Five were dead before I could wheel and run. I returned here and have not left again since. I had learned my lesson; here is home and here I would stay."

Lyria was glowering at him, but she wasn't killing him just yet, and so he took heart and continued his story.

"I know I have done bad things in my life. I know I am a coward. But believe me when I say I had no idea those men were planning to attack your village. If I had, I would have snuck away days earlier. After all, they might have wanted me to do some fighting. Now, before you kill me, if you intend to, I would like you to come to my home so I can show you something."

"Very well, we will come," Lyria, answered. "But beware, I can kill a coward as easily as a warrior."

"I believe you," Dan said with a wan smile.

They walked three blocks to Dan's home. It was nearing nightfall by then. Dan's home was almost directly behind the roadhouse, three streets away. They walked in silence with Kel to Dan's left and Lyria close behind him. He was sweating. Lyria liked that.

Wordlessly Dan opened the latch and swung the door out. They walked inside. The house was nicely if plainly furnished. Dan showed Lyria and Kel to the dining area and motioned to the chairs. Kel sat; Lyria remained standing. Her hands were on the hilts of the Teeth of the Ice Tiger. Dan walked to a cabinet by the wall and opened it. He withdrew a long wrapped object and brought it to the table.

"Before I open this, I have an offer for you."

"Here it comes," Lyria sneered. "The begging for life."

"That it may be, in truth, but you did promise to hear me out."

"Speak then."

"If you need to get into the city to look for your grandfather, you need me. Besides, we also have to try to find Noria."

"We travel alone," Lyria said with certainty.

"We trade with the Black City. I still have contact with my friends and connections there. With their help and mine you will be able to go places you would never get to without that help. Imagine, people who have lived there their whole lives, assisting you, clothing you, making documents for you should they be needed."

"If you are such a coward as you say, why are you making this offer?" Lyria was clearly skeptical.

"Mostly because of Noria. This village is my family now. She is part of my family. The dead out there by the wagons are part of my family. Yes, I am a coward—but as a coward, I know the secret ways. The silent ways. The unseen ways. Let me help, please."

With that, he unwrapped the object on the table. Lyria gasped."What you are looking at is the object I stole from the Cathedral," Dan said. "Why would a coward steal a sword? Because of its value, I'd planned to sell it, but that didn't work out. Remembering how you killed those men a little more than three years ago, I thought it should go to you. It's a warrior's instrument."

Lyria picked up the sword. She slid it from the leather scabbard and looked at the blade. It was long and double-edged though nicely balanced. The hilt was plain iron with a wooden grip wrapped in leather long enough for Lyria to hold in two hands. A large half-wheel shaped pommel made of steel was ornately engraved with complex lines that interwove back and forth across its surface.

"What is this in the steel?"

"That's called 'pattern welded' steel—it is made by twisting many pieces of iron and steel and then hammering them into a blade. The central part, in the groove, was etched with a burning liquid that ate into the softer metal and left the harder standing to give it the look of burl wood."

Lyria turned the blade in her hand, admiring the pattern.

"I have never seen metal work like this," she said in awe.

"Nor will you—you hold a sword out of legend. You hold a sword that was made across the eastern sea a thousand years before the ice moved. You hold one of the magic spirit-swords carried by a warrior from the dragon boats when the eastern men first came here. You hold a sword that is over two thousand years old. The wood and leather have been changed many times, of course, over the years, but the sword itself is as it originally was made."

Lyria again looked at the blade. "There appears to be some kind of writing here in the groove along the wooden looking part of the blade. The characters are very small and made of straight lines. Do you know what it says?"

"I do. When I stole it, I also stole the documents that went with it. This item the priests were especially frightened of. It was behind two locks and even I, the researching priest, had to pick both locks to find it."

"What do the characters say?" Kel asked.

"This side says 'I am the flame of thy spirit. I have never been defeated. I am the line. I divide worlds." The other side says, "I am the breath of the dragon. With my Light I can smelt lead or gold. Choose wisely."

"Kel," Lyria whispered, "this is one of those swords that might talk to me."

"The stories seem to say that the spirit of the blade will talk to a warrior. Needless to say, it has said nothing to me," Dan chuckled.

Kel and Lyria looked at each other.

Then Lyria used some leather cord Dan had in his house and fashioned a harness that held the sword to her back.

"Thank you for this priceless gift, you have ransomed your life, Dan Hendricks."

The man beamed.

"And you will travel with us and help us in our quest into the Black City."

Dan looked at Lyria and Kel, and then said, "I'm glad. Now I can do something to repay these magnificent people who've taken me in and allowed me to become one of them."

Chapter 21

Far below the cruising zeppelin, the tribes were gathering. The pilot of the airship was looking through the forward telescope at the ground below. The last time he passed over this area, the village had been half this size—and it appeared to be growing still. He saw homes being constructed, tents being raised, and he noticed the expansion of the corrals and horse barns. There was a slow, steady stream of horsemen and wagons flowing into the village. All of the male riders, he noticed, were heavily armed. He glanced over to the priest who'd been looking through the aft telescope. The priest looked back at him, worry clearly showing on his face.

"We must return west immediately," said Father Davis. "We have to report this to the Bishop right away."

"I agree," the commander responded. "The last time I flew over this village it was small and quiet. Things have changed dramatically since then."

"Come about and let's head back with as much speed as we safely can."

"Yes, Your Grace!"

The commander returned to the ship's wheel, turning the airship to port. It slowly made a wide turn, turning away from the village and heading to the north. When he increased the speed of the engines already running and fired up the others, he wanted to be sure to be out of earshot of the village. The engine master was standing by, ready to signal the engine room to increase speed and start the additional engines.

As they came about, the priest recommenced examining the ground through the large brass telescope. Because he was at the aft viewing station, he was looking east once the airship completed its turn. He saw yet more riders coming toward the village. He counted horses, estimating at least thirty. Looking farther in that direction, he saw a distant cloud of dust. More riders were coming—too far for even his powerful telescope to show. He was really worried now; never had he seen such a procession of half-humans. He hadn't thought they would be capable of this kind of organization.

The commander was looking out the starboard windows in the forward pilothouse. Even without a telescope he could see the dust cloud of many approaching riders coming in from the north.

"Father Davis, more horses are coming from the north as well."

"I hope whatever the Bishop is planning works. I don't know if the Cathedral has enough soldiers to fight a hoard such as this."

"I've seen a number of riders with ballistic weapons across their backs," the commander said. "A few even have telescopes mounted along the tops."

"I doubt they have ammunition to use such weapons. They're probably prestige items to make the half-humans feel ferocious."

The commander laughed, "You're probably right, the weapons must be ancient. Still, those bandoleers…"

"It wouldn't surprise me if the half-humans thought they were magical," the priest said with a smirk on his face.

The crew of the airship laughed, nodding in agreement.

The commander drew the priest to one side, whispering, "I hope you're saying this for the benefit of the crew, Your Grace. The bandoleers I saw were filled with cartridges."

"I know," the priest said in a worried tone, "I saw."

"Fire up those engines, if you will," the commander ordered. "Let's return home."

"Aye, sir!"

The engine master moved the throttle lever to seventy percent power and called for the engine room to begin supplying hydrogen to the silent engines. It wasn't long before all eight engines were roaring steadily, turning the screws that pushed the great airship through the sky. The commander looked at the airspeed gauge, the needle was slowly rising. With any luck they'd be back at the Cathedral very early the next morning.

~

"We should dig the post holes deeper here," Geog said firmly.

"They are deep enough," responded Mart. "Why do you think they should be deeper?"

"The earth here seems a bit softer than over there, closer to the barn. We would not want a corral falling down, would we?" Geog stood with his hands on his hips, facing the other man.

"If we dig much deeper, these poles will be too short," Mart responded.

Geog had not thought of that. Mart smiled. Geog noticed that it was his annoying 'superior smile.'

"Okay, you win," conceded Geog. "But we should plan on reinforcing them at the least."

"That is an excellent suggestion," Mart responded. "Perhaps some cross bracing between the poles and the ground."

"Or we can make some wooden wedges and hammer them into the earth around the poles."

"Now you're talking," Mart said enthusiastically.

Pela smiled. Those two could accomplish amazing things, but not without a bit of warfare first. She walked closer, offering them water from the bucket she was carrying.

"Drink," she said smiling. "When your mouths are full, you cannot argue."

"See! That is proof you are the wise woman of the tribe," said Pars as he wandered over.

That made them all laugh. After taking a drink, they thanked Pela for the water. As she walked away to offer water to other workers, Pars looked at his two friends.

"Can I be of help?"

"Yes, you can," Geog answered.

"Could you find a heavy wooden maul that we might use to pound in the wedges Geog said he would make to help reinforce these poles?"

Geog stared at Mart. He was smiling that superior smile again.

Pars noticed it as well and said, "I can also cut the wedges so you two don't have to stop all that fine work you are getting accomplished."

~

Adria wandered through the people gathered in the street. She was looking for the strange man who was her mentor in the real ways of magic. It seemed he wasn't here yet, but she was confident he'd come. She turned and walked home. Yes, it was her house now—it really was *her* house. She slipped through the front door into the interior gloom. She wandered into the bedroom. There was a new bed in there now. She opened the trunk at the foot of the bed, moved some blankets stored there, and took out the small black box.

She opened the lid. There it was, the necklace she'd saved from the grave. Her mother didn't need it any more. Why shouldn't Adria have it? She carefully lifted it out of its box, putting it around her neck. She rose and walked to the small mirror on the table next to her bed. She turned a bit so the light would reflect from the carved metal. It was beautiful—not unlike herself. Then she returned it to the box and hid it again. She knew she needed a better hiding place. If that snoopy old woman came again uninvited, she might find it.

~

Pela finished her rounds with the water bucket, by now it was almost empty. She took a drink and sat down on a bench in the village common area. There were a lot of people milling about. Some had just arrived and hadn't yet been assigned accommodations or even a place to raise their tents. She looked around and saw many weapons: spears, swords, and bows. She also noticed the ballistic weapons some of the men carried, wondering if they were functional.

She was wondering about other things as well. It was over a week since the mysterious deaths of Ama and Torr. She'd examined the bodies and there were too many scorpion stings for just one insect. Yet, that is all Adria said she'd seen. To give the girl the benefit of the doubt, she'd ask her if she'd killed any more in the house recently.

There was something else she wanted to do first. She pushed herself to her feet and carried the wooden bucket and ladle back to where it was kept. She walked past Ama and Torr's house…no, that wasn't true anymore, now it was Adria's house. She was saddened by the thought.

She walked to where Geog and Mart had been working on the new corrals. She smiled when she saw that they'd enlisted Par's aid. Apparently it had been decided that Pars would make the wedges they'd been discussing. He sat in the shade of the barn with a small axe, patiently shaping small sections of tree branches into wedges for Mart and Geog. He had quite a pile prepared.

"I did not know you were so handy with an axe," she said to him. "Maybe this winter I will let you chop my firewood for me."

He looked up at her and answered, "I would consider it an honor to be able to do that for you."

She smiled at him, "I may just take you up on that."

"It seems that Mart and Geog are quiet," she offered.

"Not surprising; they have taken time off to eat," Pars said. "Now they are probably arguing about what they should eat."

"True," she said, "I have never seen friends argue so much."

"Me neither, but that seems to be the way they figure things out, and they are very good at figuring things out."

"That they are," she said.

She left Pars to his work, walking out of the village toward the burial ground—she was curious about something. As she walked, she remembered how she'd enlisted the aid of Mart and Geog in quietly hunting for scorpions near the village in the days right after the mysterious deaths. In three days of admittedly only occasional searching they'd found only two, and one of those was dead—and that was odd as well. It had died in the village midden. She found it accidentally the third day after the killings. Yes, she decided, that's what they were—killings. When she went to the midden with a bucket of garbage from her home, she saw the insect; it lay right on top of a small recently dug area. The peculiar thing about the area was that the fresh earth of the dig was very small in nature; almost as if some individual thing had been buried there rather than a mass of refuse. She poked the area with a stick, turning the earth, finding shards of what appeared to have been a small, fired-clay jug. She picked up one of the shards, carefully examining it. There was residue on what had once been the inside. She brought it under her nose, cautiously inhaling the scent, and recognized it immediately. It was the poppy plant—the seeds that she used to make pain medicine for anyone seriously injured.

She continued toward the burial ground. When she arrived at the sacred rock, she said a silent prayer to the God and Goddess and walked over to the graves of Ama and Torr. She saw that the earth over Ama's grave had been disturbed recently and very carefully repacked. She didn't need to dig to know what was no longer there with Ama's ashes. She'd ask Adria about the scorpions before the day ended.

~

Adria left her house in search of her friends—her servants, actually. She found Glorr helping one of the new families raise their tent. He looked at her and then looked away as he helped several others pulling on a rope that would be used to hold the tent fast against the wind. She walked on. A little later she found Palom and Lorra with their parents preparing one of the cauldrons of food for the evening meal. She was getting angry again— she got angry a lot these days. She took some deep breaths to calm herself. The anger didn't bother her; it was the headaches that accompanied them.

She turned and walked back to her house. She was lost in thought, staring at the ground just in front of her feet—that's why she didn't see Pela until she was practically on top of the old hag.

"Adria, dear," Pela said with a smile. "How fare you?"

Adria didn't smile; she figured she should probably still be in mourning.

"I am doing well, thank you."

"If you need anything, just call on me."

"Certainly," Adria said with a small smile. Why didn't the old hag just walk away?

"If you get stung by a scorpion, come to me."

"Why would I get stung by a scorpion?" Adria was annoyed.

"Well dear, there may be more in your house that you have not found."

"I have found no more scorpions in my house," the girl snapped, feeling the anger approaching again.

"I only say this because your parents had too many stings to have come from just the one we killed, so be careful."

"Actually," Adria said, thinking fast, "I did kill another scorpion the day after my parents died. I forgot with everything else going on at the time."

"Ah…well perhaps that ends it then."

"Ends what?"

Damn the woman!

"Why, people being stung by scorpions, of course," Pela said, smiling at the girl.

"I certainly hope so," Adria responded. "There must be lots of them this year."

"Yes," Pela agreed, looking into Adria's eyes, "a lot of scorpions."

Chapter 22

The zeppelin was coming in for a landing. The wind had come up in the last several hours in the Los Angeles area with gusts over twenty miles an hour, making landing more difficult and more dangerous. They were still fifty feet over the field and the great airship was rocking and yawing in the wind.

"Open the windows now," ordered the commander. "Cast the mooring ropes."

Two members of the crew moved from their positions, sliding the bolts holding the windows in place. Once the bolts were released, the windows slid smoothly down into the frame of the gondola.

"Casting off the lines, sir," the first crewman said.

"Will we make it safely?" Father Davis was worried, and just a little nauseated by the constant rolling and pitching of the zeppelin.

"Oh, that we will," the commander said with a grin. "It'll take more than this to scare us—won't it?"

He was looking at the priest, still with that grin on his face. The priest was sure the commander thought his discomfort was somehow entertaining. He turned away, closing his eyes for a moment as a fresh wave of nausea washed over him.

The commander turned back to his wheel, watching as the ground came up under them.

"Drop our speed a bit more, if you would," he said to the engine master.

"Aye, sir," he replied, sending the signal to the engine room. In a moment, four of the airscrews turned slowly to a stop. They were thirty feet off the ground. The commander saw the ground crew scrambling to stay under the unstable zeppelin. The mooring ropes were almost within reach. The engine master eased back yet again on the speed control. The four remaining engines slowed even more. The elevators in the rear of the great ship were guiding her down.

Now the mooring ropes were dragging on the ground. Six men ran to catch them; then there were more as the eight mooring ropes were secured to the windlasses. The commander let out his breath; the rest of the descent was now in the hands of the ground crew. He shot a quick glance at the priest and was gratified to see him sitting in his chair—his face as green as the upholstery.

"Shut the engines," the commander called to the engine master.

"Shutting now," was the reply.

Suddenly, except for the howling wind, the airship was silent. The ground was now only ten feet away and approaching rapidly—they were home at last.

As soon as the great ship was moored to the cart that would pull it into the barn, the commander opened the door, finding the ladder already in place. He helped the priest to his feet, guiding him to the ladder. He watched the priest's unsteady descent. There was a steam-car waiting for him. The chauffeur helped him into the back seat, the car hissed for a moment and then rolled away toward the Cathedral. Then the commander and his crew disembarked, walking with the slowly moving airship toward the barn. Several of the crew joked about the airsick priest. The commander smiled, no point in being too awestruck by priests, they were just men like the rest of the crew at the end of the day.

The steam-car took the priest quickly to the side entrance of the Cathedral. The driver hurried around the vehicle, opening the priest's door.

"Have a pleasant evening, Your Grace."

The priest half smiled—his equilibrium was finally coming back. "Now that I'm away from that accursed airship, I believe it'll be a pleasant evening."

The driver chuckled, "Nobody could ever get me to go up in one of those things."

The priest looked at the driver and said, "I believe you're a wise man!" He turned, pushing his way through the door into the great stone structure.

The Bishop was waiting in his study. He paced nervously from one wall to the other—things were moving quickly now. There was a knock.

"Come."

"Father Davis to see you, Your Eminence," the servant said.

"Thank you, Harold, please show him in."

The priest entered and quickly knelt before the Bishop.

"Rise, Father Davis. Tell me your news."

The priest stood and the Bishop waved him to a chair near his desk.

"It's easily as bad as we had thought, Your Eminence. The half-humans are all heading to one particular village from all over the flatlands."

"How did they appear to you?"

133

"They were heavily armed, even some women were carrying spears and swords."

"What of ballistic weapons?"

"There were more than I'd thought possible in the hands of half-humans," the priest said in a worried tone. "Your Eminence, we saw some of the warriors with bandoleers around their bodies—the cartridge loops seemed filled."

"Well then," the Bishop said, "we must move quickly. Please file a complete report with me in writing. Have the airship commander do the same."

"Yes, Your Eminence," the priest said as he rose to go.

As soon as the door closed, the Bishop was on the telephone. He felt his sweat gathering around the hard black bakelite earpiece as he waited impatiently for his call to go through.

"Father Woods. I need to see you immediately."

He pulled the brass fork down, and then released it.

"Yes, Your Eminence?"

"Connect me to the zeppelin barn please, I need to speak to Franklin."

The line clicked, was briefly silent, and there was another click.

"Franklin, here."

"How're the repairs coming on my airship?"

"All finished, Your Eminence," he said in a happy tone. "Installed and thoroughly tested."

"And the paint?"

The Bishop heard Franklin chuckle as he answered, "It's as white as the face of the ice."

"Excellent. Now I want you to prepare it for flight. I want it ready for take off by very early tomorrow evening."

"It'll be ready, Your Eminence."

"Thank you, Franklin."

There was a knock on the door.

"Come."

Father Woods entered and knelt.

"Tell me," said the Bishop, "are your robes finished?"

Father Woods glanced up.

"Yes, Your Eminence."

~

It was already dark by the time Adria was able to get her companions all together with her. She looked at them, thinking how she would word what she was about to say. However, it was Glorr who broke the silence.

"We do not like this game any more, Adria."

She looked up in disbelief, shouting, "What are you saying?"

Palom answered, "He is saying we are done with this thing you are doing."

Adria wheeled toward Palom, hissing, "You will be done when I say you are."

"No! You scare us, Adria. You are not the person you were when we became friends," Palom said. "We are no longer friends, Adria. Leave us alone."

Adria looked from one to the other. The children stood firm—she knew she'd lost them. They'd been frightened of her for some time now, which she had enjoyed, but now they were gone from her control.

"Fine. Go. But you better remember your blood oath."

The children had started to turn; now they waited.

"If you tell anyone what we talked about, or what I did, the bloodsmoke will come for you and your families. This I promise."

"We won't tell anyone," Glorr promised. "But you leave us alone now."

When the children were gone, Adria sat thinking for a long time before going home and to bed. She really needed to see her mentor. Why was he not here? Where could he be? She fingered the small bag she carried containing some of her parents' ashes. She decided she'd go looking for him in the morning, among the new arrivals—at least a hundred had arrived throughout the day.

She arose very early and headed toward the new construction. She came upon a small group of individuals she hadn't seen before. She thought for a moment; how could she ask when she couldn't even remember the man's name? And then she did remember. How could she have forgotten it? How silly! It seemed as though she'd always known and that some cloud in her mind had hidden it for some reason. The headaches sometimes made things hard to remember.

"Hello," she said, smiling at an older couple who had just finished raising their tent. They smiled back at her.

"I have been looking for someone," she began. "I thought he would have been here by now."

The woman smiled back at Adria, asking, "How is he called, child?"

"He calls himself 'Floweht.'"

The demeanor of the two people changed immediately. The smiles were gone. They drew back from the girl. "We know of no one with that name."

They went inside their tent, dropping the flap.

Adria stood for a moment, unsure of what to do next. She decided to try someone who might be less rude. She walked beyond the tents into the area where new wooden homes were being built. She found a strong, young man working at sawing a board. He glanced at her, then stopped working and looked again, a flash of appreciation in his eye. Adria smiled at him; she knew she was beautiful.

"Hi," she said, "I am looking for someone, perhaps you have seen him?"

"And who might that be?"

He was smiling; he was enjoying looking at her.

"He calls himself Floweht, and I have to show him something."

The man had been standing on one leg, his left knee bent, holding down the board he was cutting. He took his leg off the board, quickly picking it up.

"I have never heard that name, girl," he said, walking away from her.

"You didn't finish cutting the board," she called after him mockingly.

"I have to measure it first to make sure I did not cut it wrong."

Then he was gone. What was going on? She turned, slowly winding her way back into the village.

~

Pela had looked everywhere. The necklace wasn't in Adria's trunk or any of the drawers in her dresser. It wasn't in the kitchen—she'd even looked in every empty jug she could find. She was convinced Adria had removed it from her mother's grave, but she had nothing to prove it. The girl was careful, that was certain. She sighed, leaving the house. She walked slowly toward her own home in the late afternoon. As she neared, she saw three people standing close to the door, waiting. There was an older couple, probably around her age, and a tall young man. She could see they looked worried. As she increased the pace of her walk, the three glanced up. The woman came several steps closer, saying, "One of your tribe has asked after a forbidden name."

"What name is that?"

"A blonde woman asked if we knew where Floweht might be. She said she had something to show him."

"I have heard the name," Pela said, "I did not know he might come here."

"He has come to the gatherings the last few summers, hiding at the edges of the group, I'm told," the older man said. "But he will be coming no more."

Pela looked surprised. Almost anyone involved with magic, healing, or the shamanic arts had heard of Floweht. He was reputed to be a shape shifter, capable of turning himself into an animal at will. He was an outcast, never daring to stay in any one location very long. He was a hunted man, sought by many villages to answer for crimes of murder and cannibalism. His reputation was that of a black magic sorcerer and werewolf. The name he chose for himself, Floweht, was 'the wolf' reversed.

"The creature was discovered about a week ago with the freshly killed body of a woman who had been passing through our tribal territory with a small band from her village. They were coming to this gathering," the woman explained. "He had also been traveling toward this location, it seemed."

"Yes, we believe he was coming here," the woman's husband said. "But his unnatural hunger for human flesh needed release, so he crept into our village a little more than a week ago and took the woman as she slept."

"He must have used some magic," the younger man added, "because her husband did not awaken during the abduction. Later that morning it was discovered that the woman was missing and a search led into the hills where we found the creature's camp."

"The missing woman had been…cut up," the woman said. "He had roasted part of her. Some of her could not be found."

"He was caught asleep in his tent and slain by warriors of her tribe. His evil ways have ended," the young man said, shaking his head in disgust.

"But apparently the woman of your tribe does not know that. I fear for her," the older woman added.

"I know who she is," Pela said with certainty, "I will look into it in the morning."

Chapter 23

The zeppelin left the airfield at dusk. The crew was hand picked by Father Woods himself; he wanted men who would remain calm even in the presence of half-humans. He explained to them that they probably wouldn't have any contact with the creatures; that would be his job. They were, however, to maintain a non-aggressive attitude, showing no weapons unless they were actually attacked. As a precaution, each man was issued a Mauser semiautomatic pistol to conceal on his person—just in case.

The crew was smaller than the usual complement of a spy ship; there were only three men besides the priest. Fewer people meant fewer problems, the Bishop had said. The priest was looking over some notes and thoughts he'd written. He wanted his 'presentation' to go smoothly and naturally.

The nose of the airship tipped up slightly as the engines revved. Each was fed by a small tube descending from one of the great gasbags of the airship. The hydrogen was forced past a valve under pressure into a small copper cylinder attached to each engine. The cylinder supplied a constant, even flow of gas to the engine. It was an easy way to power the zeppelins. The gasbags had been deliberately designed to hold forty percent more hydrogen than needed. Some of this, of course, was for safety reasons, but some also was used to feed the engines. The airship was kept much lighter without the need for large pressurized metal tanks of gas to feed the engines.

The commander of the ship turned the wheel slightly to bring the nine hundred foot airship about to starboard—now it was facing east. The control surfaces were trimmed, and the white ship began moving forward. The weapons that had been aboard were dismantled and dismounted, making the ship lighter and faster—everything not necessary for this mission had been removed. The airship began picking up speed.

Looking west, the priest was able to witness a second sunset. The great ship was climbing and it appeared as though the sun had risen again in the west and was now setting one more time. Father Woods smiled, he always enjoyed that odd phenomena. He sat, reviewing his notes one more time. Soon it was too dark to see inside the gondola. Small gaslights were lit around the cabin—twelve in all. They supplied enough light to read the instruments and keep people from stumbling over each other, but not much more. Father Woods sighed, putting down his notebook. *It was just as well,* he thought, *if he wasn't ready now, he'd not be ready in the morning either. Perhaps a good night's sleep would be the wiser thing right now.*

Father Woods rose from his seat, walking to the central portion of the gondola. It was even darker back there. He unhooked one of the cots attached to the wall and lowered it. It was hinged to the cabin on one side while the other side was kept from falling beyond the horizontal by canvas web straps near the top and bottom of the cot. The system worked well; they had sleeping accommodations for forty men when needed, but the cots could be conveniently folded against the wall, strapped in place and out of the way when they weren't in use. He lay down, closing his eyes. He knew morning would come fast and now that he was lying down, he realized just how tired he actually was. He glanced briefly ahead, past the chart room into the forward cabin. The small gaslights flickered, reflecting off the polished brass instrument cases and glass faces of the various gauges. Through the forward windows he saw the moon in its last quarter against the featureless velvet of the night sky. He closed his eyes again and in a moment he was asleep.

The great ship slid through the night sky like some vast predatory beast. The commander was keeping a sharp eye out for clouds that might indicate an impending storm. Storms were much harder to detect at night, especially when the moon gave as little light as it was giving on this night. Still, stars could be seen all around the vessel with no dark patches indicating clouds. The ever-present Aurora flickered and flashed its ghost lights above the ice far to the north. It looked like it would be a smooth and uneventful flight.

The commander glanced at the altimeter; they were cruising at two thousand feet, which would probably be as high as they'd go for this mission. If any of the half-humans were to see them, they'd see a white ship rather than a black one. He made a slight correction in heading and relaxed at his post. He had a small crew, but it was the best the Cathedral had to offer and he was confident in their abilities. The droning of the engines lulled him as it always did on night missions. The engine master came forward to report.

"The engines are running smoothly commander—gas pressures are steady and well within safety parameters."

"Excellent," he responded.

The engine master returned to his position and listened to his engines, always seeking the stutter or misfire that could herald an engine failure. He heard none of those things. The ship had been tested after it was refitted for this mission. He sat back and smiled to himself, this would be a quiet mission.

~

Just after dawn, Pela went for her usual early morning walk, though today she was looking for Adria. The young woman was probably still asleep at home. Nevertheless, she'd keep an eye out for her at breakfast. Adria never missed a meal, it seemed. Pela smiled, greeting Palom and Lorra's mother, Ress. She and her two daughters were working at the cauldron this morning, helping prepare a stew that would give both warmth and energy for the coming day's work. Many strangers were already up and about, gathered in small groups discussing the day's labors. To one side, several men laughed at some quip. She estimated that there were now over three hundred people living in her village, and more would undoubtedly be arriving today.

Pela noticed the two girls with Ress seemed quiet this morning and that they wouldn't meet her gaze. She'd ask them later what might be wrong for she knew they were Adria's friends and she was worried about them. Hopefully they weren't too involved with the woman. She smiled at them and they smiled back wanly—then looked away again. Pela could see the pall of fear that hung over the children. It saddened her; children should be happy and playful. Today she'd get to the end of it, one way or another.

Adria awoke a short time after dawn. She still felt just as annoyed as she had when she went to bed. Her friends had deserted her, just like everyone else in her life, even her parents. To make matters worse, the hag had been in her home again. She'd placed one of her long blonde hairs across a blanket in the top section of her trunk. Her hair was gone when she looked into the trunk the next time; obviously the old woman was snooping. Adria smiled, the hag hadn't found the necklace and she never would; she was sure that's what she was looking for. The meddling old fool must have gone to the burial grounds. Adria figured that the old woman might even have dug into her parents' graves. That made her a grave robber, did it not? Was that not a crime?

Once she was dressed, she walked to her dresser, looking between it and the wall. In the darkness she just barely saw the box holding the necklace. She had nailed it to the back of the dresser the day before the snooping and then pushed the dresser as close to the wall as she could. She smiled, nodding; she was still on top of things, even if those horrible children had deserted her—even if that horrible old woman was spying on her. Pela would pay for her obnoxious snooping; it was long overdue. She smiled and opened her door. It was time for the morning meal.

~

The airship descended to a lower altitude once they'd crossed the mountains; they'd reach their destination in approximately two hours. It was still night on the ground, but from the vantage point of altitude, Father Woods saw the brightening rim of the Earth far to the east. He was nervous, but that was to be expected on a mission such as this. As much as he revered the Redeemed God, he wasn't especially anxious to find himself in His presence—at least not today.

Father Woods dressed in his new white robe. He rather liked the feel of the open collar as opposed to the high, tight collar on the standard priestly robe. He looked out the window again and saw that the land beneath them was relatively flat. He guessed that they were flying under a thousand feet at the moment. He told the commander to come in low and slow—making his approach as different as possible from the tactics the black zeppelins used in raiding.

"Father Woods," the commander called, "could I have a word with you?"

The priest walked to the front of the gondola.

"I just wanted to inform you that we might be a bit early. We've had a fair tailwind the last few miles and if it continues we'll arrive about an hour early."

"That'll be fine," answered the priest. "In fact, it might be better to be grounded by daylight. Perhaps the half...I mean the tribes-people will not be aware of our arrival."

"As superstitious as they are, I'm sure that would awe them," the commander said with a snicker.

"Just remember," Father Woods said, "your weapons must be hidden at all times. We don't want any incidents here by the airship."

"The men have been well briefed and they have already concealed their handguns about their persons—we'll be ready."

"Excellent," Father Woods beamed. "Excellent!"

~

"Good morning, dear," Pela said with a smile.

Adria had been expecting Pela, but her happy demeanor was a surprise; she'd thought there would be a confrontation.

"Good morning, Pela," she responded with a return smile. "It is getting a little warmer, is it not?"

"Yes it is. High summer will be upon us soon."

Adria ladled some of the stew into a bowl for Pela. The old woman thanked her as Adria filled her own bowl next. Bread was waiting at the table, along with jars of butter, which had been laid out ahead of time due to the large number of people eating at the communal gathering. Many, of course, ate in their tents and homes, but the newcomers were not yet established enough to do that, so the growing village got together and produced community meals for the new arrivals.

"Someone told me you were asking after someone," Pela said evenly.

"Oh, it was just someone I had seen at the last summer gathering. He seemed interesting and I was wondering if he would come to the village."

"Maybe I can be of help," Pela smiled. "Who is the person? I might know him."

"I do not think you would know him. I actually do not know him either," Adria lied. "He had promised he would make me a gift the next time he was here."

"A gift? Is he a suitor then?"

"Oh no, he is much older than me," Adria said, "I do not know why he said that, but I thought it would be interesting to see what he would bring to me."

They stopped talking when two men sat near enough to overhear their conversation. They ate slowly, in silence, and finally the two men rose, walking away, leaving the two women alone once again.

"Well, what does the man call himself?"

That damn woman was persistent! *Well*, Adria thought, *I can be as well*.

"I am not sure of his name."

"I do not believe you, dear," Pela said with a flat voice. "I know who it is you seek. I beg you to give up that way; it will only lead to your destruction."

Adria snapped her answer, viciously hissing, "What do you know about it? Why won't you just leave me alone?"

"Because, dear," Pela said quietly, "I know."

Adria sneered and said, "What do you 'know'?"

"Three things," Pela responded. "First, there were not enough scorpions to account for all those stings."

"What…"

Pela cut her off.

"Second, the grave of your mother has been…disturbed."

Adria sneered again, saying, "With all the newcomers, who can say who might have done that?"

"Third, Floweht."

Adria paused for a moment as she was rising.

"The Wolf is dead," Pela said evenly. "Killed with a cannibalized woman in his fire."

"You lie!" Adria spat. "You lie!"

She rose, tossed her bowl to the table, and ran toward her home.

Suddenly there was a clamor from the west side of the village beyond the new construction. Several people came running up shouting that a white airship had landed a short distance away and a man was approaching.

"The airship is white?"

Pela had only ever heard of black zeppelins.

"White as snow, as are the clothes of the man approaching."

"Only one man?"

Pela was confused. She rose, going with the gathering crowd to see what was really happening.

Chapter 24

Adria heard the shouting, but she waited a minute before leaving her home. She didn't want to see that nasty old lady again this morning. Perhaps by this evening, she'd no longer be a nuisance. She followed the crowd at a distance, keeping buildings and tents between herself and the milling crowd.

The people were all streaming west. This might be entertaining.

When the people passed the last of the construction and were beyond the village, they stopped and waited. Over the tops of the scrub trees they saw a vast white circle. It was like the moon had settled to the Earth just outside their village. Pela lowered her gaze and saw the man walking steadily toward them. He was all dressed in white. The low murmuring of the crowd sounded like bees swarming in spring flowers. Even from this distance, everyone could see that the man was smiling, the sunlight reflecting from his teeth.

When the man was close enough for conversation, he raised his hand in greeting. "I bring you greetings from the Cathedral and a message from the Bishop."

"Stand and speak," one of the warriors said, lowering his spear.

The man stopped, raising his hands in a supplication gesture.

"Please, I mean you no harm. That's what we must talk about."

"Where are the rest of your men," the warrior demanded.

"There are three men with the ship. They're the ones who know how to fly it. I am just a lowly priest."

"Lowly enough to command an airship," the warrior growled.

The priest looked at the warrior who'd spoken and actually laughed.

"Believe me, I have nothing to do with the airship. I'm merely a messenger."

There was silence for a moment.

"May I enter your village? I have important things to tell your leaders."

A number in the crowd looked at Pela.

"Very well, you may enter, but you alone."

"That is my intention, good woman," the priest said. "The crew must stay with the zeppelin to control it if the wind comes up."

~

Adria looked from her concealment at the priest—he was young and really handsome! He also had an airship. She thought it would be grand to fly in one and maybe own one. She wondered if priests were allowed to marry. Surely they must be, even great shamans and healers had wives and families. Maybe....

She wandered back to the village, following the crowd. People were chattering excitedly, nobody paid much attention to her. For an instant she saw Lorra, but the girl quickly turned her head. Fine, she didn't really need any of them. Still, the news of Floweht's death had stunned her—he was her teacher and her first lover. At his request, she'd given herself to him repeatedly last summer. He explained how some of his magical power would flow into her, making her stronger and more powerfully in tune with her scorpion spirit.

Her teacher had been murdered. No doubt jealous shamans who couldn't compete with him in the magical arena instigated it. The cannibalism charges had all been made up to justify his brutal murder. She knew now she had to get away from here if she was ever going to be able to make something of herself. If she was ever going to achieve real power, she had to be far away from these murdering, suspicious people.

She watched the priest as he walked in the center of the crowd, ethereally white amid all the browns and greens of the tribal attire. She looked down at herself—for the first time in her life she hated her clothing. She was far too beautiful to have to live in these rags. In the Black City, however, with a rich priest for a husband, she was sure she could have whatever she'd want. She smiled. She knew she was smart enough to carry this off, but there was one bit of work that had to be attended to first.

~

The sun was almost at its zenith by the time the leaders and shamans of the various tribes were gathered to listen to the priest's message. The priest had eaten a late breakfast with some of the villagers—he seemed very open and cordial. He ate the food with relish, thanking everyone for being so kind to him. He was overwhelmed, he said, by his welcome into the village.

Now, however, the difficult part would begin. Father Woods had no illusions that he could charm the shamans and war leaders as easily as he could the ordinary population of half-humans. He worked very hard not to gag at just the thought of sharing a filthy table of barbarian food with them, and he'd pulled it off. Though he knew a challenge lay ahead, he was confident he was up to it.

145

The crowd gathered around the three shamans and dozen or so warriors who comprised the tribal leaders then present. Some stood on tiptoe to see over the heads of those in front of them; some just wandered to the rear of the crowd figuring they'd hear what was said afterward, if not now. They knew everyone in the village would share this news by nightfall. In the second row off to the left, near the benches, which were already filled, a young blonde woman stood listening intently. She was fingering a small leather bag she carried at her waist.

The crowd quieted. They knew important words were about to be spoken, and they all wanted to be able to hear what was said.

Pela began the conversation. "I am Pela, wife of Garn and tribal healer. Tell us why you have come here."

The priest flashed his biggest smile, looking around not only at the small group he'd be talking with, but also the crowds, 'the herd,' as he thought of them. Part of his plan was to include them; if the masses liked him, the leaders would recognize this and it would help sway their opinion as well.

"For some time now, the Bishop of the Cathedral has been concerned over some of the activities of the city of Los Angeles. You probably don't know this, but with twelve million mouths to feed…"

The expression of surprise and awe temporarily drowned out the priest's words. He waited patiently.

"You say there are millions in the city?"

It was Geog who asked the question needing verification for himself, as well as for everyone else in the crowd.

"That is, in fact, correct." The priest continued when the hubbub had quieted, "You have to remember that when the ice came, the people of many cities eventually congregated in Los Angeles—much as you appear to be doing here. As time went on, more arrived. The city wasn't prepared to feed such masses and the population, being city people, knew nothing of farming."

He stopped a moment, letting his words sink in.

"The city began using science to feed its people. They call it 'hydroponic gardening' and it consists of growing vegetables and fruit trees and all kinds of edible plants inside tall buildings using chemical nutrients instead of soil."

"You grow without dirt?" Mart was shocked and for the first time in his life, virtually without words to say.

The priest smiled, answering in the affirmative. "The problem for the city is finding enough workers for this kind of work. The hours are long and the odors from the chemicals and sewage before they're mixed can be noxious—that is, they smell very bad and can also be poisonous. Not many will do that work voluntarily. The city doesn't want to pay much for the work either, which doesn't help the situation. This is why the city has resorted to using slave labor. This is why your tribes have been raided and people taken."

Pela asked anxiously, "What of the last raid?"

"The city is an odd mix of people," Father Woods answered. "Many people from many places bring with them many ideas. While we of the Cathedral try to help people find the way to the Redeemed God, not all wish this, which is fine. Perhaps they'll come to us later. There are four main faiths present in the city, and a fifth that's the most noxious of all when it comes to antagonistic behavior."

The priest paused for a breath and asked if he might have a drink. A bowl of water was quickly brought. After slaking his thirst, the priest went on.

"While most religions desire conversions to their way of thinking, the non-believers are by far the most bitter and hostile. The people who believe in nothing but the power of their minds and their science are like rabid animals when it comes to trying to force everyone to their way of thinking. It's like they have a hole in them that they constantly try to fill with anger, rage, and hostility."

"People who believe in nothing?" Pela was shocked. "How can they look at the wide world and the heavens and think that?"

The priest shrugged, "Frankly, this I don't know, but what I'm saying is the way of things. The city's in the control of the unbelievers—they make the laws and enforce them. If they thought they could get away with it, they'd outlaw all religion, forcing children to learn only their ways in school. Needless to say, we of the Cathedral, and the leaders of the other faiths represented in the city, are fearful. The only thing saving us right now is that the unbelievers don't yet have sufficient votes in the legislative body to pass such laws—and for the time being they fear the possibility of a revolt. It's a precarious balance though, to say the least."

Once more, Father Woods stopped to sip some water. He was thinking fast, wondering if the 'herd' believed him and, more importantly, the war leaders and shamans. Now was the time for the final ploy.

"You mentioned the last raid on your villages in which your shamans were kidnapped. We know of this, and we are appalled. We know why it was done. The unbelievers apparently don't believe in the Divine, but they do believe in magic. They intend to use your shamans' magic somehow to consolidate control over the city—this is why we're certain they're still alive."

"Garn would never agree to help with this," Pela said indignantly.

"Nor would Galv or any of the others," someone in the crowd shouted.

The priest held up his hands for silence, and gradually the crowd subsided to a gentle murmur.

"This we know, too," Father Woods said in an assuring voice. "We've taken steps to prevent it happening again. We've taken it upon ourselves to scuttle the city's zeppelin fleet."

A surly warrior with feathers in his long braid asked, "What does that mean?"

"It means simply that we were able to severely damage their airships. We even destroyed several, though to be honest, that was an accident."

Farther Woods smiled for the crowd. He had them eating out of his hands! How simple these half-humans were.

"It'll be a very long time before any of the black airships will be airworthy. As for your shamans, priests of the Cathedral are searching for them as we speak. I cannot guarantee success, but every byway and dark hole is being examined."

Geog asked, "Why would you care?"

"It's simple," the priest answered, "because what they're doing is wrong. We don't subscribe to your religion, but you have the right to your own destiny. If at some future time you become members of our faith, we will rejoice, but until that day you have the right to make your own path."

The priest smiled inwardly—he really had them now. It was obvious they knew nothing of the city, the religion of the Cathedral, or anything else for that matter. This was going to be easier than expected. His plan was perfect.

He continued, "If and when we find your shamans, we'll bring them back to you in our own zeppelin. In the meantime, we ask that you be patient with us. If you move on the city, their army will crush you. I am not disparaging your brave warriors, but against automatic rifles...ballistic weapons, you'd be cut to pieces. Wait. Leave things to us for a while—at least until we find and rescue your shamans. There's no point in losing many of your people only to find they've spitefully killed…Garn and Galv, was it?"

The crowd was silent. He'd won.

"So you would have us wait to see if you can find our lost shamans?" Pela was still a bit skeptical, but the priest seemed sincere—and if anyone would know how to search the city, surely it would be someone who lived there and was familiar with its surroundings.

"That is what I ask," Father Woods said. "Give us six cycles of the moon. We'll strive to keep you informed as to what is going on."

"We will wait," Pela said, "but no longer than six months."

The priest caught her use of the word 'month,' realizing they knew a bit more than he'd been led to believe. Still, months, moons—it was a little thing.

"Very well, we thank you sincerely," Father Woods said. "I have hope of finding your lost tribesmen. As I said, the search is going on right now."

"Are you staying the night?" Geog looked at the priest and continued, "If you wish, you could stay the night and leave at dawn—surely it must be easier to fly in the light."

The priest smiled. How little they knew of navigation and science. Still, staying might not be a bad idea; it would give the aura of trust he was so carefully trying to build.

"That's most kind of you, sir. I'd be delighted to spend the night in this fine company."

"We have some extra rooms right now," Mart said.

"Yes, you could look at several and choose among them," Geog returned.

The priest smiled at the two saying, "I'm certain the first will be just fine."

Geog and Mart looked at each other as if to say, how could something this complicated be solved so easily?

"Why do you not show me my quarters, so I know where they are, and then I can come back here and talk for a while with anyone who might wish to converse."

Geog and Mart led the priest away as the others watched them depart.

~

149

"What think you?" Pela asked, addressing the question to the small group of leaders.

"He seems sincere," one of the shamans from a more easterly tribe said. "Perhaps some investigating in another world might give us more information."

"We must be secretive around him, nevertheless," admonished the tall warrior with the long braid. "If he thinks we are looking into things, he may flee and then we will never know the truth."

"That is good thinking," another war leader said. "The best way to get past an enemy's defenses is with trickery and stealth."

"We will do this in secret," the first shaman said. "Tonight when the priest is in his quarters we will travel a distance beyond the village. There we will conduct the ceremony and see what we will see."

"So be it," Pela stated. "He seems sincere, but he comes from another world and we do not know how the people of that world view such things as honor and truthfulness."

It was decided that three of the shamans would quietly leave the village just after dark and travel some distance into the wilderness to journey between the worlds. There they would invoke their animal spirits to reach for the truth. Pela was satisfied as well; there wasn't much else they could do right now. The priest said all the right things—it is true. Still, she didn't completely trust him; a fact she made known clearly to those around her. She didn't notice that Adria was listening intently from the second row of onlookers and had heard every word.

Chapter 25

Adria returned to her house to think. She found she liked the priest more and more; not only was he very handsome and rich, he was incredibly knowledgeable about many things. A husband such as this would bring her prestige, power, and importance. She deserved these things. With the fine strong priest with her, someone like Pela would never be able to interfere with her again. Damn that old hag! Well, this would be her last night on this earth just as it would be Adria's last night in this accursed village.

She had something to offer the priest as well—beyond her beauty and her body. She had some information she was certain this 'Bishop' would want to know. Bishop…was that a title or a name? Well, it didn't really matter. Whoever he was, he'd be immensely grateful for what she could tell him. She felt she finally had it made. Perhaps the scorpions were guiding her—she didn't know. She could feel their presence constantly now, almost like they were crawling under her skin, giving her the deadly power they possessed.

She left her house, slipping around the back. She wanted a look at this zeppelin everyone was talking about. Imagine, actually flying through the air like a bird. She smiled at the thought. She wound her way between some scrub brush and the backs of various homes. She had to pause once, ducking behind a broken cart as three figures passed close by on their way to the center of the village. It was the priest and Geog and what was his name? It didn't matter, he was Geog's friend and that was close enough. *Oh yes,* she thought, *Mart was his name.* When they'd passed, she resumed her skulking way out into the wilderness west of the village. She moved cautiously now. She didn't want any of the airship's men to see her if they were about.

She saw the massive thing over the scrub long before the lower part came into view. She couldn't believe something so huge could just sail through the air like a cloud. It was a marvel and truly demonstrated the priest's power and prestige. The last hundred feet she moved cautiously and quietly, watching where she stepped so she wouldn't break a twig or move any stone. When she wanted to, she could be as stealthy as a scorpion.

Then she was there, crouching behind a thin screen of brush, staring at the great zeppelin. Below the huge ribbed upper structure she saw what looked to her like a long 'building.' This part, probably where the people lived when they were aloft, was the length of three houses. It certainly could hold a lot more than the four who'd traveled here. This again showed the power and assuredness of her priest. She was so proud of him—and of herself for having the boldness to claim him.

She saw the three crewmen sitting in chairs they had obviously removed from the airship. They sat at a small table and seemed to be playing a game with small pieces of…something. She knew that they were occupied and not paying attention to what was going on around them. She decided to sneak a closer look at the great ship. She crept farther to the rear of the thing and moved forward. She froze in her tracks when one of the men shouted suddenly. She glanced fearfully in their direction. The man was slapping the things he was holding down onto the table and hooting. This was a strange game indeed. She watched for a moment as the other two men handed something to the first man. Then it seemed the whole thing started over. What the point was, she had no idea. Her priest could teach her, she was sure.

She crept stealthily to the last window on the left side of the airship. She saw that the airship was floating there, as if by magic. What a wonderful object. She stood on her tiptoes, looking through the large window. She was seeing into the sleeping compartment and saw the cots strapped to the wall and guessed what they were. As she moved along the outside of the gondola she looked into what might be called the chart room and saw two tables with a chair. On the tables were rolled parchments, they looked like, with lines both straight and meandering in heavy black ink. In a container toward the back of one of the tables she saw several brass instruments. One looked like it had two legs with sharp points for feet, but no body where the legs met—how curious.

She withdrew from the window, dropped to her belly, and slithered under the ship to the other side; she wanted to see how one would enter the airship. Her question was quickly answered when she saw a ladder made of heavy rope, most of it coiled on the ground because the zeppelin was close to the earth. Obviously, they could enter and leave from even higher in the air. She saw the door was standing open. Satisfied, she faded back into the brush, jumping once more when another of the crewmen shouted loudly as they played their strange game.

~

At dusk, Father Woods sat by the fire in the center of town. He spoke to anyone who spoke first, but he was primarily listening. He was hoping to get some sense from the ordinary half-humans of how they felt about everything he'd said earlier. Several people asked him about the beliefs of his religion and he glibly lied to them. A lie was merely a trick, much like the trick the Redeemed God played on His evil female counterpart.

"You mentioned ballistic weapons," the warrior with the long braid said. "Tell me of them."

The priest looked at Vorth. He'd made a point of learning the big man's name.

"They're not much more than what I've seen some of your people carrying on their backs around here, Vorth. The big difference is that they have many. They've been making them for many years and they're all in top working order. Do you suppose the weapons I've seen here today are functional?"

"I know that the men who carry them would not do so if they did not work properly."

"But surely ammunition must be a problem for the tribes?"

"I do not know for myself," Vorth said, touching the hilt of the short sword at his side. "But I have been told that the ammunition they carry was bought with trade by a far eastern tribe from one of the great cities in the east."

"I didn't know there were any cities left besides Los Angeles," the priest lied.

"I have been told," Vorth said, "that there are many, and trade with them is constant for some of the far eastern tribes."

"I'm hoping we can come to a trading agreement ourselves," Father Woods said smiling. "The women of the city love the tribal jewelry and we, in return, probably have much we can offer you in trade."

"Let us wait and see," was all Vorth said as he rose to leave.

The priest wished him a good night and the wish was returned by Vorth.

The priest hoped the warrior wouldn't be so antagonistic to him now that they'd actually met as men.

Father Woods rose, stretched, and yawned. He was tired. He decided he would head to his abode for the night and if bugs didn't eat him alive in his sleep, in the morning he could leave this filth pit and return home. He walked slowly away from the fire and didn't turn back when three men and a woman approached the communal fire to converse. The priest's home for the night was a small house that had just been finished. He preferred it that way; no half-humans had yet contaminated it with their sleeping thoughts or their obnoxious living habits. All in all, it had been an eventful but fruitful day. He was sure he had the half-humans convinced he was telling the truth about everything. His mission was a success. He lay on the bed fully clothed—just in case he needed to make a quick exit. He lay on his back with his hands behind his head. Soon he was asleep.

~

The three shamans and their drummer gathered by the fire with Pela.

"The drum will have to be used quietly," Pela warned. "We do not want the man in white to hear you and come to see."

Marger, the female shaman, agreed. "We shall be quiet as the hill lion," she said with a smile.

"Then you had better be off," Pela said. "When should we look for your return?"

"We have talked about this and we believe we should stay until dawn. This way we can journey, discuss it, and then dream. It is the best way to find the most complete answer."

"Very well," Pela said to Marger, "we will look for you near dawn."

The woman nodded, and the five people rose. Pela turned and walked home. She was tired and didn't envy the shamans the long night ahead of them. The others walked to where the new corrals were being built—then headed out into the scrub. They walked an hour before stopping to be sure they were far enough away that the muffled drum wouldn't be heard in the village.

On this spot they built a small fire and spread their blankets. All three shamans would journey at the same time bringing back three times the information. The seers spread their blankets out and lay on their backs, moving around to make themselves comfortable. The drummer was a young man of about eighteen summers—a shaman in training. He sat on his blanket with a small drum in his hand, waiting for the order to begin. The drum was much smaller than what they'd ordinarily use, but it would make less sound. It had been made for just such a contingency as was now present.

After a short interval, the three were breathing shallowly and regularly. From years of practice, they were already almost in trance. The drummer struck the drum with the small baton. The sound thrummed out, washing over the shamans. Then there was another drumbeat, and another, and another…

The drummer was sweating—he'd been working the drum for almost an hour. It must be close to the middle of the night. He glanced up, never losing the rhythmic beat. By moon and stars he saw that he was right about the time. Now it was time to bring them back from between the worlds. The drumbeat halted, began again and halted one more time. Now the young man was striking the drum very quickly, it was the calling back from between the worlds.

One by one the shamans awoke. When the third was finally conscious and fully back in the physical world, they moved closer to the fire to discuss what they'd seen. This discussion took about an hour; there was much to interpret and many decisions to be made. In the end it was decided that the priest couldn't be trusted. He was lying about something, perhaps about everything. They decided to wait and sleep on it; sometimes dreams would come from their spirit animals that might further clarify the issues they'd already discussed. Once again the shamans lay on their blankets. This time the young drummer joined them. It wasn't long before they were all asleep.

~

Adria listened to their conversation. Imagine, saying her priest was a liar! Well, she'd expected something like this. One shaman or another, it seemed, interfered with every aspect of her life. This time, she had a positive response. She waited, watching quietly to be sure they were all asleep.

~

The older couple that had told Pela of the woman asking after Floweht was waiting by her door when she arrived.

"We were wondering about the woman…" the man began.

"I know positively who it is, and I must think of how to handle this situation."

Pela was worried and wondered if she should go to the tribal elders for advice in the matter.

"We are sure that what you decide will be the right thing," the woman said. "It just gave us a fright to hear that name mentioned by that lovely young woman."

"I agree," said Pela, "in the morning I will consult with some of the tribal elders. We have enough of them here right now."

"Perhaps with that evil man gone, she will refrain from thinking of him and his ways," said the old man.

"If only I could believe that," Pela said. "I believe things will get much worse before they get better."

"We hope you are mistaken, Pela," said the woman with sympathy. "We will go now and leave you in peace." They turned and walked into the night, heading back to their tent.

Pela went into her home and prepared for bed.

"Adria, my dear," she said softly, "what have you gotten yourself into?"

She shook her head sadly, sat on her bed for a moment, and then lay down. She didn't know if she would sleep or not.

~

Adria watched as the fire burned lower. She crept a little closer, listening to the steady breathing of the four sleepers. The firelight flickering across her features gave her eyes an unwholesome glitter while turning her blonde hair into a cascade of fire. Slowly she brought up her short bow. She moved to within twenty feet of the sleeping shamans; no point in taking any risks at this point. She removed three arrows from her quiver, gently pushing them point down into the sand so they'd stand ready in an instant. She placed a fourth arrow on the string, selecting the elder shaman as her first target. He was, after all, the one who had said the most against her priest, her betrothed. This wasn't murder—it was defending the honor of the man she loved. She drew the arrow back to its fullest extent, taking careful aim at the center of the old man's chest. She exhaled, took a calming breath, exhaled again and released the string.

~

"Did you hear something?"

The engine master set his cup upon the small table where the airship crew had earlier been playing cards.

"I may have," said the engineer. "There're many strange noises in the wild."

The third crewman looked at the other two with a scornful smile.

"It was surely an owl or one of the other night animals that keep the half-humans company."

The others laughed, returning to their drinking. The rum they'd smuggled onboard was taking hold of them, and they were enjoying the feeling too much to be concerned about what might be happening to some small rodent far afield. Their fire was bright, and the rum was strong. There was nothing to be concerned about.

~

The arrow struck the old man, penetrating deeply into his body. He gasped louder than Adria thought he would. She quickly pulled another arrow from the ground, firing again. This arrow pierced the old shaman's neck from side to side severing the carotid artery. The razor-sharp point sheared vessels cleanly and blood spewed from his torn throat in a scarlet fountain—pulsing three, four, five times. The old man fell back to the red earth and was silent. By the time the old man settled back to the ground, Adria had already pulled another arrow from the ground, nocking it. She strained at the bowstring, pulling it to its maximum before releasing it toward the sleeping Marger.

Chapter 26

In the village, Pela turned restlessly in her sleep. She was dreaming she was standing alone in an open area of sandy ground surrounded by low scrub... *There was a small fire burning and interestingly there were four animals gathered around the fire—four animals and something else. The cave lion lay dead in a pool of its own blood, pierced by two arrows. A hare lay next to the lion, it was waking up, it seemed. It lifted its head and another arrow came whistling from the darkness, striking the hare in the temple—killing it instantly...*

~

The third arrow was well aimed, Adria thought, it struck the female shaman squarely in the side of her head. Though the point didn't exit the other side, she saw that only two thirds of the shaft remained visible. She knew the wide, sharply barbed tip had to be lodged against the inside of the lying fool's skull. This one didn't make a sound but slumped quickly and quietly as jets of dark red blood shot from her head, making a small pool two feet from the body.

She grabbed another arrow, drawing the bow to its fullest once more. *Half done*, she thought with glee. *Such men of knowledge,* she thought scornfully, *had been brought down by the queen of the scorpions.* She almost laughed out loud at that. Instead, she released another deadly arrow into the temple of the third sleeper. This one didn't even raise his head; it was like he never realized he was dead. This was real power—the power over the lives of great shamans, and the queen of the scorpions was the one wielding that power.

~

Pela saw a dark shape moving closer to the animals as they slept and died one at a time by the fire. Why would wild animals sleep by a fire, she wondered? The third animal to be struck down in its sleep was a large boar. It never made a sound as an arrow transfixed its head. This time the arrow came through the skull, protruding from both sides. Then there was a commotion, the fourth animal had awakened, and it was a fox. The fox scrambled to its feet, facing a darkness that Pela couldn't seem to penetrate with her vision. The shadow moved quickly pouncing on the fox with a savage growl. The shadow had a hand, she saw. In that hand a dagger rose and fell, rose and fell, rose and fell....

~

Adria got unsteadily to her feet. The drummer and the three shamans lay dead before her—she just barely recalled what had happened. She looked down at herself numbly, seeing blood on her clothes and hands. Yes, she must've been the one who killed the four lying here. Her plan was coming back to her now—there was no turning back. There was one final act that needed to be accomplished before she was free, this one would be an act of revenge. She turned her head, looking back toward the village, and began walking slowly, thinking how she'd do it.

She skulked back into the dark and silent village. She stayed in the shadows in case anyone might be about. There were no sounds but crickets and the muted crackling of the communal fire. She moved cautiously nonetheless. She rounded the central meeting ground and now she was next to the hag's house. She looked around for a moment; then picked up a short, heavy tree limb that had been cut for firewood. She hefted it. Yes, this would do nicely.

Stepping up on the porch, she quietly approached the entrance. She carefully lifted the leather curtain that still served as a door to the old woman's home. Then a thought struck Adria—the old lady wanted to die. Of course! Why would she not have installed a wooden door that she could have barred? She wanted Adria to come in and do this thing.

The old lady was mourning her lost husband and wanted to join him in the Otherworld. How could she have been so stupid as to not see this before? The accusations and questioning the old hag had done was simply to lead Adria into the act that would relieve her of the burden of doing it herself—the old lady was simply a coward. Adria quietly slipped past the leather flap of Pela's home. She was in the living area now, and she knew the bedchamber was just ahead of her. She moved forward cautiously, quietly.

~

Pela saw the shadow rise and leave the scene of slaughter. All four animals were dead—lying in pools of their own blood. But wait. Now they didn't look at all like animals! They were human! One she recognized—it was Marger. She moaned in her sleep, turning fitfully toward the wall, she could see that odd blackness now. It was in the village, it was in her house.

~

Pela awoke with a start. She lay for a moment with her eyes open, listening. She heard nothing. Perhaps it was truly just a dream brought on

by all that had happened in the past few weeks. She swung her legs over
the side of the bed, sitting there a moment. She found the pitcher on the
table by the bed and poured some water into a cup. She saw her hand
shaking. She laughed nervously and brought the cup to her lips.

~

Adria heard the gasp of Pela awakening and froze just beyond the
entrance to the old woman's bedchamber. She heard the soft laugh and the
clink of the pitcher striking some hard object—a cup probably. Well, it
was now or never. She stepped into the room and there she was sitting
with her back to the door. Adria was certain the old woman really did
want to die. She was sitting calmly sipping water as Adria crept closer—
closer. The young woman raised the heavy piece of wood in both hands,
bringing it down on the back of the old woman's head. She made an odd,
grunting noise and slumped forward.

She quickly raised her weapon to strike again, and she froze. What
was that? A dog was barking, and right next door too. She quickly ran
around the bed. She saw the old woman lying very still on the floor near
the wall. It didn't look like she was breathing.

She wanted dearly to make one more strike, even if just for the fun of
it, but she knew the rest of her plan required speed. She dropped the log on
the bed, running out of Pela's home.

Adria ran to her house as quickly as she could. She quietly shut her
door and lit her lamp. She quickly stripped off her bloody clothing and
proceeded to wash the blood from her skin. Some of it was partly dried
and was harder to remove than she'd thought. She scrubbed savagely at
her skin until she was clean. There was no time to waste. She dressed
quickly in her finest ceremonial garb. The shirt was longer than her
everyday clothing and it was fringed at the bottom. She reached for her
trousers, and then stopped. No, she would just wear the shirt—it hung
halfway to her knees anyway. The priest would be able to admire her legs
as they traveled together, that would probably help him realize how much
he loves her. She put on her doe hide boots and turned to go.

She stopped for a moment, looking at her dresser. She pulled it away
from the wall, retrieving the necklace Pela had stolen from her. She
opened the box, put on the necklace, and ran out the door and around
behind the building. She headed toward where she knew the zeppelin
waited. At one point, she halted, squatting in the heavy brush as two men
walked past talking. Adria had seen the men before—they were warriors

who had come in a few days earlier with Vorth. They were headed back to the village from their dialogue. Adria discovered they'd been watching from a distance to see if the airship crew would leave the area. She breathed out once they were past. She was lucky she hadn't run into them the first time she'd come this way. The scorpion power was really with her tonight.

~

At first there was no pain, just a deep, numb disorientation. What happened? How did she end up on the floor? Pela turned, and the pain hit her. She was suddenly very dizzy. She vomited, almost passing out again. It was coming back to her slowly—the dream, the sense of being stalked, and the attack. She managed to get to her hands and knees. She moaned in pain, thinking she would vomit again. The wave of dizziness passed and she began crawling slowly toward the door of her bedchamber. Her hands were slick with blood—more of it dripped from her head. As a healer, she knew she was seriously wounded. Slowly, painfully, she managed to leave the bloodstained bedchamber. She collapsed in the living area and, for a short time, lost consciousness again.

~

Adria could see the vast airship now. The very earliest hints of dawn were streaking the eastern sky with subtle pinks. She crept quietly to the vast machine. She saw the table where the men had been playing that peculiar game. They were gone. They must be inside. She'd have to be very quiet. She moved to the rope ladder; most of it was still coiled on the ground. The gondola was about three feet above the ground—just floating, as if by magic. Her priest was indeed a powerful wizard.

She cautiously mounted the ladder, peering into the doorway at floor level before entering. There was no sign of the three crewmen. She climbed inside, turning to the front of the airship. She marveled at the instruments, the brass devices with black faces and white lines under the glass fascinated her. The great wheel of the ship attracted her attention, as did the large brass telescope protruding from the front of the gondola on the left side.

She turned quietly, gazing into the chart room—nobody was there. Where were the three men? Carefully she looked into the next compartment. It was there she found the three crewmen fast asleep on the beds that could be folded down from the wall. She crept quietly past them—the rum she smelled on them made them insensible to her presence.

In the next compartment she found a large trunk. This was obviously a storage area; there were hooks mounted to the walls and straps with buckles neatly rolled and stored in one corner. She opened the trunk, as it had no lock. Inside were an assortment of winter style clothes, parkas with fur hoods and the like. It was only half full. She climbed in and closed the lid. This would be the safest hiding place aboard, she was sure. She smiled to herself in the darkness. Her plans were working smoothly—just as she knew they would.

~

At dawn Father Woods arose, washed quickly, and walked out the door of his little cabin. He hoped he hadn't picked up any parasites while he slept; it was enough to make one's skin crawl. He stretched, stepping off the front porch. Across the street, two warriors moved away toward the center of town. The priest smiled, he figured he'd be watched. He followed them into the waking village. Vorth was already talking with the two warriors he'd posted outside the priest's dwelling. There were also two others, conversing together.

He walked up, smiling. "Good morning, Vorth," he said jovially. "I hope you slept well."

"I believe we all must have," Vorth replied, eyeing the priest, "I know you did not leave your quarters all night."

"Why would I have?" He played confused, as though he didn't understand he was not completely trusted.

"Something happened last night," the war leader said. "You know Pela?"

"Why yes, of course, a lovely woman," he answered, now truly confused. "Why?"

"She was attacked last night by someone. The healers are with her now."

"But this is terrible," Father Woods said. "Who might've done such an evil deed?"

"We do not know yet," Vorth said, "but I know it was not you or your men."

"I should certainly hope not!"

Just then a young man came running up to Vorth. They conversed in hushed whispers. The newcomer shot his eyes several times to the priest, but he didn't seem hostile.

"Pela is awake," Vorth stated. "The one who attacked her is known. We must search for her immediately."

The priest looked worried, hopefully his work yesterday would not be undone by some savage half-human assault.

"It would be best if you left us now," Vorth stated evenly. "It is dangerous here at the moment."

Father Woods was given an armed escort to his zeppelin. He smiled inwardly at the warriors' obvious awe. The three crewmen had already begun preparing for take off. Everything was packed inside, and the engine master and the pilot were at the wheel.

Father Woods thanked the warriors for the escort and climbed up into the machine. The engine master pulled in the mooring ropes one by one as the crewman still on the ground freed the lines from the grappling hooks. Once the pressure of the straining airship was off, the hooks could be easily picked up. The machine hovered now four feet from the ground—it was rising. The crewman climbed the ladder with the four hooks tied together, slung over his back. Father Woods lifted his hand in a farewell salute to his warrior escort and closed the door. When the engines were fired up, the warriors below quickly backed away. Father Woods smiled. The engines revved to quarter speed and the great ship rose steadily into the air. When it was at five hundred feet, it began its slow turn to the west and the Cathedral.

Chapter 27

"What about war?"

"War is only just when it allows you to remain you, it is never justified when used to attempt to make others into you."

Dan and Kel looked at each other briefly, and then continued to write. Lyria's whisper was barely audible, "What of the sword?"

"The sword is the tool of the warrior, the warrior is a tool of the Gods."

"A tool of the Gods or of other men?" Lyria was almost, but not quite, in a trance. Both Kel and Dan were transcribing as she spoke, making sure they recorded every word, both questions and answers. The sword across her lap spoke again.

"Spirit is a tool of no man! A warrior's spirit is the Spirit within the mountain, they are one."

"But warriors fight for warlords and other men," Lyria insisted.

"There are many who call themselves warriors, most are just fighters. A warrior raises his sword for the Gods and only for the Gods. The river of flame flows through him, even if he dies the river will carry him back to the mountain and to the Gods."

There was a pause as Lyria's head lowered, then rose again. The voice of the sword suddenly thundered in her brain.

"Hear my words, young one, for this is the burden you must accept if you are to carry this sword. Take witness."

Again there was a pause, allowing Lyria to whisper what she had heard. Then the ancient sword spoke again.

"In the blackness of battle I am the rising sun. I bring Light or I am defiled. Dishonor me and you will surely die on my steel."

Lyria thought about this, and then answered, "This burden I do accept, for it is my way and my belief as well."

"That is good."

"Tell me more about learning to properly wield your strength," Lyria whispered.

"I stand like a mountain. I divide the winds."

"You mean like the 'Four Winds'?"

"Yes. The winds of fate and chance. In fire I am cold. In water I am hot. From the mountain, all can be seen as distant."

"So you are saying that in battle I should stay aloof from the fight so that I can calmly evaluate what is happening?"

"Like a cloud at the mountain top, rest until it is time for the lightning."

"What of the patterns I see in your steel?"

"It is day and night. It is light and dark. It is life and death."

"You are strong," Lyria whispered, "I can feel it."

"The mountain stands against the ocean and the air. I give form to sea and sky. I am not my dress. I am the flame that resides within..."

Lyria opened her eyes; gradually they regained their focus. She looked around confused for a moment for she'd been very far away. The fire in Dan's room burned low, reflecting red as blood on the steel of the naked sword still in her lap. Slowly, reverently, she slid the razor-sharp blade back into its scabbard. She exhaled softly looking up at Kel and Dan. She smiled tiredly.

"So," Dan asked eagerly, "was it really a voice?"

Lyria thought for a moment, and then said, "It was a voice, but it was inside my head somehow."

"This is the way totems speak as well, with words that are not words," Kel said.

Dan laughed, "You would not believe me if I told you how many times I have held that sword in the same manner waiting for something—anything—to happen."

He laughed again, saying sheepishly, "I told you I was no warrior, this pretty much proves it."

Lyria rose. She turned to the two men and said, "This talk of mountain, ocean, and sky—what do you make of it, Kel?"

Kel read over what he'd written on the parchment.

"The sword is very old, it comes from a people dead a very long time. Perhaps their thought was different from mine, but I believe the message was simply as you stated while you were...away. In battle it is important to not let things happening close to you give you fear. Fear slows us, makes us indecisive. If in battle we can face our enemy as though he is a distance away from us, we will believe we have time to respond to what he is doing with his weapon, and with that 'seeing' we find we actually do have all the time in the world."

Dan smiled at her and shrugged. "While I'm as far from being a warrior as a man can be, what I see is this. The river spoken of, the river of

165

flame, is the connection between time and place—connecting everything we think, do, and say."

Dan looked at his two new friends and said, "It seems to me a Divine thing, flowing eternally from the mountain, which is clearly the Otherworld where we will reside once we die. Water, fire, mountain, and cloud symbolize the elements I believe—Fire, Earth, Air, and Water. A warrior must be able to balance these in his or her," here he smiled self-consciously at Lyria, "mind and spirit to keep that mountain-top clarity."

The other two looked at Dan, clearly impressed. He laughed self-consciously.

"I'm something of a philosopher."

"What is a 'philosopher'?"

Dan looked at Lyria. "A philosopher is an individual who likes to give advice to people who are happier than he is."

At that they all laughed.

"The first comment, about making others me—what do you make of that?"

"I believe," Kel responded, "that the sword was telling you that war is only just when it defends. When it is used in aggression, to conquer, it becomes evil."

"That is well put," Lyria said. "Fortunately, I already believe that."

"Well, I think we should retire, it's getting late and we have traveling to do tomorrow," Dan suggested.

"I have been reading this book," Kel said, holding up his copy of *The Way Things Were*. "Perhaps as we travel, you can answer some questions I have about things I find confusing."

"I would be delighted! If I have read it or heard of it, I will be happy to answer your questions."

Kel and Lyria said good night to Dan, retiring to their room. It was comfortable, clean, and had been prepared for them while they were in Dan's room. There were two beds, as they'd requested—difficult as that was after spending so much time in such close proximity. They held each other warmly, kissing briefly. They parted reluctantly to lie on their beds. It didn't take long before both were soon fast asleep.

In the morning they arose early and met in the roadhouse. They were serving, among other things, quail egg omelets that morning. After they'd been served, Lyria looked sidelong at Kel and said, "Oink! Oink!"

Dan looked up in surprise, and seeing both Kel and Lyria laughing, he joined in, commenting, "I would swear I heard you say oink, oink—I must be missing something."

Lyria snorted in merriment, "What you are missing is the first part of our journey!"

"Yes," Kel retorted. "Imagine, my betrothed thinks I always eat like a pig!"

"No, I do not, just when food is present."

That set both of them off again. Dan could only look on bemusedly.

After breakfast, they gathered their things and loaded the cart. Kel saddled the horses while Dan hooked Morning to the cart. It took about fifteen minutes to finish loading. Dan noticed with pride that Lyria was already wearing her sword, in spite of the fact she'd never wielded a blade of this size before. He was glad he'd given it to her. Sure, he could have sold it in Los Angeles or to one of the larger tribes, but he felt the sword 'belonged' to Lyria. Kel checked their water supply one final time before they mounted up to begin the final leg of the trek to the Black City.

"It seems amazing to me that this sword could actually talk to me," Lyria said in wonder. "It seems it really does have an indwelling spirit."

"From what I have read," Dan responded, "when the swords were forged, a spiritual force was deliberately housed in the steel."

"The makers of these swords must have been great magicians," Kel commented.

"I am certain they were. But the information is so far lost and misinterpreted, it is hard to separate fact from supposition."

And so, they traveled slowly through the awakening village heading ever westward toward their destinies. Of the people in the streets, very few seemed to take notice of their passing. Kel was happy about that; from now on the journey would get progressively more dangerous.

"When we arrive," Dan began, "we have what my friends call 'safe houses' where we can rest and make our plans. I know of several near the edges of the city. We'll need new clothing so we don't stand out too much as we enter the heart of the city."

"I suppose there aren't many in the city who dress like we do," Lyria said.

"There are some, but they are outlanders—traders or merchants. We don't want to look like that, we want to look like we belong in the city."

"I can see the reasoning behind that," Kel stated with a nod. "Nothing is more invisible than a grain of sand hiding in the desert."

"Woo-hoo. It looks like I'm not the only philosopher traveling with us this day."

Lyria laughed, "Well, Kel is a shaman's apprentice, after all. Remember, his grandfather is one of the shamans we seek."

Dan became serious at hearing that.

"I'm sorry. We'll find out what's going on and bring them home. I believe they must have some use for them. If they'd meant to harm them, they could have killed them when they attacked the villages."

"That is true," Kel answered with hope in his voice, "I had one more trial before I could be considered a man of wisdom, but with my grandfather taken that cannot take place."

"And," Lyria added, "until then, we cannot be wed."

"Then we had better find them quickly," Dan smiled. "I would hate to see either one of you become deranged with love, especially the lady with the sword!"

Again, they laughed.

Chapter 28

Finally they were clear of the village, once again in lightly forested terrain. Here the path was actually a road that ran fairly straight and was easy to follow. Ahead of them a steep climb awaited, then they would be in the hills overlooking the Black City. Kel wondered if it would look as it had in his dream.

They rode on along the wide, even pathway toward the darkness. The sun was at its zenith when they stopped for their midday meal. Their larder was well supplied from the generosity of the people of Mountain Village. They had fresh meat and bread, and now there would be butter for several days. Lyria had a half smile on her face when she handed Kel the butter, but she refrained from making any 'butter hog' comments. He accepted the butter, took some for his bread, and passed it to Dan. They ate in silence and soon they were ready to resume their travel. They mounted up and were off.

"I have a question about history," Kel said in mid-afternoon. "You say Los Angeles contains millions of people."

"That's correct. There are other cities as well, as you have heard. It's my understanding that there are at least five great cities very far to the eastern part of this land. What is your question?"

"I have been thinking that even if the cities contain many people and the villages few, it seems that there should be more people—it seems that many people are missing.

"What I mean is, in ancient time this entire land was populated. From the book I read of the war with the men of the Black Cross, the warm areas of the world were filled with cities. I know the ice has taken many, but it travels slowly and would not account for a seemingly almost empty world."

"That's a perceptive observation. You may not yet officially be a 'man of wisdom,' but you sound wise to me."

Kel said nothing, temporarily embarrassed by the praise.

"I do know the answer to that question."

Lyria looked from one man to the other. This was a question she hadn't considered, simply assuming things were the way they were because, well, that's just how they were.

"When the ice began moving almost two thousand years ago, there was a great war. The warriors of the lands across the sea came westward to conquer this land. They failed. They killed many and destroyed the great cities along the eastern coast with their bombs and ballistic weapons. This war raged for over ten years, and then something happened. There was an illness spreading through the people. I've read of this—the illness they called 'influenza.' It was a new kind they weren't used to and had no way of stopping. People began dying by the hundreds. The illness spread quickly and for a short time, the raiders from the lands of the Black Cross redoubled their attacks claiming that somehow this illness was made by the military in these lands to kill them, our enemy. Well, that didn't last very long. The great crystal ships the Black Cross sent across the sea arrived with only dead men aboard. Eventually the fighting stopped, not because one or the other side won, but because so many were dying so quickly they could no longer supply their armies with trained soldiers."

"That is terrible," Lyria said in a shocked voice.

"Indeed, by the time the illness ran its course, it killed eight out of every ten people in the world—even the tribes were hit hard by the illness. It was this illness that crushed civilization and the ice just buried empty cities."

"Does anyone know why it stopped or why it didn't kill everyone?" Lyria was still awed by what she had heard—the possibilities were frightening to contemplate.

"It's known that some people couldn't catch the illness; it seemed it had no effect on them." Dan continued, "So, if you got it, you died. If you didn't get it, you lived. It's said the reason the illness stopped is because it had killed everyone it could kill. Either it's still around, though powerless against the descendants of the ones it could not kill, or somehow it died. Perhaps it was not being fed whatever it was it needed from the deaths of humans."

"So, with so many people dead, it took a very long time to breed enough people to fill the land."

"That would be a correct supposition, Kel. And the cities for a very long time afterward were pestholes filled with rotting corpses and rampant with rats. Many people left the cities, moved out to the country, and were absorbed by the tribes that accepted them freely and without reservation."

They rode on in silence, Kel and Lyria shocked by the magnitude of what they'd heard. Almost everyone killed by a disease. Could it happen again? It was clear nobody knew the answer to that question. What other horrors from the past might they run across as they traveled? It wasn't pleasant to contemplate. Lyria put her hand defensively on the hilt of the sword—if they had to face flesh and blood enemies she was sure that the sword would fight with her. That gave some confidence, at least.

"I think it would be a good idea to tell you a bit about the Black City," Dan said. "Don't you agree?"

"By all means," Kel responded. "If we are to move about unseen, it would be useful to learn all we can before we arrive."

Lyria nodded in agreement.

"Well then, in general, the people of the city go to their various jobs, go home at the end of the day, and primarily mind their own business. But it's not the ordinary citizen of the city we need to worry about, it's the Cathedral and their spies we need to fool—and that will not be easy. Fortunately, nobody knows we're coming, so we'll have surprise on our side."

"How are we to disappear?" Lyria asked, looking at Dan.

"The first thing we'll do, as I said before, is change our clothing. We want to look like we belong in the city, and these clothes will mark us as outlanders no matter how familiar we seem to be with the city. My friends will provide us with clothing. I'll have to make the arrangements after we arrive, but it will be done quickly and secretly."

"Tell us something of the city," Lyria said. "How does it look, how does it work?"

"The outer part of the city is made of many small dwellings, much like a tribal village—individual family homes with shopping areas close to the various neighborhoods so people can purchase clothing, food, and whatever else they need without having to venture into the center of the city. As one moves toward the center of the city, the buildings grow very tall. Some are residences, some are places where people work, some are the hydroponic gardens—those are high towers of stone where the city grows its food."

Kel said, haltingly, "Hy..hydringpondics?

"Hydroponics," Dan corrected. "They grow food in towers using chemicals and sewage to feed the plants—that's where most of the slave labor ended up from the kidnapping raids."

Lyria and Kel stared at each other. They'd never heard of such a thing.

"In the city," Dan continued, "the streets are all paved with cobblestones and there are walkways on both sides against the building faces. The entire city is powered by gas. As I mentioned, some homes in

Mountain Village are also powered in this manner. One important thing to remember is this—the gas they use is very flammable, so do not let a quantity escape from a gas jet and fill the room you're in. If that happens and someone strikes a flame, you'll be immediately incinerated in a ball of fire."

"Well," Kel said, "that is reassuring!"

Dan laughed, "It isn't bad if you remember this rule—make sure the main gas valve to your home or room is turned off when you leave. The outside is lighted by gas as well; there are poles at long intervals along most of the streets in the central part of the city. They are lighted each evening and extinguished each morning. They don't supply much light, but there's enough to see you around even on the darkest nights. But rest assured, my friends or I will be with you at all times, helping you deal with whomever you may meet."

They stopped at last by the bank of a wide stream. It would've completely blocked their passage had there not been a stone bridge spanning the rapidly flowing water. Dan helped Kel unsaddle Fog and Mist as Lyria freed Morning from the cart. Dan's horse seemed not to have a name—at least they never heard him mention it. She was happy to be relieved of her burden, and snorted, tossing her head as she cantered down to the water's edge to join the other three horses calmly eating grass by the stream. Kel and Dan secured their guide ropes to small trees and returned to the wagon. Lyria had a fire lit and the men helped her get the food and cooking utensils from the wagon.

They ate in silence and when the meal was finished, Dan walked to his saddle and opened one of the leather bags. He withdrew a bottle—then walked back to the others. Kel and Lyria looked at each other questioningly. Dan sat down with a smile, showing them the bottle. He'd brought wine from Mountain Village. He poured the wine into their cups.

He forced the cork back into the neck of the bottle and spoke, "In the city, we would be using wine glasses made of actual glass, but this will do for now. I propose a toast to the success of our mission and the safe return of all to their families."

Kel raised his cup, "That is a worthy toast!"

Lyria nodded, raising her cup as well. They drank down the wine, and set the cups on the ground. They were tired, and the wine quickly took its toll. They wished each other a good night and retired to their respective tents. It didn't take long for sleep to come.

At dawn they rose, eating a quiet breakfast—each alone with their thoughts. Lyria washed the plates and cups as Kel and Dan saddled their horses for the day's journey. They all knew they'd reach the Black City the following day. Kel folded the canvas and leather tents, packing them in the bed of the wagon while Dan poured water over the remains of their fire, making sure the ashes were cold. They then mounted up, turned their horses toward the west, and were off once again.

As they rode, Dan told them of the ways of the city dwellers. He discussed their clothing and headgear—hats they were called. Both Lyria and Kel were astonished that people who lived and worked in protective stone structures all day and night would wear as much clothing as they apparently did. The men wore belted trousers and shirts, as well as vests, ties, and coats. The women fared no better with long dresses or gowns with tightly cinched waists and shoes on their feet that were fastened with many buttons. The women also wore hats everywhere they went. The two of them looked at each other, then down at themselves and laughed. The whole concept seemed quite silly and almost unbelievable to them. Dan laughed as well, making the comment, "I told you it would be a strange new world and that we could never fit in dressed as we are now."

"You will be able to dress us in the manner which you have described?" Kel was incredulous.

"Oh, you bet and you had best become used to the attire quickly so we may begin our searching."

"What of our weapons," Lyria asked, looking at Dan now, narrowly.

"We can carry small, hidden weapons but your fine sword will have to be hidden at the safe house for the time being. In the city, women don't carry swords."

Lyria wasn't happy with the idea of leaving the sword, but she'd find a way, one way or another, to carry Llo's gifts—the Teeth of the Ice Tiger. On this she knew she wouldn't budge.

It was nearing the time of the midday meal when they heard a distant sound. Dan immediately began scanning the skies, a worried look on his face.

"What is that sound?" Kel asked, also beginning to look upward.

"That, my friend, is the sound of a zeppelin. We should consider getting under that grove of trees for the time being."

Lyria looked over. The trees were only a hundred feet from the trail. She guided Fog under the canopy. A moment later Kel and Dan joined her with Morning and her cart safely in tow. Dan was still looking up into the trees. The humming sound was growing louder now.

"I believe it'll pass directly over us," Dan remarked. "Have you ever seen a zeppelin?"

Kel and Lyria answered in the negative.

"Well, let's quickly dismount, tie the horses, and we can have a look."

Kel tied Fog, Mist, and Morning to the trees while Dan tied his horse. He then joined Lyria and Kel by the edge of the grove. As the horses calmly grazed, a shadow passed over the small party. Kel and Lyria both gasped in disbelief as the great airship drifted overhead. They'd never seen any single object of this size made by man, and it was flying.

"You say this...this thing is held up by hydrogen gas?" Kel was almost at a loss for words.

"That's correct. The bag that makes up the top part that we can see is a light shell. It holds and protects a series of inner bags, for lack of a better word, that contains the gas. The gas from one of the bags is fed in small amounts to the engines along the sides. The engines have propellers which turn rapidly and push the thing through the sky like the screws on a ship or boat push it through the water."

Lyria said, breathlessly, "There are really people in that thing?"

Dan laughed, "That long box at the bottom is called the gondola—it's where the people live when they're in the sky. The ship you're looking at is almost a thousand feet in length, and the gondola could hold as many as thirty or forty men."

"That is why you wanted us to hide?"

Dan looked at Lyria and said, "You may be able to take on thirty soldiers, but I would have to run and it's a long way back to Mountain Village."

They watched in silence as the great white zeppelin cruised directly over their heads, perhaps several hundred feet above the earth. It seemed to move slowly to Kel, but that could be deceiving he realized, due to the monstrous size of the thing.

"I thought zeppelins were black," he said in awe. "We have never heard of white airships."

"Nor have I," said Dan in a worried voice. "That's surely an airship of the Cathedral, but as far as I've heard, they're all black. We'll wait until they're well past before we move on. They have large telescopes on board that can see a very long way, there's no point in letting them know we're here."

"That is a wise choice," Kel commented.

Dan snickered, "Not wise, cowardly!"

"Do not mistake reluctance to fight with cowardice, Dan, even the great ice tigers and cave bears avoid a fight if at all possible, but they still carry tooth and claw."

Dan had nothing to add to this and kept thoughtfully silent.

They decided to eat their midday meal here, under the spreading green trees. It would be at least an hour before the zeppelin would be far enough away to ensure they wouldn't be seen—they made no fire, eating cold salted pork and venison with bread and the last of the butter. As Kel buttered his bread, Lyria snickered but said nothing. He smiled at her, making an elaborate ritual of not using too much butter *and* making sure she watched his every move. When they'd finished eating, Lyria said she would like to see if she could talk to her sword again. Dan glanced into the sky. The zeppelin was receding, but he knew the large telescopes would be able to see them for about another half hour.

"We have the time, if you wish to try."

They moved into a circle and Kel began talking to Lyria in a low, calm voice, beginning to prepare her for her communication as she withdrew the great sword from its scabbard. The blade flashed in the sunlight. She set it across her lap, turning her attention to Kel.

"As you sit holding the sword, I want you to feel its presence, feel its weight. Put your hand on the blade and reach for the life that is within it."

Lyria touched the cold steel of the blade, laying her left hand lightly upon it.

"Reach inside the steel, Lyria. Reach for the spirit indwelling. You can feel it, can you not?'

Lyria's response was slow and dreamy. Kel knew she was there and became silent.

"Who are you?"

Again, Dan and Kel were transcribing the whispered questions and answers.

"I am honor, strength, protection, and victory," the sword whispered inside her mind.

"What do you call yourself?"

"I am the Guardian of Light."

"Are you fire?"

"I am the flame, not the fire. Fire is chaos—directed and controlled, my flame brings order."

"How can fire protect if it is chaos?"

"I am two edged. I bring Light and divide Light."

"By your inscription you call yourself the Light of the Fire Dragon?"

"The dragon contains the chaos of fire. Fire, like your spirit, can be directed."

"Will your spirit give me courage in battle?"

"Spirit and courage are yours. I am the channel and the means, not the source."

"How can I relate more to the flame?"

"Heed your instincts, learn how fire burns. "Do you merely need light or a torch? Do you need heat or a conflagration? The choice is yours."

"Well then, can you tell me anything about water?" Lyria's mumbling could barely be heard now so Kel and Dan leaned toward her to hear what was being said.

"Water and fire are similar. If they are not moderated and directed, both can engulf you. Fire makes water. Water makes fire."

Lyria had an image flash though her mind of a volcano and a lightning bolt. The sword spoke one more time.

"Fire and water are primary. Air is an expression of their mix. Air is the child of fire and water and earth are these three manifested. The triad resides in the fourth, by mastering the three, you master the fourth...."

Chapter 29

Lyria's head dropped to her breast, and Kel gently roused her. She opened her eyes, staring around in a confused state. She smiled when her eyes finally focused on Kel.

"I was really gone that time," she said.

"Yes, you were," Dan responded.

Lyria asked them to read back to her what had transpired. Dan read his notes with an occasional addition from Kel. When they'd finished, Lyria looked up.

"I understand some of this. It is a mistake for a warrior to try to control a battle on the physical level—that is the earth level. By knowing and mastering how the spirits of fire, water, and air are manifesting in a battle, the combat simply cannot be lost—the three reside in the fourth, the sword said. By mastering the three, I master the fourth."

Kel laughed, "You have just learned one of the basic concepts of magic. If this keeps up, you will not only be a fearsome warrior, but a wise woman as well."

Lyria laughed, saying, "Let us first complete this journey before we praise ourselves for our wisdom."

"There!" Kel shouted, looking at Dan. "Did you hear that? See? She's...she's doing it again, getting all wise on us."

As they all laughed, Fog issued a loud snort. That brought the three into more gales of laughter. Finally, with the zeppelin a mere speck in the western sky, they saddled up the impatient horses and were on their way again.

By evening they were moving into a more mountainous region. They stopped for supper near an outcropping of rocks that shielded them from the view of anyone who might be traveling on the pathway. The four horses grazed amiably side by side, hidden by the massive boulders. Kel thought they could risk a fire, and Dan agreed. Lyria started gathering sticks and twigs while Dan lit some tinder with a bit of flint and a piece of steel. By the time the tinder was smoking, the bright flame flashed up and quickly spread, igniting first the small twigs, then the larger ones. Soon they had a cook fire going and Lyria prepared the food while the two men spread blankets to sit on, arranged the plates, and filled their cups with cool fresh water from the small stream flowing nearby.

"By midday tomorrow we should crest this mountainous area and then we will have our first look at Los Angeles," Dan commented between mouthfuls. "From then on, it'll be a simple downhill trek into the city."

"Will there be a lot of people where we will be traveling?" Kel was worried about how their arrival might be viewed by the city dwellers.

"We will not have to worry about that," Dan explained. "We'll be entering through a residential area of small houses with single families dwelling in them. People will see us, but they will not bother us."

"I suppose," Lyria said, "that for the time being, if anyone asks about us, we can say we have come to the Black City to trade."

"That's not a bad idea. Then later, if by chance someone should look for us, they'll be looking for outlanders—and by that time we'll be finely dressed city folk." Dan snickered at the idea of fooling people. This was something he'd enjoyed immensely when he lived as a thief and later as a member of the resistance.

"You mentioned the so-called safe house. How long will we be staying there before we begin our search inquiries?" Kel asked.

"Oh, I suspect you two will have to stay hidden for a day or so. That should be enough time for me to get into the downtown section and find some of my old friends. We'll need proper clothing first and foremost."

After eating, Lyria decided to try handling her new sword. She withdrew it from the scabbard. The blade seemed heavy compared to her daggers, but it was well balanced; the steel pommel helped balance the blade. Kel placed several stout tree branches in the ground to serve as targets. Lyria faced her three enemies. She moved slowly to her left, visualizing in her mind's eye the movements of her foes. She maneuvered herself so two of the branches were more or less behind the one closest to her, lining them up. She raised the blade, bringing it down diagonally from right to left, severing the tree branch easily.

She stepped in with a snarl, engaging the second foe, bringing the sword up from the low position it had assumed after her first cut, again with an angled cut that parted the branch as though it was made of nothing more substantial than air. Withdrawing the hilt toward herself, she made a quick, straight thrust with the tip of the blade, striking the last branch squarely. The blade was so sharp that the point slid into the wood, coming out the back before the pressure of the blade snapped the branch. The combat took three seconds.

Dan clapped his hands in delight. "That was fantastic. I've watched soldiers practicing in a similar manner many times. I've seen none complete a test such as this as quickly as you just did—and they're used to their swords."

Lyria was standing by the stump of her last target, staring at the blade in awe. "I would not have thought any metal could be that sharp. The easy way the blade cuts makes it seem even faster, somehow."

"You have a natural talent for this anyway," said Kel. "Now you have a sword equal to your talent."

She smiled at both men, sheathing the ancient sword.

"Now I really see why I never sold the sword. You truly are a warrior in the most ancient of traditions. I believe the men of the dragon boats who made this sword would be proud for one such as you to wield it again after all these years. I know who I will be standing behind if we ever have to do some fighting."

Kel banked the fire so it would burn low through the night and be ready to reignite in the morning. He climbed up on a low boulder surveying the countryside in all directions.

"Do you think many pass this way?"

Dan looked up from pitching his small tent. "I do not think many. This road is seldom used, as it leads eastward. The northern road is more heavily traveled. People from small cities and villages frequently come to Los Angeles to trade—and to stay. Many of the tribes who live closely have lost many of their young men and women. The family comes to trade, the youngsters are delighted by the strangeness and 'bigness,' I guess you'd say, of the city and they 'run away,' deciding to stay in the city."

"What happens to them?" Lyria sounded apprehensive.

"Sometimes something good, sometimes something bad," Dan responded. "In many cases, it depends on the person—how well he or she was taught basic virtues such as honesty. In such a large place, with so many diversions, it's easy to become lost—both in body and in mind."

"That I do believe," she responded.

"What I was wondering," Kel said, bringing the conversation back to his initial question. "Should we post a guard and take turns at watch?"

"I don't think so," Dan responded with a shrug. "Few pass this way and even bandits don't travel at night except when they're in the midst of a raid."

"Then this will be our last night sleeping under stars, and we may all sleep."

So they pitched the other two tents. Kel went to check on the horses and returned to his tent. All of them were tired, and tomorrow they would pass into the borders of the Black City of the West.

The night passed peacefully and at dawn the three travelers awoke refreshed and ready for their final day of travel. The horses were peacefully grazing as Lyria went to the stream to wash. Kel and Dan busied themselves with restarting the fire and preparing the utensils they'd need for breakfast.

"By tomorrow we'll be eating city food," Dan stated. "Once we're safely in our hideaway, I'll go out and get us some food."

Lyria had just returned; her hair was still wet and her face glistening with moisture. Kel rose and put his arm around her, taking a towel and patting her face and hair. She smiled at him and Dan smiled as well.

"Is the city food safe to eat?" Lyria had heard Dan's comment earlier and was worried about the safety of the hydroponic gardens.

"It must be, millions eat it every day."

"Millions…" Lyria said with wonder, "and I thought Mountain Village was large."

"You will need a new concept for the word 'large' once you see the city," Dan said. "It extends for many miles in all directions from its center."

"Still," she said, "with so many people, three outsiders would hardly be noticed."

"That's what I'm hoping," Dan said. "That's our one big advantage and our detriment—with so much space, finding one or two individuals could be difficult."

"I suppose so," Kel interjected, "but if your friends are as good as you say at finding things, there is still hope."

"There is always hope," Dan answered.

Kel cooked their breakfast that morning and both Dan and Lyria approved wholeheartedly. They quickly washed their utensils after eating and packed them in the cart. Soon all was in readiness, so they mounted up for the last day of riding. They reined their horses out onto the trail, turning west. To Kel it seemed they'd been traveling west for a lifetime. Dan was whistling a merry tune as they rode. Lyria looked at Kel and he at her. They both began whistling along with Dan. Their horses didn't seem to mind.

They traveled without incident the rest of the morning and by the time they stopped for their midday meal they were well into the low ridges and hills that led ever upward. After eating, they rested for a little while, mostly to let the horses eat and drink. When they resumed their journey, they led the horses for about an hour so they could move up the hills a bit more easily. The brush was denser here, as were the trees. Dan led both Morning and his own horse, and he stayed close to Kel and Lyria.

Fog was restless—nervous. He stopped, pawing the ground, neighing. Everyone stopped and listened. They heard nothing but the sound of a distant stream and the birds in the trees. Dan heard the sound first, the low rumble that could almost be felt rather than heard. His horse reared and bolted.

"Watch out!"

Kel's warning came just in time as Dan's horse ran closely past Lyria. Fog and Mist were agitated as well. Both Lyria and Kel had their bows drawn and ready. The next sound was not a low rumble; it was a roar. All three turned to face the sound. A huge, tawny shape leaped upon a boulder not thirty feet from them. It was a cave lion, and it was huge. Standing four feet at the shoulder, the massive beast stared down at them. It snarled, its golden eyes flashing as it crouched for the attack. As it leaped, twin shafts of wood tipped by razor-sharp iron struck home. The lion gave a sort of growl and gasp, collapsing on the earth not eight feet from Lyria. It was still alive, though just barely. Kel went forward and straddled the animal. It was breathing heavily—wetly. Their arrows had pierced both heart and lung.

"Great Mother of all," Kel said, "bring the spirit of this noble animal into Your Otherworld in peace."

He quickly thrust his dagger into the lion's throat—a gush of blood rushed out, the golden eyes closed, and the beast was still.

Lyria looked for Dan, expecting that he had run. She was surprised to see him still standing nearby, holding Fog and Mist and Morning's reins. She looked at him and he shrugged sheepishly.

"Well…you two were busy and somebody had to hold the horses."

Lyria and Kel laughed, and a moment later Dan joined in.

It took the better part of a half hour to find Dan's horse and bring it back to the trail. All the horses were acting nervously from the smell of blood. They decided it would be best to be quickly gone from this spot. They mounted up and rode off, ever west.

It was late afternoon when they finally reached the top of the ridge and found themselves gazing down on Los Angeles. Their destination finally in reach, they paused to savor the moment, gazing in wonder. Kel thought the city looked remarkably like he'd seen it in his dream, though the sunlight reflected off of shiny objects and occasionally from windows. The tallest buildings—several hundred of them—towered over the rest of the city.

"They are down there somewhere," Kel said. "Garn, Galv, Noria, and all the rest."

"I think we will find them," Lyria said with conviction.

"If we don't, it will not be for a lack of trying," Dan stated with a flat voice.

Chapter 30

They coaxed their mounts down the other side of the ridge. In an hour they were traveling on a rather wide road. They passed an occasional farm, though they were small and probably supported only the people living there. Once in a while they'd hear a dog barking as they passed a gate or a pathway leading to a distant house. They saw no one as they traveled.

"Soon it'll get a lot more populated. We should act like traders and otherwise mind our business."

Gradually the number if not the size of the dwellings grew. As they rode down the road, there were now homes along both sides. Children played in front fenced yards. There were a few adults around, but other than watching suspiciously as they passed, nothing was said to them.

"They want to make sure we don't steal from them. Those tribal types are often up to no good, you know."

Lyria laughed.

Any adults they came near scrutinized them until they were past, then returned to whatever it was they were doing in the first place. Lyria thought it was most annoying. "They don't like us and they don't even know us," she said in disgust.

"It's how they were taught," Dan said. "And there are many people who simply find it easier to believe what someone has told them rather than to find out for themselves. In actuality, I feel sorry for them, for all the richness of life they miss or ignore in their bigotry."

"I had not thought of it in those terms," Lyria said thoughtfully.

"You know," Kel added, "in the tribes we are told the same thing of the people of the Black City. In that respect we are alike. Some find it easier to simply hate and mistrust, rather than to look and see for themselves—I, myself, am guilty of that."

"To a greater or lesser extent, I believe everyone does it. The priests of the Cathedral have taken it much farther than that," Dan warned. "Don't underestimate the hatefulness that can come from religion once it's codified in so-called ancient and holy books that must be believed simply because someone says that they are ancient and holy."

"Garn taught that religion and the Spirit are two distinct things. Things spiritual are simple and straightforward, while religion is a product of men created to give those men power over others."

"Garn is a wise man," Dan said with a nod. "Each exists separate from the other."

Three children suddenly darted into the street between Kel and Lyria who were leading and Dan who had fallen a short distance behind them. Dan's horse shied and he pulled back hard on the reins.

"Whoa, Daisy!"

The horse stopped instantly and the children passed unharmed— oblivious to the potential of what might have been. Dan sat for a moment, took a breath, and then continued. When he'd pulled up next to Kel, Lyria glanced over at him and questioned, "Daisy?"

"It's the name of my horse."

"I have never heard you call your horse by any name," she responded. "I am glad she has one."

Dan smiled wistfully, "Everyone should have a name."

"So," Lyria persisted, "why Daisy?"

"I like the flowers," Dan said almost defensively. "That is reason enough."

Lyria let it go at that, knowing in her heart the answer was more complex.

After another hour riding into the city, Dan suddenly reined Daisy in and pointed to a small home to his right. Though the house wasn't large, it was located on its own plot of land about an acre in size. Past the house was a small barn. Dan led the small party to the barn where they unsaddled the horses and freed Morning from her cart. They put their horses into four side-by-side stalls, filling the food troughs with the grain they'd brought in the wagon. Dan had gone outside to fill three large pails with water. He brought the pails into the barn one at a time, pouring them into a large cauldron-like ceramic container. Kel and Lyria watched, fascinated, as he used the pump, again to fill the three pails. This time each of them carried one into the barn. With five trips finished, the ceramic container was finally filled.

Dan pointed to the copper tubing running from the cauldron to the individual water containers in each of the horse's stalls.

"This brings the water from the tank to the troughs," he explained.

He pointed to a copper box attached to the backs of the troughs.

"See that round thing on the copper rod? That is called a 'float.' When the trough is filled, it automatically stops the water flow and opens it again when it gets too low. This way we can fill the main tank and the horses will always have a full trough of water."

"Won't the water also go into the empty stalls and just evaporate?" Kel was looking down the line of six stalls.

"Watch," Dan answered with a knowing smile. He walked to the tank and began turning small valves located at the base of the tank. As the valves opened, water flowed into the four stalls where their horses stood, but none into the empty stalls. "This way, we can just fill the stalls that have horses."

"That is very clever," Kel said in awe. "It makes watering the horses much easier. I see now why Mountain Village is willing to trade with the Black City. I'm ashamed I was critical of them for that trading and ashamed of having been so blind as to think nothing but evil could come from the city."

"Friendly monsters," Lyria said, referencing Kel's past journey.

They proceeded toward the house, carrying their personal things. The door was locked, but Dan had a key.

"I um…never gave it back," he said self-consciously. "I'm glad they didn't change the locks."

After they'd placed their belongings in their rooms, Dan called them together into the living room.

"I'll show you how the water supply works in the house and show you the generator that runs the automatic pump, but there is something else I want to show you first."

On the wall that backed up to a large storage room just outside the house, were shelves that extended almost to the ceiling. Without comment, Dan removed several books and slid off the wood trim at the back of the shelf. He pressed on some hidden lever and the center shelf section swung out on hinges. Kel and Lyria looked at each other in amazement.

"Come," Dan said, gesturing with his hand.

They followed him into the wall. It wasn't into the wall actually; the wall of the storage room was a mere two feet away from the wall of the house. Between the walls, a staircase descended into darkness. Dan picked up a lantern from the floor and examined it. It was full of oil. His friends maintained it constantly since the house might be needed at any time. Next to the lamp was a stack of wooden crates that seemed tied together with heavy cord.

With the lamp lit, they walked down the stairs into a room half the size of the house above it. There was a table in the center with three chairs and four cots along the walls. On one wall was a short doorway.

"This doorway leads to a tunnel that traverses about two hundred yards and ends under the house behind us. That house also belongs to my friends. In fact, a family lives there all the time. That house has another stairway leading up into yet another bookcase like the one we just went through. If you come under attack while in the house, this is the escape route."

"But won't the attackers find the stairway and the room—and the other house?"

"If they have the time," Dan answered enigmatically.

"They will take the time, I am sure," Kel stated.

"They will try, of course. But, when you enter the bookcase, you'll pull it shut behind you—it locks automatically. After you light the lantern, you use the flame to light the cord on the crates you were examining earlier. The crates are filled with explosives."

"Explosives," Lyria said in confusion, having never heard the word before.

"In the crates there are fifty pounds of a chemical that burns so quickly, it's literally consumed instantly. The blast will be like a thousand thunderclaps and the fire will be like the breath of the Celestial Dragon…you'll need to be far away in one minute after you light the fuse. The explosives will completely collapse the tunnel and completely destroy the house, and all the invaders inside and standing outside as well."

"Like the 'bombs' I read of that were dropped by the zeppelins of the Black Cross tribes on the eastern cities," Kel said, proud of having that knowledge.

"Very perceptive, Kel. That's exactly what it is like."

They retraced their steps, pausing long enough for Dan to show them the end of the fuse they must light if they had to flee the house. He then showed them how the secret-latch on the bookcase worked; they each tried it.

"If you'll come with me outside for just a moment, I'll leave you in peace," Dan said.

They walked around the side of the house and Dan showed them the generator that ran the automatic pump for the house. He showed them how to turn on the gas jet and light it to heat the water that would eventually make the steam pressure needed to run the pump. After this was explained and the pump was activated, Dan took them back inside and showed them how the faucets worked in the kitchen and bath—Kel and Lyria were amazed.

"Something else worthy to come from the City," Kel said, impressed. "Llo was right, when you travel in the wide world, vision must widen with it."

"I must change clothes now," Dan said. "I'll have to leave you for a short period of time and I believe my old clothing will still fit me. I'll also need one each of your clothing."

"Why is that?"

Lyria, he thought, *always suspicious*.

"I'll need them to match sizes so when I bring city clothing back, it'll fit you."

"That is sensible," Lyria mused. "We can do that."

Dan paused, then added, "I must go into the city to see if I can find my friends to let them know we are here, staying in one of their houses. They also need to know about what we're doing here."

Kel and Lyria nodded, and then Kel said with sudden realization, "It is dusk, and the city is far…how will you get there?"

"Oh," Dan answered with a smile, "I'll take the bus!"

"Bus?"

"Certainly," Dan responded. "It comes by every three hours to a stop about a mile from here."

"No," Kel laughed, "I mean, what is a 'bus'?"

"Ah," Dan said, "a bus is a large steam-powered…wagon, you might say, with many seats. For a fee it can take you almost anywhere in the city if you have the patience to wait out all of its stops."

Kel looked at Lyria and said, "We do have a lot to learn, don't we?" Lyria nodded and Dan laughed.

"Most of the time I'll be able to guide you, but yes, there's much you must learn to blend in."

Dan left them to their own devices, going to his room to change. When he returned, they almost didn't recognize him. He was dressed in dark clothing of precise fit. On his head he wore a low top hat. His short coat was worn over a white shirt and a dark green silk vest. A gold chain ran a short distance from the center of the vest and disappeared into a pocket. His feet were shod in leather boots that shone dully, not highly polished but not shabby either. His trouser legs covered the tops of the boots.

Kel asked incredulously, "Will I dress like that?"

Dan laughed, assuring him he'd have to, then adding, "Wait until you see what Lyria will have to wear and you'll not object at all to your attire."

"What will I have to wear?"

Lyria sounded defensive and Dan laughed, "All in good time, Tiger Lady, all in good time."

He turned, leaving the house, walking briskly down the street carrying the bundle of clothing. Kel and Lyria watched him go, and they then went in to explore the wonders of their new dwelling. They tried the faucets and to their delight they also worked for them. They went to their bedrooms to lay out what personal possessions they'd brought with them. The cart would be safe in the barn until morning when the trunk could be brought inside. Lyria went into the bathroom and called to Kel. When he entered, she was staring at the bathtub. She turned the faucets and water flowed, beginning to fill the tub.

"Imagine taking a bath in this. The water is even heated!"

"It is big enough for two people," Kel said, and then blushed at the unintended implication.

Lyria laughed, "Perhaps when we are wed, we can get one of these and try out your idea."

Kel laughed.

"For now, though," Lyria said, shoving Kel out the door and closing it. "I will bathe alone, but I will be thinking of you," she shouted playfully through the door.

Kel mumbled something and Lyria inquired, "What?"

"I'm going to go read a book."

She laughed, and so did Kel in spite of himself.

~

Dan only had to wait a couple minutes for the steam bus to arrive. He was lucky he got there when he did; he wouldn't have relished the three-hour wait if he'd missed it. He stepped onto the bus, telling the driver he'd be going to the center of the city. He paid his fare and walked down the aisle about halfway. Sitting on the green leather seat, he forced himself to relax. He'd never dreamed he might be involved in something like this. In the past he'd taken incredible risks, but it had always been, almost always been, only himself he was putting at risk. It bothered him to hold the lives of other people in his hands. The last time that happened, it hadn't been a happy ending. He sighed, forcing himself to think of something other than Daisy.

The bus moved slowly toward the center of the city, stopping every mile to drop off or pick up riders. Dan watched everyone who entered the bus, scrutinizing them with the years of expertise he'd gained as a criminal and thief. He was certain that none of the individuals currently aboard were law enforcement. He'd been gone from the city a very long time, but he also knew the Bishop had a long memory—and his own dungeons.

Chapter 31

After Lyria had taken a long and leisurely bath, she dressed in a fleece robe that was hanging in the closet. She felt wonderful—truly clean for the first time in almost half a month. Feeling refreshed, she opened the bathroom door and called to Kel. He put down the book he was reading and walked into the next room. Lyria tossed him another robe; it danced through the air and came to rest over his head. She giggled as though she were six, watching Kel struggle with the fleece fabric. He took a playfully threatening step toward her.

"No you don't," she said, "you can only hug me once you are clean, get in there and take a bath."

"How do you know I was going to hug you?"

"What else could you have possibly been planning," she teased. "Certainly not revenge for the robe ending up on your head—that was clearly your fault."

He sighed, bundled up the robe, and headed into the bathroom.

"Make sure you wash well." Lyria taunted him, "even if you are a butter hog, you don't have to smell like one."

She heard him laughing behind the door. Gods, how she loved him!

While Kel bathed, she wandered into the other room, noticing the book Kel had been reading. Though Lyria couldn't read, she was delighted to find the book filled with amazingly realistic pictures. She was familiar with the wood cuts she saw on occasion in Kel's books, but this was something else altogether. She turned the pages, staring in amazement at the photogravure prints of huge cities, marching armies, and skies filled with zeppelins.

~

At long last, the steam bus arrived at the main terminal in the heart of Los Angeles. Dan dismounted, standing for a moment, orienting himself. It'd been a long time since he'd been here. He found he still remembered, and started off down the street, mindful of the young boys who came near. They reminded him of himself from his days as a pickpocket. He was determined not to be a victim of the crime at which he'd been so proficient. He withdrew his silver watch from the vest pocket, opening the case. It was nearly seven, plenty of time to find the tavern where his friends used to gather. He hoped they'd still be there after all this time.

As Dan walked down the street, the lamplighters were busily lighting the gas jets for the streetlamps. The yellow-orange glow gave Dan a sense of familiarity and comfort. Though there were dangers in the city, he knew them firsthand and was not afraid. He rounded the corner and saw he was on the right street. Ahead was the dimly visible sign of the rooming house near the tavern. He knew about the tall structure and what the priests sometimes did in there—in the rooms reserved by the Cathedral. He walked past the building. As he approached the tavern, he saw two young women lounging in front. He knew what their profession was and he suddenly realized he was aroused. He hadn't been with any woman in years, with one exception—Daisy. He pushed the thought from his mind. He might have time for the hookers, but first he had something more important to do.

As he approached the tavern, as expected, the girls wandered up to him sinuously. One ran her hand gently down his cheek, dragging her red painted nails lightly against his skin. She smiled at him. "I think I know you," she began, putting another hand between his legs. She smiled when she realized how ready he was. "Now I'm certain that I know you."

Quick money, she thought.

Dan gently removed her hand, saying, "It could well be that you know me. I have business to attend to, but if you're still here when I leave, I'll be sure to get to know both of you even better."

He brushed his hand lightly over her breast, turned and entered the tavern.

"I'll be right here, honey," she promised.

The inside of the tavern was dark, as was expected. The gaslights that ran around the wall didn't supply enough light for so big a room, but that was as intended. Dan glanced around, and to his surprise he saw someone he knew. He casually walked over to the table where his friend from his former life sat and looked down at him. The man glanced up, and then suddenly a broad smile crossed his face.

"I'll be damned!"

Dan smiled, saying, "Yes, you probably are."

His friend waved for a waitress. She came up quickly, asking Dan what he would like to drink.

"Make it a whisky, please."

"You got it, sir," she responded, walking off toward the bar.

"Dan Hendricks, by all the Gods!"

"It is I," Dan responded. "So, what has ol' Lawrence been doing with himself these past years? You don't look too much worse for wear."

Lawrence laughed, sliding his chair closer. Just then the waitress approached, setting a glass in front of Dan.

"Leave the bottle, if you would be so kind," Lawrence said to her. "Put it on my tab."

The young woman nodded, walking away, looking for another customer.

~

Kel finished a very long soak in the tub. He climbed out, feeling amazingly refreshed. He toweled off and slipped on the robe. He marveled at its softness, thinking he'd take some back to his village when his business in the city was finished—he could trade for them. He smiled, pulling the drain plug from the tub, watching as the water just disappeared, apparently right into the floor. He watched the wood for a moment, expecting to see the water soaking back up to the surface, but that didn't happen. He walked in bare feet back into the living room. Lyria was curled up on the sofa, the book he'd been reading open in her lap. She was sound asleep. He gently picked her up in his arms. She moaned a bit, settling back into her slumber. He carried her into her bedroom, carefully placing her on the bed, and drew the blanket up over her. He leaned over, brushing a strand of hair that had come out of her war braids from her forehead. He leaned over a bit farther, giving her a gentle kiss on her cheek. She smiled in her sleep. He left her room, closing the door, and walked back into the living room.

He picked up the book and looked at the engraving Lyria had last looked at before falling asleep. It was a two-page spread showing a huge, menacing zeppelin very close to the ground. There were men in the gondola firing ballistic weapons from the windows at the people on the street. There were dead and dying women, children, men, and soldiers scattered in its wake. There were two wet spots on the page. Kel touched them, tasting them. They were salty. Lyria had cried when she saw the images of the civilian carnage wrought by the zeppelin in the picture. Clearly visible on the side of the zeppelin was a large black equal-armed cross. Below the engraving were the words, "Philadelphia devastated by strafing zeppelins." Lyria's tears made a poignant counterpoint to the cold, stilted words under the picture. Kel closed the book, went into his own room, and was soon asleep.

~

Lawrence looked amusedly at Dan, "I'm doing well. I even have a tab at the tavern now."

Dan laughed and drank down the whisky. It was as good as he remembered.

"What of your work?"

Lawrence looked around nervously and said, "Priests come in here nowadays, priests of the Cathedral. Talk is more guarded now than in the old days."

"Believe it or not, I'm still working with you…in a way, that is."

"Really? After all these years on the run?"

"I was never very far, Lawrence. I was living in a village a couple days travel by horse from here."

"That'll make an interesting tale, I'm sure," Lawrence said, pouring Dan a fresh drink.

Dan quickly swallowed the whisky, poured another, and then went into his story. He told of his alliance with Mountain Village and the attacks on the tribes, and about young Noria and his mission to bring her home.

"This sounds like something just about anyone would attempt except you."

Lawrence looked skeptically at Dan and asked, "What's the real play?"

"This is the real play, Lawrence," Dan insisted. "I also have two travelers waiting at the safe house in section four."

Lawrence again glanced around. There was nobody within earshot.

"Outlanders? Here? Looking for lost shamans?"

"That's correct. It would seem the Cathedral is responsible for all the kidnappings of the magic men. With their belief that magic is the work of the evil Goddess, now bound and under control, I cannot imagine their interest in such things."

"I can."

Dan looked surprised; he'd expected a bit more resistance, considering how long he'd been away.

"Tell me," he said.

"There've been rumors coming from the Cathedral over the last few years. They're financing and building cities far south on the edges of The Green Hell."

"That doesn't seem a smart thing to me," Dan commented. "Everyone knows what happens when city dwellers enter that wild area."

"Nevertheless, they apparently have one city completed and are beginning work on several others. Also, a priest was murdered a while ago. We heard of it from a connection that actually viewed the body. Inquiries led us to a family who was missing a favored son who'd become a priest a number of years back. The priest's name was Caven and he'd been spreading some very interesting rumors."

"Rumors?"

"About the new cities. It seems the Bishop wants to move the Cathedral down south and set up cities that only allow members of their faith to dwell there."

"Why?"

"That part's easy," Lawrence said. "The teachings of the Cathedral are no longer popular with most of the population of the city. The abuse of women and children, the secret buying of businesses and properties—it's all getting more attention than the Cathedral likes."

"I wonder how that could've happened," Dan said with a smile.

"We've not been sitting by waiting for your return," Lawrence said with a grin, pouring Dan yet another drink.

They drank in silence for several minutes, two friends from long ago simply enjoying each other's company.

"There's something else going on," Lawrence said, "and it's very confusing."

"Tell me. After the last few years nothing seems strange to me."

"The city's now in the control of politicians who aren't particularly friendly toward the Cathedral. They're preparing to enact civil laws that'll make much of the behavior of the followers of the Redeemed God criminal acts."

"Wow! That really is big news."

"It certainly is. Now, there's no telling if they have the strength to enact these laws, but the Bishop is worried."

"As he should be," Dan nodded. "What else?"

"Simply this, rumors about the southern cities include more than suggestions of the Cathedral moving entirely down there—that's their backup plan. There's something else they're doing down there, but we haven't been able to figure out what it is."

Dan was silent, knowing Lawrence would continue.

"The shamans you've spoken of—they aren't here," Lawrence said.

"What? Where are they, do you know?"

"Not for certain, but it's probable that the Bishop has had them sent south into The Green Hell. We can't imagine why, but it has something to do with a shaman's purported connection to animal spirits."

"So the Bishop is using magic for some secret end?"

"That's what we think, though what he's planning is anyone's guess."

They shared another couple of drinks, and then continued their conversation.

"Your friends need to meet with the magician. If he likes what he hears, he'll devote the energies of the resistance toward that end."

"I can arrange that," Dan said, downing his drink. He felt a bit fuzzy; it was a good feeling. He thought about the hookers waiting outside, wondering if they'd still be there.

"One other thing," Dan said, "we'll need clothing for my friends."

"I can arrange that, do you know the sizes?"

"I've brought some of their clothing with me."

"Very clever, but then, you always were very clever."

Dan handed Lawrence the clothing.

"I'll have clothing ready by morning. I'll have a steam-car ready to take you back so you won't have to juggle all the boxes."

"That's thoughtful of you. When should we come back to see the magician?"

"Today's his day off. He'll be here most of the day tomorrow, so if you can get your friends dressed, just show up. He'll be waiting for you."

"That will work. I was thinking—should we get a priest robe for Kel? It'll help him get around—and you say priests come here nowadays."

"That can be arranged as well. You have somewhere to spend the night?"

"Most of it," Dan smiled, "and I'll improvise the rest and see you in the morning."

"You'll not see me. However, the car will be waiting in front with the clothing and other things."

Dan downed his last drink and got unsteadily to his feet.

Lawrence laughed, "Lightweight! Only a few years pass and even I can drink you under the table."

Dan laughed as well, "I'm not under the table yet."

He rose, meandering toward the door. He hoped he wouldn't be too drunk to enjoy the company of the prostitutes.

As it happened, he wasn't disappointed. The women walked over to him immediately, putting their arms around him—the first letting her hands rest on his hip. Dan handed her a roll of paper currency. She smiled and did not pull away when he put his hand on her breast. She wasn't wearing anything under the thin top. They walked a short distance around the corner to the rooming house that so much was spoken of. They walked in, going immediately to the lift, then to the third floor. Dan smiled as he felt the young woman's warmth against him, for that much money, this should be a night to remember.

Chapter 32

Kel arose early, as was the way of the tribes. He stretched, went to the sink in the bathroom, again marveling at the spigots and the water they seemed to magically conjure. He washed his face and returned to his room to dress. By the time he was finished, he could hear Lyria moving about in the bathroom. He waited for her to return to her room to dress. While he waited for her to come out of her bedroom, he moved about in the kitchen area, surprised to find no fire pit or cauldron. How did the city people cook their food? By the time Lyria presented herself, he had prepared a cold breakfast of the last of their salted meat and bread. There was no butter left, so the bread would be eaten plain. Neither complained; any food was always good food. As soon as they were finished, they went to the windows. Both were eager for Dan's return; they wanted to be on the search and they were wondering what manner of clothes he'd bring back with him—and if they'd fit.

~

Dan also woke early. The women were gone and he was alone. Women? He tried to think back; yes, that was right. There were two women. He smiled to himself—at least he was no coward in bed. He dressed quickly, wanting to be on his way. His old habits were returning. He desired not to stay in any one place very long. Instead of taking the lift, he used the stairs. He knew there'd be nobody on them this early and he wished to see no one. He swung open the door of the building, walking quickly through the large stone arch that was mirrored on almost all the buildings in the area. The iron portcullis was raised; though most buildings had them, few were lowered at night.

As promised, the car was waiting by the curb, it's engine running—its steam at full pressure. He walked to the passenger side. The driver's side door opened and a small, older man stepped out. He handed an envelope to Dan and walked away. Dan shrugged and went around to the street side. He wondered if he still remembered how to drive a steam-car. With some trepidation, he stepped into the vehicle. He sat for a moment familiarizing himself with the instruments: steam pressure, water level, boiler temperature, and velocity gauge. He nodded to himself, released the hand brake and pressed the accelerator. The vehicle slid smoothly into the street.

There was little traffic this early in the morning and for that he was grateful, he'd like a bit of practice handling the car before he faced busy traffic. He made a turn back the way he came, and drove slowly down the street heading back out of the downtown region. He was whistling again. He was back in his old domain—back on the hunt. This time he'd be stealing lives back from the Cathedral. That thought made all his other endeavors as a thief pale by comparison. He was almost ashamed of his past life. *Daisy*. He pushed the thought aside. He shook his head, began whistling again, pressing the accelerator to the floor. He was back.

~

"I can hear something," Kel said eagerly. "Do you hear it?"

Lyria strained her ears and she too heard the sound of an approaching vehicle.

"I see it. It must be Dan; it's slowing down and turning into the lane."

They watched as the automobile cruised slowly up to the front door. It stopped with a hiss, and then went silent. They saw Dan through the windscreen. He seemed to be adjusting something on the panel by the wheel that apparently was used to control the vehicle. The door opened, and Dan stepped out, a big smile on his face. He was whistling again as he opened the back door and removed a large trunk. It was heavy, so Kel came out to help him lift it into the house.

"What is in here?"

Kel felt the weight of the trunk straining his arms.

"Clothes," Dan said between clenched teeth.

They carried the trunk into the house, setting it on the floor of the living room. Dan grinned at his two friends and opened the trunk. He'd not been lying. It was filled to the top with clothes. They each began lifting out the clothes, stopping here and there for a moment, holding a garment up in front of themselves or each other. Another bundle held underwear and at the bottom were several pairs of shoes.

"I guessed at your shoe size," Dan said apologetically, "I got four pair for each of you in various sizes—hopefully there's something that'll fit you."

Lyria and Kel bundled up their clothing and retired to their bedrooms. Dan sat in a chair, glancing through the book that told of the war between the nations. He heard a door open and looked up. Kel was standing there, but he wouldn't have recognized him. As it happened, the suit fit him perfectly. The dark red silk vest stood out in contrast to the white shirt beneath it and the black tie made a nice accent for both.

"It took me a minute to figure out how to fasten the shoes," Kel grinned, "I never saw crisscrossing lacing done exactly like this on footwear."

"Well, I think you look very natural. If anyone were to look at you, you'd not get a second glance. Welcome to Los Angeles!"

Just then the other door opened and Lyria stepped out. She wasn't as happy as Kel and Dan. She was wearing a dark green dress that hung almost all the way to the ground. She had to lift it to walk. What kind of garment was this for a warrior? Suddenly Dan started laughing. She whirled toward him.

"What do you find so funny?"

She stood with her fists on her hips, a determined look on her face.

"It's the dagger, dear," Dan said with a grin. "It looks...out of place. Perhaps you should carry it strapped under your dress. You know, I had an extra opening put in the front of the dress just so you could access your knife quickly should the need arise."

Lyria looked down, groping at the skirt, and found the secret opening. With her dagger hung low on her left hip, it would be reachable. Still, it was no way for a warrior to dress.

"Humph," she snorted.

"I told her she wouldn't be happy with her new clothes," Dan said to Kel, and then he burst out laughing again.

"I suppose my hair will have to change too, won't it?" Lyria sounded defiant and Dan grinned.

"Actually, no, women wear their hair any way they like in the city, so long as they think it's attractive."

Kel smiled and said, "I think your hair is very attractive, Lyria."

"Well...alright then. When can we leave to meet these friends of yours?"

"Soon," Dan said. He looked at Kel and continued, "First, though, I want you to change into the priest's robes I brought you." Kel looked at him quizzically.

"Even though the religion of the Cathedral is losing favor in the city, they are still very powerful—people fear and respect the priests. Dressed as one, you'll be able to move about completely unmolested by any you may approach."

"What about me? Am I to pose as the priest's wife?"

Dan laughed, "Priests don't have wives, they have servants, prostitutes, and slaves."

"So I am to be a servant?"

"That would be the best choice of the three," Dan joked. "It's simple. You walk next to Kel with your eyes lowered; you must be submissive at all times. Remember the teaching of the Cathedral regarding the evilness of the Goddess and of all women by association."

"Where will I carry my daggers?"

"You'll be able to take one of them," Dan answered, "under your dress as we discussed."

Kel returned to his room and, a short time later, reappeared wearing the floor length black robes of a priest. He pulled at the tight collar.

"How is anyone to breathe with this thing so tightly grasping the throat?"

Lyria grinned wickedly, "Whiner."

Kel looked at her, a half smile on his face. "Whiner? I'm a whiner?"

She laughed, "I think you look nice in a dress, my dear." She looked behind him and said with a laugh, "Where's your handbag?"

Dan roared with laughter, and the other two joined in.

"We should be on our way," Dan said, glancing at his watch. "We don't want to keep the magician waiting."

"The magician?"

Kel and Lyria looked at each other as Dan opened the front door and motioned for them to exit.

Lyria got in first, and then Kel entered the car. They were looking around at the leather seats and wooden trim; it seemed an admirable work of craftsmanship. Dan worked the instruments, firing up the boiler once again. When the pressure was high enough, he released the brake, and with a hiss the vehicle began moving.

He spoke to Lyria first, "From now on, you must hold doors for Kel, not the other way around. Remember, you're a servant, not an equal."

"I will remember," she said.

"When we get there, I'll park the steam-car about a block away. You'll get out and walk up the street on the same side as I park the car. You'll see a tavern called the Green Hyena. Go in and sit at the table by the back wall that's in the center of the room. Set this on the table."

Dan handed Kel a large leather book. The clasp shone brightly of polished brass.

"With this he'll recognize you and come to your table. Don't rise or go anywhere until you speak to the magician."

"How will I know him?"

Dan grinned, looking up into the rear view mirror, "Oh, you'll know him!"

They drove on into the city. The buildings seemed to grow blacker as they grew taller. Kel surmised it was simply because less light penetrated to street level. *Imagine*, he thought, *living in narrow stone canyons built by your own hands and seemingly designed deliberately to block out the sun.*

As they approached the center of the city, traffic grew steadily heavier. Both Kel and Lyria were amazed at the profusion of steam-cars, delivery trucks, and what certainly must be the 'busses' Dan mentioned. Kel glanced up into the sky above them. The ice lights appeared close today. He watched the red and purple curtains of the Aurora flickering and weaving their cold magic in the sky. He shivered.

"It would be best if Kel went into the tavern alone," Dan said. "Lyria can wait with me. Inside the steam-car she'll be safe."

"I will not let him walk up there alone," she said with determination.

"Very well, you can walk him to the door but then you must return. Priests do not take servants to their entertainments."

"So shall it be," she said.

At long last, the steam-car slid to the curbing and stopped. Dan put on the brake while lowering the steam pressure. He turned, looking over the seat at his new friends.

"Lyria, just keep your head down," he warned. "Kel, you must walk head high—you are the master and better than anyone you may meet on the street. You should stay aloof if you wish people to think you a priest."

Kel nodded.

"Remember, if we become separated for any reason, come back here. I'll be waiting for you. If I had to move the steam-car for some reason, wait—I'll return shortly."

Now there was nothing left to do but walk to the Green Hyena and see what there was to see. Lyria stepped out of the vehicle, crossed to the sidewalk, and opened the door for Kel. Once the door was open, she stood back with her head lowered. Dan smiled. *She'd be fine*, he thought. Kel stepped out of the vehicle and immediately began walking away. Lyria had to shut the door and run a few steps to catch up with him. *That was a nice touch*, Dan thought. He watched them walk away from him and kept an eye on the street, always scanning for police or someone who might recognize him—or even potential marks eager to have their pockets picked. He grinned to himself—old habits die hard.

Chapter 33

The airship was now at six hundred feet. The 180-degree turn to bring the airship about carried it well south of the village. The engines were running at quarter speed for the moment as the zeppelin slowly gained altitude. Everyone inside was relaxed now. The strain of wondering what might happen had passed—everyone could breathe more easily. The pilot watched his heading carefully. With only a three-man crew, it would be easy for something to go wrong. He glanced over at the priest. Whatever he'd set out to do, he hoped the result would be worth the risk they were taking.

"So, how did things go?"

Father Woods glanced up from his reading, smiling, "We exceeded expectations, Commander!"

"That's excellent, Your Grace, we were worried that something may have gone wrong."

"Something almost did," Father Woods answered. "There was some trouble in the village, a woman was assaulted and almost killed. It could've ruined everything."

"Did they catch whoever did it?"

"I doubt it, they're all half wild at best and to my mind any of those warriors looked quite capable of attempting murder. Apparently, this woman is someone of importance to these tribes. It's well that she survived and will probably recover; we can use her allegiance."

"It's well they didn't think you had anything to do with it," the commander laughed.

"Actually, they didn't think I was involved, I was under guard all night. These half-humans are very cautious, except when dealing with their own kind. They felt whoever did the attack was one of theirs."

"Frankly, I'm surprised they didn't think we might have done it."

"Oh, you fellows were watched all night as well. Be glad you obeyed orders and didn't go wandering around; your heads might be on sharpened stakes by now."

~

Adria, from her hiding place in the large storage bin, was dismayed to hear that her attack on Pela hadn't resulted in the old woman's death. Well, she was hurt pretty badly; she'd felt the impact the wood branch bludgeon delivered to the hag's head all the way to her shoulder. She hit her good and hard—too bad she didn't have time to hit her several more times. Damn that dog! Oh well, she was away from them now—on her way to a new and exciting life. She could hardly wait to see the look on her beloved's face when he found out she was aboard the vessel.

She relaxed a bit, turning to find a more comfortable position. She needed to wait until they were so far from the village that they wouldn't consider returning her. Oh, she knew the priest wouldn't, but the other men might force him to do so. For all she knew, there might even be some law against having strangers on the zeppelin. No, she'd wait. Maybe she could get some sleep—that would be nice. Sleep didn't come as readily these days as it once had. It was probably the headaches that were doing it. She hadn't thought that transitioning into divinity, as she was now doing, would be painful—but however it worked was how it worked. She smiled. The Scorpion Queen was on her way.

~

"The rear port engine's heating up a bit," the engine master said to the pilot. "We should lower its RPMs for a while; I think if it cools off it'll be fine."

"I thought this airship had been checked out by the maintenance crew before we left," Father Woods said with annoyance. With such a small crew, something like this could be a disaster. He glared at the engine master.

"I'm sorry, Your Grace, it's one of the older engines. Things like this happen sometimes."

"Not on airships that I fly on."

"Yes, Your Grace, it's only a minor inconvenience. It'll slow us a little, but with a bit more rudder we'll stay on course, and we'll be home only about twenty minutes later than scheduled."

"See that this is so."

The priest turned his gaze away from the engine master. Nothing like putting a little scare into the help once in a while to keep them sharp. He turned his attention back to his notes. He went down each point he'd wanted to make, checking it against his other list of what he felt he'd accomplished. He smiled; he'd probably saved both the Cathedral and the Black City a lot of expense and time by forestalling an attack by the half-humans. All this mess regarding the kidnapped shamans—he sighed, hoping it was worth the effort.

"We're now at eight hundred feet, Commander," said the first mate, Barney. "Do you want to maintain that as our ceiling?"

The commander glanced over at the priest. He was fast asleep in his chair. Good, that would make the flight home that much easier.

"Yes, Barney, I think eight hundred feet will do nicely. We've no need of altitude, and the engines seem to work better at lower altitudes."

"True. By the way, that engine's cooling nicely. I talked with Jim a minute ago and he thought we could bring it back up to speed in maybe ten minutes."

"Give it fifteen; then try it," the commander said with a smile. "No point in taking any more chances than needed—if you know what I mean."

Barney smiled at the commander. He liked being assigned to this flight crew; everyone seemed to work together smoothly and efficiently. That was especially important when a priest insisted on flying cross-country with a crew of three.

~

Adria was thinking and planning. She hadn't really figured out how she'd make her presence known once she was aboard the flying machine. They hadn't mentioned the four shamans she'd killed; that was a good thing. It seemed that she wasn't connected with the assault on Pela—that old hag. Why didn't she just die like she was supposed to? It was aggravating, as the Scorpion Queen, should she not be getting her wishes? She paused. Maybe she didn't have her full powers yet? That could be. If only Floweht had lived. Well, so far she'd gotten almost everything she wanted. True, the old lady wasn't dead, but she was on her way to an exciting life as the spouse of a very powerful and wealthy man. Perhaps with the help of that wonderful Father Woods, she'd finally attain the Godhead she so richly deserved.

~

"By the Redeemed God!"

Father Woods, startled, looked up and asked, "What's wrong?"

The first mate was standing by the locker that held the winter clothing, staring into it in disbelief. He was speechless.

"What's going on?"

The pilot's command voice cut the silence.

"We have ourselves a stowaway!"

Father Woods leapt to his feet, hurrying to the storage room. A stowaway? This could complicate things. What if the people of the village thought he'd kidnapped someone? His anger was seething now. The pilot called for the engine master to man the wheel for a moment as he hurried to the rear portion of the gondola. A stowaway?

Father Woods reached the first mate before the commander. He looked into the locker in amazement. There was a young and rather pretty—for a half-human—girl lying among the winter gear.

"Who are you and why are you on my airship?"

The commander finally arrived and he too was furious.

Adria looked up at the three men. This wasn't what she'd been planning, but she'd better make the best of it.

"I...I..." she stammered, fumbling around in the material and fur of the crew's parkas. "I have important news for you."

She stared directly at Father Woods.

"Don't just stand there, man, help her out," the commander shouted. The first mate jumped at the command from the pilot, reaching into the trunk to help Adria climb out. She noticed both he and her betrothed were looking at her legs. That was good, she praised herself—her last-minute decision to not wear her trousers had been wise. The one called 'first mate' lifted her from the trunk, setting her on her feet. He stepped back, allowing the commander to face the girl. "Well, speak up, woman, didn't you hear my question," he shouted. "What're you doing aboard my zeppelin?"

"Now take it easy for a moment," Father Woods said. "She must have a very important reason for being here. Don't you think in all fairness we should hear what she has to say?"

"Very well," the commander conceded, "I have an airship to run in any event."

Without further comment, the commander returned to his station at the wheel.

"Come over here, young one," the priest urged. "Sit. Tell me what's so important that you risked sneaking aboard this vessel."

He lowered his voice to a conspiratorial whisper, "You know, if I hadn't been here, the crew would probably have used you and then thrown you overboard. You took a big risk. Why?"

Adria quickly formed her thoughts. Father Woods was being kind to her. Winning his affections should not be hard for someone as beautiful and powerful as she.

"There are several things I have to say, but first would you answer a question?"

"If I can," Father Woods said.

"What is a Bishop?"

Father Woods laughed out loud at that.

The commander and the first mate glanced over; then turned back to their duties. They knew better than to interfere in Cathedral business.

"Bishop is the title of the head man in our Order. It's rather like a tribal chieftain, you could say."

"I see, then it is to him I will need to speak."

Father Woods stared at the young girl. He thought she was pretty enough. Still, she showed a distinct lack of respect and subservience to her male betters. Well, that could be changed with time.

"The Bishop is a very busy man, you know. When we arrive, I'll have to make a report. Can you tell me anything that I can include in my report that would make him want to take the time to see you?"

"I think he will want to see me."

Father Woods spread his hands in a supplicating gesture saying, "But surely you can give me something I may take to him?"

Adria thought for a moment and then said, "I know of a plot to maybe murder him. I know who the assassins are and I know what they look like."

Father Woods was taken aback. Assassins? Could the half-humans even plan for something that complex? Surely it must be that they've no inkling as to how hard it would be to get near enough to harm His Eminence. He took a long, hard look at the young woman. She seemed determined and she acted like she truly knew something. He decided to play along, just in case.

"Very well," he said, smiling, "I'll urge the Bishop to see you when we arrive."

"Thank you. I am sure he will want to know what I know."

"You seem very knowledgeable about things for a young person."

"Oh, I have ways of finding out things," she responded with a knowing smile.

"Very well, if this subject is not to be discussed for now, then tell me why you hid. Surely if you'd come to me, I would've listened."

"I was afraid of the people in my village. They do not like me."

"Why is that? You seem a beautiful and charming young woman."

Adria, incapable of blushing, answered, "Thank you. You are very kind."

"So tell me why your people don't like you," Father Woods asked, thinking it would make an interesting story. The flight back was going to be boring anyway, after his performance for those tribal creatures.

So Adria told him tales of her persecution at the hands of Garn, the kidnapped shaman. She explained that there were several women who wanted the title of tribal healer. These other women were jealous of Pela and of her close and loving relationship with Adria. With her husband Garn kidnapped, Pela had nobody to turn to except her good friend. She explained how these other women tried to gain control of the tribe by trying shamanic journeying on their own without sufficient training and had gotten into trouble. She told him how kind, loving Pela came to their aid and how, as a sign of their gratitude, they attacked her while she slept—attempting to murder her with a cut tree limb. Why, they even went so far as to implicate her. She had to flee for her life, and the zeppelin and Father Woods was the only refuge of safety she could find. If she went back, she'd be immediately killed—both for supposedly attacking Pela and for finding out about the plot to kill the Bishop.

Father Woods smiled at her. He caught her reference to the cut branch that'd been the weapon, and knew nobody aboard the zeppelin knew of it. In fact, he didn't know the nature of the assault himself until this half-human clearly implicated herself in the crime—care must be taken with this one. Perhaps she herself was intending to kill the Bishop. Well, they had a little time yet, perhaps he could find out a bit more before they arrived at the Cathedral.

"I apologize," the priest said suddenly, "have you eaten? You look hungry."

Adria smiled at him, he was so very kind.

"Actually, I am a little hungry."

"Well, let's see what we can do about that, come with me."

Chapter 34

She followed him into the next compartment behind the storage area. This was the galley, and although there was no cook on this mission, there was food and drink. She sat at the small table as Father Woods brought her a glass of water and a prepared sandwich of roast beef with lettuce. She devoured the sandwich quickly, drank the water, and smiled again at the priest.

"Thank you so much," she said. "You are very kind."

The priest smiled back. What foul eating habits these half-humans had; it was almost enough to make one throw up.

The priest guided her past the chart room into the pilothouse. She walked to the starboard windows, looked out, and took a quick step back. She was pale.

"H...how high are we?"

Father Woods glanced at the commander, who had been watching this little scene with amusement.

"We're currently cruising at eight hundred feet with a ground speed of about twenty-eight knots."

Adria didn't know how fast that was exactly, but she was impressed nevertheless. She had never dreamed of moving this fast, much less through the air. She walked carefully back to the window, looking for the first time in her life at the tops of the trees. She thought of Kel. She knew that his hawk totem allowed him to see like this any time he wished. Well, she was seeing it for real. A small stream flashed past, then they were climbing again. She felt the airship rising, but the ground stayed the same distance away. She asked the priest how that could be. He explained that they were climbing over a ridge and would soon be on the other side.

Once they were over the ridge, she could see smoke rising from a dozen or more spots. Father Woods explained that she was seeing the cooking smoke from a very large village and that it was the last of the tribal outposts before the Black City. Adria stared in fascination. She never dreamed that the airship her betrothed owned could travel this fast or this high. He'd be a fitting husband for the Scorpion Queen.

"I think there are travelers ahead," the first mate announced.

Father Woods walked to the forward telescope in the flight control cabin. He looked out ahead of the airship. He saw nothing.

"Tell me what you saw?" he asked.

"I saw what looked like three people on horses, leading a fourth horse that was pulling a cart. It was very far ahead and the mirage is strong today."

Father Woods looked again. The ripples of ground mirage distorted his vision through the telescope—he saw nothing.

"Well, if someone's there, they're under the trees, it's no concern of ours."

"Just thought you might like to know, Your Grace," the first mate said.

"Thank you, I want to know of anything unusual on this flight."

"Yes, sir," the first mate answered.

The zeppelin passed over the grove of trees, continuing on its way. Adria was engrossed with the port telescope, studying the ground intently. The first mate and the priest walked up to where the commander stood at the wheel.

"What should we do with her?" The commander's whispered question was on everyone's mind at the moment.

"Well, if it were up to me, I'd toss her out the window," the first mate sneered.

"Now, Barney," the commander chided, "she might truly have some information that's vital to the Bishop. No, we will not throw her out the window, we'll remand her to the custody of Father Woods." He smiled innocently at the priest.

If his intention had been to upset the priest, he failed dismally. Taking control of the half-human was the priest's priority, at least for the moment. If he could find out what she knew, they wouldn't have to bother taking her back to Los Angeles. However, she could be of use even if her information proved to be lacking in merit. He glanced over his shoulder, watching how Adria's bottom moved beneath the short-fringed hem of her shirt. He wondered if half-human creatures such as this one even knew what underwear was. He snickered, the other two men looked at him.

"I'll gladly take control of the thing," Father Woods stated flatly. "What she may know is potentially too important to pass over."

That ended the conversation as far as the commander was concerned, at least the girl was no longer his responsibility. Getting the zeppelin back to the Cathedral would be responsibility enough. The first mate walked back to his station as the priest moved farther back, standing next to Adria.

"It's quite an amazing view, is it not?"

Adria jumped in surprise, quickly standing up, accidentally pressing her back and shoulder against Father Woods. She lingered there, just for a second—his body was firm. She stepped away, smiling.

"I'm sorry to have bumped you."

"It's all right," he responded, "I startled you and for that I should be sorry—but for some reason I'm not."

They both laughed at his little joke.

"How long will it be before we arrive?"

"Well, I'm not the commander, but my guess from other flights would be that we'll be back at the Cathedral the day after tomorrow."

"I am so excited to see your home," she gushed. "I bet it is really beautiful!

"Oh, it is that, our building is about as large as much of your entire village."

Adria gasped, "Can any building be so big?"

Father Woods spread his hands, indicating the airship, and asked, "Did you believe anything of this size could fly?"

"Truly, no. You must be a very powerful and rich man to afford such a device as this."

Father Woods paused a moment, thinking. Actually, it wasn't surprising that someone with such a simple mind might believe him the owner. He decided it would help if he allowed her to believe he owned the vessel.

"It was very expensive," he said, leading her on. "Why, just the white paint on the outside cost four large silver coins."

Adria had no idea what silver coins were worth, but obviously they were worth a great deal—and her betrothed parted with four of them just to make his airship white. She was certain she made the right decision to leave the tribe forever and seek her fame and Godhead elsewhere.

The day passed quickly for Adria, engrossed as she was with the telescope. She never realized that shaped glass could make you see things far away as though they were close. This was true magic. As night fell, the zeppelin continued relentlessly toward the rapidly darkening west.

"Will we land for the night?"

"No, we'll fly through the night. Ordinarily there's a larger crew for such a ship, but I was afraid so many people might scare the members of your tribe, especially with what has happened with zeppelins in the past."

"I suppose we really can't hit anything," she mused. "Maybe just a bird, and I expect those things are too small to harm us."

The priest gave a start, saying, "What things?"

Adria laughed, pointing out the starboard window. Father Woods' gaze followed her finger to the tiny points of light headed in their direction.

"Commander! Look to starboard and tell me what you see."

The airship pilot looked out into the falling night. He squinted and looked again saying, "They appear to be fireflies, Your Grace."

"They're very bright for fireflies," the priest commented.

"Aye, they are," stated the commander, "what else could they be?"

Now it was Adria's turn to comment, "Can fireflies go this high?"

That gave the commander and the priest something to think about. They'd never before seen fireflies from an airship in flight. The commander shrugged, looking at the priest. Neither man had an answer.

Everyone watched as the small, brilliant points of light suddenly dove, falling quickly until they passed under the zeppelin, still heading relentlessly south.

"How many do you make?"

The commander looked again, this time to port. He paused as he estimated the number of sparks of light, then said, "I'd say somewhere in the vicinity of forty."

"That's what I believe as well," the priest agreed. "Look at how straight they're flying—only the slightest variation."

"I never saw fireflies fly that way," Adria commented soberly. "They flit around, they fly in circles, and frequently land."

The commander watched them until they were out of sight and said, "Well, whatever they are, they're harmless."

The priest stared thoughtfully out into the now black sky, turning when he heard Adria's yawn. The priest folded down a cot from the wall, securing it in the lowered position, gesturing for Adria to lie down.

"Tomorrow will be a very busy day and you look tired. At least now you have a real bed to sleep on."

Adria lay on the bed and Father Woods put a light blanket over her, watching how her breasts moved beneath the clothing she wore. She noticed that as well and was pleased. Her body interested him; it was good her betrothed found her desirable. She closed her eyes and slept dreamlessly for a long time.

As they continued on their flight, Adria spent much of her time looking through the various telescopes, crying out in delight when some new land feature came into view. The priest engaged her repeatedly in conversation, but she remained steadfast in her silence about the plot against the Bishop. It was frustrating, but not unexpected. Though she'd been greeted in a friendly manner, she was still a stranger surrounded by men she didn't know way up in the sky. He guessed her silence about the plot was more a way to protect her life than an attempt to annoy. That was fine. In the morning they'd be landing and then they'd get to the bottom of things one way or another. Assassinating the Bishop? The idea seemed far-fetched, but with the recent kidnappings and all, he thought the attempt posed a real possibility. Carrying it out, considering the number of priests and soldiers surrounding the Bishop, would be another matter altogether. He sighed, stretching before he reclined on a cot across the gondola from Adria. He didn't want to seem too eager to get at her. There would be plenty of time for that later. He smiled to himself, slowly relaxing into slumber.

By noon, the airship was in sight of the Black City. Adria was beside herself, imagining the clothes and jewelry her betrothed would shower upon her once they were settled. She watched the city approaching through one of the telescopes. The priest and crew left her alone, as they were busy. It was nearly two o'clock in the afternoon when the zeppelin was at last over the field. Everyone was glad they made it home in one piece. Imagine the stories they could tell—they'd run a ship with three men. It was unthinkable, but true.

As their airspeed diminished, the control surfaces were used to lose altitude as they drifted toward the ground. They briefly ran the engines in reverse to halt the airship's forward motion. Now it hung virtually motionless in the sky about fifty feet from the ground. Adria hadn't said a word through the whole process. The commander was glad of that; the last thing he needed right now was a bunch of questions from a creature that was incapable of understanding the answers. He glanced at Adria in disgust.

At twenty feet, the mooring lines were lowered to the waiting ground crew. Eight men moved efficiently and quickly to attach the lines to the windlasses that would bring the zeppelin the rest of the way to earth. The tractor was already in position on the ground and it was a simple matter to bring her down into the cradle, securing her for the haul back to the zeppelin barn.

Chapter 35

As the ship finally came to rest, a wheeled stairway was pushed up to the door and the crew and passengers descended. The ground crew stared at Adria, not knowing what to make of the pretty young girl in the odd apparel of the tribes. Still, it was none of their business and they knew it. They kept their comments and supposition for discussion later in the dining hall. The priest was right behind the girl and the commander, as was traditional, was the last man to leave the great airship. There were two steam-cars waiting.

One of the cars was for the crew; they were quickly borne away toward the zeppelin barn and the barracks next to it. The priest walked with Adria toward the second car. He watched her closely as the driver opened the door to the back seat. Adria was about to climb in, when the driver, putting his hand on her shoulder said, "His Grace always enters first."

Father Woods put a gentle hand on the driver's shoulder.

"Let things be this time."

The driver nodded, "As you wish, Your Grace."

The priest followed the girl into the vehicle and the driver shut the door. In a minute the steam pressure was up and, with a slight hiss, the vehicle started on its way toward the Cathedral.

They arrived a few minutes later. The driver lowered the pressure, opening the door for Father Woods and his odd guest. This time he made no comment. The priest smiled at him as the two walked away without a word. The driver watched them go. *Strange days have found us*, he thought, *priests and female half-humans going into the Cathedral together*. He shook his head in disbelief. What was the world coming to?

Father Woods opened the door at the side of the Cathedral allowing Adria to enter. It galled him to allow any female to precede him into any room, and this was the holiest building in the entire region. Well, soon things would be explained, and then the situation would change. He smiled to himself at the thought.

The priest led the girl up several flights of stone steps. She was so awed by the size of the building she said nothing all the way up to the Bishop's rooms. A soldier happened to be passing and the priest jerked his head in a 'come here' gesture. The soldier walked over to him. Father Woods turned to the girl.

"You must wait here. Remember me saying that I had to make my report first and then he'd see you?"

She smiled, "Yes, I remember."

"This man will stand with you to make sure nobody bothers you while I'm inside, okay?"

"Yes."

The priest turned, knocking on the door. Harold answered almost immediately, allowing the priest inside. He cast a very quick glance at the girl, but befitting his position, he said nothing.

While Father Woods stood outside the office, the Bishop's servant announced his presence. He was quickly admitted. Before he even had time to kneel, the Bishop was in front of him with his hand on his shoulder.

"So tell me of your journey, Father Woods, was our mission successful?"

"That and more, Your Eminence!"

"Well, don't just stand there, tell me."

The Bishop was beaming. His plan implemented by Father Woods had worked. The Bishop motioned the priest to the sofa by his desk. After he was sitting, he began his tale. There was a short interruption while Harold served them some warmed wine. Father Woods drank some with gratitude and continued with his story. The Bishop frowned when the priest got to the part explaining Adria's presence outside and her claims of an assassination attempt.

"Do you think she speaks truthfully?"

"I suspect she believes so, anyway. I can think of no reason a half-human would come anywhere near a zeppelin, especially with the reputation that surrounds them these days."

The Bishop laughed and agreed.

"Well, let's see the creature and find out what it has to say."

The priest nodded, rose, and left. Harold was told to leave the door to the Bishop's room open. He nodded and left to attend to other business.

"The Bishop said he'll see you now, but he's asked me to search you. He fears you may be the assassin."

Adria didn't hesitate, "I understand, being careful about this makes sense even to me."

The priest walked up to her, asking her to turn away from him. She was now facing the soldier. The search began relatively routinely, but

Father Woods' exploring hands lingered on her breasts, feeling them beneath her clothes. The guard was grinning as the priest pressed himself against the girl. Adria didn't like the guard watching, but perhaps it was the way of the very rich and powerful—she didn't know. The other part was nice though. Father Woods ended the search by asking her to spread her legs. He probed deeply with his fingers. The guard licked his lips, watching intently. Then the priest was finished. She knew he'd enjoyed it, and she was happy. Her spouse liked touching her. That was how things should be, wasn't it?

She smiled at him as he led her into the Bishop's chambers. Inside she finally got to see the man called 'Bishop.' She smiled at him, but his face remained stony. He gestured to a chair—she sat facing him behind his desk.

"Father Woods has told of your story of a plot to kill me, I'd like to hear the whole story in your own words."

She glanced at Father Woods and he smiled at her, nodding encouragement. Then she began the story she had worked out on the trip to the city.

"The story began when a girl from another tribe was allowed to replace me in the shaman training I was undergoing. This other girl slept with the old man to gain his favor. Once I was ousted from my training, I began training on my own, discovering the secret of the scorpions."

She looked eagerly at the Bishop, "I told the old man I'd gained mastery of scorpion magic but he wasn't interested. The other girl was keeping his bed too warm for any changes to be made. I demonstrated the scorpion magic I'd learned to members of my tribe—how it allowed me to read people's minds, and how the voices I heard crowded even my own thoughts on occasion.

"In jealousy, the wife of the shaman, a stupid old hag who didn't even realize her husband was 'mating' with the young shaman in training, decided that I was too powerful for her husband to control. The old lady had powers of her own and she deliberately used scorpions to kill my parents so she could blame me—she always claimed to be the Scorpion Queen." Adria sobbed at this part of the story, it seemed the proper thing to do.

"But the tribe didn't realize the full extent of the power of my magic. I read the thoughts of the tribe when Father Woods arrived. I found out that four shaman were going to try to kill him. I was able to sneak up on the shamans and I killed them all to protect the priest, after I'd heard them discussing the people they'd sent to kill the Bishop. I got aboard the airship so I could come and warn you—and here I am."

She looked at the Bishop, hoping she looked very sincere as she said, "The killers are people I know from the tribe and I can identify them—their names are Kel and Lyria."

She described them in detail, down to the wagon and the names of their horses. *What a great story*, she thought to herself, *the Scorpion Queen at her best*.

The Bishop stared at her a moment, then asked Father Woods to escort her out. Again, Adria had to wait with the guard who had watched Father Woods making love to her. Well, maybe this was some kind of loyalty test—something like the shadow walk a shaman had to take. She knew she'd pass the test. She smiled at the guard and sat on a chair that had been brought for her. When she sat, the fringed hem of her garment rode up on her thighs. She didn't even cross her legs. If this was a test, she'd test the guard as well and see who had more power. She opened her legs slightly.

"So, what do you think, Your Eminence?"

"I think there's something seriously wrong with the girl, if you want my honest opinion. Did she really kill four shamans?"

"I've no idea. There was an old woman who was the wife of a shaman we took earlier who'd been attacked though."

"Hmmm," the Bishop said, stroking his chin, "I think we should be careful, nevertheless. Her detailed description of the supposed killers sounds very…uncrazy. Yet this Scorpion Queen stuff…"

When the Bishop trailed off, the priest spoke.

"I agree with the caution. You should have guards outside your residence and with you whenever you leave your rooms—we dare not be too careful, Your Eminence. You're the heart and soul of the Cathedral."

The Bishop smiled, asking, "Do you think she has any further information?"

"I doubt it, and I noticed her story's changed the second time it was told."

The priest laughed, adding, "When she was on the airship, she said she was good friends with the old lady, and today her story is just the opposite. Clearly, she's lying. And I'm wondering which story, if either, is true.

"I think we should alert our spies and, as you know, in a few days she'll be out on the streets. I'm sure I can convince her to keep an eye and an ear open for those supposed killers, if they exist. I even have a plan to win her over while taking her over."

The Bishop smiled and said, "Do what you will, she'll never be more than half-human, and female at that. Use her as you see fit, she was good looking though," he said with a thoughtful smile. "I might use her myself."

They both had a good laugh.

"I'll begin her training immediately, she trusts me. I think the creature believes I love her."

"Use that to your advantage, Father Woods."

"Oh I plan to," he smiled as he rose to leave. "I plan to."

The priest escorted Adria down the original flights of steps, then down one more. He held a door for her, smiling as she walked into the room. The room was sparsely furnished with just a bed, a small table, and several chairs. He closed the door behind him, motioning her to a chair near the table.

"Before you can go out into the city and mingle with its people, there are some things you'll need to learn."

"Yes," she answered enthusiastically, "I want to fit in and learn."

"Excellent, I'll tell you a few things, and I want you to think carefully before you answer."

"Yes," she said again.

"From now on, you must refer to the Bishop as 'Your Eminence,' even I'm required to use that title in his presence. Do you understand?"

"Yes, the Bishop is to be spoken to as 'Your Eminence.'"

The priest smiled broadly at her, saying, "The rules of titles also require you to refer to me and other priests as 'Your Grace.' This is considered good manners."

"I will remember, Your Grace!" She beamed at him, she was proud of herself for responding so quickly.

"Very good, but you must use these terms at all times."

"I will remember."

"One other thing, when you're out of your room, or when someone else is in here, you must keep your eyes lowered. Here it's good manners for a woman to not look directly at a man, do you understand?"

"Yes, but…"

"There can be no buts, child, the traditions are firmly established and thousands of years old and must be obeyed."

"I will do my best to remember, Your Grace."

"Some food will be brought up for you. There'll be a guard at your door and he'll make sure you're not disturbed this night."

"Thank you," she responded.

He smiled at her again; then rose to leave. At the door he paused, turned and said, "Tomorrow your real education will begin. You'll have several teachers and they might not understand your unfamiliarity with the rules."

"I understand. I will not disappoint you."

"I'm sure you will not," he said grinning.

The priest turned and left—closing the door behind him. Adria sat on the bed, testing its feel. It wasn't too uncomfortable and besides, she wouldn't be here long. Once she understood the rules, she knew she'd be allowed to marry her betrothed and live with him somewhere else in this great house. She thought about the guard outside. She was happy. Just think of it. Her very own guards were protecting her; clearly her betrothed was recognizing her closeness to Godhead.

Chapter 36

An hour later, the door opened and a man walked in. Adria quickly lowered her eyes, remembering her instructions. The man, obviously a servant, set a covered tray on the table. He took off the cover, pouring some of the water from the pitcher into a lightweight metal cup. Wordlessly, he turned, leaving her alone again with only her thoughts for company. She tried the food. The taste was strange and different from what she'd eaten back home. No, she needed to stop thinking of that horrible place as home—this was her home now.

She finished her meal and drank a glass of water. She thought about pouring another, but she was suddenly overcome with tiredness. *That wasn't surprising*, she thought, *she'd had a very busy day.* She stretched out on the bed, planning on getting under the blanket but sleep engulfed her and she slipped into a completely dreamless slumber.

"Get up, wench."

The gruff voice startled Adria and she slowly awakened. She had a mild headache and was a bit lethargic, but she rose quickly enough.

"You slept in your clothes."

"I am sorry. I was suddenly so tired…"

The man's voice boomed in anger, shouting, "What did you say?"

Adria started, glancing up quickly at the man. Her look was met with a slap across her face.

"You do not raise either eyes or voice to me, woman. Do you understand?"

Adria was confused; her face stung from the blow. Feeling tears in her eyes from the slap, she stammered, "I'm sorry, I forgot."

Another slap was delivered to the other side of her face.

"What else have you forgotten?"

"Oh, oh," she stammered, then remembered and answered, "I have forgotten to call you by your title of Your Eminence!"

Her head jerked in the other direction as yet a third slap was delivered—though this one was not so hard.

"I…I mean Your Grace."

Adria knew the man was smiling when he congratulated her on how quickly she responded. She was confused. Did he hate her? Did he like her? Why was she being slapped for such small things? Her face stung and she knew her cheeks would be bright red if she had a mirror to look into.

"Your breakfast will be brought up shortly."

"Thank you, Your Grace."

"Very good. Now listen carefully. Father Woods is your primary teacher; he'll be up here after you eat. Remember to show proper respect, woman. He may not deal with infractions as severely as I have, but this is what you must expect if you don't fall into line and obey in all things."

"I will remember, Your Grace," she said, still confused.

The priest with no name turned, leaving the room with no further comment. Adria rubbed her cheeks; they were still burning from the slaps. She didn't know why he had to hit her so hard. He could have been gentler.

Her thoughts were interrupted when the door opened and the servant who'd brought her dinner returned with her breakfast. She looked at him, smiling. His response surprised her.

"Do not look at me, female. You've no right to gaze upon me. Servant though I am, I'm still a man, you'll treat me with the same respect as you must all men."

Adria quickly lowered her eyes. This Cathedral and city was a lot harder to get used to than she thought it would be. Still, she'd better make the best of it. Surely her betrothed would let her out of here once she'd learned the rules. How many could there be, after all? She quietly ate her breakfast. The water with her meal this morning didn't taste quite like it had the night before. She brushed the thought away; last night she was tired. Even the Scorpion Queen had a right to get tired.

After she'd eaten, the servant returned to take the tray. Adria made sure she didn't look at him. She was proud of herself—learning so quickly.

She heard the door open but she didn't look up. The familiar voice of Father Woods was reassuring. She knew at least that he wouldn't strike her.

"Look at me, child."

Adria almost raised her head, and then froze, her chin barely up from her chest. The priest laughed and said, "You do learn fast, do you not?"

"I am trying, Your Grace."

Father Woods clapped his hands several times in glee.

"Now I really do want you to look at me."

Timidly, she raised her eyes. The priest was smiling at her. She smiled back.

"There aren't many who do things the way I do, young one. What you do in my presence you must not do with the others. You may look at me when I tell you to and at no other time, do you understand?"

"Yes, Your Grace."

"We must be very careful, you and I. Others must never find out that I treat you differently than they do; they must never know that I don't hit you, as an example."

"I am grateful for that, Your Grace, and I will not say anything to anyone."

"Make sure of that because if the Bishop hears, he'll remove me from your training and probably send me far to the south away from here."

Adria felt the rise of panic—she and her spouse separated? That would be intolerable. She'd endure anything to keep that from happening.

"Today you will begin your physical training," Father Woods stated, interrupting her thoughts, "It'll be important that you do whatever the priests tell you to do."

"I will, Your Grace."

"That would be well," he answered in a kindly voice.

"What kind of training, if I may ask, Your Grace?"

"Women of the city are expected to be very open sexually—do you know what I mean?"

"I am not sure, Your Grace."

"Today you'll be taken by five of the priests here in the Cathedral and you must submit to any and all requests, do you understand?"

"Taken?"

"They're all going to have sex with you, one after the other. Tomorrow it'll be seven priests and the day after ten. You'll become used to it; you'll welcome it. Do you understand?"

"I…I think so, Your Grace," she stammered. "Will you be one of…the ones?"

"No, today I have other duties. I'm finding something very special for you, and if you do well today and the next three days, I'll have a surprise for you."

The door to the room opened and two guards entered. They approached the girl—she continued to look down, not knowing what to do next.

"Go with the guards. Follow the priests' instructions in everything you do today."

"Yes, Your Grace."

The guards lifted Adria to her feet, escorting her through the door of her room. They allowed her to walk between them. They were snickering for some reason she couldn't imagine. They walked her down a stone corridor to another doorway. One of the men pushed the door open, and she followed them inside. There were five men in black robes waiting— the priests. In the center of the room was a low circular platform. The guards led her to the platform; then left the room without a word.

"Dance for us," one of the priests said, "show us one of your tribal dances."

The others laughed.

"Well, get up on the platform and dance for us. Oh, while you're in here, you may look at us."

Adria didn't move.

"I said, look at us," the priest said in a threatening voice.

She raised her head, looking at each in turn. The one on the left licked his lips.

"Get up on the platform and dance."

Adria did as she was told. She hadn't participated in many of the ritual dances since that woman had come to the tribe, but she remembered some of what she'd learned. And so she danced. And then the priests moved closer to the platform—some sitting on the floor so they could look up at her. She knew what they were doing, she'd only worn the top part of her garment to attract her spouse, and it seemed to be attracting these men also. She didn't know if she liked that. She danced for a while and was told to do it again, but with her clothes off. Her betrothed had told her that this was an essential part of her training for city life. One of the priests got up on the platform with her. He clutched at her—feeling and probing. He forced her to the platform, removed his robe and then her real education began.

The priests were merciless. They demanded things of her she'd never imagined. They hurt her, but they didn't seem to care. One after the other, all five had their varied ways with her. While she lay under them, listening to their animalistic grunting and gasping, she looked up at the ceiling. There was an image painted there. She stared at it, trying to figure out what it represented. In the painting, a man stood with his arms lifted over his head. His head was slightly tilted back in ecstasy, a smile on his face. At his feet was a woman. She was tightly bound with what looked like a rolled piece of fabric tied tightly over her face. It was so tight it had forced its way into her mouth. The male figure gloated over the supine female. She stared at the painting throughout her ordeal; it seemed to make the pain more distant.

Afterward, the guards returned to escort her back to her room. She was very tired and sore. She sat carefully on her bed. She thought back to her time with Floweht; he'd been gentle in his lovemaking compared to these priests. He'd never demanded that she do those other kinds of things—things that hurt. She lay back on her bed. She figured if this is how women of the city behave, she'd better learn and learn well. Her betrothed told her she'd have seven men tomorrow. She decided that if this was the way things were, she'd take the lead—maybe she could teach them something. She sighed, the thought was nice, but the things she'd done today she'd never imagined. What would they require tomorrow?

The servant entered with her tray of food. She remembered to diligently keep her head lowered. He set the tray on the table and turned.

At the door, he paused and said, "After you eat, Father Woods will come to see you."

She smiled at the thought. Her spouse was coming to check up on her because he was concerned for her well being. Maybe it would all be worth it in the end once her training was finished and she was with the priest permanently. She thought about doing the things she learned of today with him. Though some of those things seemed grotesque to her, he might like it. Well, once they were alone, she'd certainly find out.

After the servant removed her tray, Father Woods entered her room.

"Hello, Your Grace," she said meekly, trying to please the priest.

"How are you feeling?" The priest deliberately put concern into the question; he had a pretty good idea how she was feeling and he didn't care.

"I am sore, Your Grace," she said quietly, "in places I have never been sore."

"It'll pass with practice," he said, not unkindly. "No one will bother you the rest of the day, get some sleep."

"I think I will, Your Grace."

The priest handed her a glass of water. She drank it down, vaguely noticing the same taste she had the night before.

"In the morning, we'll have some new clothes for you," Father Woods said as he rose, walking to the second door in Adria's room. She'd tried the door and found it locked. Now the priest unlocked it. He motioned for her to enter. She did as he wished. This was a bathing room, that much she knew. He showed her how the spigots worked, much to her delight.

"Bathe yourself, it'll relieve some of the pain. Then sleep."

He left her then. She tried the spigots several times, laughing. She filled the tub with hot water, removed her shirt and stepped into the tub. The bath felt wonderful—like she was washing away the groping hands, licking tongues, and other violations. She smiled, relaxing in the tub for almost an hour. Then she got out, drying herself. She took another drink of water; it seemed to make her drowsy, though she knew not why.

Chapter 37

There was a knock on the door. The Bishop glanced at the clock; it was seven in the evening. He heard his servant answer the door and admit Father Woods. He sat at his desk, anxious for a report. Had the beastling said anything more of a murder attempt? Father Woods entered, kneeling before the Bishop.

"Rise, Father Woods, what have you to report?"

"The girl is sore," he said with mock seriousness.

The Bishop laughed, "That's good for a half-human, is it not?"

The priest snickered, "I believe it is, Your Eminence, pain brings submission."

"Has she said any more to you of this supposed assassination attempt?"

"Nothing, Your Eminence, but I'll try to find out more tomorrow."

"When she is less sore," the Bishop said in mock sympathy.

"Then I'd better be there early," the priest said with a laugh.

"Find out what you can; I can't help but think this is all a ruse, though."

"I was thinking that as well, Your Eminence. Perhaps if she was the person who assaulted the shaman's wife, she was simply attempting to escape."

"Well, from the look of her, and from the feel of her, she ran to the right place."

They laughed again.

"So, tell me of your plan to win her over, as you put it last time we spoke."

"I'm thinking we can use this Scorpion Queen nonsense to our benefit."

The Bishop was interested and asked, "How so?"

"As you know, tomorrow she begins her injections of opiates."

"That's good. Once she's on the street, we want her coming back to us for the next one…and the next."

The priest laughed, "Once we've shown her around the places she'll be working, I thought I would add something to her injections."

"What might that be?"

"I've convinced her that I think she's something special. You already heard how she thinks she loves me."

"Yes," the Bishop laughed, "I remember that little joke!"

"Well, my plan is really quite simple. I'll tell her that I have secretly stolen something from the Cathedral that'll make her see which of her customers are divine. I'll tell her that when she fucks these godlings, she'll absorb some of their divinity into herself when they climax. I'll tell her this only works with someone already half divine—like a Scorpion Queen, for instance."

He snickered and continued, "I'll then include mescaline in her injections. The men who pay for her will seem to glow. She'll be told this means they're divine entities, and she'll work very hard to please them. I'm telling you, Your Eminence, we can make a fortune selling this one. None of the other whores we have under our control will be so lively and enthusiastic in their couplings. I want to charge a double fee for her when the time comes. I believe her customers will pay it once they see how she goes at it."

The Bishop clapped his hands with glee, "Father Woods, your ingenuity never ceases to amaze me."

The priest lowered his head humbly, "Anything to serve the Redeemed God."

"Be sure to include teachings of our religion to this one as well. Who knows, she might become a sexual missionary."

They both laughed at the double entendre. Father Woods rose, leaving the Bishop. He had some things to arrange with the Cathedral chemist. *Who knows*, he thought, *maybe this one half-human will finance a good portion of the work that was going on in the far south all by herself.*

~

Adria slept soundly that night and in the morning was as rested as she could be under the circumstances. She rose, took another bath—this one quickly so she'd be ready for the day's work. She wondered when this would all end. She didn't mind the sex, but perhaps if it wasn't one after the other like that. She shrugged, figuring her betrothed would take care of her, and guide her through this ordeal of training so they could be together forever. She warmed at the thought. She showed that Pela. She was becoming a woman of stature—of power. She smiled at her reflection in the bathroom wall mirror. When she returned to her bedroom, she found her breakfast already laid out on the table for her. She also saw the clothing spread out on the bed. She glanced at the wardrobe before sitting down to eat. It seemed all the clothes were thin and filmy—some transparent. She reflected as she ate that these clothes would be useless in the tribes—they would snag on underbrush, saddle harnesses, and any number of things. But, she thought with a smile that the dull and disgusting part of her life was over. She finished her breakfast and had just put on one of her garments when the door opened behind her.

"Well, quicken it up," the gruff voice of the guard snarled, "I haven't got all day."

"Yes, sir," she said with practiced contriteness, "I will be ready right away."

She quickly finished dressing, then turned with her head properly lowered and followed the guard out into the stone hallway. She was lead into the room she'd been in the day before. Now there were seven men present, she'd expected them. There was one other person present—a man in a long white coat of some kind. He was holding a small tray upon which something glittered. Upon direction she sat on the platform, head lowered. The man in the white coat approached saying, "This'll sting for a moment, you will not move when I do this, you understand?"

"Yes, Your Grace," she answered.

The slap came as a complete surprise.

"I am a doctor, not a priest, wench," he said. "You'd better learn the difference, and quickly."

"Yes, sir," she amended.

The doctor tied a stretchy thing around her arm very tightly. She moved a little; it was uncomfortable. The movement was met with another slap. She bit her lip, saying nothing. The doctor was looking at her arm and at the vein standing up blue against her tan skin. He stabbed her with the glittering thing, removing the tightness from her arm. Almost immediately she felt a flood of warmth and a blissful peace steal over her. She smiled, looking up at the doctor. He didn't slap her—that was very nice of him, wasn't it? She smiled again.

"She's out there now. You can take over."

The doctor turned, leaving Adria alone with the seven priests. She looked at them—at the peculiar eagerness in their expressions. One or two she recognized from the day before, the others were strangers.

"Should I take off my clothes now?"

She had to say it twice; her tongue seemed not to be connected to the rest of her head. She giggled—that was surely a funny thought.

"No," a priest answered her question. "Today you'll serve us without needing to take off your clothes—there are other ways you must learn to be of service."

"If you bite, you die," one of the priests commented.

The others laughed. Bite? Adria was trying to understand what they meant. Then, one after the other, they showed her.

~

"What have you to report?"

The Bishop was sitting at his desk, interviewing a shabbily dressed man of about sixty. It was early in the morning, but the Bishop wanted to hear what the man had to say. The man sat confidently in front of the Bishop's desk. He was a spy.

"I have all my connections listening and looking, so far we've heard nothing."

"In one sense, that's reassuring and in another, it's disturbing."

"My ears are the sharpest in the city, Your Eminence," the spy said with surety. "If there were a conspiracy being fostered within the boundaries of the city, I would've heard."

"Then perhaps the half-human is telling the truth about some tribal assassins coming here to kill me."

"That's possible, of course, but how many tribal types would you suppose have even heard of you?"

The Bishop rubbed his chin thoughtfully, "I hadn't thought of that…"

"I'd think they know very little about the Cathedral. From everything my ears have heard from traveling traders in the markets, the tribes believe the city is behind the airship attacks. It's been a number of years after all, and now that we're no longer raiding the villages, why would they decide to kill you at this time? Why would they not have tried years ago when the raids were actually happening?"

The man was smart, there was no getting around that, the Bishop thought, but then it wasn't his life in jeopardy. Ambivalence in a leadership position was never a good thing. What was he to believe? He knew his life hung, perhaps, in the balance.

"What you say makes sense," he finally responded, "I'll have the half-human questioned again, and see if she has a time in mind that this event might take place."

The shabby man grinned wickedly, "Why not let me interrogate her? I know ways that are sure and fun."

"We'll have none of that," the Bishop stated firmly. "This creature will make us a lot of money either way, I've been assured."

The spy looked crestfallen.

"Pending this next interrogation, I want your ears to remain open to any rumors related to me, is that clear?"

"Yes, Your Eminence."

"If it turns out she's lying, there's no harm. You may go."

"Yes, Your Eminence," the man responded as he rose, leaving the Bishop alone with his thoughts.

The Bishop sat for a moment, picked up the phone, and waited for a connection.

"I wish to speak to Father Woods, please."

A moment later, the priest answered.

"Come to my office, would you? I've some errands for you to run for me."

"Immediately, Your Eminence."

Twenty minutes later, the servant admitted Father Woods into the Bishop's office. He knelt, waiting for the order to rise.

"Come, Father Woods, sit."

The priest got to his feet, moving to the chair indicated by the Bishop.

The Bishop told the priest of his conversation with the spy; it wasn't long in the telling.

"I gather it would be more efficient use of a spy's time if he knew when something was supposed to happen," Father Woods said thoughtfully.

"Excellent, you should be a spy, Father Woods. You'd be very good at that line of work."

"I'll do as I am commanded, Your Eminence,"

"Very well then, I want you to interview our guest, see if she can pinpoint a time for this alleged attempt on my life. Frankly, my spies seem to think she's lying and has made everything up."

"That's surely a possibility. I'm seeing her tonight. Today was her first day on the opiates. I'm thinking she'll be more pliant mentally than in the past. I'll find out if she knows more about this."

"Thank you, Father Woods. Either way it'll put my mind a bit to rest about this issue."

"Mine as well, Your Eminence."

The Bishop dismissed Father Woods. The priest quickly left. He had much to do today before the whore in training would be ready to see him. He was glad now that she'd stowed away. She was certainly fun to play with. Perhaps when he saw her later, he could have even more fun with her—if the other priests haven't used her too roughly today. He smiled, knowing he'd take his pleasure with her tonight no matter what her feelings were on the subject—that would be simply part of her training. He knew he could explain it to her—after all, they were lovers, were they not? He laughed aloud as he walked down the corridor to the chemist's laboratory.

Chapter 38

Adria was lying on her bed. Whatever was in that sharp thing was still coursing through her body. She felt warm and cool—light as an airship and heavy as a rock. She was trying not to think about tomorrow—they told her she'd have the privilege of serving ten men. After today, she wondered if she'd be able to do that. Her supper came and went, and she'd not eaten, the food was tasteless and worse, tainted by something else. There was a knock on her door; she sat up looking toward the closed door.

"I am here," was all she could say.

She'd at least begun to get a clearer use of her voice again.

The door opened and her betrothed came into the room. She smiled, he was the first welcome sight she'd seen this day. She looked down immediately, waiting for the slap. It didn't come. Instead, the priest dragged a chair toward her, sitting in front of the girl as she sat on the bed. He knew it would be a tactical mistake to sit on her bed next to her. He'd heard how things had gone during the day. It had been hard for her to do what was required, but she managed nonetheless. He smiled at her.

"Look up at me, Adria, I've some important news for you, and some questions."

Cautiously she raised her eyes. It wasn't some trick—he didn't hit her. But then, why would he? They loved one another. She smiled back at him.

"I talked to the Bishop today. He thinks you may have made up the story you told of his impending assassination."

"It is true, Your Grace."

He smiled. She was learning fast—good for her and good for them.

"Is there any more information you can give us? Do you know the names of the killers and when they plan to kill the Bishop?"

"Their names are Kel and Lyria," she said with an inward smirk. "I already told you that and what they look like. They ride two horses, one male, and one female. The horses are called Fog and Mist."

"That's very good," the priest said to encourage her, "but what about a time?"

"I did not hear that, but do you remember when we were coming over that last ridge before we arrived here?"

"Yes, what has that got to do with anything?"

"I have been thinking about that. The man on the airship said he saw travelers and then they disappeared. It could have been them."

233

"The assassins?"

"Yes, Your Grace, I did not think of it right away because that man said there were three travelers and I knew of only two. Still, the horse and cart sounded like them. Perhaps there was a third I didn't know of, or maybe they picked up someone on the way."

The priest thought for a moment. Then he smiled at the girl again.

"That's good information, it'll help greatly."

"You said you had something to tell me as well?"

The priest could see how hopeful the girl was.

"Remember the secret I told you? A thing that allows you to see divine beings?"

"Yes, I remember, Your Grace."

"I've found it! I'll secretly make sure you get it when you receive the sting of the scorpion each morning, once you're inside the city."

"Sting of the scorpion?"

"You know, the sharp thing that stung you this morning? It's very powerful magic, but it makes you crave—so you'll need more every morning. The extra part will be secretly included as my gift to you."

The girl beamed. He smiled. How naïve and foolish the half-humans were.

"The day after tomorrow I'll take you away from here. There's a very tall building you are going to live in. There's someone there you'll meet who'll show you other places you'll work."

"Work, Your Grace?"

"Work at continuing your physical education," he said, cursing himself silently for the slip of the tongue.

"I see."

"The man who'll help you is named Larry Harper. He's a nice man who will not expect you to keep your head down in his presence; however, you must always do what he says. He's your pimp."

Looking at the priest in confusion, she asked, "What is a...pimp?"

"He's the man who'll give you the sting of the scorpion each morning in the tall building, and then you must come back to him every night, is that clear?"

"Yes, it is clear, Your Grace."

"Good. Now I'll tell you something about the pimp, so you'll sort of know him when you meet."

"Larry Harper was once what some might call a journalist. He wrote for a newspaper that was secretly owned by the Cathedral. He wrote the stories he was told to write. If the facts didn't match the story—he was very good at making things up. More than half of what he wrote wasn't true at all, and the rest were lies built up around a kernel of truth; basic journalism. He was very good at it. But then another newspaper, one owned privately and hostile to our faith, told all about it. They had a spy inside our paper—the damage was significant.

"This other newspaper exposed Larry Harper for what he was. They detailed how he'd caused innocent people to be jailed, and in some cases even killed, over things that never happened. In each of these cases, we were clearly justified in what we did. The people he destroyed with his writing were enemies of the one true church—blasphemers and heathens. They got what the Redeemed God wished for them. Nevertheless, we lost the newspaper and Larry Harper had to go into hiding for a while. He's now our primary pimp. It's quite a natural thing, actually, to move from journalist to pimp—the jobs are very much alike."

Adria listened to all of this, still in a bit of a fog, and asked, "What is a newspaper?"

That brought gales of laughter from her betrothed. He spent the next few minutes explaining such things as newspapers and journalists to the simple-minded creature. He then left her for the night. She'd have a big day tomorrow—tomorrow she'd find out what the Bishop really liked. He laughed.

The third morning of Adria's training began early. She had barely time to bathe when she heard her door open. The servant brought in her breakfast, and some other clothing. Wordlessly, he placed her tray on the table and left the room. She looked at the ceremonial costume she was obviously supposed to wear today. She thought of it as ceremonial—with no other point of reference it appeared as though it was supposed to be shamanic—although she knew her totem wasn't a cheetah. If there was a ceremony of some kind coming, she'd know soon enough. Right now she better eat, as the guards would soon be here to take her away again. This would be the last day of this kind of training, she'd been told. She was glad about that.

Adria sat at the table, picking at her food. Though she knew she was hungry, she didn't care particularly. As she ate some of her breakfast, she became aware of another kind of hunger—one she hadn't experienced before. She was confused. This feeling was strong, and she didn't know the source. She must ask her betrothed, he'd know. Satisfied for the moment, she ate quickly.

After she finished, she took off her sleeping garment and looked at the ceremonial garb she would wear today. Her first thought was that there wasn't much to it. As she tied the lacing that held the upper part together, she struggled to get it fastened—it was almost too small. The lower part was easier to get into; it was nothing more than a very short skirt-like wrap. She noticed with curiosity that the tail was still attached. She giggled and knew she better make sure that it was in back or she might get slapped again. Finally she was ready. The cheetah fur was somewhat course, but she was dressed at least, if one could call it that.

The door opened and she quickly lowered her head. She turned before the guard could say anything, anticipating his command. Still, he shoved her too hard, she thought, considering she was quickly complying with his unspoken requests. She must be reading his mind, she thought. His must be one of the voices she heard buzzing in her mind—seemingly too far away to hear. She quickly walked down the hall with the guard behind her.

"Pick up your tail, wench. That thing costs money and you'd better not damage it."

"Yes, sir," she replied, picking up the long tail.

They were at the door again. It stood partly open; the guard pushed it all the way open and shoved the girl inside. As the door closed behind her, she stole a glance ahead and was relieved to see the doctor—somehow she knew he would make that odd hunger go away.

The injection went more smoothly this time. She knew what to expect and realized she'd been looking forward to this all morning. She also knew something the doctor didn't. She was gaining power—the sting of the scorpion.

"Sit here," the doctor commanded, "and wait."

He left the room, closing the door behind him.

Adria heard the door behind her open, and then close. One set of footsteps, one person. She kept her head averted, determined to end her training properly.

"Get on your hands and knees, beastling," the man said.

She complied—even as she recognized the voice. It was the one called Bishop. The man roughly pushed her head to the surface of the platform. She heard his excited breathing as he spoke.

236

"Keep your head down, creature, bow before your master."

She felt him pushing up the fur skirt she was wearing, she knew what to expect, as several of the other priests liked it this way. Then she felt pain. What was he doing? That wasn't where it was supposed to go—didn't he realize his mistake? She gasped again in pain, surprise, and shock. He must realize what he's doing, why doesn't he stop?

But the Bishop didn't stop, not for a very long time. Even in the haze of the fresh heroin, Adria was crying. It had been a long time since she'd felt humiliated—not since the tribes. When the Bishop was finished, he shoved her roughly the rest of the way down to the platform.

"That was better than I thought it would be, beastling. I may have to try you again sometime."

Then he laughed. She knew he was laughing at her. Would her life be no better here than in the tribe where everyone laughed at her? She drew a deep breath. She'd see about that.

Then the Bishop was gone and the others came in. The rest of the morning was little more than a fog to Adria. Her mind was far away as she listened to the voices. They were telling her to be patient—once she was powerful enough, she'd be able to avenge herself. As she'd done with the hag, as she'd done with the four shamans, and as she'd done with Kel and that woman. Her time was coming—of that she was certain. The men took her, and took her, and took her. She didn't care; she was going to become more powerful than they were. She wouldn't allow anyone to do to her what that hag had done. What that woman and Kel had done. Not ever again.

Chapter 39

After, back in her rooms, she took a very long, hot bath. She had to drain the water once and refill because her first tub had turned a light pink from her blood. Finally she felt clean again. Fortunately the sting was numbing some of the pain. She lay on her bed and slept a long time. In her sleep, the voices spoke to her. She was going to be gone from all this very soon, they said. She'd get her revenge. She'd never be treated as she'd been by that hag or by that other woman—what was her name? Oh yes, Lyria. The voices soothed her; calmed her.

A knock on her door awakened her. She quickly rose and put on a nightgown. The knock came again.

"Adria? Are you awake?"

It was her betrothed. "Yes, Your Grace, I am awake."

The priest opened the door, smiling at her as he entered.

She sat on the bed and, as before, the priest drew up a chair and sat before her.

"I've heard that everything went well yesterday. Would you like to leave this place?"

"Yes, Your Grace."

"Then we'll be off," he responded jovially. "Tonight you'll have your own apartment and many clothes to choose from."

Adria clapped her hands in glee, "Will you be with me?"

"No, sadly, I have duties to attend to; however, Larry Harper will be there for you. He'll show you around and introduce you to the other girls."

"Other girls?"

"Well," the priest said, "the building is large with many apartments."

"I see, Your Grace."

"Leave everything. Let's go."

They exited the side door of the Cathedral and found a steam-car waiting. Adria noticed there was no driver.

"There is no pilot, how shall we go?"

The priest laughed, "I'll drive."

Adria was in awe, and asked, "Is this yours?"

"Of course, I own several."

She sat back into the leather of the seat, leaning her head back.

"Does the Cathedral own the city?"

"No, but we're within its borders. Up to this point we've been able to maintain our independence from the laws of the city. But the enemies of the true church are getting stronger."

"Can't you just kill them?"

"If only it were that simple! There are a number of religions present within the city, and though we are the strongest, together they outnumber us. If it came to open war, we would lose."

They arrived in a short time at the tall stone building that would become Adria's home. She stepped from the vehicle, looking upward…and upward.

"How high does it go?"

"Eighty-five levels."

He guided her through the front door and past the man at the desk, to whom he nodded. The old man nodded back, saying nothing.

The lift confused and frightened Adria, much to the delight of the priest at her side. By the time they reached the seventy-third floor, she had learned how to operate the lift. She was proud of herself for learning something like that—one never knew when it might come in handy. Looking at her betrothed, she wondered, for all of his supposed love, why he'd not taken her, not even once. Though he allowed many other men to use her, he seemed not to have interest himself. Why was that? Could that be the way of the city and the Cathedral? Was she misunderstanding something? The thought was driven from her mind when the priest spoke again.

"Here's the apartment, Adria."

She entered the room. It was rather large, really. There was more than enough room for the four beds, and dressers, and tables. It was nicely furnished, she supposed—she didn't know what nice meant in city standards. She opened the closet finding a dozen dresses and gowns. The priest watched.

"Adria? I want you to meet Larry Harper."

The man entered the room, smiling at Adria, and said, "I'm sure your stay here will be mutually beneficial."

Larry was tall and lean, in his early sixties, his eyes still sharp. He could instantly see the potential the priest had seen in this girl.

"Larry knows to give you the sting of the scorpion in the morning, and tomorrow you'll be getting your surprise as well," the priest said.

Adria glanced at Larry, then back to the priest, asking, "He knows?"

"He does what he's told to do."

Larry smiled, "I live to serve."

"I'm leaving now, Adria. I'll be back in a couple days to see how you're doing. In the meantime, remember your training. Larry will be going with you everywhere you go, you're precious to me."

Then he was gone. Larry looked the young woman up and down. What the priest said was true—she really was beautiful. She might even draw the double fees he'd been instructed to charge. *Well*, he thought, *tomorrow will tell the tale.*

Adria asked curiously, "Why are there four beds?"

Larry smiled, "Those three are for your roommates, dear."

"I am sharing the room?"

"Certainly! You'll like the girls, I'm sure. You'll meet them tomorrow; they're on an extended service. They are called Hainie, Susan, and Sarah."

"Very well," Adria answered, "I will meet them tomorrow then."

Again, thanks to the effects of the sting, Adria slept soundly—the voices a barely heard whisper. The night passed quickly and quietly. Adria awoke refreshed, but with that vague craving for something she hadn't completely recognized yet. She rose and bathed quickly—anxious to finally be able to explore the city that was to be her home. She quickly dressed in the first outfit she found in the closet. It was a very pale green flowing thing that, while coming all the way to her ankles, was thin enough to accentuate the lines of her body. She liked how she looked in the mirror. On the dressing table below the mirror were trays of various brushes and bottles. Cosmetics were something not used in the tribes, therefore she had no idea what they were for.

Suddenly there was a knock on the door. Adria lowered her head as she walked to the door and opened it. She thought it was probably Larry Harper, but she dared not look up. She heard a soft chuckle, then a gentle voice.

"Look up at me, dear," the voice said. Timidly she raised her eyes. She was right—it was Larry.

"Unless you're with a customer who wishes it, you may keep your head up inside this building. Outside, you must keep your eyes averted. Do you understand?"

"Yes," she answered simply.

"Excellent. Sit on the bed dear, and I'll give you your sting."

Adria complied—the needle didn't seem to hurt anymore. She seemed to want the slight pain of the injection for the wondrous thing that followed. When he was done, he said, "Today we're going to a tavern. Do you know what a tavern is?"

"Father Woods told me that was a place where people gather to drink what he called spirits, though I have never heard of spirits that could be drunk."

Larry laughed at her unintended joke, "Spirits is what they call various drinks with alcohol. The effect is a very mild version of what you feel after your sting."

Adria traveled with Larry Harper through the hall and down the lift. Even the loud clank of the lift gate didn't startle her this morning, as she was already drifting from the heroin. Outside, Adria remembered to lower her head. She longed to look at the city, but she remembered her teaching. For the time being, she would obey. Eventually, she knew, she'd be powerful enough to do whatever she wanted. She smiled.

They walked down the sidewalk together. Larry greeted several women on the way, but didn't introduce Adria. She didn't care—people just complicated her life. She smiled as she thought of how simply that complication could be taken care of. They crossed two roadways noisy with steam-cars and lorries. She ached to look, but one voice kept telling her to bide her time; her rise to power was coming. She listened, taking comfort. They turned off the street into a dark room. Adria heard many voices, some loud, almost shouting. She could smell the pungent odor of food, drink, and something else—something sweet. Incense she was familiar with—though this was a new aroma that was actually quite pleasant. She heard Larry talking to someone who laughed.

"Put her on the stages, Larry," the man said. "Let's see what she can do."

Adria suddenly found herself on a raised platform similar to the one in the Cathedral, though much larger. She looked up. In front of her the dark room was lit periodically with candles and along the walls jets of fire sent out a weak light from their polished metal reflectors. The room was not full, but there were probably thirty men present who were all looking at her expectantly. Larry was on the platform too. He was speaking to the crowd as Adria wondered why the place she was standing was so brightly lit. She listened, hoping for a clue.

"We've a new girl today, gentlemen," Larry shouted to the crowd. "She comes from the tribes, and I'm told she can get really wild."

The crowd looked at her, cheering and clapping. She realized she was the center of that adulation. She smiled, standing straight. Larry walked up to her with a small glass tube in his hand. Adria recognized the brightness of the needle. He smiled.

"This is the magic Father Woods told you about. Shortly after you receive this gift, you'll see who here is divine enough to…combine with you." There was a slight prick and then it was over. Music began playing—loud and fast.

"Now dance, my dear," Larry whispered. "Let the music take you— dance and slowly remove your clothing. Let these men see what a truly divine body looks like."

The music was loud and Adria abandoned herself to it. She remembered the use of the drum in tribal ceremonies. Here there was a drum as well, she let it carry her. She gyrated and twirled—peeling off her garments slowly. She almost laughed. All these men were worshipping her—her beauty. *This is how it's supposed to be*, she thought. She realized she was always meant to be the center of attention.

Now the men were lining up at the steps leading to the platform. Adria didn't care; the mescaline was beginning to do things to her. She laughed when the first man came to her; he seemed to glow. Faint colored lights seemed to flash around his body. She looked lower and saw his manhood was glowing as well. She smiled up at him as she wantonly took him into her arms. His grunting and pushing was like divine music.

Then, finally, she felt some of his divinity leave him—it was hers now. Some of his power was inside her. She reveled in it and reveled in the attention of the men who climbed to the stage that morning. They glowed—she glowed. She realized that each of them was somehow divine and that wherever they left their divine spore, it was hers. Power was coming.

She laughed when the twentieth man took her, and when the thirtieth took her. She didn't see Larry collecting money from the men as they trooped onto the stage somehow eager to leave their Godpower with her— in her.

"So, how'd things go?"

Father Woods was anxious to hear about Larry's day.

"By the Redeemed God, Your Grace, you should've seen her."

"Maybe I will soon," the priest laughed.

"This girl is a money machine, Your Grace. One time she took three men at once. Satisfied all of them she did. None of them complained about paying double either."

"I think we should keep her off the street. Let's just let her work the tavern for the time being. Let the men come to her, it'll save time."

"You're right, Your Grace. We'll be able to use this one for a very long time."

"How much money did she turn today?"

The pimp pulled a canvas sack from his jacket, saying, "Fifty large in silver, Your Grace, and…ten gold."

"Even gold?"

"There was one man there with his wife, Your Grace—she wanted to sample the goods as well, so we made a private deal for a private room for an hour.

"They paid in gold for the privilege, Your Grace, and they'll be back."

The priest smiled. Though not being a shaman, he couldn't see what was coming.

Chapter 40

Kel and Lyria approached the Green Hyena tavern. The streets were crowded in the downtown area, but virtually everyone ignored the priest and the servant woman they assumed Kel and Lyria to be. Dressing like a priest of the Cathedral had been an excellent idea—he wished it had been his. Kel looked at his surroundings—the city seemed to be all black here in the central part. Basalt and granite were the main materials of the tall buildings that rose up on both sides of the street like the walls of some great canyon. Kel glanced across the street and saw a woman and a man walking with a cheetah. The large spotted cat wore a collar of thick leather attached to a leash. The cat walked docilely at the woman's side, its long tail swishing from side to side. *The woman seems an aristocrat,* Kel thought, as she strode along with her head up. It was not the pose of a woman of the religion of the Redeemed God. As people passed her, the cat didn't seem to pay attention to them. This must truly be a tame cheetah, or the woman had a powerful totem.

In the street, two men on horseback passed. *They have to be outlanders*, Kel thought, as he studied the way they were dressed. Each man was in light iron and leather armor decorated with fur strips at the shoulders. They also carried a round metal shield about three feet in diameter hung on the left side of their saddles and short, heavy swords suspended from their belts. He guessed them to be traders from one of the more northerly tribes. A large canvas bag was slung over the rump of each horse, no doubt carrying the wares they'd trade at the city market farther up the street.

Coming from the other direction was one of the strange-wheeled wagons that moved under its own power. He'd heard Dan call them 'automobiles' or sometimes 'motors.' Though it looked like magic, Kel knew that inside the long metal covering extending in front of the flat glass front window was a water tank and a device to make a flame. Dan had told him that they ran on steam. Kel thought this was a clever idea. For a city right on the great Western Sea, using water to make steam to drive engines such as this seemed logical.

Kel and Lyria walked past the front of the huge building standing next to the Green Hyena. This building, like all the rest in the central part of Los Angeles, soared into the sky many levels high. Kel looked up, noticing that the windows were barred to eighty levels. *Very good security*, he thought, *but who could come through a window to inflict harm that high up?* It seemed the people who lived in these tall buildings were inordinately fearful. Yet very few seemed to be armed when they ventured out onto the streets. Life in a large city of many millions like this was confusing at best. He smiled to himself as they walked past the arched doorway of the building. The iron portcullis was raised this time of day; he wondered how someone might leave the building at night when the gate was lowered. He'd have to find out, as he might need that information at some point in time.

They passed a very narrow walkway between the two buildings. Two women were standing in the alley—both dressed in tight fitting silk that did nothing to hide the more intimate details of their bodies. Their faces were decorated with white and red paint. Though the paint wasn't applied like it was used ceremonially in the tribes, he thought it was still dramatic. Lyria thought otherwise.

One of the young women approached Kel, smiling at him. She walked slowly around both of them, looking at Lyria. Then she turned her attention to Kel, and ran her hand slowly down his cheek. He pulled back at the sudden touch—the woman laughed.

"Hello," she said, "I think I love you!"

She glanced down, and then looked up at him coyly through her lashes and whispered, "Won't you tell me your name?"

Kel was shocked into silence as the woman put her other hand on him—this one a bit lower than his face. He might not have been able to move, but that wasn't a problem for Lyria. She shoved the street woman roughly away with her left hand against the prostitute's chest. The woman glowered at Lyria as she tried to move toward Kel, and again Lyria shoved her, harder this time. She stumbled and sat down heavily on the cobblestones. She snarled up at Lyria, "You better watch out, servant woman. This is a protected business."

As the woman regained her feet, Lyria glanced around her, turned, and smiled at the prostitute. "I see no one protecting you. Touch him again and you will die."

Lyria half pulled one of the Teeth of the Ice Tiger from her handbag. The woman saw the knife and decided that discretion was indeed the better part of valor.

She mumbled to her friend who'd stood mute through the whole incident, "Let's cross the street. I think there are more willing men over there."

Without a backward glance, the two prostitutes crossed the street. Lyria looked askance at Kel. "You could have done more!"

"But you handled things so well," he snickered. "Truthfully, I believe you knew what she was doing before I did."

"And you are to be a man of knowledge?" She spoke with her hands on her hips and a wry smile on her lips.

Dan watched the encounter between the prostitutes and his friends. He was leaning casually against the front of a building near the auto. When Lyria shoved the woman, he gasped. This could go very badly. The Cathedral ran some prostitutes, and some were more or less freelancing. Still others were controlled by the criminal element of the city, and those people were not the least bit afraid of the priests. He hoped these women weren't gang affiliated, or at least that their pimp wasn't present to see this interchange. He sighed with relief when the two women crossed the street to ply their trade in a safer locale. Though he didn't hear the exchange between Lyria and the woman, he could imagine how it'd transpired. With the danger over, he laughed. Several young men passing on the sidewalk never even glanced at him. Dan had said that in the city, everyone was invisible.

Kel and Lyria walked on a short distance until they were at the tavern's entrance. As agreed, Kel entered alone, but not before Lyria said, "If you let another one of those women touch you, I'll know."

"You know—I believe you," Kel responded with a grin.

He pushed open the two swinging doors that led into the Green Hyena. Lyria turned and walked slowly back to the steam-car and Dan.

She opened the door of the auto and sat inside. Dan, entering the driver's side, said with a smile, "I saw that little combat you engaged in."

"She had no right to touch him like that."

"She was just doing her job, Lyria."

"She should find a safer way to make her living."

"For some, this is the final answer. Many of these women come from very bad beginnings. They come from homes where their parents began selling them when they were little more than children. Many of them have addictions to the drugs they can find on the street."

Lyria opened the door, glancing up and down the roadway. "What do drugs look like?" She questioned. "I see only paper and horse dung in the street."

Dan laughed at her remark, "Drugs are chemicals, Lyria. Some are like the poppy plants the tribes use to relieve pain and give sleep to the injured. There are many who use them for fun, but then come to need them. This 'need' rises above all other desires— even eating."

Lyria thought about that for a while and said, "We know of such cravings, that is why the healers only use a small amount and only in the most serious cases."

"That's the wise way. But wise people are scarce in the city. Many have schooling and are smart, but true wisdom isn't often found here."

"That is too bad. Where are the city's shamans? Or is that why ours were being kidnapped?"

"We're hoping to find that information. I would guess that if the Cathedral is involved, they aren't wanting to help the people of the city, but rather to gain power over it."

~

Kel looked around the Green Hyena as the door closed behind him. The inside was smoky and dim. There were no windows to let in the daylight or any fresh air. The place smelled like stale drinks, sweat, and smoke. A thin copper tube ran around the walls close to the ceiling. At intervals, small brass jets spewed out steady, small flames reflected in round metal mirrors. Though the gaslights ran around the entire room, they supplied only a minimal amount of light. *Regular lanterns would have worked better*, Kel thought.

Men and women sat at the tables, some ate but most seemed to be here for the fermented drinks being served. Most of the people looked like city folk—here and there were rougher types—some with long braided hair and light iron armor. A man standing near the wall even had what he knew to be a ballistic weapon. In days long past, these weapons had been very common. From his reading, Kel knew that when the ice crushed the large manufacturing centers to the north, most complex mechanical creations ceased to be made. Attrition must have taken its toll on weapons as well as other machines of the old age. Still, the black weapon the man had hung from his chest certainly didn't look to be a thousand years old. He imagined that in a city the size of Los Angeles, the production of this type of weapon had once again begun. He wondered what that might mean for the free tribes to the east of the city.

Kel wrinkled his nose—what an obnoxious place. He was glad he wouldn't have to be here long. He walked to the table by the back wall as he'd been instructed, winding his way past tables and the various patrons of the place. He was virtually ignored by everyone, though two men sitting at one of the tables nodded politely in his direction— obviously acknowledging his priestly garb. He sat down, making a mental note of where the two men sat. Glancing in their direction, he realized that they seemed to be ignoring him now like the rest of the crowd.

On the stage, a steam organ was playing. Kel looked at the instrument in amazement. He thought this was another interesting way to use steam. Along the top of the organ large ivory teeth and tusks were arrayed. He recognized some as the teeth of ice tigers, but some of the larger ones he couldn't identify—they had a look of great age to them. At either end of the organ, making a sort of arch over the instrument, were massive ivory tusks of a giant mammoth.

While the organist worked the keys of the organ, two other musicians stood nearby. They were playing guitars that were fashioned from the skulls of alligators. Kel knew from reading and discussions with Llo that these big lizards didn't live in these parts. He figured either the bones or the instruments were trade items from the more southern, heavily forested regions. The music, though strange to his ears, was nevertheless interesting and stimulating.

A young woman approached Kel at his table, and he looked at her warily—thinking about what Lyria had said.

"What would you like?"

Kel thought for a moment, and then ordered a mug of beer. It would be safer to drink something with less power, considering his mission. There was no point in ending up stupefied by drink.

The woman smiled. "I'll be right back."

She walked off and he sat back in his chair. He wondered when the magician would make his appearance and wondered what kind of magician he might be. Dan was conspiratorial and vague in his description. Kel noticed with some satisfaction that most of the people were still paying little attention to him in his priest's attire. It seemed that priests spending time in disreputable taverns drinking wasn't all that uncommon an occurrence. He marveled at the seemingly untouchable nature of the priesthood, it concealed a great power.

Chapter 41

Just as the young waitress returned with Kel's drink, the steam organ gave a flourish and was silent. Kel paid for his drink with coins Dan had given him, and he looked up at the stage expectantly. An older man came out from behind the curtain and people began clapping and banging their mugs and bottles on the tables. The man set a small table in front of him, raising both his hands, palms toward the audience. Smiling broadly, he said, "Thank you! Thank you!"

Eventually the clapping and hooting was reduced to a low murmur as the man spoke, "Tonight I will try something new. Tonight you'll see something that has not been seen since the dawn of time."

More hooting and clapping ensued. They all seemed to be enjoying themselves and Kel found that he was as well. The man on the stage looked around the room. His eyes stopped on Kel for an instant, and Kel raised his mug and nodded. The man on the stage nodded briefly, and then turned his attention to the audience.

"Since man has walked this Earth, he has wondered how all of this," he gestured with his open hands to the room, seeming to indicate the people therein, and the greater world outside, "could have come to be. The old religions and the new have held that God made the world and the stars."

He looked around at the audience, gauging their understanding of what he was saying. "Because this presentation is going to be something special, a round of drinks will be served...on the house."

The audience was clamoring and shouting as the bar girls quickly moved through the crowd, replacing half-finished drinks with new ones, occasionally adroitly avoiding the groping hands of already drunken men. The steam organ played softly until the drinks were all served. Kel found a new drink on his table as well. He'd just ordered his drink and had hardly sipped it—this seemed like a waste.

Now the man on the stage continued, "We know that God made great, celestial dragons and that as the dragons danced to the music of the Divine, they shot out jets of fire that made the spirals of stars we see in the night skies." He paused and the steam organ and guitar players began their music again.

Kel lifted his drink to his lips, tasting it. It wasn't right somehow. He carefully sniffed at the brew, running his tongue over his lips—then he knew. The reason the drinks were replaced was that these held a mixture

of herbs and a certain root that could make the mind open to the
suggestions of others. He knew from his training with Garn that it could
facilitate the production of a sort of waking dream state. People would see
what someone told them they'd see. This man was a magician all right,
and a stage was where he belonged. Still, it would make a perfect disguise
for someone who liked to listen to the careless words of men who'd drunk
too much.

Kel sat back and decided to enjoy the show. The organ was playing
louder now and the accompanying guitars led the way. The magician
waited, watching the people below him drinking the beverages they'd just
been served—he smiled. Kel smiled too—he knew the show was about to
begin.

The magician spoke loudly to be heard over the quickening music.
"Ladies and gentlemen, I happen to have two small dragons with me
tonight." Kel saw that some of the audience stopped in mid-drink at that.

The man continued, "I have a green and a blue dragon—yes they have
wings and can fly." He paused for effect, and then said, "But don't worry,
ladies and gentlemen, these dragons are very well behaved." He made a
show of patting various pockets and said, "Now where have they gotten
to?"

The crowd, beginning to feel the effects of the drugged drinks,
laughed as the magician fumbled around onstage.

The laughter stopped all at once when suddenly the magician
removed two small dragons from his pockets. They were about a foot tall,
serpentine, with bat-like wings. In short, they reminded the audience of all
the dragons they'd ever seen in pictures since childhood. He set them
carefully on the table. The green dragon hissed, blowing out a thin jet of
fire and smoke. The magician scolded the dragon, admonishing, "Now,
now, be nice to our friends out there."

He looked out into the audience, "You are our friends, are you not?"

The audience shouted, "Yes, Yes," and made a variety of other
comments, some more pleasant than others.

The magician laughed. "We cannot hope to know what the music of
the Divine might be, so we'll have to make due with our local musicians."

He gestured to the band—everyone hooted and clapped. Kel had to
admit the man knew how to play an audience.

The band began slowly and then started playing at a ferocious pace.
All at once, the dragons started dancing. At first they danced on the little

table, but as they danced and pirouetted more quickly, they became airborne. They twisted around one another as they rose into the air over the table. They separated from each other, beginning to twirl. Round and round they spun and suddenly they were spewing fire. The flames from the dragons' mouths and nostrils spun with them as they turned—the flames becoming spirals of golden light. The spirals gradually added arms as the dragons moved. Now the spirals were spreading out, growing larger. The audience was mesmerized. The spirals looked just like the spiral star clusters one could see some nights in the skies when the moon was dark.

Kel didn't exactly see the dragons or the spiraling flames as he'd foregone the hallucinatory drink. In his mind's eye and with his shaman's training, he could almost see through the eyes of the others present. He could see the group's image of all their waking dreaming. The dragons he saw were not like the ones any individual saw. He saw the general thoughts of the audience and their 'collective' dragons. It was still impressive and he was almost tempted to take the drink and see for himself.

The music lowered a bit and the magician was again addressing the audience, "Well, ladies and gentlemen…what do you think?"

The audience roared. Kel thought they almost sounded like a dragon themselves.

"Should we feed them as a reward?"

The crowd hooted, stomped, and shouted. The magician smiled. "As you wish, so shall it be."

Reaching into his vest pocket he withdrew two small squares of raw beef. He held them aloft for the audience to see. He set them on the table in front of the two dragons where they'd come to rest.

The dragons stalked over to the bits of meat, sniffing them. They walked around each other and sniffed the meat again, hissing at each other. The magician said impatiently, "Oh go ahead and roast it, we haven't got all night!"

The audience laughed. Suddenly both dragons expelled columns of fire and the meat charred. Then the dragons pounced on the meat and began eating ferociously.

The music picked up a little, then calmed. The magician spread his arms to his side, and bowed. As he did he passed his sleeves in front of the dragons and said, "I am the dragon king! I can do anything!"

He lifted his arms and the dragons were gone. The steam organ crashed out a finale. The two chunks of roasted meat remained on the table. Kel smiled, he'd seen the man cleverly drop two real chunks of roast meat on the table to replace the thought projections of the raw ones as he swept his arms around the dragons. The man had talent; there was no doubt. He also had some ability to control the minds of those around him, even if herbal assistance was needed. That, Kel realized, was probably his most valuable asset considering the real business he was engaged in.

The magician left the stage, slowly winding his way through the crowd accepting copper and silver coins as tokens of appreciation from individuals for the spectacle he'd shown them. He lingered a bit at a couple of tables, even sat for a moment here and there. Though he was taking his time, Kel knew he was working his way gradually in his direction. He waited patiently, sipping at a new mug of beer he'd ordered. He tasted it cautiously, sniffing before he took a drink; he wanted to make sure he didn't get another drugged drink.

Eventually the magician was standing before Kel's table. He bowed at the waist, "What did you think of the show, Your Grace?"

"It was magnificent, actually. Perhaps it will inspire some to join the Brotherhood or at least spend more time in prayer."

The man smiled.

"Please sit," Kel said.

The magician sat down in the chair across from Kel. Hardly anyone was paying attention to the two of them. Most had gone back to their drinks and though a couple of individuals casually glanced over, it seemed that once again his priest's robes allowed him to pretty much do whatever he wanted. He handed the man a small silver coin and said, "Thank you for the show."

"No, no," the magician said, "thank you for coming and enjoying our company this day, Your Grace."

He handed the coin back to Kel along with a tightly folded piece of paper. As he returned the coin, he said aloud, "Use this for your missions, Your Grace. I'm certain you can use all the help you can get."

"You are most generous," Kel replied smiling. "Since I have newly come to your fine city, can you offer a suggestion of where one might go to see new sights?"

"A couple blocks down is the amphitheater," the magician said, gesturing with his head to the West. "They're having jousting tournaments today. I'm sure you'd find it interesting."

"That does sound interesting, I haven't seen that event before."

"You might also like to go down to the harbor. A large crystal ship from the Far East has docked and is being unloaded this afternoon. We don't see as many of those as we used to. If you've never seen one, you'll find it interesting."

"Thank you so much!" Kel rose. "May blessings be upon you and your house, magician."

The man smiled and walked to the stage, disappearing through a large curtain. Kel casually slipped the coin and the note into his pocket and turned toward the exit. A crystal ship—now that was something he'd really like to see. He knew the concept was very old and trusted, but he still thought it was a dangerous way to travel. First you build a gigantic floating city made of wood and iron. Then you put a large steam engine inside heated by an open flame. And then you sail it out over the deep, wide ocean. He shook his head; a wooden ship with fire inside of it on an ocean so large you couldn't hope to be rescued if something went wrong. Still, Kel thought it would be worth seeing. He turned toward the exit, winding his way between tables.

~

"What could be taking so long?" Lyria was anxious—she hadn't been separated from Kel like this in some time. She was worried about what might be happening inside the tavern.

"Relax. The magician will not let anything bad happen to him. Besides, he has to wait for the show to end before he can even talk to the man."

"Well, if he doesn't hurry up, I'm going in looking for him."

"That wouldn't be advisable, Lyria," Dan said anxiously. "It would endanger both of you and the magician as well."

"Very well, I will wait." Lyria slumped into the leather upholstery of the vehicle.

Dan smiled at her reassuringly. "First, your man can take care of himself, I'm sure. Second, this is too important to blunder at this stage of the game. Think of how far you both have come just to be here at this moment."

"You are right, Dan," Lyria conceded, crossing her arms, "you know the ways of the Black City. I will abide your advice."

Dan relaxed, no longer concerned that Lyria would inadvertently make a fatal mistake. He remembered one of his from many years ago. *Daisy.* Again he pushed the thought from his mind.

~

As Kel was nearing the tavern door a man tugged on his sleeve. He stopped, looking at the man—he was short and rather nondescript. His clothing fit well and Kel thought it was probably fashionable for the city. The stranger looked him up and down, and then in a conspiratorial whisper said, "I see you're a man of the cloth, Your Grace. I happen to know where several of your brethren are right now…with a wild thing. Think you might be interested in joining them?" He winked and smiled.

Kel, confused, asked, "A wild thing?"

The man gave an impatient shrug. "You know…a girl thing from one of the wild tribes just to the east of us. Traders brought her here from that area. She's only partly human and has the most wonderful white hair. She's nine summers by her own words. Amazing, isn't it, that half animals can actually talk? She's made me a great deal money from the priests, and others as well."

The man patted his vest pocket, nodding knowingly at Kel.

Kel suddenly realized who the man was speaking of—the comment about her hair, and when and where she came from. The man was clearly talking about Noria, the young child taken from the mountain tribe.

Forcing himself to smile, he said, "I do believe that would be of interest after all."

"Good. Good. The uh...fee is five silver—you pay me now, of course."

The man smiled wickedly, and Kel only said, "Of course."

He handed the man five small silver coins thinking, *"So this is the price of a child of the tribes in the Black City."*

As they reached the doorway, Kel inquired, "I have a friend, a woman, that I would like to bring along. Not to participate but simply to watch."

The man responded jovially, "Of course, of course. If they don't touch, they don't pay. A woman you say?"

Kel swung the tavern door, stepping out into the afternoon sunlight. He heard a low rumble and looked up. A black zeppelin was cruising overhead just a bit higher than the rooftops of the buildings. Kel was still amazed at the size of the things. It seemed to blot out the very sky. Behind the craft, the Aurora flashed and flickered in purple and green curtains in the sky to the north. He glanced at his companion. The man was standing with his head bent reverently. Kel understood why. He now knew the black airships were the property of the Cathedral and that the girl was in their custody. Dan was right about that. What kind of religious men would sell children? He shook his head.

Chapter 42

Dan and Lyria simultaneously saw Kel exit the tavern. They both quickly exited the vehicle and stood on the sidewalk anxiously.

"I am going to him," Lyria said.

"No, dear, Kel knows we're here. He'll let you know when he wants you to go to him."

"You are right," Lyria said, "I keep forgetting I am supposed to be his servant."

Dan laughed, "Well, you can serve him now, he's looking this way and he just gestured for you to come to him."

Lyria composed herself, preparing for her role as a demure serving woman.

Dan snickered, whispering to her, "You better sniff his clothing, Lyria, to make sure no other prostitutes have been handling the merchandise."

Lyria glared at him a moment, then smiled in spite of herself.

"He knows better than that," she said confidently, "I have the magic sword!"

Dan laughed as Lyria began a slow pace down the sidewalk toward Kel. She was proud of herself when she didn't even glance up to see the zeppelin that must be overhead, judging by the sound of the engines.

By the time the zeppelin passed, Kel saw Lyria approaching at a slow, dignified pace—he smiled. She was learning how to pass for a woman of the Cathedral very quickly. While his companion was momentarily distracted by a shout coming from an alleyway, Kel held his finger to his lips, making a gesture with his left hand—a closed fist with index finger raised and then bent back into the fist. He knew Lyria would know the meaning of the tribe's hunting hand signal—that she should proceed silently, and that their game was just ahead.

Lyria walked up, saying nothing to Kel. She stood with her head lowered, as was expected of a servant of a priest. Kel's companion looked at him quizzically. "She's a bit old for me—does she have a name?"

"Her name is of no interest to you."

The man bowed and said, "As you wish, Your Grace."

As they walked past an amphitheater, Kel told Lyria about Noria. A large crowd must have been in the amphitheater, the roaring and shouting drowned out her disgusted remark. Two blocks past the amphitheater, the man showed them through the entrance of what appeared to be living quarters for some of the city's residents. The great iron portcullis was raised and people could be seen coming and going in various styles of dress.

~

Dan sat for a moment, deciding on a course of action. He watched the three individuals walking away from him. He raised the steam pressure in his vehicle, sliding smoothly from the curb. He was pleased with the ease in which he'd readapted to this aspect of city life. He glanced into his mirror and slowly proceeded down the street, following his friends and their strange companion. Dan was too far away to see the man distinctly, but he knew this wasn't part of the plan. Something had changed and his companions were without his guidance in the very center of the city. He followed cautiously, staying in the curb lane.

"Damn," he said to himself, "why would they be going in there?"

He pulled to the curb in front of the tall building. He was only there for about two minutes when a man in a uniform approached his automobile.

"Hey, fellow," the man said as he leaned on the passenger side of the auto, looking through the open window, "you can't park here, this is a loading area. Move it along, please."

Dan cursed under his breath again and turned the auto into the street. He'd have to go back to where he'd dropped Kel and Lyria off and hope they'd remember that he'd be there until they showed up. He drove quickly around the corner and up to the next street, and then wound his way cautiously through traffic. Twenty minutes later, he was back where he'd started. He pulled once more to the curb, easing the pressure in the boiler. He had no choice—he'd have to wait for his friends here. He wasn't happy. Why, he wondered, would they go into a place such as that? He hoped they'd be all right and was glad Lyria was with Kel. He shook his head in wonder—Lyria was truly a force to contend with. He laughed, settling in to wait.

~

The foyer was lit by the large, barred windows facing the street. An older man in a shabby, greasy looking uniform was standing behind the beat up wooden counter. Kel's companion simply nodded at the man and the man nodded back.

"He's paid well not to see things," the man chuckled, "he's good at his job."

257

On either side of the desk were open doorways. One led to a stairway, the other into a wooden box. The man said, "We'll take the lift."

He stepped into the box and after a second's hesitation, Kel followed with Lyria right behind him. The man pulled a gate closed behind them that was made of slats of brass held at joints by rivets so it would fold and unfold as needed. Kel marveled at the simple construction, thinking how such a gate would work for the small animal pens back home. Lyria stood with her head bowed and said nothing. The box they were in started moving. Kel and Lyria looked at each other with surprise, saying nothing. They knew that if it were dangerous, this evil little man wouldn't have entered. They rode up in silence. Lyria noticed the dial above the door showing what level they were on and nudged Kel—he nodded in understanding. They watched the dial climb until it reached the number 77. Their guide slid back the brass gate and bowed, he gestured for his guests to exit. Kel and Lyria stepped into the hallway.

Though it was daylight, the hall was illuminated with the same kind of gaslights Kel had seen in the tavern. Both sides of the hallway were lined with doors—some with more space between them than others. Kel guessed that people who possessed more money probably owned the larger living quarters. It seemed that in Los Angeles, everything depended upon money. He was glad he'd brought as much as he had. Their guide again assumed the lead, walking down the carpeted hallway. Lyria looked down at the floor. It was covered with a heavy kind of fabric—it felt soft underfoot. Lyria wondered if something like this could be put in her and Kel's home when they were finally wed. She smiled more at the thought of being united with Kel than with the idea of carpeting. Still…it would be nice in the winter.

They stopped outside a door. The man again bowed to Kel and said, "There're three of your brethren inside. Here's a key. Just leave it on the dressing table—or should I say the undressing table—when you're finished."

He chuckled at his little joke and decided to say no more. Kel handed the key to Lyria, who was already unlocking the door as Kel pushed his dagger into the chest of the man who'd led them there. He shoved the dagger between ribs, cutting the left lung and piercing the heart. He gave the dagger a violent turn, pushing it up and down and side to side in the wound. The tip of the blade cut repeatedly through the man's heart, stopping its beating almost instantly. Though the front of his shirt was reddening, nothing showed on the carpet. Lyria shoved open the door as Kel pushed the dead man into the room. He followed right behind with Lyria. She shut the door, locking it.

The three men inside stood in shocked silence in their underwear. Scrawny limbs and pasty pale skin showed their lack of physical endeavor and lack of sunshine. Their priestly robes lay in a black heap like an evil shadow on a low table with a large mirror standing at its back. One of the men held three bits of wood in his hand. Kel knew they were drawing lots to see who would get the girl first. These were men of religion. Kel couldn't understand how this could be, but he knew what he was going to do.

The priests were staring in horror at the pimp's corpse on the floor as Kel drew a second dagger from the belt under his robe. The three men, pale and shaking, sank to their knees in front of the barred window.

Sunlight streamed into the room. Kel was drawn to the illuminating light that fell on the face of the child tied to the railings of the bed— revealing her startlingly white-blonde hair. Kel thought it was as if a star had fallen to Earth and dwells in this blackness.

The girl was wearing a small costume made of the spotted fur of some exotic cat— horribly inappropriate for her age. Her real clothing lay in a heap by that of the priests.

The girl looked at Lyria pleadingly and said in a barely audible voice, "Kill me...kill me, please. Don't let them do it to me again."

Kel turned back to the three priests with rage in his heart, clutching his daggers so tightly his knuckles whitened. He took one threatening step toward them. When suddenly a voice like thunder spoke. "Touch them not! They belong to Me!"

Kel whirled, looking at Lyria. She stood there, but her eyes were blank—only the white showed as the pupils rolled back under the lids. The very air around her shimmered and flashed with power. Lyria raised her arm and her index finger pointed toward the three men cowering by the wall.

Then the 'Other' spoke again—this time to the three priests.

"You have violated the Maiden! You have defiled the Mother! You have turned away from the Wise One!"

The 'Other' gazed at them through Lyria's unseeing eyes, laughing mirthlessly.

"You have turned your back on The Three…now you must face ME! And I am the One you cannot defile—or ignore."

Kel snatched a glance at the three men. They were even paler than before, if that were possible, and they were clutching at each other like frightened children in terror.

One of the priests shouted, "Mercy! Have mercy on us!"

Again, the 'Other' laughed.

The priest babbled, crying out, "There must be something we can do to make atonement."

'Lyria that was not Lyria' laughed yet again. "Scorpions that walk like men. There is nothing left for you to do but run. Run! RUN!!"

Kel looked at the priests—suddenly his vision doubled. He looked at the barred window, over it and somehow through it he also saw a wide doorway leading to a cobblestone road—though Kel knew they were up 77 levels. The three priests didn't hesitate. They scrambled to their feet, bolted out the door, and began to run down the road. Suddenly, the barred window was all that remained.

'Lyria that was not Lyria' raised both arms and the thunder spoke again, "Not to see the Sun! Not to touch the Earth!"

The sky turned black. It was as though the sun had been extinguished. The room plunged into darkness as Kel ran to the window. Suddenly the sun was back and a great cloud of ravens passed by. Kel looked down and saw the three priests hanging in the air one level below. A thousand ravens swirled and dove at the men. The men seemed suspended by the lifting power of so many birds clutching at them—or it may have been something else. Kel didn't know.

He then saw the ravens pluck out the eyes of each man. They were shrieking in pain and terror—calling on their God. Kel knew nothing Divine would help men such as these. Now the ravens attacked the screaming men in earnest. They swept down with cries of hunger and rage—shredding the three men's clothing, and then shredding the shreds. When they were naked, the ravens attacked in waves—eating the genitals of each man. They shrieked in agony as the swirling black cloud enveloped them once more, until the screaming finally stopped.

Suddenly the black cloud exploded into a thousand individual ravens—each flying off in a different direction. When the cloud parted, all that remained of the three priests were three picked-clean skeletons that plummeted toward the street to shatter on the cobblestones. Kel turned back into the room—he was numb.

The 'Lyria that was not Lyria,' now spoke softly, the voice almost but not quite that of a mortal woman said, "Free her, Kel."

Kel walked to the bed, cutting the young girl's bonds.

The 'Other' spoke to the girl, and gently said, "Arise, child of pain and come to Me."

The girl slid off the bed, timidly walking over to stand in front of 'Lyria that was not Lyria.' They then laid their hands upon the girl's startlingly blonde head.

"Hear me now, little one—I speak the truth. From this day I am your Totem! From this day I am your Protector! From this day you shall call yourself Raven and no mortal will ever touch you again and live if you do not wish it."

The little girl shivered, and the 'Other' continued, "You shall become a force in this land such as the world has not seen in an age. Both power and mercy travel with you, child. Choose wisely."

Then the 'Other' was gone. Kel saw a shape that might have been the shadow of a raven, and then it too was gone.

Lyria sank to her knees and Kel was afraid she'd pass between the worlds as she'd done after the bandit raid. The little girl who had been Noria, who was now Raven, gently touched Lyria's shoulder saying, "We should go."

The glazed look left Lyria's eyes. She looked up at the girl, and then she looked at Kel in awe.

"I know!" Kel said. He helped Lyria to her feet as the girl quickly put her clothing on over the obscene fur costume. There was pounding on the door.

"What's going on in there," a voice shouted through the door.

Kel and Lyria looked at each other.

"We've called the City Police. They're coming!"

Kel said, "We should go."

Chapter 43

Lyria unlocked the door and the three of them calmly stepped into the hall. Lyria locked the door behind her. Five men stood together in a crowd.

One of the men said, "I don't care if you are a priest! I run this place and I want to know what's going on in there!"

Lyria calmly handed the man the key, whispering to Kel, "Only five of them." She smiled wickedly, knowing Kel would know why that number, in this instance, would be humorous. He smiled, saying to the landlord, "Three men jumped out the window just now. I don't think this building is safe for the Brotherhood to use any more. It's getting so that violence seems to be everywhere."

The landlord paused with the key in the lock.

"Now look," he began apologetically, "I didn't know you were a priest trying to save the lives of some people intent on destroying themselves. Please don't mention this in the Cathedral and I'll make it worth your while."

Kel looked at him and seemed to consider. Then he said, "No word of this shall reach the priests from my mouth...but you had better tell the police they are not needed here, as they will surely tell everyone what has happened here today."

The landlord thought about this for a moment, turning to one of the other men shouting at him, "You heard, you dunce! Phone the police immediately and tell them this was just...just a prank call by some troublemaking kid...or something."

The man nodded, running down the hall to a black box that hung on the wall. He put part of it against his ear and spoke urgently into the wall. Kel shook his head, thinking aloud, "Amazing. Simply amazing." He wondered how the talking box might work.

The landlord opened the door.

"You said three men jumped from the window in here?"

He turned, but Kel, Lyria, and Raven were already gone. The rest of the men crowded into the room, staring blankly at the firmly barred window and at the corpse of the pimp lying sprawled on the floor.

~

Kel and his companions quickly ran down two flights of stairs to the 75th level and called the cage the dead pimp had called a 'lift.' When it arrived, the three of them entered, riding it all the way to the ground floor.

They hurried out the front door into the street. There were enough people about that they would lose themselves in no time.

Just down the street from the front door a crowd gathered. They were looking up and then down. Kel hid his smile and whispered, "Let them try to figure this one out."

One voice in the crowd said, "They must have come from the roof."

Another said, "They didn't walk up there by themselves. Someone must've thrown 'em down."

"Getting so it ain't safe to walk the streets no more without gettin' a skeleton dumped on your head," a third man said.

Neither Kel nor Lyria saw Raven pause just outside the crowd, stooping to pick up a bone fragment. It was twelve inches in length. It was part of an arm bone. It was broken at a steep angle leaving a razor point at one end and a blunt knob at the other. She hid it in the folds of her garment as she walked away to rejoin Kel and Lyria.

They turned, walking back the way they'd come. Kel wanted to get some distance between them and the crowd. Glancing back over his shoulder when they were about a half block away he saw some people in the crowd staring after them. Kel recognized the landlord and two others who had witnessed the confrontation inside the building; they were now pointing in their direction.

"Let us hurry along," he said to his companions, "they are talking about us."

They were approaching the entrance to the amphitheater when Kel said, "Wait a moment."

He slipped into the alleyway, quickly slipping his priest's robe over his head, rolling it inside out. He tucked it under his arm and returned to the street.

"Let us go in and see the show," he said, "if they think we are guilty, they will think we will run."

"You are right, "Lyria said. "Since they will be looking for a priest, they will not be able to spot you from a distance with that black robe rolled up."

Kel led his party to the gateway into the amphitheater. A turnstile with four iron arms blocked the way. Kel watched several others enter and then approached.

"How much for three," he asked the woman who was taking the money.

"One half silver each for adults and a copper for the child."

As Kel handed her the money, he heard a loud whistle approaching. He glanced behind himself and just at that moment a steam-car rolled past. It was venting some of its steam through a small pipe fitted with a reed. It was like a flute but it would only play one note—and that, very loudly. Raven moved a bit closer to Lyria as the vehicle passed.

"Must be something bad happened up the street," said the woman who'd taken Kel's money. "We don't see too many police automobiles around here."

She stretched, trying to see around the edge of the building, but of course she couldn't. Kel waited patiently for her to tell them to proceed.

Finally, she looked back at Kel and his companions. "Sorry, you may go inside."

She pulled a lever and Kel saw the iron turnstile move—he knew the mechanism had been unlocked. He turned it by hand as Lyria went through.

Raven touched the turnstile, quickly pulling back her hand. "The iron is so hot!"

Kel touched the turnstile; in the shade of the awning, it was really quite cool. He looked at Raven, confused. She stared vacantly—seeing something not yet come to pass.

"I didn't know he could boil," she said simply.

Without further comment, the little girl passed through the turnstile. Kel came through last, just as another howling police automobile steamed past. They walked down a corridor that was lit only by the sunlight streaming in from the open amphitheater.

Inside, there were young men all dressed alike with green vests and pants and white shirts. One politely offered to help them find a seat. Kel nodded and they walked down the aisle with the man. He led them up a flight of stone steps—three tiers up, gesturing toward the empty seats in front of them. He smiled and said, "I hope you enjoy the show! They are cycle jousting today!"

He turned and walked back down the steps, looking for someone else to assist.

"He seems a nice fellow," Lyria said. "I can't imagine that everyone here is an evil person."

"Only some," Raven said, "and they are far from us here."

Kel glanced at Raven, but she said no more.

Across the arena, a man standing at the top of a tower began speaking through a flaring tube that amplified his voice enough that everyone present could hear him.

"We have two shows for you today," the man shouted. "First we're having the local champion cycle jousters compete to see who'll represent the central part of the city in the upcoming grand tournament."

The crowd roared, stomping and clapping. While the man was waiting for the crowd to settle down, Lyria noticed that young men and women were walking slowly up and down the stairways selling drinks from trays suspended by straps over their shoulders. She nudged Kel and he obtained bottles of water for them to drink while they watched the show.

Then the announcer spoke again, shouting, "We have six competitors here with us for this tournament. Come forward, contestants!"

Six young men walked onto the field. They were in full iron armor. The armor was obviously fairly heavy as the men walked slowly. Each carried a helmet under his left arm and each helmet was painted a different color. The armored men raised their hands as the announcer spoke their names. Different segments of the crowd cheered for each man in turn. Obviously the people of the Black City had favorites. Finally, all but two walked off the field to stand behind the low wall as four very fit men rolled two large steam-cycles onto the field.

Each cycle had two wheels and were controlled with a cross bar with handles at each end. Below the seat, a small steam engine was huffing and grumbling. When the bikes turned to face each other, an armored man swung a leg over the seats of each bike, straddling the machine as though it were a horse.

Kel, Lyria, and Raven watched with interest. They had never seen anything like this before.

Both men were handed long wooden lances that they lowered toward each other over the handlebars of the bikes. At a shouted word from the man in the tower, the two men disengaged the braking mechanisms on their machines and went hurtling toward each other.

Kel heard Raven gasp when the roaring machines came together. The bikes barely missed hitting each other head on. One man's lance struck his opponent low on his chest, sliding off. Although the impact must have been fairly heavy he remained on his machine. The other man was not so lucky. His opponent's lance struck him just below his helmet and it literally lifted him out of the saddle. He tumbled over backwards, striking the ground with an audible thump. The crowd cheered and hooted. The defeated jouster's bike wobbled along for a few feet and fell to the side. The water in the reservoir spilled through a safety valve dousing the flame that produced the steam and the engine quit.

The victor rode slowly around the field to the cheering and booing of various factions in the crowd. The rider didn't seem to care; he'd been victorious and that was all that mattered. Finally he returned to the center of the field, turned off the flame to his bike, and dismounted. Two men rolled the bike off the field as two more ran to the fallen bike to remove it as well. The fallen jouster was helped to his feet and he limped off the field, obviously injured but not seriously.

Kel, Lyria, and Raven watched the show as it progressed. Each competition progressed much as the one before it until only two men remained. The first man they'd seen competing would challenge the man who won the third bout. Raven seemed especially interested and asked, "What happens with the last man who wins?"

Lyria said, "He will go on to compete against more men who won other contests."

"So there is no end to it?"

"I don't know," Lyria said, "I imagine that sooner or later he will no longer have anyone to compete against."

"It seems sad," the young girl said, "to finish your life work so quickly."

"I am sure he will go on to do other things," Kel said. "I imagine someone with these kinds of skills would be welcomed into the warrior society of the city or as a trainer for young riders who also want to be champions."

"I hadn't thought of that," Raven said.

It didn't, however, turn out that way. As the two steam cycles roared toward each other for the last engagement, the engine on the first man's bike sputtered for a second. He looked down for just an instant as the engine reignited. He looked up, but the machines were coming together at a very fast speed. He lifted his lance but his opponent struck him hard and low on his abdomen. The lance tip dropped, puncturing the steam chamber immediately below the seat.

An explosive eruption of steam enveloped the rider. Boiling water and steam shot up under his armored chest, spraying over his body. An instant later, a spray of steam and boiling water shot out of the eye openings in his helmet. Though he surely screamed, nobody heard him. He remained on the bike for a moment and then collapsed off the saddle onto the ground. His opponent dumped his bike, turning back to help the fallen rider. Removing his helmet, he tossed it to the field, hurrying as fast as his armor would allow. He was unbuckling and dropping various segments of his armor as he ran. By then, several other men were out on the field. They removed the unconscious man's helmet and the flesh of his face pulled in long red strings where it adhered to the faceplate of the helmet. The man's face was boiled, as was the rest of his body—it no longer resembled a face. Fortunately he'd died quickly.

The crowd was howling as Raven said, "I think we should go."

Lyria responded, "I agree." She rose to leave and Kel and Raven followed her example.

As they were walking out, Kel saw a giant animal being led into the arena. Amazed, he paused for a moment. It was a wooly rhinoceros. Lyria saw it and stopped as well. The attendants had already cleared out the body of the jouster and the steam machine he had ridden to his death. The announcer was shouting something, but Kel couldn't hear him on the ground floor.

Kel looked at the animal—it was huge. Kel stood almost six feet tall and he could see that the animal's shoulder would be much taller than he. The animal's back sloped slightly to his hips, which were still over five feet in height. The large animal was almost fourteen feet from the tip of its nose to its rump. The reddish-brown shaggy coat was a rough pelt that covered the animal's flanks and hung down between its eyes. Its head carried two horns—the first stood a bit over two feet tall from nose to tip. The one behind it was less than half that length.

It seemed to Kel that the animal was sick. The great beast slowly turned its head from side to side. Its eyes seemed to not be focused on anything in particular and when the animal herders began to coax it into the amphitheater, it stumbled, and then regained its footing. Lyria tugged on Kel's sleeve and he looked in the direction she was pointing. Three men on horseback rode into the open arena, each carrying a heavy spear with a long iron point. These were killing blades, not jousting lances, Kel realized.

Raven whispered, "Are they going to kill it?"

"Look at it," Kel said to Lyria; "they have given it something to make it clumsy and slow."

"This is not a fair contest," Lyria stated in anger, "they are slaughtering an innocent beast for entertainment."

"Let us wait a moment, Lyria, and see if we can change that."

Kel attempted to reach the mind of the great beast. The animal's mind was clouded—unsure of itself, hard to reach. He tried harder as the first man began his charge. The man tried to bury his spear deep into the animal's side, but it struck the heavy shoulder bone of the great animal causing a relatively minor wound as the spear cut flesh, then rebounded out of the animal's hide. The impact was great enough, however, the rider lost his grip on the shaft of the spear and it fell from his hands. He turned his horse quickly to the right and rode off, circling back to where the other two riders waited their turn. As the second man prepared to attack, the first was handed another spear.

Kel tried again to reach the great animal, but it was Raven who finally touched its mind. The beast suddenly looked up alertly at the horseman approaching with his spear raised into the air—focusing for the first time since this brutal display began. Not waiting for the rider to lower the spear, the great rhinoceros charged with a bellow. Neither man nor horse had a chance. The great hairy beast literally ran the horse and rider down—grinding them both into a red pulp on the ground under its huge, elephantine feet.

The animal didn't wait. Under Raven's guidance, the rhino wheeled and charged the last two of the three riders. The long horn on its snout pierced a horse's belly exiting high on the animal's side. The tip struck the horseman on the inside of his thigh, ripping a hideous gash, tearing the femoral artery. Horse and rider were lifted bodily into the air and flung over the back of the galloping rhino to the packed earth floor of the arena. Neither horse nor rider moved. The last man, who'd actually been the first to attack the great rhino, took one look at the thundering beast…turned and fled.

"Coward," the audience shrieked.

"The beast wins! Free him," others shouted.

"Free the beast! Free the beast! Free the beast!"

The auditorium shook with the demand of the crowd. The entire arena was on its feet. People raised their fists into the air, shaking them in time to the chant.

"Free the beast! Free the beast! Free the beast!"

The rhino looked up at the crowd and they cheered him. He snorted and they cheered again. Then he looked at Raven and his wild gaze softened. He slowly nodded his head in her direction as his handlers removed him from the arena.

When the crowd was finally calmed down, the announcer once more picked up his megaphone.

"People of Los Angeles—you have decided and so it shall be. On my honor, I'll have the animal taken by steam engine back to the north. He'll go back to the ice and there he'll live out his life unmolested by us."

The crowd roared.

"We shall put a tag on his ear so that any who venture to the ice will see this mark and not touch the animal again. He has won his freedom."

Cheering and chanting rose like an audible cloud from the packed crowd inside the amphitheater.

"Well," Lyria said, "it seems that several people in Black City have some kind of honor!"

Chapter 44

As they walked out of the amphitheater, Raven seemed very pleased with herself. She was smiling for the first time since she'd come to be with Kel and Lyria. They walked down the street, away from the building where the police automobiles were just now pulling back out onto the road, heading off in various directions. No point in pressing their luck.

"I'm hungry," Raven said, looking up at Kel and Lyria.

"Surely there is a place here in the center of town where one can buy food." Lyria smiled, recalling her wonderment the first time she'd seen a shop selling nothing but food—it was even ready to eat. This brought home to her how many people lived in the city. She shuddered to think of living in such a crowd.

Kel said, "Here's a place now."

They walked through the entrance of the restaurant and sat at a table near the front where they could watch the street.

A woman came quickly to the table carrying menus. Kel took one, thanking the woman. They ordered three glasses of tea and the woman walked away.

"That was close—we were almost captured leaving that living quarters building," Kel said.

"You do not have to tell me that," Lyria said emphatically.

"They deserved it," Raven commented, "I would like to see that happen to all of them—the men and the women."

"Women?" Lyria was clearly startled by that comment.

Raven lowered her eyes and her voice, obviously embarrassed. "Sometimes women come with the men. They like to do things to me too, or make me do things to them, while their husbands watch," she whispered.

Kel and Lyria stared at each other in shock. They were almost unable to comprehend what the girl was telling them. Raven fell silent for a moment and the waiting woman reappeared, asking for their orders. Raven ordered eggs, toast, and bacon, even though it was late for breakfast. Without so much as a hesitation, Kel and Lyria ordered the same, much to Raven's delight. As they ate, they discussed their next move.

"We need go back to where we started," Kel offered. "Dan will be waiting there for us."

"I agree," Lyria said with a nod, "we will just walk back the way we came; there are too many people on the street for anyone to recognize us."

Raven spoke around a mouthful of toast and bacon, "The men should be back inside by now. They need to attend to their business."

"Oink, oink," Lyria said with a smile, looking at Raven.

Raven looked back and Kel burst into laughter, "Lyria thinks that if you talk with your mouth full of food, or eat too much butter, you are either a plain old hog or maybe even worse, a butter hog."

Raven giggled, "How can you eat too much butter?"

Both Kel and Lyria laughed at Raven's remark.

They finished eating and walked back outside. In the early afternoon light, the tall buildings on the west side cast shadows into the street. They walked cautiously, watching the people around them. Raven walked with her head held high. It was obvious her conversation with the 'Other' had worked a transformation in the young girl's mind. She didn't seem afraid, even when they passed the doorway of the building they'd fled several hours earlier. They walked by in silence, Raven secretly clutching the bone fragment in her fist, hoping one of the men might still be lingering outside.

There were loungers in front of the building, but not the men they'd confronted earlier. As they passed, Kel and Lyria listened to their conversation.

"The coppers say someone must have thrown the bones from the roof," one man offered. "Said it was a crime, of sorts, but certainly not a mass suicide as that one fellow claimed."

"How could it be? There was just bones in the street!"

"Hey, I know," a third man offered, obviously quite drunk, "they jumped so fast they lost their skins!"

The first man shoved the fellow roughly, laughing, "Then where are the skins?"

The third man scratched his head, pondering. "I hadn't thought of that," he said in wonder, sitting heavily onto the sidewalk.

When they were past, the three of them began laughing.

"Apparently, nothing of significance happened here," Lyria said.

"That may be," Kel responded, "but the Cathedral will know they lost three priests today—they will have their robes as proof."

"I fear you are correct," Lyria said with a sigh. "We best get away from here."

"Where will we go?" Raven asked, looking up into Lyria's eyes.

"We have a safe place to live while we are here, and you can stay with us if you wish," Lyria answered.

Raven hugged her, "I want to go with you, Lyria. I can't go home again, you know. Not after what they did to me. I would be too shamed."

"It was not your fault, honey," Kel offered, "you were kidnapped and your family slain."

"That is another reason I cannot go home," Raven answered, "somebody has to pay for what they did to me."

They arrived at the corner, and true to his word, Dan was waiting in the steam-car. They heard him firing up the engine as they approached.

"I want to sit in front," Raven said emphatically.

They laughed, and Kel said, "You may sit in the front."

Raven giggled with glee as she opened the door, and then froze for a moment. But before anyone could question her, she leaped into the vehicle and began hugging Dan.

"Dandan! You're here!" she shouted in joy as Kel and Lyria got into the back seat.

"This needs some explanation," Kel laughed. "Dandan?"

Dan smiled self-consciously as Raven explained what was going on.

"Dandan is from my tribe. He was always nice to the children of my village," she enthused. "He was always willing to take time to play with us. To teach us new things and help us with anything that needed help."

She laughed, continuing, "We used to call him Dandan. It was a special name we gave him."

Lyria looked at Dan. "Should we call you Dandan now?"

Dan and Raven both laughed, then Dan said, "No! Just keep things the way they are." Dan opened his pocket watch, glanced at it, and said, "You know, you were gone for almost three hours! I was beginning to think I might not see you again."

"As were we. We will tell you the story," Kel replied.

Dan started the steam-car and pulled out into traffic. As they drove back toward the safe house, Kel and Lyria told Dan in brief terms what had happened. He glanced several times at Raven, giving her encouraging smiles.

"Lyria is amazing," the girl told Dan. "The Splendid Lady came Herself to rescue me, and She spoke through Lyria. They saved me, Dan, the three of them."

"Kel told us he dreamed of you, little one," Dan said. "Long ago he knew he was coming here to find you."

Kel looked at Dan in surprise, and Dan laughed. "Remember the dream you told about the star in the Black City you thought might be Lyria? It could've been no one other than Nor...er...Raven."

The young girl looked at Kel and said, "Thank you, Kel. Your coming here saved my life. I didn't want to live anymore—I was so ashamed. I was planning to kill myself this very night, after..." She looked quickly down, tears forming in her eyes.

"Do you remember the time you nearly set my house on fire?" Dan asked.

The girl looked at him, laughing in spite of her tears. "I was going to cook some food for you, Dandan—only I didn't know how your oven worked."

Dan glanced in the mirror, and looked at Lyria and Kel, "My oven was one of the new gas kind. She managed to get the gas turned on, but she didn't know how to light it. By the time I got home, she had found the fire starter and was about to strike a spark."

"He stopped me just in time. Dandan turned it off and opened all his windows. He had to come to my house for dinner that night." She giggled at the memory, "But I still got to make dinner for him."

"That she did," Dan verified, "and she was only seven summers at the time."

"After that I wasn't allowed to touch the gas things people have in their homes in the village."

Lyria said, "I do not think I would want to touch them either."

They all laughed as Dan drove down the street, heading away from the tall buildings and the threat they seemed to pose.

"Having Nor...I uh mean Raven here will complicate things a little," Dan said. "We'll have to take her with us to see the magician. Our group must know everything if we're to be able to help."

Kel removed the folded bit of paper from his pocket. He had almost forgotten he had it in the rush of events that had just transpired. He unfolded it, reading aloud, "We are to meet the magician at eight in the evening in two days, Dan. I assume you know where this meeting will take place?"

"In fact, I do. It will be somewhat away from the center of the city, so that worry is lessened."

Kel asked, "What time is it now?"

Dan retrieved his pocket watch from the vest pocket, opening the cover. "It's now three in the afternoon. Why?"

"I was told by the magician that a crystal ship had come in from the far eastern lands across the great sea and I was thinking it might be interesting to see it."

Lyria immediately agreed with Kel, as she was also eager to see one of the great vessels he had described in his reading from the book on the trail.

"Very well," Dan said, "we have the time, and I know the way to the waterfront."

Raven looked at Dan thoughtfully for a moment, and said, "Have you been to see her, Dandan?"

Dan looked quickly at the little girl, attempting to evaluate what she meant, fearing the truth.

"I think we should go see her first," Raven said in a very serious voice. "Have you been yet?"

"Who are we speaking of?" Asked Kel.

Kel was confused at the interchange between his friend and the young girl.

Dan didn't hear him, though, as he was totally focused on the young girl beside him.

"How do you know of that?"

Dan was glancing at the girl, barely keeping his attention on the road.

Raven smiled slyly, saying, "Sometimes grownups think children are asleep when they are not."

She giggled and Dan responded, "You spied on us?"

"When you lived in the city you said you spied," the girl answered defensively. "I was in my room listening to you and my mother and father talking. I was in bed, but I was not asleep."

"But, you couldn't have been more than five when that conversation took place," Dan said, somewhat confused.

"It was sad and I remembered," the girl answered simply.

Kel and Lyria were at a loss. Whatever was happening in the front seat didn't include them—but it bothered them nevertheless. They sat silently, listening to the exchange between Dan and a very mature sounding nine-year-old girl.

"You shouldn't wait, you know," Raven said. "Bad things happen and everything changes and sometimes you never get to do what you thought you would."

"How well I realize that," Dan said with a quaver in his voice.

"Then it is decided," the girl said firmly, "let us go see her right now; we'll see the crystal ship another day."

At the next intersection, Dan made a left turn. He glanced in the mirror and in a tight voice said to Kel and Lyria, "I hope you don't mind."

"It's important," Raven added somberly.

Kel nodded to Dan in the mirror and they drove on in silence for a while. Soon they were in open country with small farms and homes standing on large sections of land—although there seemed to be no farming going on around many of the homes they passed. Then Kel and Lyria saw a row of trees lining the roadway on the right side of the road, and an arched gateway. Dan drove through the arch as Raven put her hand on his. He turned, smiling sadly at her.

"You will not be sorry, Dandan," she whispered. "This needs to happen."

On both sides of the narrow winding roadway were carefully tended shrubs and trees. Lyria marveled at the large expanses of grass that seemed to never change height. She looked quizzically at Kel—he'd never seen grass like this either. But beyond the mowed lawns, the regularly placed slabs of stone took their attention. Rows upon rows of them—some very large, some very small. Dan drove on in silence and when he finally arrived at his destination, he lowered the steam pressure, and sighed.

"I imagine this is a new kind of place to you," he began. "This is what is called a cemetery—it's a burial ground for the people of the city. Here they bury their dead in caskets—fancy boxes, if you will. Each stone marks the resting place of someone who was loved."

He opened his door and stepped out. Raven opened her side as well, joining Dan in front of the vehicle, holding his hand. Lyria and Kel followed, still confused.

Dan began walking slowly between the rows of stones. Kel saw that each bore an inscription dedicated to the deceased person who resided below the ground. It was a sobering display.

Dan turned to the left, Raven still holding his hand. They moved up two more rows— then Dan began crying. Raven sobbed with him. Dan sank to his knees in front of a stone laying flat to the earth. Lyria and Kel saw that it bore no inscription and was quite small. Dan caught his breath, and between sobs, began his story.

"I told you something of my reckless youth—the thieving and spying I did for the resistance organization."

Kel and Lyria nodded mutely as Dan slowly continued, "In those days I believed I could do anything—be more than one person and that it would all work out just fine. I discovered I was wrong."

He sobbed again, and Raven hugged him. He hugged her as well, drawing support from the simple understanding of the child.

"If you remember, Lyria, I mentioned once in answer to a question, that everyone should have a name. The person who lies here has no name. She did at one time, but no more. Her stone is blank."

"Daisy," Lyria said in a flat voice.

"Yes," Dan answered, "Daisy—she was my love. It was like…there was a light within her that would dispel all the darkness my life held. She…she made me…real. She didn't know what I did for a living. She never knew about the stealing and the spying. But then I took the sword and some other things from the Cathedral. I was warned that the priests would come for me. The resistance offered me a safe house, the one we abide in, as a matter of fact."

He paused for a moment, "But I had another house. Actually it was Daisy's house, I was living with her then. I did this to her," Dan sobbed, resting one hand on the cold, blank stone. Raven hugged him again encouragingly and he continued.

"She was living in a house of love—my Daisy. It was a house of love. She never questioned me and never knew. When they came, I wasn't there. I was in the safe house with the magician, being very cautious and safe—trying to figure out what I should do. I was safe when the priests came for me, and when they didn't find me they took my dear Daisy instead."

Dan was openly crying now, telling his story between racking sobs. Raven was crying silently at his side.

"When it was decided that I should take Daisy with me into hiding, I returned to her house. It was as though an evil storm had passed within. Every piece of furniture, and every precious tiny glass animal she loved so much was smashed and in ruin on the floor. The priests had relieved themselves on our bed. But that was after they raped her. The place stunk. They left taunting messages, written on the walls discussing her reactions to what they were doing to her—each one adding something as the next one took her. I was a spy living secretly in her house of love, and she died for it."

Dan paused for an instant, looking up beseechingly at Lyria and Kel as though hoping they could somehow help him get her back. He looked back to the stone and finished his story.

"I knew where they'd take her. It's the place where the priests do these deeds. There's an enclosed area behind the zeppelin barn that's their abattoir. I climbed the wall, dropping down behind some bushes where I could hide. From where I was crouching, I could see the priests and about a dozen soldiers. The soldiers were in a ring around the steel post. My Daisy was there with the priests. They'd put a steel collar around her neck that was chained to the pole with a chain about twenty feet long. They'd stripped her naked and everyone was watching her—staring at her. Then came the oil. They poured it over her head, making sure she was covered completely. They took their time spreading it over her body with their hands. They were laughing. How I wished I'd had a weapon.

"By the time I realized exactly what they were planning, it was too late. Still, I should have done something—anything to try to save her. But there were all the soldiers, you see; I knew I wouldn't be able to pass them by without dying. So to save myself, I sat and watched as they took bets as to how many times she'd be able to drag the chain around the pole before she died.

"They interrogated her once more, hitting her in the stomach, making her collapse to her knees. But she stood right up again, and that was when they put the flame to her."

Dan broke down again, crying uncontrolled. Finally, he was able to tell the end.

"They all lost their bets that day. She stood there, a column of fire and smoke, and did not run. My beautiful Daisy stood without crying out until she finally dropped to the ground and could no longer move. The priests laughed, called her a witch and half-human. I heard the soldiers say they'd gather her remains in the morning when they'd cooled and feed them to the pigs. That night I went back over the wall and I stole her body from them. I brought her here, buried her with the help of the magician, and put the unmarked stone over her. I dare not mark it. If they found it, they'd dig her up and commit more foul acts with her bones."

He looked from Kel to Lyria in a pleading manner and said, "Can you not see now why I am a coward? I stood there, watching that horror, and did nothing. Nothing!"

It was Raven who spoke first, "All you could have done back then was die, Dandan. By living you carry a burden, and you retain the right to avenge her death. You could not save her, but you can make them pay for what they did."

Dan looked down at the somber girl and said, "And I planned to do just that, little one, I wanted to find the priests and I wanted to kill them all, but somehow I never quite did. Things just never seemed to be…right. Days later, I fled the city and the hateful Cathedral like the coward that I am. I fled into the wilderness, abandoning my Daisy and all thoughts of vengeance. I ended up finally in Mountain Village, and there I stayed. I was afraid to go back, afraid to even think about why I didn't go after the priests right away."

Raven squeezed his hand. She understood more than anyone what Dan was facing, and what he must do to cleanse his spirit and save his life.

They returned to the steam-car in silence. Dan raised the pressure and they were back on the road. They traveled over an hour before anyone spoke.

"We will help you, Dan," Lyria said in earnest, "we will help you avenge your woman now, if you wish it."

"All in good time," Dan said, "I have been eaten alive by this. I'm a hollow vessel, no spirit remaining, and no soul left to save. I am no longer afraid to die. It would be a blessing to just cease to exist. If indeed there is an afterlife, and Daisy is there, I don't deserve to be in her company."

"Would you still wish to avenge her?" Raven's question was whispered.

"I would, and I will this time regardless of whether I live or die. A coward matters not in the scheme of life. If I pass, it will be as though I never existed, and that is how it should be."

Raven was crying again and said, "That is not true, Dandan, you have been like a light to the children of Mountain Village—we all love you. You matter to us. We don't want you to die."

Dan looked at the girl and smiled, "I wish I'd been born in your village and never had to come to this turn of events."

"Then you would have been a different person, Dandan," Raven replied wisely. "We love you for who you are now."

Dan returned his attention to the road, thinking about what had been said before he spoke. "Very well then—my road will be the road of vengeance until they are as dead as my lovely Daisy. This must be done carefully, though; the reckless youth I had been died in the flames with Daisy, along with my life and my spirit. I will have vengeance, but it will be planned and carefully accomplished. I don't wish to die just yet. I would wait, if I could; not dying until they're all dead, every one of them."

Kel considered for a moment and asked, "Do you know which priests committed this hideous act?"

"Yes," Dan answered, "all of them."

They drove on in silence until they reached the safe house. They drove down the unpaved drive to the small house, carefully watching the roadway behind them, making sure they hadn't been followed. Once inside, they allowed themselves to relax. Raven sat with Dan on the sofa, telling him children's stories he most likely had heard before. Still, he listened with rapt attention—gasping or laughing where appropriate. Kel and Lyria watched them from across the room, and she then looked at Kel and smiled. He knew she longed for children of her own—he smiled back wishing their journey had already ended. It was, of course, only beginning.

Chapter 45

"So? What's your determination?" The Bishop sat upright in the big chair behind his fine wooden desk. He held his hands together on the blotter paper, afraid that Father Woods might see them trembling. Was he afraid? Was he angry? He couldn't yet ascertain the answer. He did know he was worried.

"Well," Father Woods began, "We don't have to worry about the police. They found the bones, but we cleaned the inside of the building quickly. As it turns out, the police never searched any of the rooms, and they were convinced the bones came from the roof. When they went up there, they found one jawbone—dropped by the prankster who hurled the rest of them into the street." Father Woods smiled reassuringly, though he was far from reassured.

"Well? Was it pranksters then?" The Bishop wasn't happy, Father Woods noticed. That was to be expected.

"No, Your Eminence, the jawbone they found on the roof was placed there by me personally—to assist the police in…solving the crime." He laughed, but the Bishop did not.

"What of Fathers Janzen, Hurley, and Jamison?"

Father Woods sighed, "They are indeed missing, Your Eminence. It truly was their clothing in that room. Their identification papers were all there as well—they were definitely in that room with the half-human child."

The Bishop rose to his feet, staring hard at the priest. "Then where are they?" he demanded. "Why have they not been found—any of them?"

"The men in front of the building, who were our only witnesses, told me a priest and a woman came out of the room with the beastling child," the priest explained. "They claimed three men committed suicide by jumping. That is, of course, ridiculous—the windows are barred."

"And your pimp was dead," the Bishop said with mounting fury.

"Yes, Your Eminence," the priest said, bowing his head. "He was stabbed."

"And all those brave, loyal men just let those two leave with my property? That child-thing was making us money," the Bishop shouted. "Are you thinking what I'm thinking, Father Woods?"

"You're wondering about the comments made by our half-human stowaway, are you not?"

280

The Bishop struck his fist on the desk and said in a measured tone, "What else in the name of the Redeemed God would I be thinking of?"

Father Woods winced and bowed his head again, "They left no names, Your Eminence. But there were two—a man and a woman. It could be the assassins we've been forewarned about, but how would experienced assassins make three men just disappear? Or worse, dissolve their bodies into nothing and cast their bones to the street?"

"Perhaps," the Bishop said coldly, "you should consider asking an assassin."

The Bishop sat again and more calmly said, "You must bring those witnesses here. We must let the beastling whore hear what they have to say."

Father Woods bowed his head a third time. *This is getting tiresome,* he thought, *the Bishop shouldn't treat me like some unimaginative underling.* "Yes, Your Eminence. I'll bring them in the morning so they may speak with the half-human before she goes to work."

"Very well," the Bishop said, "Make it happen."

He gave a dismissive wave; Father Woods rose and quickly left the room. He clearly had work to do.

~

Adria awakened early and found she was thinking about the sting. It seemed to be becoming more and more important. That was fine—it meant her Godhead was imminent. She wouldn't have to stay here doing this kind of work, sharing her life with roommates. She deserved better. She knew it would happen—the voices had said it would happen soon.

There was a knock on the door, and her betrothed entered. She quickly lowered her head. The priest walked up to her and said, "Come with me. We must see some men before you work today."

"More men to service, Your Grace?"

"No, people you must listen to. They'll describe two people and you must decide if they're describing the assassins you told us of."

"Very well, Your Grace," she responded, rising from her bed.

There was a steam-car from the Cathedral waiting at the curb, its engine hissing, standing at full pressure for an immediate departure. The driver exited the vehicle when he saw the pair walk out of the building. By the time they were at the vehicle, he was holding the door for the priest. After Father Woods was seated, he shut the front passenger side door and returned to his position behind the wheel. He wouldn't demean himself

281

opening a door for a woman, much less a half-human. Adria said nothing—she opened the rear door for herself, sliding into the interior. The car pulled quickly from the curb, barely giving the young woman time to shut her door.

No words were spoken as they sped toward the Cathedral. Traffic was light early in the morning, so they made good time. Adria occupied herself looking out the window at the sights of the great city. *Imagine*, she thought, *millions of people—all waiting for the Scorpion Queen*. She smiled at her secret thoughts. Her time was coming—the voices had reassured her only this morning.

The auto came to a halt by the side door of the great black building. The driver opened the door for the priest. Adria waited until he was out before opening her door and exiting. They walked wordlessly toward the big bronze door. Adria kept her head lowered, but she let her eyes rise surveying the building and her betrothed—if that truly is what he was. "*Why would she think a thing like that*," she wondered? Sometimes it was so hard to keep things straight.

Once through the door, they climbed the stairway to the Bishop's waiting room. Harold already had the door open for them. Father Woods and Adria entered the room and the man closed the door behind them.

"You're to sit here and wait, Your Grace," the man said. "His Eminence will be with you shortly."

"Thank you, Harold," Father Woods said, motioning Adria to a chair in the corner. She sat, head lowered. She wondered what they wanted. She was late for the sting of the scorpion and she really needed it this morning—she felt itchy.

The door opposite her opened. She heard people entering; they were all men. Were they going to take her again like they did in that room with the painting on the ceiling? She found she really didn't care just as long as they'd brought the sting with them. She was disappointed when she found they hadn't.

"You may look up, beastling," the Bishop said.

Adria raised her head. There were two men with the Bishop. They clearly were not priests, nor did she recognize them. She waited, knowing they'd make their desires known one way or another.

"These men saw two people under mysterious circumstances, beastling," the Bishop began. "They will tell you what they saw and you're to tell us if they're the two you told us about."

Adria nodded, but didn't speak. That seemed to please the Bishop.

One of the men described the priest and his serving woman to her in as much detail as he could remember. The other man nodded in agreement, but said nothing. Adria listened patiently.

"These two were young," the man began. "Eighteen summers or a little less."

Adria nodded, "That would be the right age for them."

The man continued, "The man was tall, he had long straight brown hair and brown eyes. The woman, now, she was…special."

At that Adria raised her eyes to the man, who quickly looked away from her, uncomfortable in the presence of something not human. Adria was pleased.

"The woman had black hair and blue eyes. Her eyes stood out against all that black hair tied up in many braids."

At that Adria looked up again and said, "These braids, sir, were they tightly done with not much hair in each so that the look might be that of a helmet?"

"That's exactly the look," the man said enthusiastically. "She looked strong as well; much too strong for whom she was claiming to be."

Adria turned to the Bishop, lowered her head and said, "They are the ones, Your Eminence. The braids gave her away in truth. Years ago when we were children, that woman told me of a tradition in her birth tribe. When the women prepared for war, they tied their hair like that, in many braids to keep it short, close to the head, and out of their eyes. Apparently it is a very efficient way of keeping one's hair long yet out of the way in battle."

"The women go into battle?" The Bishop was thunderstruck. Who ever heard of such a thing! Women warriors? Ridiculous! He turned to the priest. "We've heard enough, Father Woods. Take her into the hall and let Harold watch her for a moment so we may talk."

He turned toward the other two men, "You've done well today; too bad you couldn't have been that assertive on the day they stole the beastling child."

The two men hung their heads in shame.

"You may leave us now," the Bishop said.

Both men left the room as the Bishop turned to the priest who had just returned. "Well, now we know for sure, do we not?"

"Yes, Your Eminence. Now all we have to do is find them."

The Bishop smiled, "I've an idea for that as well. First, take that creature back to where she belongs before she fouls my anteroom with her waste or something."

"Yes, Your Eminence, would you wish me to return after that's done?"

"Yes, we've a couple of matters to discuss."

"As you wish, Your Eminence," the priest answered.

Adria waited silently in the next room. Harold was standing over her with a short knife in his hand. The priest laughed, "It's all right, Harold, I'm taking her away now."

The servant sighed with relief, returning the knife to the silver tray that held the remains of the Bishop's breakfast. Father Woods almost laughed again—the servant had been trying to threaten the half-human with a butter knife.

"Come. We're leaving," he said to the girl.

She rose, silently following him out the door.

"May I speak, Your Grace?"

"Certainly," he responded.

"Will...will I be able to get my sting this morning? It is so late."

"Don't worry, child," he answered. "You'll get your sting, and more."

He nodded knowingly at the girl—she understood she was to get the magic as well. She lowered her head and said nothing more on the way to the steam-car.

~

The Bishop picked up his phone and spoke to his servant.

"I want to see Father Anderson, Harold. Would you ring him for me?"

Harold answered in the affirmative, and the Bishop hung up.

Twenty minutes later, Harold admitted Father Anderson. The shabbily dressed man entered quietly, kneeling, as was the custom.

"Rise Father Anderson," the Bishop said. "What has the best of spies learned?"

The sixty-year-old priest looked up at the Bishop and said, "There's absolutely no chatter in the city whatsoever regarding assassins sent to kill anyone—including you, Your Eminence."

The Bishop told the spy about the identification made by Adria, but he wasn't impressed. He just shook his head, "Those people may be the ones the half-human spoke of, but I don't believe they're assassins, Your Eminence. I still find it very hard to believe that any of the tribal creatures know of your existence, where you might be, or even what you might look like."

The Bishop shifted uncomfortably in his chair.

Father Anderson continued, "I believe those two came perhaps to rescue the child-whore. It wouldn't surprise me if they weren't halfway back to their tribe by now. They were damn lucky finding her like that, though..." he trailed off.

The Bishop tried a new approach to the problem.

"Can you, or anyone with your craft, dissolve a body, leaving only bones?"

"Certainly, Your Eminence, with a vat of acid and a little time. The odor would be extreme, and the air in the room poisonous from the acid fumes. It'd take several hours and require many safety precautions."

"That's what I feared," the Bishop said. "How did they do that to the priests? There were three of them against two—could they not defend themselves?"

Father Anderson cleared his throat before continuing. "They may well have tried to defend themselves, we don't know. Considering their robes were all on the table in the room, it's possible they were enjoying the whore and were taken by surprise."

"That may be," said the Bishop, "but this business with the bones bothers me."

"Frankly," Anderson responded, "I'm wondering if they took the three of them somewhere else in the building as captives—perhaps drugged. Now that's something the people of the half-human tribes would be capable of. You'll remember the shouting that drew all the attention didn't happen immediately. It's possible in the confusion they not only took the child-whore, but the three priests as well. Nobody saw them actually leave, you'll remember."

The Bishop's head was whirling—would it never stop?

"So you think the priests were kidnapped?"

"It's one possibility, Your Eminence," the spy responded. "They might be interrogating them right now. Remember that the blonde-thing said there were three on the trail. Perhaps it was the third person who threw the bones from the roof to frighten us."

"Yet another possibility," the Bishop shouted. "How can I be sure they aren't here to kill me?"

"There's a very simple solution to this problem," the spy said. "Have someone impersonate you. Then you go into hiding for several days while the imitation Bishop spends time in the city going for walks, visiting museums, and going to the theater."

The Bishop smiled at Father Anderson—comprehension coming at last. "If they try to kill him, even if they succeed, they would only kill the imposter. With your people following him everywhere, even if he's killed, you'd have the killers and I could go back to being me."

Father Anderson smiled, "I take it, Your Eminence, you approve?"

"By all means," the Bishop enthused, "but where do we find an imposter?"

Father Anderson stood, pointing at himself.

Chapter 46

After receiving her injections, Adria returned to the tavern, ready for the divine work of the day. As usual, Larry went with her, marketing her to any and all customers. Adria began her day by dancing on stage to get the attention of all the men. She'd slowly strip until she was naked—at that point, the men would be lining up. Larry noticed with some satisfaction that he recognized many of the day's customers, some having been there only the day before. Adria's wild abandon and the lure of her half-human nature created a big draw. By afternoon, Larry Harper's pockets were bulging with coins and paper money. This looked like it would be the best day yet, and they had started late.

Afterward, on the walk back to the rooming house, they stopped at a restaurant. Adria was now dressed to look simply like a woman of the city in a long skirt that came down to her ankles. She thought the dress was hilarious, but knowing the rules, she allowed Larry to show her how to put it on—with a lot of touching on his part she noticed. She smiled smugly to herself and waited for him to take her. He didn't, which made her somewhat angry; she wondered if he thought he was too good for her.

Larry decided to buy her dinner that evening, as he was happy with her performance that day. After the food was served and they had begun to eat, Larry said, "You're doing very well, Adria."

Adria looked up with a mouthful of food, but she did not speak. Larry continued, "We've some very important clients I'm thinking about introducing you to. Would you like to meet some of the real society people of the city?"

"I imagine they fuck like everyone else, don't they?" Her comment made several people look in their direction.

"You must watch what you say in public, Adria. We don't want unfavorable notice, do we?"

Adria considered that and said, "Very well, I shall watch my tongue, although I have become used to the language the Godmen use on the stage."

Larry smiled at her, "That language is for that time and no other."

Adria shrugged indifferently. She'd obey, of course, because she'd heard from one of her roommates about a whore who disobeyed and wasn't allowed to have her injection for several days. The results were horrifying, Sarah told her, and that was something Adria didn't want to deal with. She knew she was getting stronger every day—she would do nothing to impede her coming Godhead.

Larry continued, "In eight days, we'll take a trip up a hill to a giant house—inside you'll find they have servants. Watch your manners around both the servants and city folk."

"I will remember," Adria said a bit petulantly. She was tired and wanted a bath and then sleep.

"These people are very important to both our income and the Cathedral, Adria," he said seriously. "The man owns the arms manufacturing factory that makes weapons for the Cathedral soldiers."

"A blacksmith," Adria said dismissively.

"No, Adria, not a blacksmith. He runs a large factory that makes all the ballistic weapons we use, from the Mauser pistols to the Maximum rapid-fire guns. He's wealthy and important."

"I will take good care of him," Adria said as she stuffed more food into her mouth. "I take good care of all the men, don't I?"

Larry looked around nervously and fortunately no one seemed to be paying attention to them. "Yes, you do, Adria, which is why you're being chosen for this job. You'll stay in the house three days, servicing the man of the house, his son, and any guests he may have—who knows, his wife may join in as well. I'll make the financial arrangements ahead of time— all you'll have to do is perform."

Adria nodded.

"You do this right, Adria, and you'll get to move up in the world, believe me."

As they walked back to the rooming house, Adria had a lot to think about. Some things did indeed seem to be going her way, but where was her betrothed? He hadn't taken her once, could it be that he didn't love her after all? She shook her head. If that was the case, it probably didn't matter. The voices were getting stronger again. They warned her against everyone—even her betrothed. They argued that they and Adria could do anything they wanted to do without anyone's help. The power was coming fast, and soon Adria would move up in the world without Larry Harper's help.

They arrived at the rooming house and Larry left her there. She'd become accustomed to the lift, using it with deftness. She stepped out and walked to her apartment. She knew that probably two or maybe all three of her roommates would be there by now. She unlocked the door and entered.

Sarah, Susan, and Hainie were all sitting at the table eating. They invited her to join them, but she declined, explaining that Larry had taken her to a restaurant. The three women looked at each other—the newcomer was getting a bit high and mighty, wasn't she?

"So what did you and Larry talk about," Sarah queried casually.

Adria preened, "He wants me to do a big thing in a week."

"A big thing?"

Adria thought Susan sounded a bit catty—well this would put her in her place. "Yes," she said casually, "I am going to spend three days in a big house with a weapons maker. Larry told me it would bring me up in the world, as though I needed anything beyond the sting of the scorpion to bring me up in the world."

Adria turned, smiled, and left the three women to their dinner. She was tired and wanted a bath. She went into the bathroom, ran some hot water, and got in the tub for a long soak.

"Well," said Susan, "what do you think of that?"

Hainie glanced at the closed bathroom door, "I've worked for Larry a lot longer than that wild girl—we all have."

She looked toward the other two women, commenting, "I grew up on the waterfront—my parents were selling me by the time I was ten years old. Here, at least, we get a slightly better clientele and protection. One of us deserves that job. We aren't half-humans like her, and we deserve the best jobs, not her."

"I heard Larry telling that priest that Adria is really wild—she does her jobs on a stage in a tavern rather than in the privacy of a room. He seemed to favor that," said Sarah.

"And I heard that Larry charges her men twice what he charges for us." Hainie was indignant. Though the women didn't get any of the money, they had their pride, after all!

"It isn't fair," Susan said, "we don't even use that horrible drug she's on. We're clean and decent. In a few months she'll be worn out and used up—the heroin will kill her sooner or later. Larry has her convinced that the heroin and mescaline she takes is some kind of divine medicine that'll turn her into a Goddess. Imagine!"

"She won't die soon enough, if you ask me," Hainie remarked.

The three women laughed together.

Sarah looked at the other two women and in a conspiratorial tone said, "Larry says Adria thinks she's special—half divine or some such rubbish.

He gives her mescaline, telling her it's a big secret thing he steals just for her."

"Really? I have two clients who make the stuff," Hainie said. "The Cathedral doesn't know their secret 'magic' is being produced outside their control. Or know that people not even of that religion are selling it. And you know that's given me an idea!"

~

The Bishop quietly made the arrangements with Father Woods. He'd hide in the Cathedral in another location away from his rooms while Father Anderson would wander the city, living in his quarters, blatantly pretending to be the Bishop. It was a brilliant plan—both he and Father Woods agreed.

"We need to get this finished—things are progressing in The Green. I have reports that what we're seeking has been found, after a fashion." The Bishop said.

Father Woods grinned, "I'll believe it when I see it, Your Eminence. It's such a fantastic story, I find it very hard to believe."

"But there've been so many stories and reports, we must at least try."

Father Woods sighed, "I agree, Your Eminence, I just think you shouldn't get your hopes up until we know for sure."

The Bishop waved his hand impatiently. "You're right, of course, Father Woods, those half-human magic men we sent down there have been of no use to us as yet. It was difficult work getting them that far."

"Yes, Your Eminence, I do know," Father Woods said, remembering the zeppelin raids and the sleeping gas. He was there, for each of them. "With Father Anderson out there, we'll know soon enough."

"I agree," the Bishop responded. "I hope if it does happen, they get the killers before they can kill Father Anderson. He's a real asset to us."

"That he is," Father Woods agreed.

"On another topic," the Bishop began. "I've heard from Larry Harper that the whore you brought on your airship has been working her ass off."

"I certainly hope not," the priest quipped. "She'd be worth little without that bit of anatomy."

"Larry thinks she's ready for something big. He's sending her to Reichhardt's in about a week to service his clients and even a few representatives from the city of Atlanta, perhaps."

"Really?"

"Yes indeed, she works with wild abandon. Larry tells me that the mescaline magic is doing wonders for the girl."

"Maybe I better try her on for size before she's all used up," the priest said with a grin. "I've been so busy, but maybe I should take a turn."

"Might as well," the Bishop quipped. "Everyone else has!"

~

"I'm going to let you go home by yourself tonight," Larry said to Adria. "I have business I must attend to. Will you be all right?"

"Oh yes, I can do that all by myself."

Larry smiled at her, turned, and left her there in front of the tavern.

Adria took her time getting home. By the time she got there, Hainie and Sarah were already home. The two women looked at Adria when she came in.

"So, did Larry take you out to dinner tonight?"

The tone was conversational, and Adria didn't notice Hainie's veiled sarcasm.

"No, I guess I'll be eating here tonight. What are we having?"

"Whatever you make, sweetie," Hainie said. "Tonight is your night to cook!"

"Very well," she answered complacently, "I can come up with something."

"What's that on your arm?" Sarah asked. "It looks like blood!"

"Oh that," Adria said, casually glancing at the smear on her left arm, "My last client today cut himself with a broken glass in the tavern. He was trying to fuck me and drink at the same time."

The three women laughed at the image.

"I will bathe first, and then make dinner." Adria turned and walked into the bathroom, shutting the door.

After bathing, she dressed and returned to the living quarters. Hainie used the telephone in the hall to call up meat, cheese, and other ingredients stored in the office icebox. Adria began cooking and preparing the meal. The other two set the table, each glancing at the front door from time to time.

Finally, Adria asked, "Where is Susan? Does she have a late job tonight?"

"We've been wondering that ourselves," Hainie said. "She's never late for dinner, even if she has to go out again."

"Isn't the night work done by a different group of women?"

"The women who work the streets at night are all heroin addicts, you know that." Sarah answered.

"I know; I wonder why she isn't here? I have made enough food for four. Maybe she stopped to do some shopping," Adria offered.

Hainie snorted, "Larry takes us with him, he has all the money."

"Yes, but Susan has something she could trade," Adria answered.

There was a short pause in the conversation, and then Hainie said, "You know very well that we're bound by the priests and Larry. We don't freelance for any reason, it's frowned upon."

Adria responded, "Who would know?"

She looked from one to the other. Neither girl had an answer to that question.

~

"She's still missing," Larry said to the priest. "She hasn't been seen in two days now."

Larry was clearly upset. He didn't like having one of his girls unaccounted for. In a huge city like this, if she ran off they might never find her. She was a moneymaker, not as good as the half-human, but good.

"Could she have run away?"

"Not likely," Larry answered, partly to convince himself. "She likes the work and she's safer here than if she worked the streets on her own, and she gets more in the way of benefits. No, she wouldn't run off."

"So, Susan Henley is officially missing then?"

"So it seems," answered the pimp.

"Very well," Father Woods said, "I'll contact our man in the police department and have him begin looking for her. She must be somewhere."

"If she is, Sergeant Jinks'll find her," Larry answered confidently.

~

"Hello?" Larry Harper's wife had picked up the telephone in the hall.

"Is Mister Harper available?"

"Yes, sir," the woman said with proper respect. "I'll bring him to the telephone. Who shall I say is calling, sir?"

"Sergeant Jinks with the police department."

She set the handset down on the small table in the hallway and walked quickly toward the bedroom. Larry was already awake, but still in his nightshirt when his wife came into the bedroom to tell him of the call. When he heard who the caller was, he leaped out of bed, hurrying to the phone.

"This is Larry Harper, John, what have you got?"

"We found your woman, Larry," the policeman said. "You'd better come. I'm at the corner of Third Avenue and Thompson. We'll be in the adjacent alley, come now."

"What is it, dear?"

"Oh nothing, just something work related," he said distractedly, getting into his clothing. He fastened his shoes, picked up his pocket watch, and stepped out of the bedroom.

"I called a cab for you, Larry," his wife said.

"Thank you," he responded.

He grabbed a hat and was out the door, waiting at the curb for the taxi. He didn't have to wait long. The cab slid to the curb with a hiss and Larry quickly opened the rear door—not giving the driver time to open the door for him.

"Where to, sir?"

"Take me to Third Avenue and Thompson, please."

"Ain't a good part o' town, if you don't mind my sayin'."

"I realize that. I'll pay extra if you hurry."

"Already there, sir," said the driver, pushing the accelerator to the floor. The cab shot from the curb into the street almost striking a delivery lorry coming up behind him. The lorry's driver gave a blast of his air horn as the cab driver made a rude gesture out the window of the cab as they quickly accelerated away from the lumbering truck. In an instant they were far down the street.

Chapter 47

"This is where she was found," the policeman said, "she was behind that trash bin, which is why nobody noticed her until she began to smell."

Larry grimaced, seeing the dead woman was bad enough. The body had begun to bloat slightly, making the purple gash in her throat bulge obscenely. The front of her dress was brown with dried blood. "Anything not obvious?"

Sergeant Jinks looked at Larry, and then wordlessly lifted the dead woman's skirts. High up on her right thigh, right next to her underwear, was a savage bite. A piece of flesh seemed to be missing. There'd been substantial blood flow from the wound, the policeman pointed out. "Her femoral artery was chewed open and since her heart had already stopped there was no explosive fountain of blood. We didn't find the piece from her leg," the policeman said, having guessed the next question. "Nor from this one."

He turned the dead woman's head. On her throat was also a bite wound with the flesh missing. "Got the jugular vein and carotid artery with that bite," the policeman offered. "We think the killer drank quite a bit of the blood. Looks like we have a cannibal on our hands, eh?"

"So it seems," Larry responded. "How did she actually die?"

"She was stabbed in the back, sir," the Sergeant said. "The knife's right here, it looks like a butcher's knife, sir. Appropriate, isn't it?"

Larry looked at the policeman. He said nothing about the comment, knowing the police and their sometimes-morbid sense of humor.

"What makes you think someone drank her blood?"

"Well, if you'll come over here," Sergeant Jinks said, "there's something I want to show you."

Larry followed the policeman a short way down the alley. The Sergeant pointed wordlessly to a discolored spot on the ground about thirty feet from the slain woman's body.

"That's a pool of vomit," Jinks said, "with quite a bit of blood in it. My guess is this was the killer's first taste of blood and it didn't sit well on the stomach."

Larry nodded, turning away. He'd seen enough to know that his whore was dead and the Cathedral would want to know why—and by whose hand.

"One funny thing, though," the policeman offered once they returned to the corpse. "Somebody reported seeing a naked woman in the alley about the time this woman died. Freelance hookers frequent the area, so we didn't pay much attention. But now that there's a body, that sorta' changes things."

"Can anyone identify the naked woman?"

"No, sir," the sergeant answered. "She was seen at a distance from three floors up. She was standing by the trash bin right here, like she was waiting for someone. We figured she was meeting a client and let it go."

Larry looked again at the body of the dead hooker. Who could've done such a thing? She worked this area, but a bit further up the street. He knew she was a streetwise woman and never would have come down an alley like this. Especially not when the sun was already setting and with the shadows of the buildings darkening her path, hiding what or whoever lurked here. No, she would have stayed on Thompson, of that he was certain. That was the way back to the boarding house—this alley wouldn't have been a shortcut.

He shook his head. He knew the women's work was dangerous, but he hadn't lost a girl in five years and he was proud of his record. He started counting up the prospective revenue the Cathedral would not now make from this woman over the next year. Again he shook his head, turned, and walked back to the street. From a general store on the corner, he called for another cab. He needed to consult with Father Woods.

~

The next day when Hainie and Sarah got home, they made a quick meal for themselves and settled in to wait for Adria. The women didn't have to wait long before she came in. She seemed distracted, as though listening to a voice the two of them couldn't hear. She smiled, though, when she walked through the door. She plopped herself down in a vacant chair to relax. It had been an eventful day. She'd overheard a conversation that one of Larry's women had been murdered. The news shocked Adria, making her glad she didn't work the streets. She decided to tell the other two, to see how they reacted—that might be fun. Now that the Scorpion Queen was this strong, she could control the emotional responses of others. It must be true—the buzzing inner voice told her so.

"Did you hear the news about Susan?"

The others looked up, startled.

"No? It is not good news."

"Won't you tell us?" Hainie asked.

"She's dead."

"What?" The two women shouted in unison.

"She was murdered in an alley on her way home. I overheard Larry talking about it to some man in the tavern."

"By the Redeemed God! That's terrible news," Sarah said.

Hainie was pale. Adria knew this would be their response since she could sometimes predict the future.

There was a period of shocked silence. Adria noticed that Hainie was crying softly—the two had been close. Adria didn't particularly feel sorry for them, and she knew she'd be safe in the public tavern. She wouldn't be foolish enough to walk down some unlit city alleyway at night. She was a higher-class whore than that. She silently made something to eat, settling back into her chair, enjoying the other women's fear and worry. It was nice being divine, to be above all that.

Adria, Hainie, and Sarah were allowed to attend Susan's funeral. It was a simple ceremony conducted in a secluded part of the cemetery. Besides the three women, Larry was present, as was Father Woods. The priest conducted the ceremony with little fanfare and no family members to grieve. By eight in the morning, it was over. They left the cemetery before any other people might show up to be with their loved ones, as birds chirped cheerily in the trees and grasshoppers buzzed in the bushes—seemingly an affirmation that life goes on.

There were two who didn't leave immediately. Hidden in the shrubbery to the east, a shabby older man watched with keen eyes. Unknown to him, a police sergeant in plain clothes was also watching from concealment nearer the road. Each man was doing the same job, though they didn't know it. Both were watching to see if anyone else came to the woman's gravesite. Now that the principals had left, stragglers would be evaluated critically as potential suspects in the woman's death.

The policeman waited an hour, then left. The older man stayed a bit longer, noticing the policeman as he came out of hiding—noting his description and build in his notebook for future reference. Father Anderson knew vaguely who Sergeant Jinks was, but he'd check up on him nonetheless. The policeman didn't raise any real suspicion in the mind of the spy, but a spy had to remain suspicious if he was to remain alive. The old priest waited another half hour, and then he too left. Apparently the killer wasn't going to show that day after all.

Back in the city, the women broke their fast and then went off to work to their various haunts—Adria to the tavern, the other two on the street.

Adria wasn't afraid, as she knew she'd spend the day servicing men in a safe place with people who'd protect her—even if it was only because they wished to fuck her. Her power was growing quickly now. It was amazing how fast Divine Godhead could be achieved if one shed the inhibitions and taboos of the merely mortal.

~

Hainie and Sarah met as planned for lunch later that day. Both had been cautious this morning, refusing customers they'd normally have taken without a second thought. The money they made wasn't going to make Larry happy, but that was his problem. If they were dead like Susan, he'd be making nothing. Hainie was waiting in the restaurant and had already ordered a drink by the time Sarah arrived. Sarah also ordered a glass of wine and the two women began studying the menu.

After they ordered, Hainie turned to Sarah, looking around to make sure nobody could overhear her. "Remember when I said I had an idea regarding Adria?"

Sarah snorted in disgust, finishing her wine and calling for another.

"Since she thinks that the heroin and mescaline are making her sacred," Hainie continued, "we could use that against her."

"How would we do that?"

Hainie grinned at her friend, finished her glass of wine, and ordered another. After the food had been served, Hainie explained her idea. "It's simple, actually. We tell her that the priests are lying to her, that the magic elixir—or whatever it's supposed to be—can be bought on the street. We'll tell her she can buy it herself, speeding up her divinity on her terms."

"That's a good idea," Sarah said enthusiastically. "She'll have to go freelance, then, as she'll need money to buy the junk. She'll go away from us, Larry, and the Cathedral—and be out of our hair."

"We can meet here after work today," Sarah suggested. "Maybe we should talk to one of your friends and find out how we can get him to meet Adria."

"That'll be easy to do," Hainie said. "One of them works a corner just a few blocks from here."

"Then we have a date," Sarah said. "I'll meet you here tonight."

The two women parted company happily. Now that they had a plan to remove the half-human from their lives, things were finally looking up. Maybe, if they worked it quickly enough, Adria would be gone before the 'big thing' she'd talked about with Larry. Perhaps then they'd get the recognition they deserved. It was too bad that Susan wasn't here to see it happen.

~

"Larry, how are you?" Father Woods asked, rising from his chair. "I heard about your whore, it's a real pity. I understand she was a good moneymaker."

Larry shook his head sadly, "She was indeed, Your Grace."

"I assume you talked with your friend in the police department. Does he have any thoughts on the matter?"

"There's not much to go on," Larry replied. "Some witnesses saw a naked woman in the alleyway about the time the woman was killed, but nobody could identify her."

"That's a pity," the priest said, "I would have thought a naked woman would always attract attention."

"That neighborhood is a good one for whores—ours and some independents."

"Were there any clues left at the scene? Anything at all?"

Larry described the murder in graphic detail to the priest. Even though the priest was trained in the ways of the half-human tribes, cannibalism and vampirism were well beyond his area of knowledge.

"I'm at a loss as well, Your Grace. I know of no one who specializes in such things."

"There is one," the priest said. "A priest who now works in the zeppelin barn used to deal with that kind of crime until he finally had his fill and couldn't handle it any longer. It's a rare kind of crime, as you can imagine, but too horrific for a person to deal with over the years. I'll consult with him today and see if he can give us insight into who would do something like this."

"I'm concerned that whoever did this might kill again. We don't want any more of our women injured or killed, there's no profit in that."

"I'll inform you as to what my friend has to say on the subject, for what it's worth. Maybe what he tells me will give us a hint or a clue to the killer's identity—assuming it's not just a complete stranger to us."

"Sergeant Jinks will help us as well. He's good at ferreting out the criminals from society."

"How're your plans for the half-human Adria and the arms manufacturer coming along?"

Larry smiled. This was a subject he didn't mind discussing. "The old man has agreed to the price, Your Grace. After we make him, his family, and his friends happy, he'll make two thousand Mauser pistols for the army. I cannot fathom why the Bishop wants such a large army, though."

"Those questions are not your concern," the priest said sternly. "That's the Bishop's business."

"Certainly, Your Grace, I was just thinking out loud."

"Not a good thing to do too frequently," the priest warned.

"I understand."

Father Woods dismissed the pimp and sat for a moment in thought. He picked up his phone and called the zeppelin barn.

"Father Jackson, please," he said.

Twenty minutes later, the old priest arrived. He was old beyond his years from the psychological stresses brought on by years of viewing violent crime scenes, trying to find the motive that led a killer to commit his crimes so that he might be stopped.

Father Woods explained the situation to the old priest, giving him each detail as he'd heard it from the pimp. The telling took almost twenty minutes, and the old priest's face was showing stress by the time he had finished.

The old man sat and thought for a long time. Slowly and reluctantly he brought up long ago memories, crimes, and observations. Finally he spoke. "I believe you'll find this person to be rather mentally disturbed," he began. "This kind of savage, inhumane killing is a clear indication of that fact."

"So the person is crazy?"

"Well," the old priest said, "yes and no. He—or she, as this case might lead us to believe—is mentally deranged but might not show anything on the surface. As a rule, these types have something seriously wrong with them. If you're with them for any length of time, the outside shell they project will begin to crumble and the rottenness and madness will begin to show through."

"What should the police be looking for?"

The old man again took a pause as he thought about the question.

"I believe this person will be young, in their teens or early twenties. Usually, they eventually show themselves and are caught before they live much beyond that age. They'll seem to like people, but will nevertheless stay by themselves with minimal interaction."

"Anything else you can think of?"

"Yes," the old priest said, "seldom are these kinds of killers female. Your killer should be easy to spot by the police. She won't like other women; she'll act independently and not care about social mores. She may use inappropriate language for a woman. In the end, these types usually give themselves away. Think about your killer—she attacked a person in public and she was naked while she did it. If anyone had been close enough to see her clearly, she'd already be in custody. That's what will happen. That's how she'll be caught."

~

"Adria? We have news for you," Hainie said.

"Really? What?"

Some surprises were nice; maybe this one would be, too.

"You know those special things the priest said he would get for you? The Sting of the Scorpion?"

"Yes," Adria answered guardedly, this wasn't sounding like a nice surprise at all.

"Well, he lied to you, sweetie."

"What do you mean, he lied?" Adria asked, more in surprise than anger.

"We know someone who makes it—both the thing called heroin and the 'magic' thing. It's called mescaline and he makes that as well."

"Why are you telling me this?"

"Why, we thought that with your coming divinity, you might not want to remain attached to the Cathedral. You might not want to let Larry take all the money that you earned without giving you any."

Adria thought about that for a moment. What the woman said made sense. Why were they not trusted more? Why wasn't she trusted more? Why could they not simply require an oath as was done in the tribes? Suddenly the answer was obvious—the priests really didn't trust them. They were simply merchandise to be sold for profit—their profit. She was angry now. Did her betrothed fall into this category as well? She wasn't prepared to answer that question, so she shoved it away into a little drawer in her mind, and it was promptly forgotten along with many other things in many other little drawers.

"We can introduce you to the man who can supply you with the stuff, if you like," Sarah cajoled. "Then you can go out on your own and be independent. Fuck the men you choose and keep all the money."

Adria liked this idea more and more. She should be in charge of her own life—her own body. She was a Goddess.

"Very well, when can we meet this fellow?"

Her two roommates looked at each other—their plan had worked!

"We can go right now, if you like. He'll let you try the stuff to see if you like it before you have to pay for it."

"That sounds reasonable," Adria agreed. "Let us be off."

The three women left their apartment, riding the lift to the street. From there they walked out into crowded anonymity.

Chapter 48

The Bishop was waiting for Father Woods and Larry Harper. He didn't wait long. Harold allowed the two men to enter the Bishop's office. When he departed, after serving a tray with glasses and wine, the Bishop announced, "Reichhardt called today."

Father Woods and the pimp looked up, they knew the name, of course. Franz was the wealthy arms maker who'd requested a special 'private show' with the wild half-human whore he'd heard so much about at the plant.

"He's not backing out is he?"

The Bishop smiled at Father Woods. "No, no, nothing like that. He has to leave town soon, he's taking a zeppelin to Atlanta for a meeting with the Abbot of the Church in that city. He'll be gone for weeks. It seems they have some new engineering something-or-other they want to share with us."

"That sounds intriguing. What has this to do with the job at hand, Your Eminence?"

"Simply this—a zeppelin from Atlanta arrived yesterday. He'll be traveling next week, so he wishes to have his party this weekend. Can that be arranged?"

The pimp looked at the priest, shrugging.

"Of course we can," Father Woods said with certainty, "the half-human is always available and at my bidding. Remember Friday is two days after tomorrow. I assume you have already been paid?"

"Oh, most certainly," the pimp replied. "I put the money in the bank yesterday morning, in the special account."

The Bishop smiled. They had several secret accounts at the bank to hide the money coming in from prostitution. It wouldn't do for that bit of knowledge to get into the press. Their plans for Green Hell—and something else—relied on it.

"Excellent. You may go. Make sure the beastling puts on a good show for them."

"Oh, you can count on that, Your Eminence," the pimp replied with a smile. "She's the wildest sexer we've ever had. Men who've had a sample keep coming back, and for twice the usual fee. Perhaps we should have asked for three times the fee."

The Bishop held up his hand, "Let's not be greedy. Remember it was the Feminine who was the greedy one, instilling love and beauty in the world so men would worship Her instead of the true God."

The pimp bowed his head; he knew he'd been chastised.

"Yes, Your Eminence."

The two left the Bishop, each going their separate ways.

~

Adria and her two roommates returned to the apartment. She was very excited, as she looked at her stuff—as the anonymous man on the corner called it. Inside the small pouch were the free sample drugs, a glass syringe, several needles, and material for processing the heroin as well as the mescaline. She was anxious to try it out. She had one worry—how would she pay for the chemicals when the free stuff ran out?

"Oh, that's easy," Hainie answered. "He likes your looks. He told me he would front you the stuff until you were making your own money. Whenever you want some, so will he, if you know what I mean."

Adria laughed, "Men are so easy, aren't they?"

Sarah agreed, "Yes they are."

Hainie and Sarah were thinking how easy some women were as well—but Adria was, after all, only half-human.

Adria decided to try some of the mescaline, since the heroin being supplied by the pimp was still running in her system—no point in using up her free stuff until she was free herself. She followed the dealer's instructions, making sure there was no air in the needle. She injected herself. The effect came on gradually but steadily. Soon she was seeing strange geometric shapes within the glowing lights that flashed and shimmered around her roommates. This stuff was much better than what the Cathedral was supplying. She sat for several hours, enjoying the show. The other women eventually went to bed—they had to work tomorrow. They no longer cared about Adria; she'd be gone from their lives in a couple days.

The next morning, Adria carefully hid her stuff. Although she knew the other two women were afraid of it and wouldn't bother with it, secrecy was always best. By the time Larry arrived, she'd eaten and bathed. The other two were already out trolling the streets for men with money and an early morning itch.

"Our plans have changed, Adria," the pimp said when he arrived. "We'll be going up the hill tomorrow morning, early."

"I will be ready, sir," Adria responded.

"Today we'll leave the tavern early—we don't want you tired out for the weekend. You'll be servicing the man, his son, and probably his wife. His other child is still too young."

"Are you sure?"

"Leave the child alone, Adria."

"I was just joking, sir," she answered.

"Just see that you're ready, I'll pick you up in a steam-car at six in the morning."

~

"Any further word on the killing?" The Bishop asked anxiously.

Father Woods just shook his head, what could he tell the Bishop?

"The police are looking at some leads," he said. "Sergeant Jinks said he arrested a man near the alley the next day. He was simple minded, and didn't seem to know where he was or who he was. He did have a lot of blood on his clothes. The Sergeant thinks he may be the killer."

"What of the naked woman then?"

The Bishop was furious. No one had answers to any of his questions. Was he being stalked or not? Who killed one of his whores? Would the nosy journalists somehow connect her to the Cathedral? No one seemed to know a thing.

"They think now that the naked woman was just an independent whore looking for a mark and probably was long gone by the time the killer arrived."

The Bishop sighed in relief, maybe this problem, at least, was solved.

At that moment, his phone rang. He picked up the handset.

"Yes?" He listened for a moment and then smiled broadly, hanging up the receiver.

"That was your policeman," the Bishop announced. "He said the man has confessed to the killing."

Both men sighed with relief—at least that was out of the way.

~

Sergeant Jinks and the priest met for lunch in a restaurant near the police station. Both men were elated.

"Since we found the killer so quickly, none of this even made the news," the policeman crowed. "I think it can be swept under the rug, like it never happened. Since the man confessed, I see no need in a trial; he'll be dealt with this evening in the way murderers are dealt with. He'll hang.

The two men who were with me when we arrested him heard him confess and are willing to keep silent about all of it—even the hanging. We'll hang him in his cell and make it look like a suicide. That'll keep our superiors happy and ignorant—it's been done before."

"How long did it take him to confess?" The priest was curious; the policeman had told him the man didn't even remember his own name, much less where he'd been.

"Not long," the Sergeant smirked, "we found some of the dead woman's belongings in his pockets."

"Really?"

The priest was impressed.

"Yep, he had a gold bangle bracelet and some other personal stuff from the woman. No doubt he did it."

"So you confronted him with the items in his pockets and he confessed?"

"Well, not exactly," the policeman chuckled, "he had to lose a few more teeth and crack a rib or two, but he confessed, all right."

Father Woods was silent as their food was served. He was worried again. A confession taken by beating from a feebleminded individual was problematic. He didn't care about the beating, but about the veracity of the confession. What if the killer was still out there? Still, it'd be best to let this ride—best to keep the Bishop happy.

"Very well," he said, "I'll tell His Eminence. You're hanging the man quietly tonight, are you not?"

"Certainly, no visitors allowed, Your Grace," the policeman stated sarcastically. "As for family, well, he doesn't even know his name, how could we find his family even if we wanted to…which we don't."

"You're right about that," the priest grinned. "Why is he the way he is?"

"We found many needle marks on his arms, Your Grace. The man has been using street heroin for a long time. You know as well as I do that street stuff is not as pure as what the Cathedral uses."

Father Woods did know. Street suppliers cut their illegal heroin with any sort of chemical that might produce a euphoric feeling, whether it was safe or not. If an addict died, there seemed always to be some eager newcomer ready to follow in the dead man's footsteps.

After lunch, the priest returned to the Cathedral. The policeman walked to his precinct house to finish his day's work. He would have to come back this evening to put the final touches on this case. He knew it wouldn't take long to drop the prisoner into oblivion. Too bad this wouldn't appear on his job rating, solving a crime this fast would look good on his record. Still, he knew the concerns of the Cathedral came first. He opened the large door, walking into the cool interior of the station—another job well done. Good thing his superiors didn't know.

Father Woods was still worried by the time he returned to the Cathedral. He knew what he'd tell the Bishop, and he also knew he didn't believe a word of it. Well, sometimes the truth is best kept to oneself. Who knows, maybe the killer will stop, go away, or try to kill someone stronger and die in the attempt. The last would be the best option, he decided. He parked the auto, walked to the door, and pushed his way into the dark, cool interior of the Cathedral. Instead of climbing the stairs immediately to see the Bishop, he paused. He turned and walked into the aisle to sit in one of the pews. The large church was almost empty. He saw two women on the other side, they were lighting memory candles for a deceased relative. He turned back to the altar. He looked up at the image of the Redeemed God—magnificent in his virility—standing with one foot on the back of the bound Goddess. He thought next time he took his pleasure with a woman maybe he'd tie her up and gag her. He relished the thought—her tied securely on her back, her legs splayed, and helplessly exposed to whatever he may wish to do.

The back door of the church softly clanged shut, disturbing his erotic reverie. He sighed, rising. That would have to wait, because now he needed to talk to the Bishop.

Chapter 49

"So, how was your meeting with the policeman?"

The Bishop sat tapping his pen nervously against the desktop. Tap. Tap. Tap. Father Woods always found it annoying, but he held his tongue. He sighed and gathered his thoughts, "Sergeant Jinks has done an excellent job, Your Eminence."

"That's good to know," the Bishop responded.

"The man in custody was covered with blood and had some of the whore's possessions in his pocket. He apparently hadn't gotten around to pawning or selling them yet. I'm not surprised, at that, though."

"Why is that?"

"Well, the man can't even remember his own name. If one is so befuddled on narcotic drugs that one's identity is gone, forgetting something like that isn't surprising. He was surprised that he had blood on his clothing."

"I find that hard to believe," the Bishop said. "Surely he would have gotten rid of that kind of evidence."

"Well, the jewelry was evidence as well," the priest answered. "And he was still carrying that around with him."

The Bishop sighed, "Did he say why he did this—why he drank her blood?"

"I didn't get to see him myself, Your Eminence," the priest answered. "But Jinks told me he didn't even remember the killing at first—at least he said he didn't. When Jinks showed him the jewelry, it jogged his memory and he confessed."

"Well then," the Bishop said in a satisfied way, "that takes care of that little problem."

"By tonight, anyway," Father Woods said, smiling.

"Tonight?"

"Yes, Your Eminence," the priest answered, "tonight the nameless vagrant will be found hanging in his cell."

The Bishop laughed, it was a nice, tidy ending to a problem. If only all his problems were so easily handled. He thought about his potential assassination.

~

Sergeant Jinks looked left and right, and the only person he saw was Patrolman Thomas Spellman. Spellman was one of the officers that helped make the arrest; he also helped in the interrogation. He agreed to cover the desk in Cell Block A of the police station that evening, graciously allowing young Officer Martin to take the night off so he could spend some time with his wife and newborn son. The ploy worked perfectly, Spellman was a devout follower of the Redeemed God. He too looked left and right from his vantage point at the end of the cellblock, nodding.

As it happened, Cell Block A was currently uninhabited—well almost. The other prisoners had all been moved this morning to Cell Block B on the other side of the wall. This was standard procedure and would raise no eyebrows. Block B was for prisoners who'd appear before a judge in the next two days—moving the nine suspects was easy and uneventful. Most were there for public intoxication and urinating in public. Sergeant Jinks had Block A all to himself—himself and good ol' Karl Sweeney.

Jinks walked past the empty cells on his way to the one farthest from Spellman. Everything was in readiness, and yet he held just the tiniest regret for what he was about to do. Unconsciously, he touched his left jacket pocket. He felt the hard roundness of the bottle concealed within. He shook off his regret, realizing this is what the Redeemed God wanted—what the Bishop wanted.

"Hello, Sweeney," he said with a smile.

"Hey, Sarge, come to let me out now? I did what you asked, you promised to let me go tonight."

"That's why I am here," the policeman said reassuringly. "I want to talk a bit first, though, and then I'll set you free."

Jinks unlocked the cell door with the large iron key, swinging the heavy barred door outward. He left it open slightly, walking into the cell. Karl Sweeney smiled at his old friend.

"We've known each other a long time, now, haven't we?"

"That we have, John," Sweeney responded, "since school."

"I remember when you tried out for the wrestling team, Karl," the Sergeant said with a laugh.

"I always felt that wasn't fair," Sweeney chuckled. "You were the captain of the wrestling team and they made me fight you."

"Well," Jinks laughed, "might as well start with the best."

"Yeah," Sweeney said, "but you were so strong, working with your blacksmith father at the anvil every day, I didn't have a chance."

He never had a chance, the policeman thought, *he was drunk all the time.*

"I didn't mean to hurt you, back then, Karl."

Sweeney made a dismissive gesture with his hand, answering, "Oh, I know that, Johnny boy," he said with a grin. "Besides, I was not my best that day. I'd started my drinking campaign recently and I was…not meself at the time."

"I could smell the whiskey on your breath," Jinks laughed. "Never understood why none of our teachers could smell it on you."

Sweeney chuckled, "Prolly 'cause they all had the smell on their breaths too!"

Karl threw back his head, laughing. Jinks noticed the gap in his smile—the teeth that'd been knocked out in the interrogation.

"Sorry I had to hit you so hard, Karl," he apologized with a shake of his head. "Hadda make it look real—for the paperwork…you know…"

The man just laughed and said, "Well, when you let me out and you reward me, I can get a dentist to fix me up and still have plenty left for whores and booze!"

Sergeant Jinks hesitated. This was the moment of truth—it was now or never. He smiled at his long-time friend and said, "Which brings me to this, Karl, ol' buddy."

With a flourish, Jinks pulled a bottle of whiskey from his coat pocket, waving it tantalizingly in front of the prisoner.

"Ah, Johnny," the man said fondly, "you're a true friend."

Sweeney yanked the cork and took a long pull. How sweetly it burned going down. He smacked his lips, holding the bottle out for his friend.

"Oh, I can't drink tonight," Jinks said with a smile. "I'm on duty."

"Ah yes…duty…" Sweeney said vaguely.

Sweeney took another drink, and set the bottle on the cell floor. Jinks glanced at it briefly. He needed to drink more of it—the special ingredient wouldn't work unless he drank more. Sweeney laughed, "Booze makes me horny."

"Well, we're taking care of that shortly, my friend," Jinks laughed. "I have a really wild whore waiting for you."

The man picked up the bottle again, eagerly taking another long drink—a look of lust in his eyes.

"Yep, she's seventeen and so hot you might burn your fingers on her breasts."

"Ah, now that's a risk I'm willing to take," Sweeney said, lifting the bottle in a toast to his friend. He took one more very long drink and hesitated. He seemed confused. He rubbed his left hand over his eyes, shaking his head. When he looked up at his friend, the policeman saw that his eyes were no longer focusing. His hand opened, releasing the bottle. Jinks deftly caught it, putting the cork back into the neck of the bottle. He stood, dropping the bottle back into his jacket pocket.

Sweeney rose unsteadily to his feet. He swayed and slumped against his friend.

"Whoa, there," Jinks said with a laugh, "let me help you a bit." He lifted him back to his feet and said, "You're not turning into a lightweight on me are you?"

Sweeney laughed, "I…I ain no li…lightweight, buddy boy."

Jinks helped him stand again, leading him to the door of the cell.

"You lettin' me go now?" Sweeney's speech was slurred and hard to understand.

That was good, as it would make the next part easier. Jinks hiked up Sweeney's shirt, unbuttoned it, and pulled it off his body. Jinks wrinkled his nose in disgust—the man hadn't bathed in quite a while.

"Yes, Karl, I'm letting you go now," Jinks said.

"Waacha takin' my shirt offame for?" He asked in a befuddled voice. "Ya got the whore with the hot tits right here?"

He was laughing as Jinks twisted the sleeves of the man's shirt tightly to form a sort of rope. He looped it around Sweeney's neck and slipped the knot against his throat.

"Thash a good idea, there, buddy boy," Sweeney slurred, staggering. "That way I won't lose it."

Jinks smiled, as he brought the cell door closed with a clang.

"Hey, I thought yous gonna let me go now?"

"I am," Jinks said, "right now."

He loosely tied the remaining portion of the man's shirt over the topmost horizontal bar of the cell door, leaving enough slack. He quickly opened the door and stepped outside. He slammed the door quickly, and pulled hard on the shirt. He was strong and Karl Sweeney weighed but little—he was an emaciated drunkard. He pulled hard again and Karl's feet left the floor. As Jinks quickly tied the knot over the horizontal bar, Sweeney began kicking his feet—gagging. He looked surprised, but he could no longer say a word. His tongue was already protruding between his lips, which were turning blue as his face turned a deep red. The secret, Jinks knew, was properly placing the knot against the man's windpipe. Sweeney gagged once more and slumped, his feet making a fatal, final drumming on the hard stone floor. Saliva dribbled from between his lips as his eyes glazed. The drumming stopped. Jinks locked the door, and left his silent friend.

"I told you I'd set you free, didn't I? I said I'd reward you, didn't I? What better freedom from your excesses of drink than death? What better reward than being in the presence of the Redeemed God. May you rest in peace, old friend."

Jinks walked back down the corridor, his feet echoing slightly on the stone floor. At least that job was finished. He smiled grimly. When he reached the desk, he nodded at Officer Spellman.

"Make sure you don't inspect the cells until morning."

"No worries, sir," the young policeman said with a smile, "I already have my log entries done for the night. My last inspection of the prisoner with no name was at nine this evening, that's two hours from now."

The officer grinned at his joke, and Jinks chuckled.

"You know, Patrolman Spellman, I believe you're the kind of man who can move up quickly in the department."

"I'm sure you'll do the right thing," the officer said in mock humility.

They both laughed as Jinks patted the young man on the shoulder.

"See you tomorrow," Jinks said with a smile.

"Good night, sir," the desk officer said. "Have a nice night."

Jinks walked out of the police station. By this time, he was whistling to himself. He'd done the right thing. Now he was about to reward himself. He turned left, walking down the silent street. There were few pedestrians, but being a policeman, he knew where to find what he was looking for. *Another advantage of being a copper*, he thought with a smile, *was that all the fucking was free—one of the benefits of allowing the pimps to operate in his district*. He was already becoming aroused.

He had one hooker especially in mind; he liked the games she played. He snickered to himself—she liked to hear naughty copper stories. Well, he had a good one this time. He knew she'd be hanging out in a small tavern around the corner from her apartment. Since she was a freelancer, he needn't worry about anything he said getting back to his superiors, or the Bishop.

He walked into the bar and as he suspected, there she was, talking to a young man, touching him and leading him on. He strolled casually up to the bar. He stepped between the young man and the prostitute and flashed his badge.

"Move along, you," he said gruffly, "me and the woman have business."

The man took a look at the badge and quickly turned away. The woman laughed.

"Johnny," she said, shaking her head, "You have such a way with words."

"If you're interested, Marielle, I have some words you can have your way with."

She looked at him appraisingly. While she was no longer exactly young, she wasn't on narcotics and still carried a good figure.

"My place or yours," she crooned in his ear, nuzzling her face against his cheek.

"It better be your place," he answered. "It'd be very hard to explain to my wife."

She put one hand between his legs, and said, "I think it's very hard already."

"All the more reason we should leave now," he said with a smile.

They walked out of the tavern arm in arm, taking their time as they strolled in the cool air toward the woman's apartment building.

"So," she said, smiling at him, "What kind of words do you have for me tonight?"

"Can't tell you," he said, shaking his head, "you're gonna have to torture me."

"That can be arranged, I know just the right kind of torture."

"I'll bet you do," he said, patting her on her rear.

Inside the apartment, she led him into the bedroom. She lit several candles, but not the gaslights. She turned to him, expectantly.

He pulled a wad of bills from his pocket, and then put them back. She looked at him, confused. She knew he didn't have to pay. He smiled and reached into his pocket again. This time he withdrew a gold bangle bracelet. The metal glittered in the candlelight—he could see he'd gotten her attention. He handed her the bracelet. He knew it was worth more than her fee, but then he hadn't paid for the bracelet, either. It had once belonged to someone named Susan…something-or-other. Since she didn't need it any longer, it might as well go to Marielle. She snatched the bracelet from his hand, looked closely at it for a moment, and slipped it over her wrist, cooing, "I think this might be all I'll be wearing in just a few minutes."

She sat on the bed, undoing her shoes. He sat down next to her, and removed his shoes as well.

In a few minutes, they were both naked on the bed in an embrace. Jinks was lying on top of the woman, kissing and stroking her body with his hands. Suddenly, she rolled over and was on top of him—sitting up, smiling down at him.

"I know you've been a naughty policeman, haven't you?"

"Oh, very naughty, I assure you."

"Tell me."

"No way, it's a police secret."

She raised herself a bit, and then he was inside her. She rode him quickly, and then slowly—alternating the pace. She was truly an expert; he knew that from his wide experience with other hookers.

She watched his eyes. She brought him right to the brink, and then stopped. He was gasping. He looked at her naked body, glistening with perspiration.

"Now tell me," she cajoled.

"Nope. Can't," he answered.

Then she started again and stopped again. She did this three times before he said, "Okay, okay…I'll tell you."

She moved herself a little bit—making sure he knew she was in control.

"There was a murder a few days ago," he said. "A…woman of pleasure run by the Cathedral. She was stabbed to death, and had been bitten."

The woman, shocked, almost rose off of the policeman—but he held her to him.

"The naughty part," he confessed, "is that I beat a confession from someone who might have been the killer. He had blood all over him, and he had some of her stuff in his possession."

She grinned at him, rising and descending several times to convince him to continue.

"He was someone I knew—from our school days," he whispered. "The Cathedral needed a quick resolution, you see."

She squirmed against him and he concluded his story.

"He hung himself tonight in his cell. I guess he couldn't take the shame."

His mirthless laugh told the woman all she needed to know about that part. She smiled at him and began moving again, quicker, harder. It didn't take very long…

When Sergeant Jinks left, the woman rose, cleaned herself up and dressed once more. She slunk down the hallway of her apartment building, down the lift and into the street. She kept a wary eye out for the policeman. He was nowhere to be seen—probably on his way home to his wife. She hailed a cab and gave an address to the driver. In twenty minutes, she was in another neighborhood in front of the Bloomgarden Apartment building. She used the lift, rising to the fourteenth floor. She was dressed respectably, so nobody gave her a second look. She walked down the hall, stopped at a door and knocked. She knocked twice, then once more. The door opened, and the magician motioned her inside.

"I've further news regarding the Cathedral," she explained. "Though I don't know if it'll be of interest to you…"

Chapter 50

The sun had set an hour ago and the sky was now a deep purple, turning to black. Light clouds scudded across the sky, occasionally obscuring the crescent moon. Stars shone like bright diamonds in the blackness. The steam-car rolled from the drive onto the roadway leading back into the heart of the Black City. In the distance, the lights of the city put a luminous glow into the sky. It was as though the people of the city feared the night so they created a false light to dispel the darkness that dwelled between the tall granite and basalt buildings.

Dan, glancing into the mirror, said, "Our destination is several miles away—close to downtown—it's a region of apartment buildings and businesses."

"Will we be safe? Won't people see us?" Lyria asked.

Dan laughed as he answered, "Oh, we'll be seen, all right—by dozens of people, in fact. But they'll all be concerned with their own lives and destinations—we'll be invisible among them. It is probable that even if I wore the horns of a rhinoceros attached to my hat, nobody would even notice!"

Raven giggled at the image, "Do you have a rhinoceros hat, Dandan?"

"No, I do not," he answered, glancing at the young girl sitting beside him. "I meant it as a figure of speech."

"City speak, then," the girl answered, nodding in understanding. "At home most everyone would say what they meant, but not here. Here everyone pretends. They try to hide who they are—even what they look like."

Kel responded with a chuckle, "I have noticed that. I have seen women with paint on their faces and lips as though they are ashamed of what they look like."

Raven laughed, "That is what I mean, Kel."

"You better not let any of them touch you," Lyria added menacingly, but she was smiling.

"Oh, I have learned that lesson, my love," Kel answered. He paused a moment, and then added, "You are the sun in my day, the moon in my night, and the constant light that always guides me true."

Raven giggled, "That's not city speak—even I know what you said."

After they both looked at the little girl, Lyria looked almost shyly at Kel and said, "I did not know you were also a poet, Kel."

Kel looked back at her with a twinkle in his eye and responded, "You are the music of my song of life. You are the rhyme and meter of my soul."

"Kel," Lyria said, blushing, "that was beautiful!"

"Not as beautiful as you, my love."

Everyone was looking at Lyria, waiting for her response. She finally said, "Your love is an arrow that has pierced my heart, Kel—the barbs have held fast. If it were now withdrawn, I would surely die."

Now they were simply looking into each other's eyes.

Finally Dan said, "Please. Do we need to pull over for a couple minutes?"

At that, everyone burst out laughing.

Lyria lowered her head to Kel's shoulder, sighing as he gently stroked her hair, smiling down on her.

They traveled in silence for a while, each keeping to their own thoughts. Everyone was looking forward to and fearing the coming meeting. Who could tell what the future held in store for them? Only Raven seemed complacent, as though privy to some secret inner knowledge that perhaps even she wasn't consciously aware of.

A lorry passed them on the way to a late delivery. The truck rumbled past—the dark canvas covering over the back flapping in the wind like the wings of some trapped bat. The lorry was going very fast and was soon lost to sight. In the distance, the Black City, under its false day, grew closer every minute.

In a half hour they were once again amid tall buildings, driving through black canyons of basalt. Dan maneuvered the car through the city streets. Finally, they arrived at their destination and he drew the steam-car up to the curbing, lowering the pressure. Dan wordlessly guided them to the low stairway leading into the building. Kel noticed the seemingly odd name, "Bloomgarden Apartments" and asked Dan about it—having noticed neither garden nor blooms.

"Oh, that's more of what Raven would call city speak. They make up names for buildings to make them seem exotic or favorable."

"I do not know if I could ever get used to living in a place like this," Lyria said. "Nothing seems what it appears to be."

Dan shrugged, "I didn't think I'd be able to live in Mountain Village when I arrived there either. You get used to new ways to live, I suppose."

"Maybe," Lyria said, "but I prefer the canyons made by the Earth Mother to the ones made by men."

Raven was tugging at Lyria and Dan's hands, eager to be off the street.

They climbed the four steps to the front door and entered. The inside was well lit with reflected gaslights and had a warm feeling overall. The man at the front desk seemed to recognize Dan, nodding in his direction as they headed to the lift. Dan opened the metal gate and they filed inside. He set the lever for the fourteenth floor and the lift began to rise. The thing still made Lyria and Kel nervous—they would have preferred the stairs. Raven seemed to be enjoying the ride.

When the lift stopped, Dan opened the gate to be greeted by Lawrence, his long-time friend.

"I see you brought your friends with you," he said, smiling.

"We're all here," Dan said.

"And who is this, if I may ask?"

He was pointing at Raven, who shrank back behind Lyria.

"Her name is Raven," Dan said. "She is with us also."

"Come out, sweetie," Lawrence coaxed, but the little girl was having none of it. He laughed and then gestured down the hallway. Dan and Lawrence went first, while the three others followed silently. Raven stayed behind Lyria, holding her hand.

Ahead, a door opened, letting a glow of yellow light out into the hallway. Lawrence motioned toward the door, and they all hurried inside. An older man that Kel knew only as the 'magician' shut the door.

The magician looked over the odd band of individuals who'd entered the room. He gave each an appraising look—smiled and pointed to a table where several chairs awaited. He sat at the head of the table, with Lawrence and Dan on one side and Kel and Lyria on the other. Raven walked to the sofa, sat down silently and watched.

The magician began, "I heard that one of you can read, is that correct?" He looked from Lyria to Kel expectantly. Kel nodded, and the man handed him a sheaf of papers.

"You can read these at the safe house later," he explained. "They outline the exact details of what we've learned and how we learned it."

Kel flipped through the eight pages of closely written ink. It was script, of course, but he was sure he could piece it together.

"The child will be a complication, I think," the old man began. "But there is one way she might be to our advantage."

Lyria looked at Raven. She was sitting silently, looking at the heavily draped window across the room. "We won't leave her," Lyria said firmly. "We are obligated to return her to her family."

"Perhaps we'd better start at the beginning," the old man said with a smile. "Problems usually seem easier if they are completely understood."

Lyria nodded in agreement and began an explanation of why they'd come from so far away. The magician listened carefully and would nod on occasion, but was otherwise silent. Lyria told of their journey, carefully editing the portions of the narrative covering the discovery of Raven's slaughtered family, and then the taking of Lyria by the 'Other' in the apartment building where they'd discovered Noria—now called Raven.

When she'd finished her explanation, the old man nodded again as though accepting the story, and then he glanced at the girl on the sofa.

"It's fortunate for her that you came when you did, that's obvious," he observed. "It's also fortunate that one of you is a shaman, is it not?"

Kel laughed, "Well, almost. My grandfather, who is also my teacher, was one of the shamans taken by the zeppelin and brought here. We intend to find him and free him."

The magician glanced at Dan, who shrugged.

"Well, Kel," he began again, "I'm afraid I have some bad news for you."

Kel and Lyria looked closely at the old man, and he continued, "Your grandfather and the other shamans aren't in the city."

"Of course they are," Lyria interjected, "where else would they be?"

The old man paused, and then answered, "They're in The Green, far to the south. That's where the Cathedral took them, that's where you must go to seek them."

"Then that is where we will go," Kel answered firmly.

~

"It's dark."

The five adults were startled by Raven's sudden comment. Lyria looked around, the girl was no longer on the sofa—she was standing at the window. She pulled a corner of the heavy burgundy drapes back to look out into the night, her nose pressed against the glass. Lyria rose, going quickly to the girl. She put her hand on Raven's shoulder, saying softly to her, "Of course it's dark, sweetie, it is nighttime."

The little girl looked up at Lyria, "The dark has legs, you know," she said in an emotionless serious voice. "It bites."

The magician and Lawrence looked at each other nervously, not knowing what to say. Dan watched the young girl closely, a worried look on his face.

Lawrence cleared his throat, "Uh…we should get back to business— we all know it's dark outside." He gave a disgusted look toward the girl. Dan looked at him in surprise. He didn't remember his friend being so callous or so sarcastic—he was clearly disappointed.

"Raven, honey," Lyria queried, "are you all right?"

The girl was looking out the window again. Lyria also looked, noticing nothing but the apartment building across the street, its sign almost obscured by the night. She felt Raven's hand pull from hers as Raven turned. She walked listlessly back to the sofa, sat down, and slumped into the soft cushions.

"It's all right, Lyria," the girl said, almost in a whisper. "It's not right here yet."

"What is not right here, honey?"

"The dark," she answered cryptically and was silent once more.

Lawrence once again cleared his throat and said in an annoyed voice, "We um…should get back to the actual, real, important business. As I said before, everyone knows how dark it is out there."

"Do you?" Raven had spoken again—now she paused. She seemed to be looking vaguely into a corner of the room, seeing something there that none save she could see. "Do you really know how dark it is? Do you really want to?"

She stared at Lawrence with a look of complete, piercing sincerity in her eyes.

Lyria quickly gathered Raven into her arms, and with a look of mystified sorrow, she ushered the little girl into the next room, which turned out to be the kitchen. "We will be in here talking for a while," she explained. "You all go ahead. Kel and Dan can tell me about it later."

She closed the door and led Raven to the table. After seating the young girl, she looked around. She found bread and jelly and then made a sandwich, which she put on a plate and brought to the table. Raven was shaking, holding her hands to her face and crying, "I don't know what I am saying," she sobbed. "The words come out, but there is nothing behind them."

319

"It's all right, dear," Lyria said sympathetically. "We will figure it out. Why don't you eat now?"

Raven ate one bite of the sandwich. Some of the strawberry jelly oozed out onto her hand and she shrieked, flinging the sandwich across the room where it stuck to the wall, then slid to the floor leaving a sticky red trail.

"It's all bloody! It's all bloody! They're both going to be dead!"

Lyria looked at the girl in shock as the men who'd heard her scream threw the door open. Raven was curled up in a fetal position on the floor, sobbing.

"What's going on in here," demanded the magician. "We cannot have so much noise, it'll attract undue attention."

"The white lady with the flame will save her." Another cryptic, though very calm, remark uttered by the girl.

Lyria sat on the floor, cradling the crying child in her arms. She motioned with her head for the men to leave. When the door was again shut, she bent down, kissing Raven on her forehead. The girl was still quietly crying. "Why am I saying these things," she asked in a pleading voice. "Make it stop! Make it stop!"

As Lyria and the girl cried together, she attempted to soothe the girl.

"It's going to be all right," Lyria whispered to the girl.

Raven, her hair covering her face, vehemently shook her head. Tears flew. "No it's not," she wept. "It's going to get much, much worse—those children…"

Chapter 51

"So," the magician concluded, "that, in essence, is what we know. The Bishop and the Cathedral have some master plan involving the Green Hell. We haven't been able to find out what that plan may be. We know several small cities are being built down there and that they're recruiting soldiers from other cities, a few from as far away as Atlanta and New Orleans."

He looked around at the other men, stopping his gaze on Kel.

"We know for a fact that the kidnapped shamans are gone from the city. They were taken away aboard a crystal ship many weeks ago. Our most reliable source of information was the gossiping of a priest named Caven. He has since been killed—that cannot be a coincidence. Whatever is happening has something to do with religion, the hunger of the Bishop to rule the world, and the kind of magic that involves animal communication. That's all we know."

Kel thought for a moment and said, "How will we be able to follow? I don't know how far The Green lies from here, but we cannot walk there!"

The old man laughed, "No, you can't walk, but you can travel there nevertheless."

Kel just looked at him and said nothing.

The magician laughed again, explaining, "We know they're recruiting soldiers from very far away. I know someone who can make false documents for you and Lyria...and Raven. How would you like to be a military liaison officer traveling with your family from...oh...New Orleans?"

Kel reacted with surprise, "How does that work?"

"Simple," Lawrence interjected, "we get documents forged by an expert. In the city, you are what people think you are. If you act like a military adviser from New Orleans and have papers to prove it, well then...that's what you are!"

"We'll need you here in the morning," the old man said. "You should all stay here tonight, so we can get an early start. All of you will have to come with me to the document maker. He'll need your descriptions and you'll need his photographs and papers."

"Photographs?" Kel had never heard the word.

Lawrence rolled his eyes in disgust, "It's a process that puts your images on paper so you may show them to others—that way they can see that you are who you say you are."

"Because of a picture?"

"The documents will be very professional and I doubt many have seen the military identification papers of someone from New Orleans."

Kel was satisfied with that answer. It didn't make much sense to him, but then not much in the city did.

After a half hour of conversation, Dan entered the kitchen. Lyria and Raven were seated again at the table. The young girl was eating an apple, seemingly calm.

"We have finished here. Are you ready to go?"

"I believe so," Lyria said, smiling at Raven. "We've licked the jelly off the wall!"

Raven giggled, "We did not! Lyria washed it off with a cloth."

"Whew," Kel said, having entered the room with Dan, "butter hogs don't do well with wall lickers!"

Raven burst into laughter, the previous strangeness forgotten.

Everyone left the kitchen and headed to the door that the magician held open for them. They thanked him for his hospitality, and he put one hand on Raven's head affectionately.

Lawrence smiled at the girl, but she again moved behind Lyria. "Bashful thing, isn't she?"

"Sometimes," Kel answered.

The magician gave a key to Kel, motioning to the room across the hall.

"That also is one of ours, you may stay there tonight. I'm afraid we don't have extra clothing, but it'll only be the one day."

"I am sure we will be fine," Kel answered with a smile.

Kel opened the door, allowing the others to enter first. He looked both ways down the hall, and then entered himself closing the door behind him.

As Lawrence proceeded to make dinner, they discussed the day's events. He explained about the journey south and the assumed location if not the fate of the missing shamans. Raven was ready for the journey, fairly bursting with eagerness to not only see but actually sail on a crystal ship. Kel wasn't so sure about the last part.

Dan and Lawrence were quartered in the two-bedroom apartment next to Kel and Lyria's. Everyone was tired and so bid each other good night, going to their assigned rooms after eating. They lay in their clothing, having no other option. Tomorrow they'd return to the safe house to retrieve their belongings.

It wasn't long before everyone was asleep, or very close to it. Kel and Lyria shared the same bed, with Raven between them.

"A barrier to love," he commented with a smile.

Lyria laughed softly, "A time and place for everything, Kel."

Raven said nothing, as she was already asleep.

In his room next door, Lawrence was also asleep and dreaming. Something tickled his face—it was annoying. He moved his hand across his face, but a moment later the odd sensation returned. His nose was being tickled as well—he could feel light, rhythmic puffs of air. In his dream, a large black bird stood on his chest, looking down into his eyes. It leaned forward, striking his forehead once with its beak. He started awake, jerking his head back against his pillow.

Raven stood next to his bed, bent over at the waist, staring fixedly into his eyes. He pulled back again, even farther.

"Get away from me, girl," he hissed. "What's wrong with you?"

"I can't see your face in my thoughts."

Lawrence pushed himself into a seated position. He quickly rose, shoving the young girl roughly away from him. She staggered back, sprawling on the floor. She got quietly to her feet and, without a backward glance or complaint, left the room.

"Damn sleepwalker," Lawrence muttered. "She'll wake up the whole damn building with her strangeness."

He walked to the door of his room, watching Raven as she quietly opened the door to Dan's room right next door, and snickered. "He wants to fool around traveling with an idiot child," he muttered on his way back to bed, "might as well let the idiot child fool around with him too."

Several hours later, Dan arose sleepily.

"Drank too much water," he said to himself, shaking his head as he climbed out of bed. In the darkness, he almost tripped over a small bundle lying on the floor near his door. He stopped, pausing to light a candle on the table by the door. It was Raven, who was sound asleep.

"Raven, honey?" The child didn't move. He tried again, a little louder. "Raven?" The child rolled over, sat up, and finally stood. Dan noticed she held a long white bone fragment in her hand—she clutched it, her knuckles white with strain.

"He's not who you think he is."

He looked hard at Raven. She was asleep, yet she spoke.

"Who, honey?"

"Him."

She was pointing, arm outstretched, with her index finger. He followed her gesture, seeing only the bare wall of his room. There was nobody there.

"I see no one, Raven."

"Now you see him, now you don't—he wants to hurt us, but he will hurt others."

Dan looked again at the blank wall. He concluded that the girl must be dreaming, for there was clearly nobody else in the room. He walked toward her, just as Lyria knocked on the door.

"She's in here," Dan said with a whisper. "She's walking in her sleep."

Lyria opened the door, came forward and picked Raven up. She smiled sympathetically at Dan, turned and left the room.

He shook his head on his way back to bed. *The poor girl,* he thought, *she's been through so much, it's no wonder she talks in her sleep.*

In the morning, everyone was up early. They ate a hurried breakfast in the magician's apartment and immediately took the lift to the ground level.

"Are you sure you need me this morning," Lawrence queried. "I don't feel well and I'd like to go home."

"I need you, Lawrence," the magician said firmly, "you're the one who knows the printer best, not I. When we've concluded, you may leave."

"Very well," the man answered sullenly, heading toward their steam-car.

It took a while for the boiler to reach its necessary heat. As they waited, they watched the few people who were on the streets at that hour. Raven suggested they take turns guessing what each of the passersby did for a living.

"I think that man bakes pies," Raven said, pointing and laughing.

Lyria asked, "Why is that?"

She turned to Lyria, "Because he is fat, so he is probably a pie hog!" With that she went off in gales of laughter, putting her hand over her mouth, looking first at Kel, and then at Lyria.

"She may well be right," Dan said with a laugh. "Look!"

They turned to see what he was referring to. The man in question had stopped by the front door of a small bakery shop, used his key and gone inside.

"Lucky guess," scoffed Lawrence. "What about her?"

Raven gave the woman in question an appraising look. She was well dressed, wearing nice though not expensive clothing. She carried a large handbag. She was walking quickly, approaching a man walking in front of her.

"She's a thief," Raven said with certainty.

As Lawrence began to protest, they watched the woman set her pace to match that of the man. There was the quick flash of a blade. The man's wallet tumbled from his slit hip pocket. She quickly palmed it, dropping it into her handbag along with her knife. She turned around and quickly put some distance between herself and her unsuspecting victim.

"Well, I'll be damned," Lawrence said, shaking his head. "How're you able to call that?"

Raven shrugged her shoulders. "My mother and father always wanted me to go with them on trading trips. I could sometimes…know…if someone was trying to cheat them or steal from them." Then she started crying.

Lyria pulled her close, attempting to soothe the girl, "I'm sorry about your parents. I know they loved you very much."

"But the one time they should have listened to me, they didn't," she sobbed.

Dan asked, "What do you mean, honey?"

"I knew something bad was going to happen. I told them, but we had to go. They wouldn't listen. I should have tried harder."

Now she was in full tears, sobbing against Lyria's shoulder.

Lawrence gasped, "She's a seer!"

"You were not responsible for that," Dan said firmly. "That was the fault of the bandits, not yours. Like Daisy's death was the fault of the Cathedral rather than mine— you told me so yourself."

The girl looked up at Dan with tearstained eyes. She snuffled, wiping her nose on a handkerchief presented, seemingly from nowhere, by the magician.

"Thank you, Dandan," she said. "I really love you."

"I love you too, little one," he answered with a smile.

In the driver's seat, Lawrence rolled his eyes in disgust, put the car in gear, and jerked it from the curb out into the street. They had some distance to go to get to the printer, and time would have to be spent getting the photos and such together. He had things to do and was impatient to get on with it. They moved quickly through the light early morning traffic, having to wait only once as a large wagon being pulled by two very stubborn mules came to a stop, blocking the street in front of them.

Dan noticed his friend drumming his fingers on the steering wheel—he didn't remember the happy-go-lucky Lawrence ever being this impatient. Years change people; he knew this to be true. He wondered why his friend was in such a hurry this morning. He turned his attention in amusement to the show going on in the street as the mules firmly dug in with their hooves, straight legged. One of the men driving the wagon got down from his seat. The whip he'd been using ineffectually from above, he was now planning to use from the ground. He had a determined scowl on his face.

Lawrence laughed, shouting out the open window, "Now we'll get some action. Whip those beasts—get 'em goin' there, guys, we have business."

Everyone watched the scene unfold through the windshield, so they didn't see Raven sidle up to the door. She quickly opened it, and before anyone could stop her, she was walking toward the wagon. The driver was still cracking his whip from the seat, while the man on the ground raised his whip, the end of it trailing on the ground. He swung, but the whip stayed where it was. He looked around in confusion, and saw a young girl with amazingly white hair standing on the end of his whip. Before he could say anything, the girl stepped off the whip, walking forward calmly to look into the eyes of the mule on the left side.

She spoke, but it wasn't to the man with the whip. "You know, if you pull the wagon to where it needs to go, they will empty it, and you can have an easy pull with an empty wagon back home."

The mule and Raven continued their eye contact for a moment—then the mule huffed, nodded, and began walking forward. The other followed and the wagon was again moving. As the man swung himself up into the seat, he said to Raven, "Little girl, I don't know how you knew which of my mules was dominant, but if you ever want a job when you grow up, come see me."

"If you are nice to them, they will be nice to you," Raven answered with a smile.

The man shook his head in wonder, and in a moment the intersection was clear.

Raven returned to the waiting auto. She quickly got back inside, with a smile on her face that said, "Aren't I clever?"

Everyone burst into laughter—everyone but Lawrence, Kel noticed. The rest of the journey was uneventful, though traffic was starting to pick up. Shops were being unlocked for the day and kids were standing around on a corner waiting for the steam-bus that would take them to school. Lawrence made three turns, ending in a narrow street that was hardly more than an alleyway. He moved slowly to avoid occasional pedestrians, finally pulling up at their destination.

Chapter 52

Lawrence parked the car along the side of a brick building. It might as well have been basalt or granite for all the color gave away, as years of soot and street grime had turned the bricks a mottled black and dark grey. He shut down the engine, and they exited the vehicle from the driver's side, the doors on the other side being too close to the wall to open. Lawrence knocked twice on a nondescript doorway with no sign to indicate the presence of a business. The door opened a crack, and ferret-like eyes ran quickly over all present. Satisfied, the owner of those eyes shut the door, slipped the chain, and opened it all the way.

Once inside, it was apparent this was in fact a home, rather than a place of business. The man led the small band through the living room into the dining room without a word. He squatted, flinging back the edge of the heavy rug covering the floor—below the rug was a trapdoor. He lifted the trap, and motioned for the others to descend. Kel looked at Lyria, she shrugged and they started down the steps.

"This basement's a secret," the ferret-eyed man said. "You are to mention it to no one."

"We'll be silent," the magician answered for his party.

First, the man asked Kel to stand in front of a drape on one wall. He moved the oak-cased camera and set it up facing Kel. He quickly loaded a sheet of film, and suddenly there was an intense flash of light. Kel blinked, but the photo was already taken. The man laughed, "It is a bit disconcerting, if you've never done this before."

Next came Lyria. The man looked at her appreciatively. "I don't get to photograph many as beautiful as you, my dear."

She smiled, and that was what he was waiting for. Flash! Lyria jumped and laughed. Raven came last and she was surprisingly placid about the process.

Afterward, Kel, Lyria, Raven, and Dan were led back into the living room where they were invited to sit. The printer, Lawrence, and the magician stayed in the basement making final preparations. The man's wife came out of the kitchen and served them hot coffee and toast. She smiled at Raven as she went back into the kitchen. In a moment she was back with a cup of hot chocolate for the young girl. Raven smiled at her, taking a sip. It was lovely! She'd never tasted anything so wonderful and wondered if they had this at home.

Dan spoke first and asked, "Raven, how come the camera didn't make you jump like the big, strong Lyria and Kel did?"

Surprisingly, the girl didn't laugh—nor smile. She looked down at her lap.

"Sometimes they took those of me," she mumbled. "In the building with the men."

Lyria looked at Kel, her heart breaking. How could anyone do such a cruel and inhuman thing and dare call it the will of the Divine? She just shook her head.

"It is all right, honey," she soothed, "all that is over now. You are with us and we will never allow bad things to happen to you again."

They finished the coffee and toast. The man's wife came back into the living room and they spent their time discussing the operation of cameras, how the films were developed, and how printing worked. She showed them photographs in a book of the gigantic printing presses used in the big newspaper offices. It was impressive. Kel had never really thought about how the books his father cherished and he loved had been made. Now he felt an even greater appreciation for them. Home. Wouldn't that be nice?

The trapdoor gave a clunk as it was lowered. The men came into the living room and the ferret-eyed man—apparently no names were used for security reasons—handed Kel and Lyria their documents.

"You're now a military adviser and observer from the city of New Orleans," the magician explained. "You'll notice that you now have last names."

Kel laughed, he'd never considered having two names. He looked at the very official document in his hand. It had various stamps and marks including eagles and numbers. His photo was inside the front cover.

"You'll notice," the magician continued, "that I've renamed you Kelley—it's a good choice since Lyria or Raven calling you Kel will seem natural. Lyria is a good name by itself, as is Raven."

"But we all have the same last name," Kel commented.

"Of course," the magician said. "You're married and Raven is your daughter!"

Raven clapped her hands with glee upon hearing that.

"Kelley Draco," Kel tried the name, it sounded good to him.

He stood, bowed formally to Lyria, "Lyria Draco, I am very pleased to meet you."

Raven giggled when they said her name.

The magician said, "Draco means dragon in a foreign tongue. I thought it appropriate considering what you two have done, and what you have left to do."

"My new mommy and daddy are dragons!"

Raven was entranced with the idea. Everyone smiled at her—then the magician clapped his hands together.

"We must be going now," he said, "thank you for the quick service."

He bowed before the printer and his wife.

"Thank you," Raven said simply.

The rest gave their thanks and the group departed. They'd been there two hours, and Lawrence was very anxious to go home. They got into the auto, this time Dan was driving. They pulled up to the narrow street that cut across the road the printer lived on, and pulled over.

"I'm afraid we have another stop to make," the magician said.

He handed some coins to Lawrence, "Here is taxi fare. You can catch a cab from here and be on your way home."

Lawrence reluctantly left the auto muttering, "Not many cabs on this street!"

But the magician had already shut the door and the car was rapidly moving away from him. He shrugged. He had time to do what he needed to do anyway. He turned to face the roadway, waiting for a taxi.

~

Lawrence stood for almost thirty minutes waiting for a cab. He was getting impatient—he had something important to do. Eventually, he saw a delivery truck heading his direction. When the truck rumbled to a stop to make a delivery just a half block away, Lawrence ran the distance so he'd be there when the driver returned.

"Excuse me," Lawrence said, gasping to catch his breath, "I need to find a taxi and there are none that travel this street. Would you be kind enough to give me a lift to the next busy street?"

The man looked Lawrence up and down and said, "The company rules is that we don't take no passengers."

Lawrence thought fast, "Well, how about this. I'll give you the amount of a taxi fare across town if you'll give me a ride of a mere few miles."

The man thought it over, undecided. Lawrence pulled the coins from his pocket that the magician had given him, jingling them temptingly in his palm.

The man looked both ways, as though he thought his boss might be lurking nearby just to catch him in the act.

"All right," the man finally said, "gimme the coins."

Lawrence smiled as he climbed into the passenger side of the lorry, he'd have his ride in no time now. The driver pulled from the curb. They rode in silence for several miles until they arrived at a major intersection. Lawrence alighted to the street, thanking the driver. The man tipped his cap in Lawrence's direction, and then he was gone. Lawrence looked around; there was a taxi waiting area just a half block down the street and there were two cabs waiting.

"Where to, sir?"

"Take me to the Jefferson Apartments, please," Lawrence said.

"Yes, sir," the cab driver answered as they shot from the curb out into the busy street, narrowly missing a bus full of people, "have you there in no time."

"One piece would be preferable," Lawrence said with a laugh.

"Oh, I never kill my fares," the driver quipped. "It's bad for tips!"

They both laughed.

The cab pulled up at the front door of the apartment building, where Lawrence alighted, paying his fare and tipping the driver.

"Remember me the next time," Lawrence joked. "I always tip, unless I'm dead."

"Thank you, sir," the man acknowledged, then pulled back out into traffic.

Lawrence quickly entered the building, walking past the lobby where several individuals lounged. One group of older men was watching two of their friends playing chess around a low table—it was a game Lawrence never seemed able to master. He rode the lift up to the thirty-seventh floor. When the lift stopped moving, he quickly opened the gate and walked down the hallway. Four doors down, he stopped and knocked on the door. In a moment it opened. A rather unkempt older man stood inside the doorway.

"Well, hello, Mr. F," the old man said with a smile, "I wasn't expecting to see you for a couple of days."

"Something's come up, sir, that I thought you should know about."

"Well, don't just stand there, young man, come on in," Father Anderson said with a smile.

~

Dan drove quickly away from the printer's secret shop. Kel was wondering what the sudden hurry was.

"For a little while, we've been…concerned with regard to Mr. Ford's allegiance," he began. "Occasionally some of our plans seemed to have come to the attention of the Cathedral. We think he might be a spy."

Dan shook his head, thinking of how differently his friend had been behaving since his return to the Black City. "I find it hard to believe, but what Raven told me last night fits in with what the magician has told me in private."

"I didn't tell you anything," Raven piped up, confused. "When?"

"Last night, honey," he answered. "You were sleepwalking, and saying things."

"I was?"

"Yes," Lyria answered, "I saw it and heard it too."

"I didn't know what you meant last night," Dan continued. "But after talking to the magician this morning, I figured it out. You were warning me about him, you said he wasn't who I thought he was."

Raven didn't comment, she couldn't remember a thing she'd said last night.

"You were guarding me," Dan said to her with a great deal of fondness. "Did you know that?"

"Guarding?"

"You were sleeping on the floor in my room with a very wicked-looking sharpened bone. You were holding it like a dagger and you were sleeping between me and the door."

They thought about this in silence as they drove rapidly down the street. It would take Lawrence a while to walk to a cab from his location—hopefully they'd be finished before he did.

Kel suddenly knew where they were headed. "We're going back to the safe house, are we not?"

"That's correct," Dan said. "We're clearing out of there. If Lawrence is a spy, that location won't be safe."

Dan turned into the gravel drive leading to the small home. No one said anything; they all knew what they had to do. Clothing was quickly packed into suitcases and loaded into the auto. Some they had to leave, as there was no more room.

Lyria clutched her precious sword to her breast as they quickly got back into the vehicle. "What of our horses?"

"They've already been moved to my stables on the other side of town," the magician said. "There they'll be well cared for. Don't be surprised if they are quite spoiled by the time you see them again."

Lyria laughed, "To spoil those horses more than they already are, you will have a job on your hands."

The magician laughed as he started the vehicle rolling.

They left the house in less than twenty minutes after having arrived. Knowing what to do, Dan quickly drove around to the next street, stopping in front of a house Kel and Lyria hadn't seen before.

Lyria, looked around worriedly, and asked, "Where are we?"

The magician had already exited the vehicle and was knocking on the front door.

"This is the home behind the safe house," Dan explained. "The people living here must be warned so they can prepare for...guests."

Kel, nodding in understanding, "They are preparing the explosives in case the safe house is raided."

Dan laughed, "Your husband is a very clever fellow, Lyria."

Lyria blushed, "We are not wed yet."

"Well," Dan said in a teasing voice, "you have documents that say you are."

They all laughed, including Raven who didn't seem to grasp the joke, but laughed with everyone else.

The magician returned to the auto and they were once more on their way.

"We must find a place for you to hide for a while until we can arrange transport."

"So we are going south?"

"Yes," the magician said with a nod, "if you've been betrayed, we must get you beyond their grasp quickly—we'll know soon."

Shortly they were again on the streets of the great city. Dan was wondering where they would go. He was slightly puzzled, his friend Lawrence had been with the resistance longer than he. The magician seemed to guess his thoughts.

"One reason we've continued to operate is that the Bishop doesn't know the name of the head of our organization. Until he does, we're relatively safe—though our plans are frequently thwarted. I believe Mr. Ford's job was to find that person. To that end, I believe he kept silent about me—he wanted to find the top man, but was afraid the Bishop would come for me and take the glory. He knew of the safe house, but we've hiding places even Lawrence doesn't know about. It's to one of these that we are now headed."

"There are so many plans and deceits within the city, how do you keep them straight?" Kel, asked.

The magician laughed, "Most of the time we don't, we just guess."

When they arrived at their final location, they were surprised—they were in the parking area of one of the local newspapers. The magician smiled knowingly at the group and said, "The paper operates twenty-four hours a day, there are always people about. The Cathedral wouldn't dare raid such a place even if they knew we were using it as a safe house, which they don't. You'll be safe here, I guarantee. Come."

The magician led his small band into the noise and tumult of the news factory.

He led them quickly up a flight of stairs, into an office. Once the door was shut, he introduced them to the owner of the paper, explaining the situation. Tom Leatham looked over the newcomers, smiling at Raven and she smiled back. He led them to the bookcase lining one wall of his office. He pulled a hidden lever and the bookcase slid silently into the room. He gestured everyone inside. Much like the secret passage in their former abode, this room was small, with one adjoining room. The bathroom, it turned out, had an entrance from the office for regular use, and a secret entrance behind a large mirror for individuals who might be hiding in the secret room.

"You'll only be here two nights," the magician explained. "We'll do our best to find you transportation away from here as quickly as we can."

"We will be fine," Lyria assured him. "Be careful."

"Oh, I'm always careful," the magician said as he closed the bookcase, shutting them inside. There were two lanterns, which Kel lit. They'd have to be reasonably quiet, especially if they heard someone come into the office. They decided to nap for a while. The night before had been very eventful, and they'd risen early that morning as well.

~

"So that's the story," Lawrence concluded. "They have the little girl everyone is so anxious to find, that white hair is a real giveaway. Did you know she's a seer? She's quite talented at that. There are two outlanders as well. The fourth is a friend of mine, I would prefer he not be harmed."

"We'll do the very best we can," the spy said with a smile. "Though there can be no guarantees, are you sure of the location?"

"Yes," he answered with a firm nod, "I've been there myself. They'll be there until tomorrow night at least."

"Mr. F," Father Anderson said, "you've done well, this time. All of this information is valuable to the Cathedral, especially the part about the girl thing being a seer. That could come in very handy."

"I thought you'd like that information," Lawrence said with a smug smile. "I expect she could do a lot to help you thwart anyone who opposes you."

With that, the old priest smiled, handing Lawrence a small bag. Lawrence grinned when he took it, hearing the jingle of many coins within.

"This will really get me off the hook," Lawrence told the priest. "Whenever I gamble, I seem to lose."

"Why then do you gamble?"

"I don't know, exactly," he answered in true confusion. "I just can't resist the opportunity to try to make some quick money."

"No matter," the old priest said. "As long as the information flows true, we'll be happy to pay you."

Lawrence left the building with the bag of coins concealed inside his coat pocket. The lesson he learned watching the woman thief that Raven had identified, stayed with him. He only had two more things to do and he'd be in the clear. First, he needed to find a telephone. He walked two blocks down the street, turning into yet another apartment building. He knew no one in the building, which is why he chose it. There were several phones in the lobby for the residents, but the desk clerk was napping so he took the opportunity. The number he called rang several times before it was answered.

Lawrence recognized the voice as that of the magician. So he was home already. He looked quickly at his watch, suddenly realizing it'd taken him longer to make this meeting than he'd realized.

"It's me, Lawrence," he said in a conspiratorial whisper, "there's going to be a raid, imminently. I heard that the Cathedral was sending soldiers to investigate an anonymous report of outlanders living in a small home—this mysterious informer called the police."

Lawrence chuckled into the phone, then continued, "The police apparently called the Cathedral, because an attack is coming at any time, only for some reason, it'll be on the other side of town."

Lawrence laughed again.

"I assume we know who made that mysterious call," the magician said. "Thank you."

"It's what we do," Lawrence said humbly, "the safe house hasn't been compromised, everyone will be safe—of that I can assure you."

He hung up the receiver.

Chapter 53

The magician looked sadly at Dan.

"Was it as you predicted?"

"It was," the magician answered, "I'm sorry."

Dan hung his head in sorrow. He couldn't imagine why his friend would turn on them. Was the Cathedral planning to ambush the whole group at the safe house? Had Lawrence felt any remorse at all? Dan could answer none of these questions.

"I'm sorry, Dan," the magician said. "We'll see Lawrence later tonight, let's wait to see what he has to say for himself."

"I'm afraid, my friend," Dan said, "that Lawrence, is a traitor."

"There's now no doubt, but perhaps we can use that knowledge to our advantage. It'll be very important he doesn't know we suspect him. If we can give him false information as to our next moves, he'll fall into disfavor with the Bishop and they'll no longer trust him for giving reliable information. He'll be free to follow whatever life he chooses, but not with us."

"I understand," Dan said.

It didn't make him feel any better—he and Lawrence had been friends for years.

~

The busses drove rapidly up the semi-rural street—it was not quite dusk. The man sitting next to the driver in the first bus pointed to a driveway.

"There it is," he said tensely, "right there."

The driver grinned at him and said, "I don't know why that child or these outlander half-humans are so important to the Bishop, but after we round them up, I'll bet there'll be a reward."

The commander looked at the driver and grinned, "We take the child to the Cathedral with the adults. What happens to the female half-human inside that house, as long as she lives, is our business. We can take turns with her, she'll be used up by the time all thirty of us finish."

The other man chuckled, "I bet they do that in the tribes every night. I bet it's just one big orgy every night."

"That could very well be," the commander said, "but we'll get only one orgy—so we'll be sure to make the most of it. I suggest that once everyone is in custody, we make the child and the man watch us use the woman. Who knows, we might teach the girl a thing or two, and the man will certainly find out what it means to cross the Bishop."

The busses accelerated quickly once they were in the driveway, kicking up gravel as they came. The first bus slowed to a stop with the right side facing the house. The second bus sped around behind the house to cut off any possible retreat. The commander leaped from the bus, quickly followed by thirteen soldiers. The driver remained in the bus, but was assured he'd get his share of the woman. He was already prepared physically—he'd never done it with a half-human before. He wondered if she'd have a tail. He hoped so.

The men from the two busses quickly surrounded the house. The commander retrieved a megaphone from the bus, raising it to his lips.

"Come on out of there," he shouted. "If you make us come in, you'll only be hurt resisting. Come out now and I'll guarantee your complete safety."

The driver grinned at the last words. *Who knows*, he thought, *maybe they'd be stupid enough to just walk out*. Nobody came to the door, however.

"Very well," the commander shouted, "we're coming in."

He gave the signal and five of the soldiers stormed the house, their .30 caliber Mauser 96 pistols in their hands. They affixed the shoulder stocks, turning the ten round pistols into short carbines. The men gathered at the front door. The lead man looked back at the commander, who nodded.

The man kicked in the door and entered, moving quickly to the left, removing himself from his dangerous position in the doorway—what they called a 'fatal funnel'—a confined area allowing no evasive action, where anyone inside could aim his weapon and be assured of a hit. The others followed quickly. The men who were stationed outside relayed information by voice to the commander as they were informed of conditions within the house.

"Nobody in the front room, sir," the man by the door shouted.

"Nobody's come out the back," came a shout from the rear of the house.

"Take the next room," the raid leader said.

Two men kicked open the second door, entering a bedroom. The other two cleared the kitchen, then kicked their way into the second bedroom.

"Nobody here," the man by the door shouted again to the commander.

"Well, let's go in and see if there are clues to where they might've gone."

The commander was disgusted. He had really looked forward to the rape he'd have been allowed to perpetrate. Rank has its privileges he liked to say, as it meant he'd be the first to take the woman.

Inside, the men ransacked the house, only finding a few items of clothing and old newspapers.

"Look at this," a voice from the bedroom called.

The commander quickly followed the voice, finding two men standing by a bookcase that was slightly ajar.

"Secret room here, sir," the first man said. "Found it myself. You think the woman and the others might be in there?"

"We'll soon find out," the commander said. "Leave your pistols here with us. You'll use your sticks as weapons. We don't want any of these...things, hurt, too badly."

The men nodded, placing their Mausers on the bedside table.

They pulled the case open cautiously. When they received no resistance, they flung it open and stepped into the opening.

"Stairway leading down," the man called. "I'm advancing."

The man took several steps, and then said, "By the Redeemed God!"

No other voice was ever spoken in that house again, except perhaps the voice of thunder. The trip cord worked as had been intended, as the soldier felt the strain of the taut cord against his leg, it had already tipped the lit candle hidden behind a crate into a pool of oil. The fuses of the explosives ignited from that burning pool of oil and burned quickly.

Three detonations occurred as the house erupted into a high velocity fireball following hard on the heels of the explosion's pressure front. The house instantly turned into shrapnel. The bus in front rolled onto its side, saving the driver, all thoughts of lust driven from his mind.

The bus parked behind the house was severely penetrated by shrapnel. The massive boiler on the military vehicle detonated at almost the same moment as the house. Superheated steam shot through the cabin quickly boiling the men inside their clothing. Uniforms and flesh fell from their bodies where they stood or sat.

As the bus driver pulled himself from the wreck, he heard police whistles approaching. They were supposed to be done with this operation and out without anyone knowing. That was impossible now. The driver tried to run, but the femur of his right leg was broken. He sagged back to the ground, quickly losing consciousness.

~

Lawrence walked a short distance, again taking a cab. He had one more destination before he could go back to the magician's home. The cab dropped him in front of a laundry. He exited the cab and, without a word to the driver, paid him and turned away. He pushed his way into the dark interior of the laundry. Though the business was shut for the night, he knew the door would be unlocked for several more hours. He sauntered casually to the door at the rear. He nodded at the very large man standing guard. *The guard held a very large wrench that matched his demeanor*, Lawrence thought to himself. The man said nothing as he opened the door with a frosted glass panel, allowing Lawrence to enter. In neat gold letters, the sign on the door read 'Manager.' Inside, there were three men. They looked up in surprise.

"Well," the fat man behind the desk said, "I didn't expect to see you."

"Hey," Lawrence said with a shrug, "I owe you some money!"

The fat man smiled. Getting paid was better than breaking legs, but either would suffice. He looked at Lawrence and opened his ledger.

"Says here you owe us five thousand."

"And I have it right here," Lawrence said with a smile and a flourish as he spread the coins on the desktop.

"I gotta say you're a man of your word—even if you are a day late, Mr. Ford," the fat man said.

"I pay my debts," he answered.

"I know that the last couple bets you placed went awry, but you've won money from us at times as well. I know of something you might be interested in." He laid his index finger against his nose, tapping it.

"I don't think I better place any more bets for a while," Lawrence said.

"Oh c'mon," the fat man cajoled, "at least hear me out."

"Very well, I'll listen, but don't expect me to accept."

"Fair enough," the bookie said.

He pulled a piece of paper from under his blotter, handing it to Lawrence.

"There's a very unusual race coming up," the man said. "Most unusual."

Lawrence looked at the flier—it was an advertisement for a race from Los Angeles to New Fresno to the north. The race would cover over one hundred miles, ending in the last city still habitable south of the ice sheet—the rebuilt city of New Fresno. What interested Lawrence was that this was a race between a zeppelin and a locomotive. It would begin tomorrow morning. That was interesting, it'd be a fast payday, but which to bet on…

"A lot of money is being bet on the zeppelin," the fat man said. "I think in the air the low mountains of the Diablo Range can just be sailed right over, not slowing the movement with uphill climbs as will happen with the locomotive. The zeppelin might be a bit slower overall, but it'll be certain to maintain a constant speed of forty-five miles an hour. The locomotive may carry a speed of seventy-five, but it'll have to make a stop for water along the way and then it'll have the mountains."

"I concur," Lawrence said, "that makes sense to me."

"Then again," the man said knowingly, "betting on the locomotive is considered a long-shot with really big payoffs."

"How big?"

"If you bet five thousand and win, your take would be…in the vicinity of nine thousand. You could almost double your money."

"Why would the locomotive win?"

"Simple," the fat man said, "the locomotive will only stop fifteen minutes to refuel. I know that its speed in those mountains on those rails will be a steady fifty miles an hour. Even at the slowest, it'll be moving five miles an hour faster than the airship, and with a fuel stop, there's no way the zeppelin can beat it."

Lawrence thought a moment, but he already knew what his answer would be.

"Put me down for five thousand on the locomotive, then."

The fat man smiled, "Sign here, please."

~

It was several hours before Lawrence again appeared at the magician's home. Dan wasn't there.

"We evaded an ambush, they hit the safe house, you know." The magician said with a smile.

Lawrence feigned surprise, "Good thing you didn't follow my bad advice. I was told that the raid would be across town."

The magician smiled again, "I'd say it was lucky for us!"

341

"So we need a new plan, do we not?"

"Yes we do," responded the magician. "It'll be too dangerous now for them to use their identifications or indeed to embark on a ship or zeppelin. No, we've decided that they'll take an auto, then horses east nearly to Mountain Village. From there, a zeppelin will pick them up and fly them south all the way across Mexico, landing them directly in The Green."

"That's not a bad idea," Lawrence said, nodding. "When will they leave?"

"In two days. They're safe for now and I have preparations to make."

"Where are they?"

"Safe. Kel and Lyria wanted complete secrecy. You must remember, they don't know you as Dan and I do."

"I understand," Lawrence said. "Then if there's nothing more, I'll be on my way."

Chapter 54
CATHEDRAL SOLDIERS RAID, BLOW UP
HOME IN LOS ANGELES

The headline screamed across the front pages of all three of the city newspapers the next morning. Why was a private army assaulting a home in the city? Where were the police? Weren't arrests and raids their job, not the Cathedral's? There was a photo on the front page of the Bishop, it was an older photo and was not very flattering. Under the photo was a caption stating the Bishop was unavailable for comment. The editor of the paper showed it to Kel, a big grin on his face. Kel almost laughed out loud as he read the article in the editor's office. Lyria, Raven, and he were out of their cramped quarters. The editor decided to claim they were family visiting from New Fresno for a few days—none of the employees of the paper seemed to care today. Everyone was furiously following up on the story. Kel read the story aloud so Lyria and Raven could hear it as well, showing them photos of the destroyed busses and flattened home. When he was finished, he asked the editor how his reporters were able to arrive at the scene of the devastation even before the police.

He smiled, then answered, "It was magic."

Kel and Lyria both laughed at that. The editor had arranged to have reporters in position just up the street, so they arrived two minutes after the explosions. The editor laughed again, turning to page two. There they saw the face of a man in a uniform in apparent pain.

"He was the driver of one of the busses," the editor explained. "He was the only survivor. His uniform in the photo proves his position as a corporal in the mercenary army of the Cathedral. This raid of theirs was highly illegal, they'll be having legal problems for the next little while or so."

"Then that would be a good time for us to disappear from the city."

"The magician has already set it up," the newsman said. "Day after tomorrow you'll embark on a crystal ship bound for The Green."

"What of the Cathedral?" Lyria was nervous about this whole operation.

"They think you're on your way back to Mountain Village at this moment," he answered. "Their plan is to have spies and soldiers there waiting. But what they'll see as they approach Mountain Village is a zeppelin just leaving the ground about fifty miles west of the village."

"They will think they're too late," Lyria said. "They will have to wait in The Green for the zeppelin to arrive."

"Only it never will," the editor said. "We'll run a story that one of our zeppelins crashed on a reporting mission near Mountain Village—there won't be any survivors. Why, we even have photos of the burned bodies," he said with a snicker.

"Not our bodies," Raven said.

"No, little one," the editor said, "we withheld a few photos from the raid, burned bodies, unidentifiable in a field. The photos look like they could've been taken anywhere. In a day, the Cathedral will think you're all dead. They'll not look further," he snickered again. "Why, we'll have shown them irrefutable proof."

"City speak," Raven commented.

"That is the truth," Kel said, hugging the girl. "City speak at its finest!"

~

Lawrence reported what the magician had told him immediately. Father Anderson called Father Woods, who in turn told the Bishop. The Bishop waited eagerly for the priest to arrive. A half hour later, they were face to face.

"You'll head this mission to find the beastling child and the others. They won't slip through my fingers now, considering everything that's happened."

Father Woods shook his head, "As you wish, Your Eminence. I must say, I find it hard to believe that trained soldiers wouldn't have looked for some kind of booby traps, all things considered."

"You must remember, Father, most of our highly skilled and well trained men are in The Green. Here we're left with half trained and newly arrived adventurers. They probably had very little training before the attack."

"We should've used Father Anderson and his people, I think," the priest surmised. "He at least would have suspected a trap."

"I agree; that's partly my fault. I allowed the commander of the assault team to convince me his men were up to the job. Now, in the news, that damn bus driver has mentioned rape as being one motive in the raid."

"By the Redeemed God! That's unbelievable," Father Woods said in shock. "We need to silence him immediately."

"That's being taken care of as we speak."

Father Anderson opened the door to the hospital ward where he knew the injured driver was being cared for—most of the ward was one open room with patients separated by white drapes. The bus driver had been moved to a private room on orders of Sergeant Jinks. It was no problem for the old priest, in his black robes for the first time in years, to enter the hospital. The bus driver was, after all, a member of his church. He opened the door and found that there was nobody else in the room.

"Well, Corporal Pliny, how're you feeling?"

"Better, Your Grace," the man answered with a feeble smile.

The priest could see he was still very weak from loss of blood. That was good.

"You've been telling stories to the press, Corporal, have you not?"

When the man didn't answer, he just smiled at the soldier and said, "It isn't really a problem you know. What the Bishop would like you to do is simply write a letter of apology for making false accusations. We can give it to the press—the story will be forgotten and you'll come back to work like nothing happened."

"Truly?"

"I give you my word," the priest said with a smile, offering a fountain pen and paper to the soldier.

The man eagerly wrote what the priest told him to; he knew he had made a grave mistake saying those things to the reporters. They confused him and made him say things he didn't mean. When he finished writing, he handed the letter to the priest, who set it on the table next to the bed. The priest withdrew a syringe from his robe, turning to the soldier.

"What is that?"

"This," the priest said with a disarming smile, "is called Atropa Belladonna. As you know, we have access to many medicines that ordinary doctors don't."

The man nodded, he'd heard of the miraculous recoveries of wounded soldiers.

"This is one of those medicines," the priest went on. "With this, your body will begin producing new blood very quickly. I estimate you'll be out of the hospital by tomorrow evening."

"Really? The doctor told me it'd be about a week!"

The priest gave an indulgent smile as he pushed the needle into the man's arm. Almost immediately the man began having trouble breathing. His pupils dilated fully causing him to squint in the now very bright light.

Father Anderson calmly took the man's pulse—it was climbing rapidly. While distilling the contents of the syringe, he used the root of the plant— making it quicker and more deadly. The man paled, his eyes moving around the room. The spy knew he was hallucinating and that it wouldn't be long. *The man's heart must be racing*, the priest thought.

He moved quickly. He took the rope belt from the man's pajamas, tying it around his neck. He lowered the man to the floor, making sure the rope was pulled tightly around his throat. The soldier was only vaguely aware of what was happening and unable to stop it, he gagged as the rope tightened. The priest couldn't tell if it was strangulation or poison that killed the man, nor did it matter—the man was silent. Now it was time for some acting. He quickly ran down the corridor, shouting for a doctor. He explained that he'd come to see the soldier, but had tarried to pray for others in the ward outside. When he walked in, the man was dead. Obviously he killed himself in remorse for the scandalous things he told the newspapers. Why, there was even a suicide note written in his own hand.

The thing went smoothly and an hour later Father Anderson was on the street heading to his waiting auto. He smiled as he remembered telling the man he'd leave the hospital tomorrow. He would, but only for the trip to a funeral home. Mission accomplished. The good Father talked to the press next, explaining how the man was delirious—not knowing what he was saying. His suicide came as a shock to all at the Cathedral.

~

"That should help some if the reporters don't dig too far into Father Anderson's history." Father Woods said, after showing the newspaper to the Bishop the next morning.

"It will not matter," the Bishop said with a smile. "I hope they do. You see Father Anderson is actually a real doctor. What he has to say about the dead man's condition will not be challenged."

The priest heaved a sigh of relief—maybe they'd be able to squirm out of this after all. He sat heavily into his chair. The Bishop looked at him, "We're in the clear now. Father Anderson and his men have sent various reports to the newspapers claiming direct Cathedral information that the raid was an impromptu attempt by the commander to curry favor and gain rank. It seems we were about to notify the police of some dangerous outlanders who might be killers, when news of the failed raid reached us."

"Smart, very smart," Father Woods said with a grin. "But now, Your Eminence, if I'm to catch that zeppelin waiting out east, I'd best be leaving."

"I agree," the Bishop said. "Have a safe flight and bring those creatures back."

"With the help of the Redeemed God, I will do just that."

Father Woods left the Cathedral, heading for the zeppelin barn. His white airship was already being towed out onto the field. This time it was fully armed and would be carrying a detachment of the best soldiers still in the city. There'd be no botched raids under his command—that was a certainty. As he climbed into the machine, he thought about the race that was going on; he felt certain that a zeppelin could easily beat a locomotive. He knew the zeppelin they were using in the race had the new, more powerful engines. It was an experimental design, but seemed reliable. Those engines had already carried the zeppelin at seventy-eight miles an hour. If they maintained that speed, they'd be in New Fresno in an hour and a half. It seemed impossible, but there it was. He actually felt sorry for the poor losers who bet on the locomotive because of its alleged greater speed. He smiled, he'd bet a hundred on the zeppelin. He knew the fat man would hold his winnings for him.

~

The news came back quickly—the zeppelin had beaten the locomotive to New Fresno by twenty minutes. Lawrence stared in disbelief at the man who told him the news. He'd gotten only five hundred from Father Anderson, with the rest promised upon the capture of the half-humans. He no longer cared about them, especially since he knew Dan wouldn't be with them. Maybe Dan could help him deal with this constant gambling he seemed to have fallen into. *In fact*, he thought to himself, *he'd bet on it.*

Lawrence avoided the bars and any haunts where the fat man's men might be found. He needed time—he owed five thousand again, for God's sake. He just paid his debt, and now it was like that had never happened. Once he thought he saw one of the fat man's bodyguards drive by. He quickly stepped into a doorway, allowing his hat to hide his face. The steam-car slid past without even slowing, but he knew he was in trouble. What if the Bishop didn't want to pay him as much as he needed? He didn't want to think about that.

He'd begun spying for the Cathedral in desperation, and he knew from reputation that the fat man wanted to be paid immediately. Nevertheless, he figured he had a few days grace. Hopefully the captives would be brought back safe and sound by that time. He snuck into his apartment building, using the stairs instead of the lift. Perhaps he should stay with his brother-in-law a few days.

Chapter 55

The zeppelin was approaching its destination—the priest told the pilot to come in low. He didn't want the half-humans to see him from too far away.

"Bring her in slow and low," he reminded the commander of the vessel.

"We're doing only ten knots right now," the pilot reported. "We're using only half our engines and those are feathered to quarter power."

"Very well," the priest answered, "thank you Commander."

They traveled on in silence for a short period of time. The first mate made the next comment, "What's that?"

The pilot and the priest looked where he was pointing—it was a mottled green zeppelin. It rose swiftly from the ground two miles ahead.

"Looks like they beat us," the first mate said.

"Fire up the engines," the priest shouted. "We need full power immediately."

The crewmen in charge of the engines sprang into action. Still, it would take time to ignite the cold engines and the four that were running would need precious minutes to come up to speed.

The green airship was gaining altitude rapidly. Obviously they'd seen the pursuing airship and were running. Could they catch them? They could certainly try. Shouting commands and threats, the pilot and the priest cajoled the engine men to hurry. They regained top speed in record time, but it wasn't enough—the green zeppelin was pulling steadily ahead. As they passed over the spot where it had rested, the priest used the telescope to look at the ground. Below he saw three horses, and a black smudge that could be nothing but an extinguished campfire, they were too late. The priest slammed his fist onto the top of the instrument panel, but that didn't increase their speed. The weapons, soldiers, and their equipment weighed the airship down. This close to Mountain Village, they dared not jettison weapons that could be turned against them, no matter how much they weighed, and the artillery pieces weighed a considerable amount. By this time the green ship was far ahead. The pilot looked at the priest. Father Woods sighed. The Bishop would be disappointed. As the airship turned to return to the Black City, the priest saw scavenger half-humans taking the horses left by his quarry back to Mountain Village. He didn't really care; it wasn't the horses that concerned him.

They took the trip back to the city at half speed. Father Woods wasn't looking forward to telling the Bishop he failed in his mission. He didn't know what had happened unless that young spy and turncoat gave them misinformation. Why would he do that? *Probably,* thought the priest, *the powers that really ran the resistance had moved up the time for some reason of their own—they'd simply been too late.* He sighed again, he'd talk to the Bishop soon enough. He walked to the back of the airship, reclined on a bunk and fell asleep.

"There's more of 'em," the first mate called out from the wheel. He'd taken command while the pilot slept that evening. The three crewmen who were awake looked out of the starboard window. Lights, there were tiny bright spots in the sky far below them.

"Fireflies, you think?"

"Pretty bright for fireflies, eh?"

"I agree," the third man said. "Fireflies don't fly in straight lines."

"Well," the first mate said, "they can't hurt us no matter what they are."

They turned their attention back to running the airship—they'd be landing soon and it would still be dark when they did. The first mate hated night landings.

~

That night Kel, Lyria, and Raven were preparing for their journey south. They did not know what to expect. Dan returned with some armor for Kel. The armor was a light iron breastplate and back plate. The lower section was a sort of knee length skirt or kilt of leather with iron laminations riveted to it, which allowed for both protection of the upper legs and movement. The helmet was of old-fashioned design with a horsehair plume. Kel removed the horsehair, and replaced it with the hawk feathers of his spirit animal.

The magician said, "Kel is the military man, he should carry the sword." Lyria wasn't so sure until Kel assured her he'd not need to put it on until they disembarked in the south. Until then, he would not wear his armor, so he wouldn't need to wear the sword.

Kel looked at the magician, "My Lyria is very possessive of her weapons."

Lyria laughed, "I am the one the sword has chosen."

The magician didn't understand, but he didn't say anything.

350

"In the morning we'll depart by auto and drive directly to the docks. There'll be a crystal ship waiting for passengers."

"How do we know the ship does not belong to the Cathedral?"

The magician looked at Lyria, nodding in approval of the question.

"The ship has been hired by me to make this run. It's from the Far East—its crew doesn't even speak our language. Only the ship's master can speak to us. He's being paid by the Bishop as well," the magician said with an ironic smile. "Their job is taking colonizers south. Nobody will give you a second glance, and the ship's master gets paid twice."

"I'm going home!"

Raven's sudden comment silenced the rest. They looked at her in confusion. Lyria said, "No, honey, we are going to The Green, after that we will take you home if you wish."

"Birds and fireflies!"

The four adults looked at each other—nobody knew what to say. The girl turned back to the hidden room behind the editor's office to pack what few belongings she possessed. As she went she was skipping, singing to herself.

"Birds and fireflies, birds and fireflies, I'm going home."

~

"I'm sorry, Mr. Ford," Father Anderson said, "we've no further payment for you. The airship left before we got there—your information wasn't good enough. The Bishop may decide to let you keep the five hundred. I don't know, but there will certainly be no more."

"But it isn't my fault," he said in desperation.

Father Anderson just shook his head. Lawrence was in a panic. What could he do? He decided to see the fat man and offer him the five hundred as a down payment, hoping he'd be allowed more time. The phone rang. Father Anderson picked up the receiver, listened briefly, and then hung up. He turned to Lawrence with a very serious expression.

"The Bishop wants the five hundred back, Mr. Ford. He said you failed him. You have until tomorrow morning."

Lawrence left the rooming house, head down. He decided to try to pay off the fat man with a down payment; the Bishop would have to wait. Perhaps he could buy enough time to flee the city. He had friends in New Fresno he could stay with temporarily. There he could make a new beginning. He was walking past a hardware store when an idea struck him. He went inside, found the manager and inquired about the purchase of a pistol. He knew the manager supplied the resistance from time to time, and he knew he'd been recognized from the time he'd been in there with the magician. He bought a small .25 caliber Mauser—1910 model. He bought a box of ammunition as well, loading the pistol before leaving the store. The store manager said nothing. He was used to this kind of behavior from members of the resistance.

Lawrence dropped the pistol into his coat pocket as he left the hardware store. He flagged a taxi, which took him to the laundry. Inside, he passed the door guard, adjusting the pistol in his pocket. The fat man sat at his desk smiling, but then he always smiled. He seemed to win all the bets no matter which side won. He opened his arms in a charade of helplessness.

"Hey," he said, "what can I say? I just found out now that the airship had new experimental engines on it that allowed a much higher speed than anyone expected. I'm afraid you own me five thousand once again."

"I can't pay right now," Lawrence said. "I can give you five hundred now, and the rest in a few days."

"How many days?"

"I dunno…three or four at the most."

"Not good enough, Mr. Ford. I heard from your money source. I know you're not getting any more money from them. Pay me."

"I was hoping you'd be lenient with me. I've always paid you on time."

"That was then and this is now, you aren't employed by the Bishop any more."

Lawrence reacted in surprise.

"Oh come, Mr. Ford," the fat man said. "He's a man and he gambles too—only he doesn't gamble money he doesn't have."

The two thugs on each side of the desk each took a menacing step forward. Lawrence raised his hands, "All right, all right, no need for rough stuff. I have your payment right here. Payment in full."

With that, Lawrence pulled the small pistol from his pocket, extended his arm, shooting the fat man right between the eyes. Surprise left the dead man's face as he slumped over his desk. Lawrence turned the pistol to the thugs; both men had their hands raised in surrender. Lawrence smiled—he could just slip…

Lawrence never actually felt the giant wrench as it crushed his skull— the brain damage was too severe and came too quickly. Even before he collapsed in a heap on the floor, he was already dead. The man who'd been guarding the door dropped the wrench and ran to the fat man, but he was dead as well. The three thugs looked at each other, then turned and left the building. They'd need new employment, and for their kind, it was always available.

~

The next morning, the newspaper carried the story of a tragic accident involving a zeppelin they'd hired to take a photographer out to the tribal regions to make a documentary on life in the wild. Unfortunately, the airship developed engine problems. From the wreckage, it looked like something had caught fire. The hydrogen bags ignited and the ship went down in flames—there were no survivors. Page two showed several burned corpses lying on the earth.

The Bishop flung the paper across the room in a rage. Father Woods winced at the outburst, and said, "Well, if they were assassins, you no longer have to worry."

"What of the beastling child? She was making us a lot of money. Now all we have are two dead whores."

Father Woods, attempting to soothe the Bishop, said, "Well, we've the other half-human. She's making more than the child was. Think of the weapons and money we either already have or will receive once old Heinrich Franz Reichhardt has his fill, or perhaps I should say, once the half-human has had her fill."

In spite of himself, the Bishop laughed. He relaxed a little—the threat against his life was over. He could begin serious planning for his trip south. He was leaving by airship in just a few days, as a matter of fact. Things in the south were progressing and he wanted to be there to oversee the project.

Father Woods picked up the paper the Bishop had flung away. He opened it to the second page, handing it to the Bishop. The man took it, shaking it once. The article the priest wanted him to read jumped out at him.

UNDERWORLD FIGURE GUNNED DOWN
IN DOUBLE HOMICIDE.

The Bishop read the story with a look of dismay on his face. It seemed one Lawrence Ford had murdered a bookie in the downtown area, and in turn the man had been brained with an extremely large wrench. By the time the police arrived, only the two bodies remained—there were no documents, money, or anything else in the office. It was surmised that Mr. Ford was in debt to the bookie and an altercation occurred regarding payment, resulting in the two deaths. There were no other clues for the police to follow.

The Bishop sat in silence, stunned.

"I'm sorry, Your Eminence," the priest began.

The Bishop cut him off, "We've lost our one spy within the resistance. Finding the true leader will now be very difficult."

"Mr. Ford was a risk, at best," Father Woods stated. "He came under our domination because of his uncontrolled gambling. It was the vice that claimed him."

"I have not missed the irony," the Bishop snapped. "But, I have missed an opportunity to crush the resistance."

"We'll have other opportunities," the priest said reassuringly.

"Before the city politics completely sway against us?"

"It could be," Father Woods said with a smile, "if you succeed in The Green the resistance won't matter any longer."

"That's what I pray for," the Bishop said. "By the grace of the Redeemed God!"

Chapter 56

Adria was very excited the next morning as she waited impatiently for the pimp to pick her up and take her 'up the hill.' She had the comfort of her little pouch of drugs hidden in her handbag. These big city clothes might be elegant, but they greatly impeded movement and took forever to put on. Since it was the way of the city, she'd wear them—they had the benefit of being voluminous enough to hide a variety of items.

In her journeys with the pimp to and from work, she noticed something else about the city—not all women walked with their heads lowered. She heard from her roommates that there were other religions in the city and that only the followers of the Cathedral practiced the abject domination of women. She found she didn't really care. After all, if they were stupid enough to allow themselves to be dominated, it was their own fault. She, on the other hand, was using the priests and their religion to achieve her goal. The voice of the scorpion buzzed louder than usual today, telling her she'd be the center of her own religion one day. It was a sign that this would be a good day for her—and she was ready.

When Larry Harper arrived, Adria was waiting at the door. Her two roommates were in a good mood, which both surprised and annoyed her. She'd hoped they'd be jealous of her prestige, at her being picked for this choice assignment. They smiled at her, bidding her good luck as she walked out the door. She smiled in their direction, knowing they'd have another potentially dangerous day on the streets.

Once the steam-car was rolling, Larry began instructing Adria on what was to happen and who her clients were.

"The man's name is Heinrich Franz Reichhardt," Larry explained. "He'll give the Cathedral a large number of ballistic weapons and money for your services."

"I've seen some of those weapons."

"Yes. He manufactures them for us and it's very important to keep him happy. His son's name is Karl and his wife's name is Susan. I hope her name will not be a problem for you? You may have to service each of them as well. I've seen you occasionally with women on stage—you perform magnificently. The divine scorpion is surely with you in those escapades."

"He is with me always," Adria said with confidence, hearing the insectile buzzing in her ear.

Larry negotiated a turn as the car moved smoothly through the downtown streets. Traffic was light as it was still quite early. He crossed a main intersection and said, "The part of town we're going to is called Hollywood. It's where actors and cinema players live."

"What are cinema players?" Adria asked. "I've seen actors in plays in the tribes."

"Cinema is a new way of doing a play—the play is captured on cellulose film so it can be played back over and over. It's quite the new rage in all the cities of the west. The actors and players live in grand mansions high in the hills where they can watch the ice lights at night and eat and drink expensive food."

"It sounds nice," Adria commented. "They must be very special people."

"They think they are," Larry said with a laugh, "and apparently the people who pay money to watch the plays, operas, and cinema think so too as they're the ones paying for all of it."

"But this Heinrich is not an actor…he makes weapons?"

"Many rich people live in the hills they call Hollywood—not just actors. You must be on your best behavior when you're not fucking one of them, is that clear?"

Adria simply nodded, she knew what was expected of her, after all. One man…or woman, for that matter…was pretty much like the next once their clothing was removed. It was simply a more adventurous way of mating. She could do that; she'd done it hundreds of times by now, in all ways possible.

They left the city, gradually heading in a northwesterly direction. At first, the buildings in the area got smaller, more humble. They passed a couple of shopping districts made up of small shops nothing at all like the huge department stores in the downtown area. Street lighting was spotty here, with gas lights only situated at intersections to help traffic safely negotiate the dark streets at night. Then the buildings became larger—with great expanses of land separating one from another. Adria looked at the land, thinking about what her betrothed told her about the food processing towers in the city. Each of these estates could feed as many people as lived in her tribe. If all this land were farmed, the people of the Black City could eat real food grown from the earth. She shook her head at the apparent waste.

Gradually, the road began to wind its way up into the hills. Though it was impossible to believe, the homes here were even larger than the ones below. Some had grounds so large, the house itself, though huge, could barely be seen between the trees as they cruised down the roadway. Nowhere were people to be seen. It looked like an abandoned land.

"Where is everyone?"

"They're mostly in the city working in the theaters and studios or they're in their homes sleeping off the alcohol they spent all last night drinking."

Again Adria shook her head. Occasionally, she saw workers outside the houses trimming the trees and mowing the grass near the homes. She marveled at this. It seemed a lot of time and energy was being spent to harvest branches and grass that would do no one any good, except maybe sheep and horses. Although a few corrals were visible, no farm animals of any kind could be seen or heard. Los Angeles was a strange place, of that Adria was certain.

They turned off the main thoroughfare onto a narrower road that wound past low-lying hills with beautifully trimmed trees at their crests. Another turn and they came to a stop in front of massive iron gates.

"Stay in the auto," Larry said as he opened his door, "I have to speak to the guard before he will let us in."

Adria watched as the pimp had a short conversation with a large man carrying a lethal looking black metal weapon mounted in a wooden frame. She had seen enough during her time in the city to recognize a ballistic weapon. This one appeared to be what folks called a 'Mouser rifle.' To Adria, it seemed unlikely that it would be used against mice, in spite of its odd name.

Larry returned to the vehicle. As he situated himself behind the steering wheel, the great gates began opening inward. They were huge, much bigger than they needed to be. Adria knew a man had to live here—men tended to build things much larger than necessary. She thought of it as male dogs urinating on a tree, the one who hit the highest spot was the winner. She giggled as the car was again set in motion. Larry glanced nervously in her direction but said nothing. They drove around one more curve and the house came into view. Adria couldn't believe only four people lived in this great building, and half of them were children. Three or four families could live comfortably within such a large structure. She said nothing, silenced by awe. There was a large garage attached to the house with the door raised. Inside was the largest steam-car Adria had ever seen. The driver's compartment was open to the air while the passenger section was covered with metal just like the car in which she was riding.

When their vehicle stopped, the pimp opened a small door on the dashboard, removing a small pouch. "This is your magic, Adria," the pimp explained. "I told you how to do the injections. This way you can stay in your divine state for the entire three days. There's also that secret thing in the bottle as well."

She took the package with an inward grin. Now she had enough for six days. That would be plenty of time.

The large paneled front door opened as they approached. Larry was carrying Adria's suitcase with her costumes and personal items. The man at the door was dressed in all black. Very formally, he invited them both into the house. The inside was cool and a great chandelier hung from the high ceiling looking to Adria like a mountain of ice—though upside down. She turned as she followed the men, staring at the chandelier.

"If you come this way, sir, I'll show you to the lady's rooms."

They followed the servant down a short hallway into a large bedroom with its own bath. The flooring was of marble slabs with luxurious carpeting to soften the tread and warm bare feet.

The servant placed Adria's case on an ornately carved wooden stand that was almost black in color at the foot of the huge canopy bed. She saw intricately carved dragons winding their way around what appeared to be flaming fruit. She thought it was very odd.

"The master will see you now in the solarium," the servant explained.

They followed him down the hall, turning into a large room with floor to ceiling windows. All the drapes were pulled open and tied back, allowing people in the room to look out to the north. Dimly in the bright sunlight of early morning, the Aurora could barely be seen. The house was on the highest hill in the area, offering an unobstructed view to the horizon—it was an awe-inspiring sight.

"Welcome to my home," an older man said, rising from a high-backed chair facing the window.

Adria hadn't known he was there, and jumped when he suddenly appeared.

"That will be all, James," the man said to the servant, "you and the rest of the staff may leave now."

"As you wish, sir." The servant turned and silently closed the massive sliding wooden door behind him. The man turned and looked Adria up and down appraisingly.

"She is beautiful, no doubt," he said, "but she looks so…ordinary."

"Adria, show the man how ordinary you are."

Without a word Adria moved sinuously toward the old man. She moved smoothly around him, gently pushing back his long hair, lightly brushing her fingertips around an ear, then briefly inside it. She ran her hand around his neck, fondling his white beard, gently brushing her fingertips over his lips. Now she was in front of him again, and suddenly she pulled open the bodice of her dress exposing her breasts.

"Feel me," she demanded.

The old man, though surprised, complied. He touched first one breast, then the other, paying close attention to her hardening nipples. Her breasts were firm and high, not too big and not too small. The old man thought she was perfect.

Suddenly she pulled back, rearranging the bodice of her dress to its former modest appearance. She turned away from him, walking over to stand by Larry with her eyes downcast like a proper maiden of the Cathedral. The old man clapped his hands in delight.

"Mr. Harper, she's everything you said she'd be. I'm satisfied."

Larry smiled at him and said, "She's all yours, if you can handle her."

The man laughed, "Oh, I can handle her, don't know about my son though…"

Both men laughed at the joke.

"My wife will be leaving with the servants—her taste in entertainment…tends more toward young men. My son will stay with us, taking his pleasure from time to time and otherwise watching over his sister."

"I understand the girl is what…six?"

"That's correct, Mr. Harper," the old man said, "and she'll have no knowledge of what we're doing here. Come. I'll explain."

They followed the old man across the room to the bookcase. Adria was confused, but when the old man pulled down on a section of wood trim on the edge of the bookcase, the whole thing swung silently outward. Adria had never seen anything like it, though the two men seemed to think it commonplace. The old man gestured for Larry and the young woman to enter. They walked into the room, followed closely by Mr. Reichhardt. He lit a lantern on the table. The room was small—perhaps eight feet in one direction and ten in the other. The bed took up most of the room.

"I use this room for a variety of purposes," the man said with a lecherous grin, "right now, it's set up for this weekend."

He turned a leering eye on Adria. She smiled demurely back at him, blinking her eyes coyly.

"Well then," Larry said, "I'll leave you two alone. I'll return Monday morning to pick up the girl and see if you and your son survived!"

Again, both men laughed. Heinrich himself escorted Larry to the door. The servants and his wife had already gone into the city in the big saloon car that had been in the garage. Larry shook the man's hand, got into his much humbler auto, and drove away whistling a happy tune. This would make the Bishop very happy.

"Well, young lady," the old man said, "let me show you back to your room and I'll bring you something to eat. When you've finished breakfast, come down to the solarium, I'll be waiting. You know how to find it?"

"Yes, sir," Adria responded with her eyes downcast. She was wondering what the son looked like—he certainly must be younger. It was obvious to her that the old man would be a quick turn—at least the first time around. It would be easy money for the Cathedral and who knows what might be waiting in it for her.

Chapter 57

Father Anderson was waiting for the Bishop in his study. He'd let himself in—even Harold didn't know he was there. When the Bishop lit the gaslight in the room, he smiled.

"Always the clever one, eh, Father Anderson?"

"I try to maintain my skills, Your Eminence," he answered with a laugh, "at every opportunity."

"Believe me when I say, you haven't become lacking in your various talents. So, tell me, Father Anderson, what's the purpose of this meeting?"

"Simply this, Your Eminence," he said, "it's been several weeks now, and as yet we've heard not a whisper of a threat against you. Surely tribal half-humans would need the assistance of someone within the city. Yet how could they possibly know anyone here?"

"This is true," the Bishop admitted.

"If they had help, it would have to come from someone capable of helping them, and we've heard nothing from any of our contacts, spies, and ears."

"What of this resistance we hear about—could they be helping them?"

"The clear answer is no, Your Eminence."

"How can you be so certain of that, Father Anderson?"

The priest smiled, tapping the side of his nose.

"As you know, we had a spy within that organization close to the leadership. We were awaiting information that would lead us to the top of the conspiracy so we could crush it. Though he's dead now, this individual would surely have heard something about an event as big as this. He might even have been asked to help them himself."

"How can you be sure he wasn't?"

"Your Eminence," the priest said, barely hiding the disgust in his voice, "if you fear every shadow under every tree and bush you will have done their work for them. You've told me yourself the half-humans with the kidnapped child are all dead—killed in the zeppelin crash in the wilds east of here. Surely if someone within the city had been planning to kill you, they'd have tried by now. The half-human outlanders' unfamiliarity with the city would have been a major stumbling block to their success and could easily have resulted in their capture and death. Your Eminence, if you fear to do your job even knowing them dead, then in death they'll have won. If word spreads in the city that you're afraid…"

361

The Bishop shifted uncomfortably in his chair, what the priest was saying was correct. He was being needlessly frightened. Surely any attempt on his life would have happened by now. Besides, if the three missing priests were killed by tribal assassins, who then would come to kill him? How could those killings help the assassins get to him? It wouldn't have helped.

All those killings, or mysterious disappearances or whatever they were, would only raise security concerns. No, the priest was probably right—they came to rescue the beastling child, which they accomplished, and nothing else. They were almost home when they were killed in the air crash while he cowered in his rooms. He sat up in his chair, having made the decision.

"You're right, Father Anderson. I will lead the service in the Cathedral on Sunday myself. We'll show the world the Cathedral is not afraid."

"Well said, Your Eminence," the priest said, "I'll be at that service myself."

"There'll be security personnel, won't there?" the Bishop asked. "Just in case?"

"We have an entire squad who'll be in civilian clothing and stationed in various locations. You'll be safe, Your Eminence."

"Thank you," the Bishop said with a sigh.

~

After eating a delicious breakfast of eggs, toast, and orange juice, Adria was ready for the next step. She carefully put on her first costume. It consisted of a sheer mint green nightdress worn over lacy black underwear. Adria looked at herself in the mirror. She picked up her handbag, preparing to leave her room, then paused. She went back to the dresser. She'd take more of the magic Sting; she was beginning to like the lights she saw. It was as if her clients had within them the lights of the northern ice. She quickly gave herself the injection, carefully packing away the needle and paraphernalia. She took a breath—she was ready.

She closed the door to her room behind her, walking down the marble floored hallway to the solarium. She marveled at the richness of everything. She knew the wife would have lots of very nice jewelry; it looked as though they could afford anything. The old man was waiting in the room. He smiled at her, and she smiled back, her head lowered, looking at him through her eyelashes. He opened the doorway into the secret room and she walked in. He followed.

When the bookcase was shut, the man motioned her to the bed. She walked over, sitting on it with her legs somewhat parted, knowing he was looking at the outline of her black panties. She smiled, opening her legs a little more. The old man licked his lips—this was better than he'd hoped.

"The room is completely soundproof, you know," he said. "So if you scream, or something, nobody will hear."

"Don't you mean they will not hear either of us?"

She opened her legs a bit more.

"Yes," he said, "that's what I meant."

He walked over to her and said, "Undress me, dear, won't you?"

She knew what part of his clothing he wished removed, and she complied. She unbuckled his belt, then the buttons on his trousers. She could feel him, already hard, with her hands. She rubbed him slowly, smiling up at him.

"You are already very hard, sir." She squeezed him and he gasped.

"You're a very beautiful woman, Adria," he said. "Let me see your beauty."

"First things first," she answered with a sly giggle. "If we don't get that thing out soon, it might burst out all by itself."

With that, his trousers fell to the floor, quickly followed by his underwear. She stood, allowing him to remove her gown. He took his time—touching, feeling, and rubbing against her as he undid the buttons down the back of her costume.

She was now standing in just her underwear.

She laughed softly, "For the first time, you should take me quickly, leaving the slower for later."

Grinning lasciviously, he said, "I agree. Leave your underwear on, would you?"

Adria giggled again. "Why not? We can work around it."

Then he was on top of her—pushing and shoving. In bed, Adria realized, rich men were just as rough as poor men. She gasped and moaned. At first in imitation pleasure, it was part of a whore's stock in trade, and then suddenly, as her hand sought the handbag on the bed next to her, a real feeling spread though her body. It began with a tingling in her hard nipples, ending between her legs where the man was pushing himself into her.

She opened her bag, putting her hand inside. Then the man climaxed strongly, pushing himself all the way up inside of her. She felt his pleasure, his divine essence pulsing into her body.

The man gasped, looking down into the bright eyes of the girl. His pleasure was exquisite, but something was wrong. Why couldn't he breathe? What was the redness squirting rhythmically onto the girl's face—into her mouth?

The man never realized he was dead. The knife had been sharp enough that, in his extreme pleasure, he hadn't felt the cut. He sagged against Adria. She opened her mouth, allowing his life-blood to ejaculate into it. Suddenly she had an intense climax. She'd never had one before, neither with the men in the tavern or with Floweht. In all those cases, it was the men who felt the pleasure, using her body merely as their instrument. Now it was different—now the pleasure was hers!

Afterward, drenched in the man's blood, she shoved his body off of her, rose, and headed toward the bookcase. There was still the son. Would she feel like this again? She hoped so.

Carefully she pulled the lever, and the bookcase slid silently open. She stepped out barefooted—silently. Across the room she saw just the top of a man's head above the back of a chair. The son was reading, waiting his turn with the wild woman. *Well,* Adria thought, *let's see how wild he really wants his women.*

She crept silently up to him, leaving scarlet footprints on the alabaster floor. Now she was directly behind the chair. The man must've sensed something, and began to turn his head. He met the knife half way. It missed its mark—cutting a deep furrow in his cheek. The man jumped to his feet, staring in horror at the bloody woman facing him with fierce expression and sharp dagger. As she leapt at him, he struck out. His fist hit her full in the face. Two teeth snapped at the root, but she didn't feel it. What she felt was her climax approaching again as she slid the dagger across his throat.

This time, after her pleasure subsided, she felt nausea. She lifted the waist of the dead man's trousers and vomited into them, covering his private parts in his own blood. It seemed appropriate. Adria knew she kept the divinity of the blood even as she expelled the physical substance.

After the slaughter, she returned to each corpse, cutting a long lock of hair from each. She thought it would be nice to eventually have a skirt of hair to wear under her dress—a secret remembrance of each act of pleasure. She imagined that skirt of hair brushing secretly against her thighs under her clothing and shivered in delight. She returned to her room. There was still the little girl, of course, but she knew the child was upstairs—the act wasn't yet complete.

Adria laid her blood-soaked clothing on the table and went to the bath. She ran hot water into the tub and climbed in. She scrubbed herself carefully this time. No point in forgetting an incriminating bloodstain as had happened when she'd slain that annoying Susan. She smiled; her quick excuse of a man cutting himself in the tavern had worked well, even though at the time she didn't know herself that it was a lie. The woman died quickly, she now remembered, although without giving her the pleasure these men gave her. Still, the biting was fun, and the hank of hair she cut from the dead woman's head was her first trophy. She was sure there'd be many more. Funny how she just remembered now how it'd been with Susan. She remembered how fearful she had been about an unknown killer, unaware that she was being fearful of herself. Her inner scorpion was guiding her.

As she bathed, she wondered if killing the little girl would bring the pleasure on again. She touched herself, trying to bring the feeling back. Though the feelings were pleasurable, there was no climax. She listened to the buzz of the scorpion. So that was it! She had to feel the blood climax of men to feel her own. Her climax was, the voices said, the feeling of her growing divinity absorbed from both the sexual pleasure of the men and their death pleasure. The combination was exquisite, but it was the blood that was important. She sighed as she stopped fondling herself—there'd be other men. There would be other opportunities. Right now, she needed to get away.

She stepped from the tub, toweling off and quickly dressing in her street clothing. She dumped her clothes from the suitcase and left the room—costumes were no longer needed. She wandered around the lower floor of the mansion, picking up coins and money she found in drawers in the servants' quarters and elsewhere. She climbed the big circular staircase to the second floor.

She went from room to room until she found the wife's bedroom. She laughed with glee as she rifled the jewelry boxes—diamonds, pearls, and emeralds. She knew not what they were, but sensed their value, so she filled the suitcase with the contents of the jewelry boxes. The lady had money as well—a dozen gold coins lay at the bottom of one box. Gold and silver she did know. All of it went into the suitcase. Adria was ecstatic! She was now wealthy beyond anyone's dreams. She could find her own place to live in the city and make even more money servicing men—and occasionally taking that beautiful pleasure. Her knife was still sharp, and she had her connection for the Sting of the Scorpion, what the other whores told her was called heroin. She was set! She was now divine, a power unto herself. The insectile buzzing in her head reached a frantic level, drowning out all other thoughts.

She quickly left the wife's bedroom, and before she descended the stairs, she passed the closed door, where a forgotten six-year-old girl still slept. Innocent and safe, the child was unaware of the darkness moving down the hallway just a few feet away from her. In her dreams, the child saw a woman of light standing over her, a great flaming sword in her hand. She knew that the white lady with the flame would protect her. The image was soothing, and she slid further into a dreamless slumber.

~

"By the Redeemed God," the Bishop swore into the phone. "All of them?" He was shouting now. The call originated in a large house in the Hollywood hills. His client had been slaughtered.

"Not all of them, sir," the police sergeant said, "just the man and his son. The man was naked; it looks like he was having sex when he was killed—probably attacked from behind. His son was killed in the next room the same way, throat cut."

After the details of the slaughter were explained to the Bishop, he felt sick. How would this affect the arms deal? The man's brother would probably take over the business. The Bishop hung up and immediately placed a call to him. Bridges needed mending, and he was just the man to do it!

"Hello? Yes, this is the Bishop of the Cathedral. I want to express my deepest sympathy..."

~

Larry Harper wasn't allowed into the house. Sergeant Jinks called him Saturday morning and told him all he needed to know. The little girl, fortunately, was safe. She'd come downstairs and found her dead brother. She ran out the back door to a neighbor's home where the police were called. She didn't see the naked body of her father—it was bad enough as it was.

Adria. She'd done it, he was sure. The bitch. That wild half-human nature of hers had finally broken loose. The police found a rope thrown over a sidewall of the estate, used by the killer to escape without passing through the gate. Why could it not have happened in the tavern? There men were armed and she would've been quickly killed. Now she was out there, somewhere. There was no way to find her. She vomited in the young man's pants. She cut some hair from each man's head for some reason he couldn't fathom. By the Redeemed God! What would happen now? These deaths couldn't be hushed up. They'd make news in six cities—even in faraway Atlanta. He needed a good story, and he needed one fast. He drove from the slaughterhouse into town; he needed to talk to Father Woods and the Bishop.

Chapter 58

Far across town, in the very center of the tall black buildings, a young blonde woman took up residence on the sixtieth floor of a nondescript rooming house with the unlikely name of Hillcrest. Adria was amused by the name. The building wasn't on a hill and certainly not on the crest of anything. It was across the street from another apartment building with the equally unlikely name, Bloomgarden Apartments. The apartment she took wasn't large, but it was one of the nicer ones, and she could afford it. She looked at the open suitcase on the bed. It was filled with jewels and gold. She could carefully sell these items in the pawnshops she heard Larry mention—she'd have her sting for a very long time as well.

She smiled in the mirror, noticing again her two missing teeth. It made her less beautiful, she knew, but who cared. She'd still service men once in a while. The man who ran this building was a choice example; his wife was over two hundred pounds. Adria admired the reflection of her young, slim body in the mirror. That would more than compensate for a few missing teeth when the rent was due. She wondered if she should try to start a church to herself. The voices warned against this and, as always, she listened to the voices. Instead, she laid out the three locks of hair on her bed. She tied a knot in one end of each of them to keep them together. She then held them up to her waist, admiring how they looked in the mirror—and how they felt on her legs. She smiled.

~

VAMPIRE KILLER STALKS CITY!

The headline that ran the next morning was in large type and the accompanying article was filled with the sordid details of the two murders. The identity of the police officer that had talked was a closely guarded secret of the newspaper's editor. Sergeant Jinks was furious, as was everyone in the Cathedral. He didn't want to think about what the Bishop must be thinking at this moment. When it came time for the press interview, he was ready. In a room with reporters from the other two papers and representatives from New Fresno still in town after the zeppelin-locomotive race, he smiled reassuringly.

"Gentlemen," he began, "these killings are being taken very seriously by the police department. We have mobilized all our forces in the hunt for the killers."

"Killers?" one reporter said, "I heard there was only one, and that it is a woman. I heard she was a prostitute."

"That information is incorrect," Jinks reassured the man. "There were two killers— both male. The motive was clearly robbery; a large amount of money and jewelry was taken. We believe the prostitute merely helped get the killers into the house—these killings were certainly not the work of a mere woman."

The reporters wrote quickly. Jinks smiled, he had them in the palm of his hand. Another reporter raised his hand, and Jinks pointed to him.

"So is the Bishop involved in any way with the killings and robbery?"

Jinks paled and said, "Absolutely not! I know that's the story the dead man's widow is telling, but she's under a great deal of stress and anguish. How could any woman in her position speak logically? Women are barely logical at the best of times."

The reporter nodded in understanding and, Jinks hoped, in agreement. He was going to want some kind of reward from the Bishop for this acting job. For now, something must be done about the widow.

It was three days before Adria left her apartment. She realized she needed to go out. She was desperate. That afternoon she had a dream; it was terrible, but it was also revealing. In her dream, she saw that woman...Lyria, and Kel—her betrothed, that wasn't exactly right, was it? In any event, they pointed at her and laughed just as they did all the time back in the tribal village. Lyria opened her hand, showing Adria her palm filled with blood. Then, as the woman exhaled on the blood, it seemed to dry up, turn flaky and blow away. Adria awakened with a start—she knew what the dream meant. That evil woman, Lyria, had cursed her! Her blood was turning dry. If she didn't replenish it soon, she'd die! That's why the scorpion told her blood pleasure was more important than sexual pleasure—she needed the blood to stay alive.

She finished applying her makeup and lip color, rose from the dressing table, and walked out, taking her handbag with her. She headed for the tavern three blocks away. It was almost dark when she arrived. She walked in slowly, appraising the patrons for a likely candidate. There he was! That young, longhaired man standing all by himself at the bar looking down at his own feet. She smiled and made her approach.

She sidled up to him, casually looking over at him. He smiled shyly at her. She figured him to be about seventeen. She returned his smile.

"You are the only one here all alone," she said. "Would you like some company?"

He smiled again, "Sure. I could use the company right now."

"Oh? Is something wrong?"

The young man sighed. He looked appreciatively at the young blonde woman.

"No," he began, "I just got a job here in the center of town and I don't know anyone here. I can't afford an automobile, and I have no friends close by."

"Buy me a drink and tell me about it," she said quietly.

He bought two drinks from the bar, handing Adria a glass. The liquid flashed with the colors of the ice lights. She looked up at him. There was an aurora around the man as well—his divine essence was strong.

"I could be a friend," Adria said with sympathy, "I know about being alone."

"C'mon," the young man said, "a woman as beautiful as you?"

She looked down, feigning shyness, and said, "I bet you say that to all the women you meet, don't you?"

"I..uh…haven't met many women," the man stammered.

She looked at him now with renewed interest.

She put a hand on the side of his face. "A handsome man like you? Surely you have many women pursuing you."

He smiled sadly, shaking his head.

"I…was raised to believe that the right woman would come along, and that we'd be wed. I was told that to run with women was a sin against God."

Adria raised her eyebrow, she thought the Redeemed God, whoever that might be, favored the sexual domination of women. He must be talking about some other religion, or some other god. Well, no matter. What she was planning didn't involve any divine beings but herself.

"I was hoping to find a man who would sin with me tonight," she whispered.

He looked at her, blushing, "I...I…uh…don't know…."

"Have you ever been with a woman?"

He lowered his head in shame and said in a low voice, "No."

They left the tavern, walking to the young man's apartment building hand in hand. Conveniently, it was next door to the tavern. They walked up the stairs to the second floor, then down the hall to his rooms. Nobody saw them. The young man's rooms were small, much smaller than hers, she noted. Once inside, she knew what to do. She smiled at him, touching him, and kissing him. Nevertheless, he seemed reluctant. She set her handbag on the bed and opened it, taking out four short sections of rope.

"I know what will help," she said, grinning at him slyly. "If you are bound, you won't be in control. If you cannot stop it, it cannot be your sin."

She pushed him backwards onto the bed, talking softly to him, straddling him, rubbing against his manhood as she bound his hands and feet to the iron bed. He was spread eagle, a twisted cloth in his mouth—the rest would be up to her.

She withdrew her knife from the handbag and his eyes got big. She laughed, "Silly. With you tied like that, I can't get at you without cutting off your clothing. See? You can't even stop me from making you naked. This can't be a sin of yours."

She saw him relax. That was good. She cut open the man's clothing with her sharp blade; then straddled him. It didn't take the young man long, and as he climaxed, she stabbed her dagger into the side of his throat. After, thinking of her desperate need for blood, she thought there might be more she should do.

~

VAMPIRE KILLER STRIKES AGAIN

The morning headlines screamed the news. Again, all the sordid details were revealed by an anonymous source within the police department. This killing was much worse, if that were possible, than the slayings of the arms maker and his son. The man was bound, stripped, and then his throat was cut. It was obvious, the paper said, that the man had just had a sexual encounter.

The worst part, however, was the condition of the man's body—he'd been mutilated. His belly had been opened, and some internal organs removed. His intestines were coiled neatly next to his body as though it had been a rope. His spleen and liver had been cut out and carried into the kitchen. They were found on a dinner plate on the table next to an almost empty wine glass. There was lip paint on the rim of the glass. The killer had eaten portions of each organ. And once more, as in the other killings, a large hank of his hair had been cut away and wasn't in the room. The seventeen-year-old man's name was Thomas Mercer. The police were seeking relatives to notify. Sergeant Jinks was quoted as saying, "This is the same murder crew as the other killing. We have no motive at this time, though we suspect robbery, as in the last instance."

"Another one?"

The Bishop was very upset. He knew, of course, who the killer was—which didn't help if they couldn't find her. Father Woods was calmer, confident that she'd be found soon. The Bishop wasn't so sure.

"She knows nothing of city life," the priest reasoned, "she'll make a mistake. We'll have her. Jinks said he was hot on the trail at the last press conference."

"Press conference," the Bishop said sarcastically. "He's just painting pretty pictures."

"Nevertheless, Your Eminence, you need to leave for The Green. Your project seems to be bearing fruit. You said you wanted to be there—so go. I will take care of any questions anyone may ask."

The Bishop sighed, "You're right. I should go and I will. I'm ready. The airship can leave within an hour of my call. I'll make that call now."

Father Woods turned to go as the Bishop raised the phone's receiver. He needed to have another discussion with Father Jackson. This killer was making too much news. He needed more information about how she might be captured or killed.

~

The old priest listened carefully to Father Woods, insisting on every detail. Father Woods decided that it would be best if the old priest knew everything about Adria— except her name. The telling took almost twenty minutes. When he was finished, the old man sat for a moment, collecting his thoughts.

"This is far more serious than I'd thought," he began, "as I've told the Cathedral, multiple killers are very seldom women. In fact, I know of only one other case of this kind of killing in all of the cities of the west combined. Now I hear that she's not even a city person."

"That shouldn't matter, should it?"

"My dear Father Woods," the old man began patiently, "yes, in fact, it does matter. You see, we've only had killers from the various cities to study—that's how we came to recognize certain patterns in behavior that might bring the killings to an early end."

"In their minds," Father Woods said, "women are all the same, that's the teaching of the Cathedral."

"The Cathedral is wrong."

"That's blasphemy," Father Woods said, shocked to hear such a thing from so old a priest.

372

"The blasphemy, my dear Father, is finding the truth, then ignoring it because it doesn't fit neatly into our preconceived notions," the old priest retorted. "We're not talking about teachings here; we're talking about human lives being cut short in a horrific manner."

Father Woods looked at the old man, deciding to listen to what he had to say. He was right about one thing—the problem was very serious.

"As I see it," the old man began, "we have two problems. The first is that we've almost no information on repeat killers who are female. The second is that she's not of the same mental training that city people have. She's from a tribe, they're all different, and they have different teachings. We don't know what they've taught her, what she thinks is right and what she thinks is wrong. For all I know, you might have a completely sane individual on your hands. Maybe this is some tribal ritual that has no relation to mental illness as we conceive it."

Father Woods was shocked. He hadn't considered the possibility that Adria might be sane and doing something 'tribal' and, in her mind, quite rational.

"So then," he began, "what do we do?"

"Wait," the old priest said. "Bring me everything you can about each of these killings as soon as possible after the fact. You need to be prepared for the possibility that you may not catch her—ever."

"I don't like the sound of that," Father Woods stated.

"You should see to it that any information you have on this individual is made public. Something about her might ring a bell with someone who might know the woman and not suspect her."

"That," Father Woods stated with a firm shake of his head, "is completely out of the question."

"Then the slaughter will continue."

"I believe we'll have her soon," Father Woods stated with confidence.

"Her level of violence is increasing," the old priest warned. "This is going to get very bad."

Chapter 59

Adria awoke from a dreamless sleep. She sat up in her bed, yawning. She felt a bit better. The extra supply of blood from the last sacrifice had done her a world of good. She knew the curse that horrible Lyria had placed on her wouldn't work. Eventually, she'd become too powerful for the curse. Until then, there would continue to be sacrifices to the Scorpion Queen.

She rose, wandering to the dining area naked. She hadn't put on her nightdress last night. Why bother? Nobody was going to come here. Nobody knew she was here, and it was important to keep it that way— though sometimes it was hard to remember why. After eating a very small breakfast, she dressed slowly, planning her day. She sat on the edge of her bed, putting on her shoes. She rose to leave her apartment, and remembered she hadn't made the bed. She noticed that the sheets and blanket were in a heap on the mattress. Perhaps her sleep hadn't been as peaceful as she'd thought. She decided that she could make the bed tonight, or in the morning.

She left the building feeling pretty good, all things considered. She'd need to purchase more heroin and the magic her supplier called mescaline. She wondered why the Cathedral made such a big secret about all of this. Again she suspected that her betrothed, Kel…no wait, Father Woods, yes, that was the one, was using false words to keep control of her. Now she was free and on her own. As she walked down the street, she saw men looking at her. She heard their thoughts. One of them just volunteered to be the next sacrifice. She decided to follow him, and see where he was going. Ten minutes later, the man caught a taxi and was whisked away. She stood, staring after the cab. She knew she could find him again. She continued down the street, heading back the way she'd come to find her nearly forgotten heroin supplier.

"Hey," the dealer said with a smile. He liked the strange blonde. She bought her narcotics with gemstones and jewelry worth many times the cash price of his wares.

"I need the usual," she said to him, "I have some more of those colored stones."

"Lady," he said with a smile, "I don't know where your stuff's coming from, but as long as you pay, I'll see to it that you get the very best stuff on the street."

She smiled at him—gently stroking his unshaven cheek.

"You know I will," she said with a smile.

The dealer sold her a six-day supply for a half-carat diamond in an antique white gold filigree ring. He was really making money off this stupid slut. He did think she had a nice rump, though. But right now, he had other thoughts. He stayed on his corner until three in the afternoon—then walked three blocks to a pawnshop where he had a working agreement.

"Tony," the man behind the counter said, "whatcha' got for me today?"

Tony flashed the ring with a grin.

"Ah," the man behind the counter said with a nod, "your odd lady friend."

"She's no friend," Tony said with a laugh, "even if she does give me jewelry."

The pawnshop owner laughed, and took a jeweler's loupe from his vest pocket. He examined the stone carefully; then he studied the ring itself.

"I'll give you a thousand for this," he said firmly. "The stone isn't perfect, and it's an old cut—not as fashionable as it once was."

"That's fine," the drug dealer said, "I'll take the money."

Ten minutes later he was out the door, pocket bulging with cash. He hummed contentedly to himself as he walked back to his corner. Some of his customers would probably be mad at him for leaving, but that was just too bad. He was right; a disheveled woman was waiting for him. He recognized her—she was a whore on the way down. Soon, she probably wouldn't be able to pay for her fix any longer. For a moment, the thought of her withdrawing from the heroin by herself made him feel sorry for her, but just for a moment. This was business after all.

"Hey, where were you?"

"Well, aren't we upset?" he joked. "It doesn't matter where I was, I'm here now."

She smiled a crooked smile at him. "Sure, Tony."

She handed him a wad of crumpled bills and a handful of coins. She got another week's supply of heroin. As she shuffled down the street, he decided he was going to cut her stuff a bit more than the average. He might as well make as much money on her as possible while she was still alive.

~

The airship lifted off on schedule. The Bishop was at the window looking down on the city. He liked this view—it made him feel like The Redeemed God himself. He smiled as the zeppelin gained altitude, turning slowly over the city to a southerly heading. Soon, all their problems would be solved. If what he planned could be achieved, he'd be the master of Los Angeles, and then the master of the world. He really liked the sound of that. It would take the airship approximately five days to traverse the six thousand and some miles to his destination of New Los Angeles. He felt a week's vacation would do him good. With no telephones either aboard the airship or in The Green, he could let Father Woods deal with the city problems back to the north. He moved to the stern, looking out the brass telescope at the wild lands passing far below. There wasn't much one could call civilization once one passed San Diego. In approximately two hours they'd be flying over that last outpost of man and into the realm of the half-human tribes.

~

Adria was content to stay in her apartment for three days. The heroin and mescaline were so good that she didn't feel like moving—much less going out. On the third night, she dreamt again. In this dream, Kel stood on a street corner trying to sell her some heroin. Standing next to him was that black-haired bitch...what's her name? She was smiling at her. As Adria felt herself walking toward them, seemingly irresistibly drawn, two figures stepped out of the shadows—her parents. They were also smiling, and when they opened their mouths to laugh, scorpions poured out—tumbling to the ground. Instantly, Kel and that woman were crushing her sacred insects, grinding them into the dirt of the alley. They never stopped laughing. Then she saw the blood in that woman's palm, it was like dried paint. She woke in a sweat.

It was late in the afternoon when Adria awoke. She must have slept for twenty hours. She had to replenish her blood, and soon—the dream was a warning. She dressed carefully, and applied her makeup deliberately even though her hand shook. She needed more heroin, a problem easily fixed. She giggled at the joke she'd made. In thirty minutes she was ready. It was getting dark by the time she left her apartment. The bed was still unkempt, the pillowcase turning gray from sweat.

She didn't have to look very far. She again entered the tavern where she'd met that delightful young man. Perhaps she could find another like him. She was prepared with ropes in her handbag curled up right next to the knife. She stood in the doorway of the tavern, hunting. *This was much like hunting game in the tribes*, she thought. The sacrifice was here—she just had to flush him out. The first criterion she was interested in was that the man would have long hair; she needed hair for her secret skirt. She saw a number of men in the tavern, but only a few with long hair. Then she saw him. She smiled to herself. She could hear his mind pleading with her to use him in her sacred service.

~

KILLINGS CONTINUE

The headline screamed in two-inch type two days after the murder. The body of the man, a transient new in the city, had been bound to his bed and savagely mutilated. He'd been gutted—some of his organs removed and partly eaten. Though he was a salesman from San Diego with a bag of valuable pocket watches, his belongings weren't disturbed. The city was in a panic, the article announced. People weren't going out at night. Why were the police not solving these crimes? Were they supernatural in origin as some were suggesting?

~

Father Jackson left the Cathedral grounds through the back gate. He turned north and started walking—an hour later he was in the city proper. It was already dark—almost eight o'clock in the evening. The streets were crowded with pedestrians on their way to shop or to the cinema. He smiled. He didn't know what part of the city was staying indoors at night as the paper suggested, but it was clearly not this part. He strolled down the sidewalk. Nobody recognized him as a priest for he wore not a robe, but the simple suit of an average man. He drew no attention whatsoever and he wanted it that way.

After crossing the street, he saw the car pulled to the curb waiting. He looked quickly around to make sure he hadn't been followed, then opened the passenger door and stepped into the back. A man was inside waiting. The car slid quickly from the curb, its steam pressure high and ready.

"So," Tom Leatham asked, "what have you heard?"

The priest looked at the newspaper editor disgustedly saying, "The Cathedral will not release the information they have—they're afraid. This woman is challenging their doctrine. Yes, the killer is surely a woman. Father Woods, who's in charge of things while the Bishop is away, told me that all women are the same. He said that their mental states are always alike because they are inferior."

"And you do not believe this?"

The old priest looked at the newsman with a crooked grin, "Why do you really think I've been assigned to the zeppelin barn? Surely you don't think I know anything at all about airships."

The newsman laughed, "So your assignment is forced retirement, so to speak? They're keeping you out of the way."

"I have come to challenge some of the teachings of my religion. I'm finding it easier to believe that men wrote the Book of the Prophets with no Divine help."

Tom's eyebrows shot up.

"Really? Is that not dangerous talk for one in your position?"

"It is," the old man sighed, "and that's the reason I have called you for this discussion. If I help you further with this story, I want safety. I'm not going back there, not tonight or ever."

The newsman thought fast and said, "I believe we can find a safe haven for you, Father Jackson."

"Not Father," the old priest said, "not any more. Call me Henry."

"Pleased to meet you, Henry," Tom said. "Now what do you have for us?"

The former priest spent the next thirty minutes talking about Adria. What he knew, which was little, and what he surmised, which was a great deal. When he finished, the newsman just shook his head.

"Why did they bring a tribal woman to the city anyway?"

"Father Woods tells me she was a stowaway from that visit the Cathedral made into the tribal regions a while back. There was apparently some trouble in the woman's tribe—some unusual deaths."

"My God," the newsman said, "she was already killing, wasn't she? Father Woods brought this demon child into our city."

Henry raised his hand in protest, "She's no demon. She's probably a dangerously mentally deranged individual, but she's human and nothing more, despite what she might think."

The newsman questioned the last statement, so Henry told him what Father Woods said about the Scorpion Queen. The newsman was pale. This was hard to believe of a woman—even for someone who wasn't of the Cathedral's religion.

"Maybe she's not as deranged as we think, either," the former priest said. "She's a tribal person and we've no idea of the beliefs of her people. We cannot differentiate between tribal ritual and mental derangement.

378

Frankly, I believe the chances the police will find her are minimal, and that Sergeant Jinks is no more than the mouth of the Bishop. I believe he might have a hard time finding himself in a closet."

The editor laughed, but he knew this was no laughing matter. The killer was an unknown quantity, and the police were in on the cover up.

"I believe you're right," he said quietly. "This might have to run its course."

"If she's truly as unstable as I believe, that may not be a long time," the former priest said. "Her crimes are escalating—the violence increasing. If she does behave like male killers of that type, she'll get progressively more careless, and less concerned with capture. She thinks she's divine. Why would a goddess care if mere mortals were hunting her?"

"Well, for now I'll take you to my office—you'll be safe there. I believe it's time for another unofficial statement from an unnamed police source."

The former priest laughed. No one, not the police nor the Cathedral, realized that he was the 'leak.' They all thought they were looking for a copper in on the investigation with a loose tongue. He sat back into the leather seat. His life as a priest was over; perhaps that loss might save the life of someone else. He fervently hoped so.

Chapter 60

For the next several days Adria stayed very high. Her consumption of heroin was increasing, and progressively costing her more of her wealth. She looked distractedly into the suitcase. Many of the smaller pieces of jewelry were already gone. She closed the case, and slid it under her bed. She was wearing the same clothing she'd worn for the last two days. The dress and blouse were dirty and wrinkled. She looked at herself in her mirror. Her face seemed gray, almost lifeless. She licked her thumb, dragging it down her cheek. The gray was dirt, she discovered. How long had it been since she bathed? She tried to remember and couldn't. The buzzing of the scorpion was a constant backdrop to everything. Her headaches were less frequent, though—thanks to the magic of the heroin.

She ambled into the bath, and ran some hot water in the tub. She knew she must bathe if she was to be able to continue finding sacrifices. She stripped, and climbed into the tub. She sat for a long time, soaking. She made half-hearted attempts to wash herself, and eventually she climbed from the tub, more soaked clean than washed. She toweled off, and almost put on the same dress she'd been wearing. That dress smelled bad, she realized. She flung it into a corner, walked to the closet, and opened the door. Only two dresses were hanging inside. Where were her clothes? She looked around the room suspiciously. Had Lyria come in while she was asleep and stolen her dresses? Nothing could be put past that conniving bitch.

Then her eyes fell on the heap of clothing on the floor in the corner by her bed. She was momentarily shocked that she hadn't taken anything to the laundry in weeks. Now she was vaguely aware of some of the looks she'd been getting when she was out on the street. She knew she was beautiful, but some looked at her as though there was something wrong with her. It must have been her dirty clothing, she surmised, deciding right then to take her laundry to be cleaned and pressed.

She bundled everything into a heap, and shoved it into a canvas laundry bag. Not all of it would fit, but she'd be able to get three dresses laundered today. Tomorrow she could take the rest, and they'd all be ready by the weekend. She hefted the bag over her shoulder, and then remembered she was not yet dressed. She giggled as she set the bag down to dress.

The laundry man accepted a rather large emerald for the job, including of course the items she would bring the next day. She was given a claim ticket, and she headed back home. For right now, there didn't seem to be any individuals offering themselves to her. That was fine, she could wait until the divine need manifested. She felt it wouldn't be long.

The laundry man closed his shop for an hour, driving to the shop of a nearby jewelry dealer. He showed the emerald to the owner of the shop. The man took the stone, and examined it carefully under his microscope. He looked up in surprise. The laundry man didn't like that look.

"This stone I have seen once before," the old man in the expensive suit said, his large jeweler's loupe swinging from a light chain he wore around his neck.

"What do you mean, you've seen this stone?"

"Simply this," the man stated, "I once owned this stone. I sold it a few years ago to Heinrich Reichhardt's wife."

The laundry man's mouth hung open in surprise, and his eyes opened in fear.

"What are we to do about this?" he asked in a desperate voice. "I took it in trade for some laundry work."

"This? You have cheated the seller by an enormous amount," the jeweler said. "This stone is worth fifteen thousand on today's market."

"What can I do, I didn't kill the man and take his jewelry!"

"I know you didn't, but I have to hold this for the police. It's the law. This is evidence in the killing of a very good customer of mine."

The laundry man looked desperate, like a rabbit facing a fox.

"I'll tell you what I'll do," the jeweler said. "I'll call the police and tell them I have known you a long time. From what I've read in the newspaper, you wouldn't match the description of the killer in any event."

The man agreed—there wasn't much else he could do.

Sergeant Jinks arrived a short time after his department received the call. His police car was parked discreetly a block away. Since the jeweler was helping him, there was no reason to scare away customers by parking a police car in front of his store. He left the vehicle, carefully locking it. There were too many criminals in the city these days, but this was his priority case and he was closing in. He could see himself standing with the mayor of Los Angeles receiving a medal.

The police Sergeant listened carefully to what the laundry man had to say. The description was vague, but it did sound like the woman they were looking for. Unfortunately, there was no telling where she lived. She dropped off the laundry, saying she'd be back Saturday morning.

"I'll tell you what," the policeman said, "you'll continue business as usual. Launder the woman's clothing, and have it ready. I'll be in your shop on Saturday and I'll either arrest her there, or follow her to see if she has accomplices."

"You think there might be more than one of them?"

"There could be, who knows?" the policeman responded.

After the laundry man left, Sergeant Jinks made a call from the jewelry shop to the police headquarters.

"This is Jinks," he said, "I believe we have a lead on our so-called vampire killer. What I want is to have several officers comb the shops and businesses in this area. If this is the woman we seek, she's probably living nearby. She may be trading with others as well."

The conversation finished, Jinks put the gemstone into his vest pocket and left the shop. He slowly drove around, looking for the woman. He made notes on the businesses in the area. Father Woods explained that their crime expert said the killer was losing control—probably operating close to home.

It was dusk by the time he passed the Hillcrest Apartments. He noticed that the front door swung closed. He hadn't seen who came out, nor could he see where the person went. He shrugged, driving on. He was happy for the first time in days. They were closing in on the killer. It was just a matter of time and he'd see to it that he was the hero who solved the case.

~

As the call was being made to the police, Adria prepared for the evening. She was going to try something new tonight—going to the bars and taverns was time consuming. There would be many possible sacrifices in the tall apartment buildings—plenty of game for the hunt. When she left her apartment building, she exited the front door and turned down the alley. She saw a police car approaching slowly. She laughed. She was much smarter than the coppers. Besides, she was a divine being!

~

The next day the police paid a visit to Easy Money Pawn—the shop was a few blocks from the laundry. It would be likely the killer traded there as well. The bell on the door tinkled as Sergeant Jinks and several other officers entered.

"Hello, Darrell," the area beat cop said.

"Officer Henley, what can I do for you today?"

Jinks and another detective were examining Darrell's jewelry display case, comparing the items with a written list of jewelry stolen in the Reichhardt crime.

The detective pointed to a white gold ring in the case. It was rather distinctive, an old design with a reasonably large diamond.

"We need to see this ring, please," Sergeant Jinks said.

Darrell walked to the case, and when he saw the ring the policemen were interested in, his demeanor changed. He became less friendly, and more cautious.

The officers examined the ring close up, looking at the design and the karat marking inside.

"We'll need to confiscate this ring for a closer examination," Jinks said. "It's possible this ring is evidence in a major murder investigation."

"What? Murder?"

Darrell's attitude changed, he was fearful, which is just where Jinks wanted him.

"You remember the Reichhardt murders, don't you? It was only about twelve days ago, after all."

"Sure...sure I remember. It was awful, simply terrible."

"Yes, it was," the policeman said. "The thing is, we believe it was the killer who sold this to you. Now you know what that means? Has she been in your shop? Can you be sure she won't come after you, especially when we put it in all the papers that you suspected her and turned the ring in to us?"

"No! You can't do that—it isn't true!"

The man was sweating profusely, and in his panic he'd forgotten that the ring had come from a drug dealer and not the woman in question.

Jinks laughed, "No, it isn't true. But she won't know, and it will just make her mad. I mean madder than she is ordinarily."

"All right," Darrell said, perspiration shining on his face, "I'll tell you what I know."

"That's more like it," Jinks said with a grin.

Jinks was not too surprised to hear that the man now remembered a drug dealer had actually been the person who sold the ring to the pawnshop. Now all they had to do was hunt down the drug dealer. Since the police knew who and where most of them were, finding a dealer in this neighborhood would be easy. They always knew who and where they were—how else would they get their money for allowing them to continue operating?

The police left the pawnshop a half hour later having gathered what information they could from a very cooperative Darrell.

"He said he thinks she lives right around here," Jinks said to the other detective. "He also said this Tony told him she's a narcotics user. He got the ring from the woman in trade for heroin."

"Shall we pay Tony a visit?"

"I think that might be in order," Jinks answered. "Darrell is a slimy fellow, but he did drop a hint that the woman is an addict living in the area."

"He's just three blocks up the street," the detective said, pointing.

They drove two blocks, and parked away from the dealer's location. They didn't want to spook him prematurely. Nevertheless, he tried to take off at a run when he saw the two policemen approaching. Unfortunately for him, the man he'd been dealing to at the time didn't want him to run off with his money until he'd been given his stuff. He conveniently tripped the dealer, who went sprawling onto the sidewalk.

Jinks hauled him to his feet and shoved him into the alley.

"All right, Tony," he began, shoving the man roughly against a stone wall. "Who gave you the ring?"

"What ring?"

"The ring that'll hang you for murder if you don't speak clearly."

"Oh…" Tony said, "that ring…"

"Yeah, wise guy, that ring."

"I thought it might be hot, but I didn't know someone was murdered for it."

"Not just someone, Tony, Heinrich Franz Reichhardt."

The dealer turned pale. He'd read the stories, as had nearly everyone else.

"I don't know much," he began. "Tell you what, you leave me alone and I'll give you everything I know."

"Oh, you'll do that anyway, Tony," Jinks said with a grin. "The question is, will you tell me here or at the station. Believe me, here will be less painful."

The narcotics dealer thought about it for maybe three seconds.

"She never told me her name, but I know she lives around here. I see her all the time. She must live in one of these apartment buildings on this block or the next. I don't think she comes from too far away, or she'd be buying from someone closer to home—you know how addicts are."

"Yes, we know," Jinks said. "Now tell us all about her."

~

The two policemen sat in the car.

"We know it must be her," the detective said. "Problem is which building does she live in? There are a lot of apartments in this part of the city."

"Tell me about it," Jinks responded. "I told Tony if he wants to stay free and healthy, he'll let us know the next time he sees her. He'll try to find out where she lives as well."

The detective looked skeptical. Jinks laughed, "Well, it could happen that way!"

They drove to the police station in silence, each thinking their own thoughts about what might happen next.

Chapter 61

It was four days later that something happened. By eight o'clock in the evening, Adria finally awoke. Her head hurt. She walked into the kitchen, found some stale bread on a plate in the sink and listlessly ate it. Absently, she looked at the piled dishes, thinking she should probably wash them. A cockroach that had been disturbed when Adria took the plate from the sink scurried under another plate. She changed her mind remembering how much easier it would be to just take them out of the sink to reuse. She sampled the bread again, but she didn't taste it. She was listening to the voices.

She dressed quickly, and took the lift to the ground floor. She had her knife and more rope in her handbag. This time she wasn't going far. The taverns were too public. Besides, now that people were willing to be sacrifices, there was a much easier way to find them. She crossed the street to the Bloomgarden Apartments. She looked through the glass front door, and saw that no one was at the desk. That, she knew, was Divine intervention. This was the place. She walked in, unseen. She rode the lift to the second floor; no need to go higher yet. She got out of the lift, turned left, and walked down the carpeted hall. As she went, she tried the door handles on each apartment. The first three were locked. She knew that meant she wasn't supposed to go into those rooms. The fourth apartment, however, was unlocked. The invitation was obvious. She opened the door, entered the apartment, and quietly shut the door behind her.

"Is that you, dear?"

A woman's voice.

"Daddy?"

A little boy's voice.

Footsteps running down the hallway.

"Daddy! Daddy!"

~

BLOOMGARDEN MASSACRE

The headline shouted the news the next morning. One Carl Peterson came home late from work to find the front door of his apartment standing open, the article stated. Inside, Mr. Peterson found a scene of horror. His eight-year-old boy lay at the front of the hallway, his head crushed by a blow from a heavy brass fireplace poker. The boy had been savagely beaten. Mr. Peterson's wife was found just outside the kitchen door. It appeared, a police source said, like she was coming from the kitchen to investigate the noise in the living room. Her attacker slashed her several times. She was alive when found, but died on the way to the hospital from shock and blood loss without regaining consciousness.

This killing, according to police sources not cited by the paper, wasn't related to the other brutal murders that had shocked the city. This looked like a revenge killing (Mr. Peterson is being investigated) or an attempted burglary, turned robbery, turned murder.

~

Adria was furious. What had gone wrong? There'd been only the woman and child. How could that be? She would have to think about this. As it happened, the killings had been too quick—she didn't have time to bleed them out. *Next time would be better, easier,* she thought. She gave herself another injection of heroin to get her through the night, and then simply lay on the unmade and dirty sheets of the bed. Her last thought was that she should get them laundered—they too were beginning to smell.

In the morning she arose early. She needed more heroin. Had it been that long already? She had enough for today, but now she was getting scary close to being without. She walked down the street toward her supplier. She was smiling. Soon everything would be back to normal again.

She made her connection, trading for the drugs. Since the first killing, she didn't bother being a prostitute. She received no money from the men she killed. Maybe she should rob the next one, no point in running out of things to trade.

As soon as she turned her back, Tony began following her. He stayed back a discreet distance, and she never turned to see if anyone was following her. She was a strange one. He watched from the corner of an alley as she mounted the steps in front of the Hillcrest Apartments. When she disappeared through the front door, he quickly crossed the street. He cautiously climbed the stairs, peering through the door, his right hand shielding his eyes from the reflecting sun. She was getting into the lift. When she shut the door, he entered the building, and ran to the lift. He watched the numbers—the indicator stopped at sixty. He quickly left the apartment building, and headed toward the apothecary two blocks away— from there he called Sergeant Jinks.

~

Adria didn't stay long in her apartment. She was eager to try something new. She'd been told that blood carried the strongest essence.

Sexual fluids, she'd come to realize, were just a stepping stone to greater wisdom. She thought briefly of Garn. She laughed, wondering if he'd be sorry he hadn't kept her as an apprentice. Look at how strong she'd become.

She left by the side door of the building, exiting into the alley. She thought she'd try her luck on the street behind her building. There were many apartments and all were filled with blood and pain. She smiled as she hurried down the alley to the next street. She looked left and right, and went right. It seemed like what she should do. For five blocks she wandered aimlessly.

Then she saw the place—The Ventura Apartments. That was as good a place to start as any, she surmised. She opened the front door, and walked into the cool lobby. In this building, there was a man behind the desk, but he just nodded at Adria and smiled. She smiled back as she walked to the lift. It was currently stopped on the tenth floor so she'd have to wait for it to come down. She decided immediately that the next sacrifice would be on that floor.

When the lift arrived, Adria rode it back up to the tenth floor. She exited, and just like the last time, paused listening for a victim. There it was, the call! A woman came out of one of the apartments with two babies in her arms. One looked to be about one summer, the other an infant. *Young blood*, Adria thought. She followed the woman down the hall and stopped in front of a door a short distance from where the woman stood. As she unlocked and opened the door, Adria gave her a hard shove, driving her into the room. Adria followed her and quickly closed the door behind her.

"What do you want?"

Adria smiled. The woman was scared. She'd known she would be. It was just another example of her amazing ability to read minds.

"Here," the woman said, handing Adria her handbag. "There's about a hundred in there. Take the money but please don't hurt my babies."

Adria continued to smile. Coming further into the apartment, she put her hand in her bag, feeling the comfortable handle of her sacrificial knife.

She pulled the knife from her bag, and the woman screamed. Adria hadn't thought of that contingency. She stepped forward, slashing at the woman with the heavy dagger. She missed her throat, cutting her upper arm severely. Nerves and tendons cut, the babies fell from her arms. One child landed in a large stuffed chair, bounced once, and lay crying. The other baby wasn't so fortunate; he landed on the floor, fracturing his right arm, squalling in pain.

"What's going on in there?"

It was a man's voice from the other side of the door.

Adria spun toward the door, which was opening. The woman shrieked again, more weakly, as her knees buckled and she fell to the floor next to her injured baby. The severed brachial artery was pumping blood from her arm at a deadly rate. Her scream hurt Adria's ears. She was in a panic. What should she do?

When the door was flung open, she made her decision. She bolted for the doorway, and when the man standing there grabbed at her, she thrust her knife into his throat, twisted the blade in the wound, and ran. Adria jumped over the man's body and was running for the lift. By the time another neighbor got to the phone to call the police, death had taken the young mother. Adria was on the first floor walking calmly toward the front door of the building.

As she walked down the alley, she cursed herself. How could she have forgotten that the woman might scream? It was a ridiculous mistake, one she couldn't afford to make again. Two sacrifices had gone awry— and she'd so badly wanted the blood of the babies. It would have been so filled with life energy. She rounded the corner, and came to a stop. Why was there a police car in front of her apartment building? She crossed to the other side of the street and watched.

~

Sergeant Jinks entered the apartment building cautiously, his Mauser pistol in his hand and his badge pinned to his jacket pocket. He walked to the desk where a worried man stood waiting.

"You have a woman living in this building on the sixtieth floor. She's blonde and is drug addicted. You know her?"

"I'm not sure," the man began. "We have many tenants."

"Well, you'd remember this one. She's pretty with long blonde hair. She lives alone and is about seventeen years of age."

The man's wife came out of the office, looking at her husband questioningly.

"The woman is a whore," the policeman added, figuring the man had used her services. He smiled as the man stammered, "Oh, that woman," he said, his memory suddenly clear. "You see her sometimes, honey," he

389

added, turning to look at his wife, "the young blonde woman in room 1007."

"Oh, her," the wife said in disgust. "What an unwashed pig she is."

"Give me your extra key," the policeman demanded.

The manager's wife retrieved it from the desk, handing it to the policeman.

Sergeant Jinks smiled at the manager, turned and headed for the lift. He thought if his wife was that fat, he'd use prostitutes too. Of course, he did anyway, but that was the prerogative of a man, and quite beside the point.

The inside of the apartment was worse than the policeman thought it would be. The very air smelled stale, and there were other smells as well: rotting food, sweat-soaked pillows, dirty laundry, human waste. He moved to the bed. His foot struck something under the bed. He stooped, bringing out a suitcase. When he opened it, he gasped. It was half full of jewelry, gold, and silver objects of various kinds and even loose gemstones. There were eight gold coins. He put those in his pocket—a reward, he told himself, for being such a diligent police officer. Then it was time to call the station and get more police in the area. The woman was around here somewhere—the ring was tightening. He knew he must be the one to find her. She'd resist arrest, however, he couldn't let her make any statements, whether she was insane or not.

He looked again into the suitcase. What was that rolled up in the corner? He lifted out an odd tangle of what he surmised to be rope. Then he realized what it was and dropped it back into the case in disgust. It was human hair, the missing locks of hair taken from the victims. He was appalled; he'd never encountered anything of this magnitude before. He had to call Father Woods in on this. He walked back into the hall to the phone, and placed a call to the Cathedral.

"Father Woods, please."

"I'm afraid I have bad news," the priest said. "The person you need is Father Jackson—nobody's seen him in days—believe me, we have looked. It seems he left the Cathedral grounds. We're concerned he went into the city and has been waylaid."

Jinks hung up the receiver, and waited for the rest of his team. It didn't take long. He turned this part of the investigation over to them, heading out into the street.

Damn! Things were never easy, were they? He thought there must be some kind of law, some kind of natural or spiritual force that stated that if anything could go wrong it would, and what one prepared for never comes to pass. He'd have to remember that, and give it a name. It might make him famous. As he walked to his auto, he passed Murphy's Drygoods Emporium. He thought Murphy was a nice generic name. He decided to call that force of constant interference Murphy's Rule—yeah, that had a nice ring to it!

~

Adria watched in dismay as more police arrived in front of her home. She crouched in the alley across the street, hiding behind a trash bin. Tears ran down her cheeks as she watched them take her suitcase with all her jewelry and money, and put it into a waiting van—her hair collection was in there as well. What would she do now? She opened her handbag and saw her pouch of drugs, and knew she could last another five days, maybe. *I should've taken that woman's money*, she thought. She could do nothing now, but move on. She turned and walked down the avenue. There was plenty of time to think.

Presently, she arrived at a surprisingly large open area. There were trees and paths much too narrow for autos. She looked at the sign, though she couldn't read it. *This might be a good place to hide*, she thought. It was big. There were lots of trees. Here and there people strolled. Some were men on their own or in groups. She smiled. She could whore these men right here in the park. Maybe kill them and take their money as well.

She left the path, and wandered into the trees. There were birds singing and shade from the sun. She sat for a moment on a large rock and looked around. The trees hid her from all passersby—she was alone again.

"Who are you?"

Adria looked up at the sudden voice. There were three children standing in front of her. They were disheveled and dirty. They reminded her of someone, but who? Palom. A name. Lorra. Another name. She knew these weren't actually her friends from long ago, but they could still be friends. They could still be servants for her.

"I'm Adria," she said. "Do you live here?"

The children looked at each other.

The older one said, "Yes, we live here. We ran away."

"From who?"

"From the city," the girl answered.

She was no more than ten perhaps.

"You ran away from the city?"

"Yes," the child answered. "We're orphans. Our parents died in a fire. They wanted to put us in an orphan home. We ran away—now we're wild."

"We're a tribe," the second girl said happily.

Adria smiled at the children.

"Well," she said, "I ran away too. Could I stay with you? I can help you get food and whatever else you might need."

The children thought for a moment, then agreed. They led Adria into some dense brush and trees. In the center was a clearing with a small tent and a larger construction made of scrap lumber and canvas.

"This is our home," the older girl said. "We welcome you."

Adria smiled at them, thinking she could train the older one at least to be a prostitute. She was home again. She was in charge of her own tribe. She had a safe spot to live and she had the city in which to hunt. Who could ask for more?

Epilogue

In the darkness, police cars cruised the nearly empty streets of Los Angeles. It was past two in the morning, the bars were all closed—even the hookers had left the streets. In every vehicle a drawing was attached to the dash. It was an artist's rendition, made from the composite descriptions of the individuals who had seen or perhaps survived an attack by the killer. The picture was of the woman they were hunting. The woman the Los Angeles Journal called 'The Vampire Killer,' as if the crimes weren't sensational enough all by themselves. Where was this mysterious blonde woman—the woman being pursued by every lawman in the city?

The officers would look at the drawing periodically as they passed women on the streets. Occasionally, they would stop someone only to discover she was not the woman they were looking for. It was a frustrating job, looking for one face in millions. None of the officers believed they would find her—although all of them hoped they'd be the one who did.

~

Sergeant Jinks struck his fist on the top of his desk, he knew it wasn't the patrolmen's fault but he had to blame someone. He'd been so very close to catching her. He was now certain that his team had raided her apartment at the wrong time. If only he had quietly waited inside her apartment once he knew where she lived, she'd be dead by now. He again read the reports lying before him.

How could this half-human woman with almost no ability to understand city life just disappear? It was almost uncanny. He stood and turned to the large map of Los Angeles on the wall—a teacup in his hand. The search grids were tight; there was no area that wasn't covered. He thought perhaps he should have foot patrols walk the many parks of the city, but then he shook his head—they didn't have the manpower for that kind of thing. Why would someone wishing to kill people go where virtually nobody ventured anymore? The damn newspaper had made sure of that. He knew searching the parks would be a waste of time. Sooner or later the bitch would show up again, and then he'd have her. He grinned and downed the rest of his tea. It was time to go home.

~

In the darkness, the Bishop lay awake in his bed aboard the zeppelin. He was thinking about the jungle, and what awaited him there. He also felt his choice for leadership in the Black City was sound. He knew a few things that virtually no one else knew—not even most of the priests asleep in the city far behind him. To accomplish one or both of his plans, he would need stable, steadfast leadership in Los Angeles for the duration. He knew Father Woods was the right man for the job.

~

Lyria and Kel, unlike a very enthusiastic Raven, were worried about their impending journey. Coming to the Black City had been a real adventure, but now it seemed that this was merely an introduction. They were now headed to a region that nobody knew. Even Llo, with his wide travels, had not been able to shed much light on what men called 'Green Hell.' What would await them in the impenetrable greenness of the unending jungle?

The books Kel had brought spoke only in vague generalities of the region called Green Hell or simply The Green. They spoke of man-eating monsters, deadly insects, and disease. There had been man-eaters here in the north as well. What made the dangerous animals there so much more frightening? Neither he nor Lyria could explain it. Perhaps it was simply that the first men who went there were city men.

City men would have thought with their machines rather than their minds and instincts. Though neither one of them had seen a jungle, they both knew it was a living thing that could think and act on instinct alone. They also hoped that during the next part of their journey they would fare better, especially with the precious child they were taking with them.

~

Adria lay peacefully on her back in the deep darkness of the park. Here there were no gaslights, and no one venturing about in the dark. Here it was safe to sleep the night through. She'd seen the patrolling police cars and assumed they were looking for her. They would have a long look, she figured, smiling to herself in the night, listening to the quiet sounds of the children breathing. This was only a minor setback, she reasoned.

This was a quiet time. But Adria knew that wouldn't last. In a few days she'd be out there once more—hunting. Though for the moment she had sufficient heroin and mescaline, she knew she'd need more in the near future—for that she'd need money, but she knew how to get it. It was easy. Adria would just take it from very willing men along with their divine life force or from her dead sacrifices. She knew she was not done. In fact, she was just beginning. She smiled again as she slid into a calm and dreamless sleep.

Acknowledgements

I would first like to thank my wife; though she's now gone from me, she taught me a great deal about 'drive' and self-starting. I also want to thank my English teachers, both in High School and College, who taught me grammar, spelling, and the attention to detail needed to write. Also, I want to thank friends Sherry Folb and Holly Chapman who have worked very hard to help me with my stories. And finally, I want to thank that inscrutable power which has placed so many people and events in my path to teach me empathy, and expand my awareness of the human condition.

About the Author

Keith Mueller was born in Tucson Arizona and is a graduate of the U of A with degrees in art and art education. He served six years in the US Air Force as a firearms instructor and competitive shooter on the Air Force pistol team at Lackland AFB, and later as an instructor at the Air Force Academy. He's had an interest in metaphysical studies, shamanism, ancient cultures and religions since the late 1960's, personally practicing some of these disciplines. Though he's had an interest in writing for many years, retirement has allowed this interest to finally manifest in this book series.

Look for Book Two *"The City in the Jungle"* in this Series Available Soon

And so the Black City slept—but its dreams are haunted, and it slept but fitfully. For the darkness can hide many things: murder and revenge, hate and blind lust. In this living darkness, forces are gathering in unexpected places—and in unexpected ways. Paths that seemed clear and straight in the daylight are now obscure and winding. Allies are found, bonds are formed—and in the heat of battle, love finds a way.

Lyria, Kel, and Raven are about to embark on an adventure that will take them far beyond anything they've experienced before—an adventure for which even Kel's foretelling dreams could not prepare them.

Green Hell—a landmass of mysterious rainforest and sky-touching mountains. It is land invaded, once again, by city dwellers. It is here the Bishop and his Cathedral brethren prepare to make their stand. It is here they wish to build a pure nation; a nation dedicated solely to the Redeemed God and His followers. In their eyes it is a land ripe for pillage with its unlimited resources and free land in plenty for all devout men. Here, their only enemies seem to be 'half-human' tribes-people; peoples given to them by the Redeemed God for slave labor and rape—the men to build stone walls, and the women for their pleasure houses both here and in the North.

But there is one more surprise awaiting them all. The Bishop and his forces have taken something precious from the jungle—and the jungle, and what dwells within it, is awakening...